CITY of

CIRCLES

Jess Richards was born in Wales in 1972 and grew up in Scotland. She studied Creative Writing at Sussex University in 2010. Her debut novel, *Snake Ropes*, was shortlisted for the 2012 Costa First Novel Award and longlisted for the Green Carnation Prize. Her second novel, the acclaimed *Cooking With Bones,* was published in 2014. *City of Circles* is her third novel.

jessrichards.com
Twitter: @jessgrr1

JESS RICHARDS

CITY *of*

CIRCLES

SCEPTRE

First published in Great Britain in 2017 by Hodder & Stoughton
An Hachette UK company

This paperback edition published in 2018

2

Map by Jess Richards and Sandra Oakins

A CIP catalogue record for this title is available from the British Library

Paperback ISBN 9781473656710
eBook ISBN 9781473656703

Typeset in Sabon MT by Palimpsest Book Production Limited, Falkirk, Stirlingshire

Printed and bound in Great Britain by Clays Ltd, Elcograf S.p.A.

Hodder & Stoughton policy is to use papers that are natural, renewable and
recyclable products and made from wood grown in sustainable forests. The
logging and manufacturing processes are expected to conform to the
environmental regulations of the country of origin.

Hodder & Stoughton Ltd
Carmelite House
50 Victoria Embankment
London EC4Y 0DZ

www.sceptrebooks.co.uk

For my father, Alan J Richards, 1947–2014
and for Sally J Morgan, with all my love.

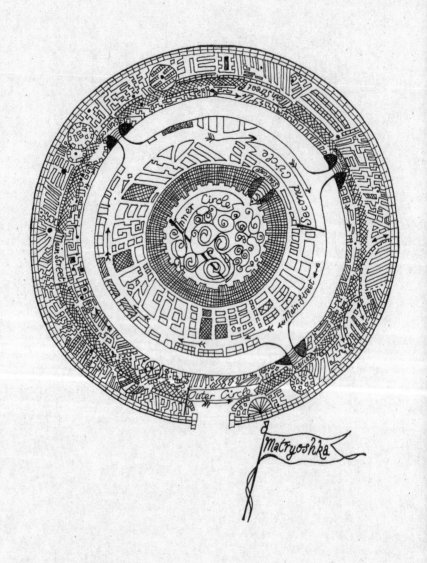

Inner Circle

Second Circle

New Street

Main Street

Main Street

Outer Circle

Matryoshka

ONE FOR SORROW

Dying faces are the colour of soiled linen. It's the eyes which shine, as if the world around the person who is dying has brightened itself, so it's fully seen and felt and known. Colours, light, emotion, air, wind, sound – all of these things have no edges. They flood into the eyes, filling them, filling them, filling them, before the eyelids eventually close.

Inside a caravan, there are two beds. There are two primrose-patterned pillows. One pillow frames the face of Danu's sick mother. The other pillow is slumped under the weight of her dead father's head. Clem and Adelaide lie on these beds, one dead, one alive, under matching blue blankets.

Danu is standing barefoot next to her mother, listening. She's spent the past two weeks trying to keep her parents calm and alive through thickened fevers. She's fed and starved them, forced water into them, added and removed blankets, cold-sponged their bodies whenever the smells were too ripe. She's snatched hours of sleep on floor cushions, and attempted to scare away the magpies which keep landing on the caravan roof. The sound of their claws cause her mother to try to sit up, when she might have a greater chance of recovery if she remained still.

The wine-coloured curtains are closed. Inside, the caravan is soaked in reds. Outside, the sun will be too bright for today.

Perhaps it will be too bright for a long time. Danu's stomach clenches. The smell of tea leaves is pungent and the spilt boiled rice needs to be wiped away. It doesn't matter that rice is left uneaten. It's not expensive. But to approach the sink to clean the mess would mean passing her father's empty body.

His corpse is in Danu's bed. She had to separate her parents when they became ill. Sharing their own bed, a blanket and fevers sent their bodies into heightened and lowered temperatures. That was when her father could still move around.

But now he's a brittle shell. Some hollowed-out thing wearing a relaxed mask of the face she loves. She can't look over her shoulder at it. At him? No, it's not him. She swallows, tastes bile. Swallows again.

Danu hasn't breathed much since Clem died. His body strained against death. She doesn't know how much he felt, as his eyes opened wide and his body slumped. She's now frozen at her mother's bedside, waiting. Will death steal whatever soul or warmth or heartbeat it wants to remove from her mother's body more peacefully?

Why has she never heard anyone speak about watching death?

All Danu can do is wait. There's a crowd of sounds in her mother's lungs: gales, whistles, scratches. As there were in her father's. Did he die a whole hour ago? She's not sure what to do. Should she know? But on any other morning she might have tangles brushed out of her hair or be asked to prepare eggs or bread or stew. Sit on the caravan steps mulling over last night's show. Flirt with another clown. Talk about everything that's wrong with flirting, but only with the horses. But none of these usual things are happening.

They're quarantined and contagious. Others in the camp are sick as well, but Danu was only ill for a short time. So some people *can* recover.

She's waiting. Hoping. Numb.

Danu hasn't told anyone her father is dead. Her parents belong to each other. Till death parts them. Yes. One is dead. But they're still wearing matching wedding rings.

Is there a word like widow or widower, for a daughter? Orphan is the word for a child. Danu is fifteen. She can't lose both parents. Not to the same illness. Not on the same day. When her mother's better, she'll know what to do.

But Danu watches her mother suffer the same worsening symptoms her father did, at the end. Between coughing fits, Danu's eyes are drawn to the ochre stains on the bib of Adelaide's nightgown. She's seeking symbols in sputum and spillages, as if these stains could give accurate predictions about whether her mother will survive or not. Small clues, or uneven blots meaning nothing? Little more than smudges – there's the shape of an egg, a feather next to a small frayed hole. The real sign is obvious – Adelaide's lips are blue-tinged. Her eyes widen, trying desperately to communicate something. As she tries to speak, her wheezes turn words into whistles.

Danu perches on the edge of the mattress and stops breathing for a few seconds to give her mother some extra breaths to use.

Adelaide moans. 'Take this.' She pats her palm against her large battered locket and lets her hand lie where it falls.

Danu says, 'Your wrist's thinner today.'

The soft thud of palm against breastbone. 'Take the locket.'

'No, it's yours. You've worn it . . . how long?'

'Always, since I . . . Clem? Clem!'

'He's not here.' Danu's eyes spring tears. She shuffles on the bed so she blocks the sight of her father from her mother. She grips Adelaide's hand. 'Don't die. I've got heartbreak already . . .' She glances over her shoulder at her father's corpse, and

3

quickly looks back at Adelaide. 'I can't lose you. Not both of you at the same time. I'll break.'

Her mother's eyes blur, filling with light.

This is exactly what her father's eyes looked like, moments before he died.

Danu releases her mother's hand.

Adelaide tries to grasp her locket again. She tries to smile, but her muscles are so weak it looks more like a grimace. She sighs. Exhales in a rattle. Inhales with a hiss.

Her fingers are the texture of wax.

Adelaide whispers, 'No, time's run . . .'

As Danu leans in to listen, there aren't any more words. She sounds like a little girl as she says, 'Don't die, fight. I'll get the brush, do your teeth—'

Above, there's a thud, and another. The scratch of claws against the wooden caravan roof.

Frowning, Adelaide strains to sit up and fails. Her breathing resumes and continues, turning to whistles, turning to silence.

Danu opens the top half of the caravan door, shielding her eyes from the noon sun. She yells to the outside world, 'More magpies, get them gone!' and rushes back to Adelaide.

Her eyes are shut. When did they close, did they stare, is she gone? No. She's still breathing. Intakes of air, a breath, a gulp.

From outside: circus people shoo away the magpies – hands clapping, sharp yells.

The top half of the door bumps, still open. Salted air blows in.

Adelaide's lungs slowly exhale, a whistle caught in the wind. Almost tuneful. Almost the ending of a song.

The song ends.

Outside: scraping of claws like thorns against wood, louder shouts.

Inside: Danu's heartbeat is too strong, too sore, too loud.

4

Everything scratches, her clothing is bark to her skin, even air scrapes her face.

Adelaide isn't breathing.

Danu pushes on her mother's chest, trying to force her lungs to inhale, trying not to break her brittle ribs. 'Don't die!' she cries. 'Don't. I've no one else who's for me. I'll wash your nightgown, get the germs soaked away. Sit up. Come on, take it off . . .' She wraps her arms around her mother's shoulders to pull her up. She yanks and rips a seam.

Danu retrieves a crumpled cloth from the floor. At the sink, she rinses it, wrings it out. She passes her father without looking at him. She sits next to her mother to wipe the stains from her nightgown. Her hands aren't solid enough. She tries to press harder yet the stains are still there. Why is this taking so long?

'Come on,' she says to her mother. 'Come on.'

There's no reply.

Someone is saying *no*, over and over again. It sounds like a storm, building. It sounds like Danu's own voice. But it can't be; she's not speaking.

They both need to be cleaned of the illness which took them away. Wipe it gone. They can't be buried in the soil with dirt on them. Why does no one ever wash the soil before putting clean bodies inside clean coffins into the ground?

Coffins. She'll need to get two. Where do they come from?

Someone else must know about coffins. She needs to wash their bodies. Would bleach stain their skin too pale? They're already pale. Or salt? She's hunting in cupboards. Flour? What is this in her hands, a bag of brown sugar? Should she cook something to share with others? Tell someone her parents are dead and give them seedcake, or flatbreads? Is that what she should be doing? This paper bag has *Sugar* written in big black

5

letters across it but anything could be in there. She rips it open to check what's inside . . .

The bolt on the bottom half of the door clacks. The hinge creaks.

Footfall.

As sugar spills onto her bare feet, hands grip her shoulders and a surgical mask is stretched over her face. She's pulled outside into sunshine, blind. More hands grip and arms restrain her. Vivid colours of clothing flash, her body thrashes, fighting against brightness. There are too many words and sympathy and sighs and sobs. Her fists thump against clothed flesh.

The three magpies are silhouettes on the caravan roof. Everything else is too light. She screams gales of '*No!*' at them.

A male voice speaks quietly in her ear, 'Danu, look away.'

She closes her eyes and the world is black. Her body stills itself but the sympathetic hands and surrounding arms scratch her tissues and muscles, the inside of her veins. Touch gets in too deep.

She has no other blood relatives in the circus; her body is alone among these bodies.

And they're hurting her without meaning to. Touch never hurt before now. Her parents hugged her all the time. Warmth. Arms filled with blood the same as hers. They always talked about blood. About sharing it. Only child.

Now she's only orphan. She's only no one.

She shouts, 'Don't touch me!' and means it. She shouts, 'This is my fault!'

The arms which enclose her tighten their grip and sting her.

She blanks her body of sensation and lets them hold on.

Throughout her childhood, Danu Mock has lived within the circus, sleeping in tents, wagons and caravans. She understands the whispers which take horses from panic to stillness and how to thaw frozen soil. She has learned to keep warm while snow is packed all around her and how to swim off the dizziness from bright sunshine. She knows how not to care when people take what they want and leave. She's travelled a long way while she's learned all these things.

Always, her parents were the backbone, the spine of this ever-shifting world. She didn't realise this while they were still alive. Without them, she is boneless. Loss has broken her body more than her heart. Her skin is raw – she's a scab, open to infection. Hollow inside? She is more crust than bone. More membrane than blood. A layer of skin over air.

Her heart, she can't yet think about.

It's there, it beats.

But every heart in the world beats whether it wants to or not.

The day her parents died, the doctor returned to the camp and pronounced them dead. Three others had also died, while Danu had been nursing her parents. The doctor examined Danu and confirmed she wasn't still contagious. She was told the virus attacked the weakest area of the body. Her mother's asthmatic lungs and her father's fused kidneys couldn't cope with the onslaught. Danu was told she was lucky she was young and healthy. Danu stared at the doctor blankly, knowing her parents caught the virus from her. They'd nursed her, and as she became well and immune, they became sick.

Her parents' bodies were removed from the caravan by someone else's hands. She wasn't allowed to wash them. She was told that unburied bodies carry a death curse. Railing against this superstition, she begged to be allowed to sit alone with their corpses. The oldest people in the circus were the ones who prevented her from doing so.

After the doctor had gone, she was taken for walks across

fields, and wrapped in blankets inside other people's caravans. She was handed sweetened milk in tin mugs, and given valerian from a bottle which warned of *a harsh and bitter flavour*. It tasted of piss. That night, she was put to bed in the caravan of two ageing contortionists.

Mag and Sandy Dougan were her parents' closest friends. Danu waited till they were asleep and tried to creep back to her own caravan. But Mag wasn't asleep. She clasped Danu's hand, forced her to sit, and hugged her too hard. Danu might have been crying. She might have been silent. It wasn't long ago. All the same, she doesn't remember all of it.

Now her parents' bodies have been removed to the nearest morgue, she stays in their caravan alone. It's been three nights now, this is the third. It's far too quiet to sleep. She hallucinates her parents' faces everywhere. They appear on each flat surface – the wooden walls, cupboard doors and bowed ceiling, the curtains and drapes, the rag rugs on the floor. Their faces appear as pencil drawings. Always side by side, disappearing and appearing again. There's no movement in their lips, no wise words mouthed. She stares, unblinking, willing them to speak.

Danu sells the caravan and horse to pay for their funeral. The sale's been agreed with a local man who wears a suit and a purple tie. He passed by after work and got talking to Hattie, the bearded lady, while she was out of costume and being demure. He wants Danu's caravan for a *feature* in his garden, and the horse for his six-year-old son.

He gives Danu a fat roll of notes when they meet beside the horses' enclosure. She's moved her caravan and hitched up the horse. All he needs to do is to check it's in good order and lead the horse away, pulling her home behind him. The horse stamps, ready to go. Sirius, her father had jokingly named him, as he'd always wanted a dog. She can't look at him.

The man says, 'I'll let you count the money.'

She nods.

He climbs the steps to the caravan and opens the door, disappearing inside.

Even as Danu sits herself on a tree stump to count the notes, focus, count them again, she knows it's the agreed amount. The man has an honest face. He's been told Danu's *lost* her parents, and didn't mention them. What is there to say? She hasn't lost them. They're dead, and she's lost. Heartbreak is homeless. Every footprint she's left in mud is a hollow thing.

The man's heavy boots echo on the caravan floorboards. She's emptied the caravan of her parents' things, divided them into bundles and given them away. Her own possessions are stored in two leather bags at Mag and Sandy's caravan. A few circus people busy themselves nearby, keeping an eye on the caravan's open door and the notes in Danu's hands. Feeling herself being watched, she stops breathing, then remembers to breathe, loses count and has to begin all over again. When she has finished counting, the caravan and Sirius have already gone.

They're not lost either. They're just somewhere else.

The walnut coffins are expensive, but not as expensive as the graveyard plots. The nearest town is a wealthy one, called Caderton. Its inhabitants grow rhododendron bushes in their vast gardens. These plants are weeds when they grow in woods and forests – Danu's seen them burning in much of the country-side they've passed through over the years.

She'll remember Caderton if the circus ever passes through it again. She'll remember it and pick wild flowers on the way there. Roses or bluebells. Ivy. Ash leaves or bunches of laburnum seeds. Catkins or dogwood stems. Whatever the season is, she'll pick something alive from it. And drop the live thing to die on Adelaide and Clem's grave-beds.

Danu will always remember Caderton, though the time the circus spends here passes in numb clouds. No shows are being performed, because everyone's in shock about the deaths, and constantly checking themselves for signs of the virus. Some people have simply taken to bed and won't get up till they *feel well again*. She doesn't believe they're even sick. The real symptoms were obvious. Raging fever and vomit followed by more raging fever and chest pains. The heartbeat weakening. Breathing problems. Not being able to eat or drink anything without evicting it again. The whole body under attack, inside and out. Her mother wheezed often, before getting the virus. Her father had a constant pain in his back, around the kidneys. He'd always said he felt *dented*.

Her parents will be buried beneath twin headstones, under a church spire which points at clouds. At Caderton, where houses are black timber and white painted blocks. At Caderton, where the riverbank's grass is mown between weeping willows by a council gardener. At Caderton where along every street, vast gardens are hidden behind privet hedges.

The day of the funeral. Her parents' coffins are side by side at the front of the church, under a gold cross. Three other coffins stand next to them. The building smells of polish and lilies. Shadows of the leaded windows criss-cross over pews and flagstones. All of the dead are spoken of in one ceremony. The minister talks first of the three others who died. He praises their longevity, says that they enjoyed full lives, and left behind many grandchildren. 'Through whom their spirits live on for evermore.'

At the back of the church a baby wails and is carried outside to be quietened.

Glancing at Danu, the minister moves on to speak of Adelaide and Clem Mock.

He tries to sound like he knew her parents, but he still gets their ages the wrong way around. He talks about Danu's parents' love story. It's what she agreed he could do. Talking to him about them the day before the funeral had made her want to stop talking. He'd softly said, *All this means is you're not ready to share your memories of them.* She'd replied, *You might be right.* He asked her how they first met each other, and she told him. So he suggested he tell their tale as – *the lady abandons every finery and runs away with the gypsy.* She agreed this was the easiest, most romantic story to tell. But all the same, as he speaks it now, she can't hear it. She's staring at the loose strands of his grey hair which catch the light from the windows. His hair is made from dust.

Their coffins have fleur brass fittings on shining wood. Inside, red velvet cushions their white-wrapped bodies. If she squints, she can see her own ghost coffin beside them. It's made of cardboard. The day she'd got sick, they'd all gone into town together. She'd stood outside a large bookshop waiting for them, knowing they were getting a book for her, and they'd hide it till her birthday. Outside the shop, a man stopped and leaned against the window, a hacking cough wracking his body. Danu asked if he was all right. He wasn't all right. He told her he was going to see the doctor. She stares at her ghost coffin, and crosses her arms over her chest.

The minister moves on to explain the deaths. 'A pernicious virus – not delivered by the hand of a forgiving god, but by the sickening fingers of the devil.' That's how he puts it. He's already told Danu he was visited by an evangelical man and is experimenting with how the devil can be blamed in a variety of linguistic styles in order to reinforce god's goodness. He wanted to check she wasn't afraid of the devil, in case he felt the urge to mention him. She told him, *No more than I am of your god.*

The locals are dressed finer than anyone in the circus. Big hats and black lapels. On the way outside into the graveyard, they mingle. They say *ya ya* when they mean *yes* or *I'm sorry.* They speak to many of the circus people, without commenting on the bright colours of their clothing, or looking too closely at their dirty boots. There's been a donation. Too late to pay for this funeral or headstones or coffins and no doubt, not enough. It's given to Gianto Shabb, the smoke-haired elder of the circus, in a sealed white envelope. He puts it in the pocket of his long leather coat. Danu won't see any of its contents.

After all the coffins have been lowered into the ground, prayers said, and earth dropped, Mag steps forward to stand at the graves. Her white hair is covered by a black shawl. She sings in a low minor key: her voice is a drone, her mouth is a circle, the tune is a tunnel . . .

> Death for the dead,
> life for the live,
> heart for the love,
> ticks for the clock,
> ticking till spent
> till spent, till spent
> ticking till spent . . .

Other voices join in. The song is low, sung in a round, goes on for an age, but doesn't last long enough. Danu keeps whispering the words after the song has ended. She turns away from the open graves and walks to the graveyard gate. She leans her back against the stone archway. Whispering, still whispering. *Life for the live, heart for the love . . .* She stops. Now she can't speak or move.

Mag approaches her. 'We'll be your family. Not the same, I know. You three were a safe little group . . .'

Danu looks up at the watermarks on the stones of the archway. She wants the damp shadows to drip on her face.

When she looks around, Mag's talking to some local man with a white-flowered buttonhole who's speaking earnestly about sympathy.

A woman with pink roses machine-embroidered on her black coat approaches Danu. 'Come to the Church Hall. We've laid on a memorial wake.'

Danu steps away from the wall, breaking her silence. She asks, 'Why, when you don't know us?'

'Out of respect for the dead. All of them. Nineteen locals died from the same virus. A bequest left by an historic landowner was to be used purely for local natural disasters.'

Danu glances at the recently swept paving stones, and an exuberant passion-flower vine which trails from the archway. She asks, 'What kind of natural disasters do you usually . . .'

The woman's short curls bounce as she shakes her head. 'I know, I know. He once lived in a tsunami zone. Left a small pot for this purpose, when quite, quite senile. Puddles and the odd thunderstorm don't require financial aid.'

'My parents' deaths aren't a natural—'

'Five strangers passing away on his land as well as so many of our own counts as some kind of disaster. Money should be *used*, not merely sit there. Come on.' She pats Danu's shoulder. 'Don't worry, it's informal.'

As Danu walks beside her, following the others towards a red-brick building, she says, 'We always have our gatherings outside. Under the sky.'

'Well you're all far hardier than we are, then. It may of course rain, or there could be a breeze. It was predicted, I think.'

The woman squints at white clouds. 'Not marquee weather yet, unfortunately.'

At the wake, sandwiches are arranged in small mountains alongside homemade cakes and a tea urn. Most of the other circus people cluster near the door, eyeing the hats of the townspeople with curiosity and suspicion. Few of them take the proffered throwaway plates, as they don't want to make a mess. The occupants of every town, rich or poor, friendly or aggressive, expect travellers to create litter.

The minister has a calmness about him. Beside him, Danu is numb. She wants to feel calmness too, but her body is too raw.

The minister eats nothing, and talks briefly to everyone in the room. In between conversations, he constantly returns to the trestle tables to have his cup of tea refilled by a lady who blushes. Danu is following him around, but he hasn't told her not to. He seems to simply accept she needs to be near him.

She edges still closer to him. He's wearing brass cuff-links and she doesn't know how they work. She wants to tug at his sleeve to see if she can undo them, but he's trying to balance his teacup, a saucer and a spoon.

The minister drops in a sugar cube and tinkles his cup. Dropping the spoon into a plastic box of dirty cutlery, he turns to her and says, 'May god be with you, child.'

Danu replies, 'He won't be. But neither will your devil.'

He nods at her. 'I understand. You've no belief. But he'll be with you anyway. You're young to lose both parents. Too young. A mere lamb.'

'I don't feel like a lamb.'

'Well that's good.' His eyes sparkle. 'I can imagine lambs are always a little chilly. All their gangly skinniness. They need a jumper knitting for them, don't they? Or a nice bright shawl.'

He nods at Danu's lopsided blanket which she's wrapped around herself. It was the one thing her father made when her mother attempted to teach him to knit.

She wants to ask the minister something. She says, 'There are church people, aren't there, who . . .'

'Yes, child?' He puts his tea down on the trestle table and turns to fully face her.

'Who live behind gates. They never marry.'

'You mean monks and nuns?'

'The ones who live in big houses with only their own sex. Do they have their own rooms?'

He speaks slowly. 'Why do you ask?'

'I want to be locked up like that.'

He smiles at her gently. 'God eases the pain of loss. It will fade. I promise.'

'It won't. I'm not even feeling it.'

'Well you think that now, but you are. These thoughts are part of your pain.'

'But how can the only people you love . . . stop being there?'

'What about the others who know you well?' He nods at the circus crowd by the doors.

'They care about me, but I'm behind glass.'

'That's often said of grief. But do you understand why?'

'They're the wrong people.'

'No, they're probably the right people. But they're not the ones you're missing.'

Danu's eyes spring tears. 'No. They're not.' She glances back at the circus people. 'I can't even see them.'

'You'll be able to see them properly again soon. It's the devil who keeps them in shadows. Forces you to feel this alone.'

'I am alone.'

'Don't let him pull you.'

Danu doesn't believe in the minister's devil any more than she believes in the minister's god. But all the same, his eyes wrinkle as he smiles. He is a gentle man who believes in goodness and its triumph over evil: he has a faith which is god-high and devil-deep, and somewhere in the middle, an even greater faith in humans. He has a straight central parting in his hair.

Danu likes him. Doesn't believe a word he says. And she's let him bury them.

She thanks him for his kindness, and leaves the wake.

The circus hold their own wake through the night after the locals have retired to their black and white houses. Danu clasps a bottle of rum to her chest. She burns her throat with it and can only drink in sips. Beside the campfire, other people's heads and shoulders blur into the black sky. She tries to sing and cries instead, tries to talk and slumps her face against her arms. It is a drunken, tearful, bleary night. Stories and songs and silences. Blanks between all of these where the drink fills her head.

She must have finally slept. She wakes at dawn with her body cocooned in blankets. The campfire is now an earth-basin of ash. She doesn't know who wrapped her up, but she's thankful. The grass is soaked.

Morrie, the tightrope walker, is watching her from the steps of his caravan. He's holding a steaming mug. Perhaps he's been there all night, watching her sleep. Her head bangs in throbs. As she looks at him, he stands and goes inside, leaving his door wide open.

Already, horses are being fed and watered, tents and poles are packed away, possessions are being stored in bellyboxes and trunks. The circus prepares to move on, leaving the dead behind them.

But as Danu looks beyond the rapid activity all around her,

at the flat horizon punctuated by organised trees and lush hedges, she knows her parents aren't really here at Caderton, being left behind in churched soil. They aren't in the clipped graveyard where the locals will strim the grass when it tries to grow tall. They won't hear the ivy being ripped from their headstones, or see its pale lightning marks on dark stone.

No, they're not really here under this blue sky with piles of neat clouds to the west.

They're not lost, or buried in soil. They're dead, which means gone.

What's left of them, the real things – the things they touched most, are now touching Danu's skin. Adelaide's silver locket is around Danu's neck and Clem's leather bootlaces are tied around her ankles. These things are hidden under her scarf, thick socks and boots.

The locket's metal is cold against her throat. The chain is linked tighter than her mother wore it, it's now a choker. The bootlaces are tied so firmly they make her ankles sting. She can't remember tying these things to her body. But she must have done.

This bruising trinket and these stinging knots. Such small, painful things.

For nearly a year, Danu's shared Mag and Sandy's caravan. Since her parents died, she won't sleep if she can't hear other people. At sixteen, she should be alive for herself, but it's this pair who've kept her heart beating.

Mag and Sandy's nocturnal breathing sounds like twinned waves. Danu lies in bed every night trying to distinguish between his breath and hers, but their rhythm is matched. The sound is like bellows being used to ignite stubborn fires.

They're kind, intelligent people. They've a stack of charity shop books in a box under their table, and often draw one of these out to refer to while talking. They talk about everything and nothing, always honestly. Their interests are as flexible as their limbs – Mag is learning about archaeology and Sandy is reading a book on cloud formations – no knowledge is out of reach when there's a book to hand on the subject. Danu's mother used to take her to libraries in every town they passed through.

Since her parents died, Danu's concentration for reading has been bad. Mag's been putting a book on her pillow every so often, to tempt her with. Today she comes back from the shops and hands her a large carrier bag.

Danu's at the table, picking at a plate of fried potatoes. She clasps the bag. 'What's this?'

Mag says, 'If nothing goes into your head, try seeing what comes out of it instead. So your mother's lessons weren't all a waste.'

Danu looks inside the bag. There are seven large hardback notebooks.

Mag nods, as Danu takes one out and strokes a thick blank page. 'They're to write and draw in.'

Danu hugs her. 'Thank you.'

'So that's that, then. I'll not ever look in them, but I want them filled, over time.'

'I'll write stories.'

'Whatever you like.' Mag puts a hand on the kettle to test its warmth. 'Tea?'

'No thanks. But can I ask you something?'

Mag swills tea leaves into the bin. ''Course you can.'

'Why does no one in the circus like it when girls leave the camp alone? I always went out with my parents. But sometimes when I go off for a walk, people glare at me.'

'Young women get in trouble.'

'What kind of trouble?'

She pats her belly. 'Girl trouble. We keep to our own.'

'What kind of trouble do boys get glared at for?'

Mag snorts with laughter as she spoons tea leaves into the pot. 'You'll find it all out when you're ready. Don't worry about glares, they're just being protective.'

When she sees Danu's confused expression, she adds, 'Take Sandy his cuppa and ask him too.' She grins to herself as she rinses out mugs.

Outside, Danu searches the camp for Sandy, and eventually finds him in a corner of the field behind Tomas's caravan. He's chopping logs for the campfire. She puts his tea on a fence post beside him.

She says, 'Sandy, why do girls need protection . . . ?'

He brings the axe down and it sticks halfway through a log. Frowning at her, he says, 'You're not knocked up, are you?'

Flushing, Danu shakes her head.

He manoeuvres the blade out of the log. 'Good. If you want to talk about protection, speak to Mag. She's always been good at it.' He smiles as he brings the axe down again, and splits the log.

There's no curtain around Mag and Sandy's bed, and they sleep with their arms and legs wrapped around each other. They're in their late seventies, and are far more tactile with each other than her parents were.

Around her own single bed, there's a yellow curtain which hangs from ceiling to floor. She keeps her possessions in leather bags under the bedframe. Each time she sits on her mattress and closes the curtain, she's as alone as she can be.

During the days, she keeps her heart so numb she's not sure it's beating any more. But at night, once she's stripped off and pulled on her nightgown, her chest fills with ragged pain.

Tonight she stares at the curtain, longing for the outlines of her parents' faces to appear. But they're not here. They weren't here last night or the night before. If she goes without sleep for long enough, she might see them again. But she's exhausted. She closes her eyes.

Like last night, and the night before, sleep grabs, pulls her in.

She runs through a nightmare in which she searches for her parents. As a hunter, she's trying to steal them back from whatever has trapped them. She hunts in lonely places:

a dump filled with rusted thick chains and broken padlocks,
a swamp made of sinking mud and icy mists,
the deserted house of god which has walls made of solid fog,
the derelict house of the devil which is made of smoked glass.

The next night, she puts a knife under her pillow and clasps its handle as she falls asleep. She will take it into her nightmares in case she finds them and can cut them free.

She hunts them night after night after night. They're nowhere.

The circus has recently moved on and pitched up camp on the edge of an old mining town called Bellclan. They're performing three shows a day – early afternoon through to night. They have to recoup their losses as the small audiences in the last few towns have left them skint.

Six locals watch the performing tent being erected. They're perched with folded arms on the drystone wall along the edge of the field. They look bored. Some flatties really must lead flat lives, especially now their mine's gone so they can't even burrow underground. Everyone outside of the circus is called a flattie, because without the highs and lows of performance and applause, what else can their lives be, but flat?

Inside the performing tent, the seating area is already roped off. People are up ladders, securing platforms to poles and tightening the tightrope wire. Danu rakes the sand, which has been laid in a wide circle. Danu stares at the patterns the rake makes in the sand. When she looks up again, she's alone, and has no idea how long she's been raking.

She goes outside. As she passes between a row of caravans she hears Mag calling her name. Following the sound of her voice, she finds her lugging a hessian sack of potatoes off a wheelbarrow.

On seeing her, Mag says, 'About time. Can you get the veg chopped, for the aftershow?'

Danu chops carrots, potatoes and garlic, and throws them all in the blackened cooking pot which hangs over the campfire. Mag brings out a plate of pale meat. Once the pot's simmering, Danu goes back to the caravan.

Her clown costume is in a crumpled heap at the foot of her bed. The costume is stained with sand from her tumbles and falls. Clem used to wash it for her. Adelaide ironed it till the parachute silk shone. Danu shakes out the dress and hangs it on a coat hanger. Wetting a sponge at the sink, she wipes smudges off the white skirt. After pinching the black pom-poms back into shape, she hooks the costume on the curtain rail next to her bed.

Danu is part of a troupe of nine teenage clowns. Everyone in the circus is part of some act, and she's been a clown since she was six. She can cartwheel, juggle, walk on stilts. She can swing from the trapeze, she can tumble, flip, bump, kick, run away. She can wave her hands and mime a joke. Her parents' acts were written off the daybills immediately after they died, and she still hates seeing the calligraphy-written list without her parents' names.

Audiences like names on the daybills. They must want to know the relationships between circus performers, whether married, or child and parent. Sibling rivalry and heartbreak is alive and howling in song and dance routines. So many members of the audience dream about running away with the circus and if they can see the performers' lives as more than an act, the more real this dream appears.

Her mother was well educated by the wealthy parents she'd abandoned to follow Clem and the circus. Adelaide was a solo singer with an extraordinary range. Clem swallowed burning swords, accompanied by the sound of drumbeats.

No one else in the circus has these skills. They won't ever be replaced.

Inside Mag and Sandy's caravan, Danu leans on the table beside a small open window. Mag has taken over at the cooking pot outside, and has donned an old shirt to protect her skin-tight glittering costume. Sandy's showing her arm gestures which look like he's doing the impression of a snake. She's leaning over the stew, smelling deeply, nose-pondering what it needs. She shoos his conversation away with a hand.

Mag used to give Adelaide a cake every year for her birthday, for as long as Danu can remember. Her and Sandy once gave Clem a bottle of whisky, but he never touched drink. He traded it in part-payment for a new saddle for their horse.

Sirius was beautiful. Strong, gentle and reliable. Is he still alive? Will he have been happy with the child he went to live with?

Danu gets three blocks of face paint, a jar of water, a sponge and a paintbrush. Squeezing into the wood-clad toilet cubicle, she stands before the mirror. The white base covers her face, semi-circles coat her eyebrows black.

She paints eyelashes on her eyelids but doesn't look into the eyes.

A red smile over her mouth is painted on, wiped off, painted on, wiped off, painted on till it's time for the show.

* * *

22

To applause from the audience, the clowns cartwheel into the main performing tent. They run around the sand circle, pushing and shoving each other. The brass instruments play as they form a human triangle. The boy clown at the top pretends to slip. He jumps forward, arms outstretched, and grabs a hanging trapeze. One of the girl clowns below him grabs his ankles and steps off the shoulders of the clowns beneath her. The boy and girl swing till there's momentum. The other clowns collapse, lie in the sand circle and watch the pair above them, kicking their feet.

The girl clown flips over and the boy clown grabs the ankles of her lace-up boots. They swap places as the music surges. The boy pretends to fall, the girl catches him by the wrists and pulls him back to her. They stand on the bar facing each other. Swinging, swinging, swinging.

The clowns on the ground roll over and under each other. They stand in two separate groups, swaying in unison as they point at the clowns on the moving swing. On the trapeze, the pair stick their rumps out, lean their upper bodies towards one another, kiss, raise their arms into the air miming an explosion, and fall backwards off the trapeze. The audience gasps. The two groups of clowns on the ground catch them. They put their feet safely on the ground, and brush them down. The pair kiss again, and this kiss makes them fall over. They wave at each other from the ground, miming flirtation. When they stand again, the other clowns cartwheel away. The boy and girl clowns circle one another as the brass music ends. Drumbeats begin and a lively tune is played on a trombone.

The girl clown sticks her tongue out, the boy slaps her face. She feigns a scream. He sticks his tongue out. She slaps his backside. They embrace and fall on top of one another. Head to toe, gripping hands to ankles, they tumble across the sand and away.

By the main entrance, they rise, take a bow, and point up at the ceiling of the tent.

High above the sand, a suspended crush of blue velvet falls away to reveal the next act descending. Hattie, the bearded woman, is sitting on another trapeze. She appears lit by starlight which shines on the spangles of her frilly indigo knickers and long scarlet wings.

She's beaming with red glittered lips as she strums a ukulele. She sings as she extends a long leg and points her toes.

> You never make me happy
> you always tell me lies
> you never kiss me hard enough
> and always like the wrong girl
> when you know that I'm the right girl.
> And I'm looking like some angel
> but I want your loving arms
> so I'm gonna kiss some devil
> just so you might notice me.
> The devil's got a forked tongue
> but I know that a forked tongue
> has a range of fiery charms . . .
> You'd best watch out or I'll go to him
> Oh, yes, I would go with him
> Mm hmm, I would go to him . . .

Beside the main entrance, the girl clown follows the smells of stew and flatbreads as she walks towards the campfire.

The boy clown grabs her hand, pulls her back, and kisses her.

She pushes him away.

He says, 'What's up, Danu?'

She wipes his kiss from her mouth and smudges makeup across her face. 'Just don't.'

'All right.' He looks crestfallen, even with the fake grin his gob's painted with.

'I don't mean to hurt you, boy clown.'

He swells to his full height, which still isn't as tall as hers. 'Well don't then, girl clown.' They're called boy clown and girl clown on the daybills – and they've called one another these nicknames for the past few years. He pushes his fist against her shoulder. 'Don't like you anyway. I trust you not to drop me, though.'

She gives him a small smile. 'Don't like you either. So is it Nadie or Posuma you'll be kissing next?'

'Oh, Nadie of course. Bigger eyes. Nice tits.'

'Good choice.'

'Or Loretta. She hates you more than ever.'

'I've not done anything to her.'

'Aye, not since you chopped her hair off.' He grins at the memory.

'We were only nine! Anyway. It was a retaliation. Not an attack.' After this, Adelaide had told Danu their feud had gone on too long. Loretta's aunt was furious, and they were made to stay away from each other. Danu can't even remember what sparked them off fighting in the first place.

She says to boy clown, 'What's she hating me for, then?'

'Because she likes me.'

'Oh. Well, she might be your girl if you ask her . . .'

He nudges her. 'So you're off limits?'

Danu nods.

'I wasn't going to ask you, or anything.'

'Good.'

25

Boy clown winks at her. 'But let me know if you ever have the urge for sex.'

A flattie staggers past, looking like he's trying to find somewhere private to piss.

Danu scrunches her nose. 'I don't have an urge for sex.'

Boy clown shakes his head, feigning wisdom. 'You will. Comes to us all. Or that's what Dad says. He said to tell you – have a chat with him, any time you're missing your folks. He misses his mum. This time last year, they all died, wasn't it.' He bites his lip.

'Missing them is constant. Too sore to chat about. But thank him anyway.'

The circus people encircle Danu, nudge her on and try to keep her spirits up around the first anniversary of her parents' death. Many speak to her about their memories of Adelaide and Clem. She's trying to listen to what they say. *Happy couple, remarkable lives, such a romance.* These phrases are sore echoes, as all she can think is that it's her fault they're dead.

She longs to remember them as happy, though whenever she does, there's a pain in her throat which feels like a lie. It's the tight chain of the locket. She imagines it's filled with strands of her parents' entwined hair. She can't bear the idea of touching something so personal to them, and so dead.

Every time she touches the locket, her heart flares, pulsing hard.

She can't look inside. It is an unexploded bullet.

When Danu is seventeen, with no parents to rebel against, her heart rebels against feeling alone in a crowd. Boy clown was right in what he said – she feels the urge for something. She's not yet sure if it's love, or affection, or sex. She often catches

Mag watching her as if she's trying to work out what she's thinking. Whenever Danu's alone behind her yellow curtain, she gets out a notebook. She writes confused stories about romances between animals, fish or birds.

Night after night she lies in her bed listening to the breathing of the contortionists. She doesn't want to move or make any sound in case she disturbs them. Over time, she realises they're not asleep. They're having sex extremely slowly. So slowly, they barely move. Would they call this *sex*, or like most married couples, would they call this *making love* as if love needs to be created and re-created?

They make love in slow tides of breath.

Her body is alert to their sounds and she hates it. Sometimes she clasps her pillow over her ears. On other nights a strange ache passes over her skin, and her lips swell as she imagines herself being kissed.

There is no recognisable face attached to these imagined lips.

But she dreams that a kiss could be something remarkable.

And when she allows herself to dream of remarkable kisses, remarkable faces appear. They are covered in dark feathers, or coarse fur, or shimmering scales.

They disappear when daylight comes, leaving her alone.

Boy clown notices Danu watching as he's kissing Nadie, and glowers at her. Averting her gaze doesn't work for long because her eyes keep getting drawn back again. On another night, she sees him kissing Loretta, who glances at her in disgust. One night, Danu changes out of her clown outfit quickly as the audience trails away. She sneaks out of the circus ground and follows the flatties to wherever they're going for further entertainment.

At a balloon-strung hen party in a village tavern, Danu lingers outside and watches strangers through the window. It's a crowded

27

party which has been going for some time. There's a band playing love songs and dance tunes. There are many local men there, and there was an empty bus outside in the car park which presumably brought the bride and her female friends from further afield. People seem to pair to one another so easily. All it takes is a few glasses of alcohol, eyes which look away and back, a few words, and at the right moment: a slight movement of a hand or a leg. She watches how women are aware of men watching them as they dance under flickering lights. Men look like hunters. They buy a drink for a woman, and separate her from the others. This is how kisses begin.

A week later, Danu is in the front room of a terraced house only a few streets away from the circus ground. There's a birthday party she followed a group of teenagers to, and the room is crammed. No one's asked her if she was invited yet. She stands near the door as couples slow-dance under revolving pink lights. She senses someone watching her.

Glancing around, she catches the gaze of a thick-spectacled boy beside the window. He comes over. She doesn't know what to say to him, and she's not sure he wants to talk to her. So she decides not to say too much, but act a part. She reaches for his hand and places it on her waist. Shyly, he glances at the floor, and back at her eyes. The music is loud. Heavy bass thuds through floorboards as he kisses her. His beery tongue enters her mouth. Their teeth bump. His inexperience makes her more confident. She whispers, 'Slow down.'

He leans away from her. 'What?' He cups his hand to his ear.

She laughs, shaking her head as the music is too loud for words to be heard.

Looking crestfallen, he shrugs and leaves the room.

Danu goes back to the circus and remembers the kiss. She enjoys it more, imagining it, than she did at the time.

She goes out again a few nights later. In a pub, she kisses a boy who's a little older. He keeps glancing at other tables, checking who's looking.

She asks, 'Is something wrong?'

'No. You're really pretty, hey.'

He bites her lip during the next kiss, and she doesn't like his face any more.

The next time he goes to the bar to order a drink, Danu grabs her coat and slips away.

Mag's sitting at the table beside two crumb-scattered plates, tugging a hairbrush through her long hair as Danu gets out of bed.

She glances at Danu. 'Do you need to talk about anything personal, now you're grown?' Brushing a strand of hair away from her forehead she ties it all back with a bobble.

Danu says, 'Not this early in the morning.'

'It's long past morning. I can smell the booze on you. Unmarried girls aren't meant to—'

'Is it late?'

'Look, do you want to ask me anything, or what?'

Danu bites her lip to stop herself laughing. 'I'd like to know about your sex life.'

Mag doesn't even blush. 'I thought we were quiet. You'll have to ask Sandy about how he does what he does to me. There's nothing you need a kind of . . . mother figure for?'

'No. And you're not really a mother figure. You do get most of my wages.'

Mag nods. 'I know, pet. But I've never been maternal.'

'I've never asked you to be.'

'But is it drink?'

'Is what drink?'

29

'That you're sneaking off for.'

Danu's cheeks flush. 'None of your business.'

'Is it sex?'

Danu shakes her head.

Mag doesn't look convinced. 'When folks die, close folks . . . Well, I'll just say it. When my mam died I wanted sex all the time. It's what the body does, to keep itself wanting to, well . . . keep on. But why not get yourself a circus lad? There's plenty of them like you. But they won't for long, if you carry on like this.'

'Like what?'

'Going anywhere with flatties after dark. Coming back smelling of booze.'

Danu doesn't know what to say, so says nothing.

Mag says, 'Well that's that done. There's been talk, so I was told to take you in hand. You're in hand now? Can you at least *say* you are, so I can say I've done it?'

'I'm in hand.'

'Good.' She goes to the counter and picks up the breadknife. 'Do you want breakfast?'

'Not yet. Just tea.'

'Pot's stewed, but you'll not mind.' She hands Danu a mug, nods at the yellow misshapen teapot, and goes outside.

Danu pours lukewarm tea into the mug. Talk is only about what people are capable of guessing.

Her curiosity is her own secret.

If secrets are kept for long enough, they become possessions.

The only things in the world which are hers.

Danu's in the kitchen at a flattie's house party. The flatties are drunk already, and no one's asked her if she's friends with anyone who lives here. She's drank too much cider and one of the flattie men comes over to her. He has brown eyes and a soft pair of hands. He glances at the leather bootlaces tied around her ankles.

She takes another swig of cider.

'Come with me.' He takes the glass from her and puts it on the counter.

Her body is like a rag doll as he leads her along a corridor and pulls her into a bathroom. He bolts the door and leans against it. 'Come here.' He opens his arms.

Laughing, she slumps against him. 'You're a bit spinning . . . I've had too much to drink . . .'

'Well, I've not. Here, lie down.'

She glances at the tiled floor. 'It'll be cold. Dirty.'

He puts his arms around her. Is she meant to stroke his hair? It's greasy. He pulls her to the ground and she lands awkwardly.

He kisses her neck.

She doesn't want to be on the floor. She says, 'I'm going now.'

As she tries to rise he grabs her hand and pulls her down on top of him.

She laughs; because his arms are so strong, she imagines he's a bear. She kisses him. This time, her lips tingle. She kisses him again.

Something hard presses against her thigh. It's sharp. She's not sure what the shape of a man's body is like under his clothes. She eases herself off him and stands up.

He's on his feet as well, and as she tries to unbolt the door, he grips her wrist and stops her.

Seeing her wince, he says, 'Sorry,' and lets go.

He pushes her clumsily against the wall.

She says, 'I don't want to kiss you.'

'Then you're a tease.' He's too tall. Too wide. Too strong.

'I'm not teasing. I've changed my mind, is all.'

He grabs her breast.

'Don't.' She pushes at him but he pushes back harder.

He's trying to get her skirt up.

She grips his wrist, but he shakes off her hand like it's nothing.

She says, 'You can't just do what you want.'

'I can.' Hand up her skirt, he moves her knickers out of the way. 'Your bound ankles turn me on, you slut.'

He smells of sweat. His body feels as hard as thick rubber. There's nothing but density inside it. No organs, no brain, no lungs, no heart. Her body feels too small to fight him, so she uses her mind. Her voice shakes as she says, 'Is your mother still alive?'

Anger makes his face look like a monster. It's dark, focused, unmoving, and the mouth has too many teeth.

She says, 'What would you think if someone touched her like this?'

He says, 'Shut the fuck up.'

There's a tap on the door. A voice from outside. 'Is the bathroom free?'

His face changes back into the face of a man. He lets her go.

Danu rushes to the door and unbolts it.

As she passes the figure on the other side of the door, the man calls after her, 'Well piss off then. You're not the only pretty girl here.'

She passes pretty girls in bright dresses as she goes back through the kitchen and outside.

As she runs back to the circus, her elbow's stinging, and there's a bruise coming up on her shoulder. Too much booze, but she doesn't feel drunk. She feels stupid and weak. She wants to swim. Float or drown. If only there was a stream here, if there was a river, a pool, a lake. If there was only an ocean.

But this town is dry.

Danu slows to a walk as she reaches the railings alongside the circus camp. Their shadows make the caravans look like they're inside a cage. She goes in through the gates and crosses shorn grass.

She opens the caravan door and clicks the catch closed behind her.

Exhaling, she leans back against the door. Two wine glasses are on the table beside an empty bottle. A stack of clean laundry is piled on a chair.

Everything is still.

Mag and Sandy are asleep under a thin sheet. She tiptoes across the rug and stands over them for a moment. Their hair is tangled together across blue pillows. The wrinkles which deepen their expressions during the daylight hours are gone while they're asleep. Mag's lips move, and are still. Sandy's eyebrows frown, and relax. Face to face, dream to dream, they could be any age at all.

Danu closes the curtain alongside her own bed and her world shrinks into a private one. She examines her body. One bruise to the elbow, one to the shoulder, a scrape to the knee. She lies down and tears run into her hair. Trails of salt burn her face.

She's been bruised often throughout her life. As a child, she scraped her elbows and knees learning acrobatics, fell on her arm while training for the trapeze, ground blisters into her palms practising handstands on sand, and few of those bruises brought tears with them.

So Innocence, and its twin, Ignorance, are to blame. How might she take revenge on them? She sees them as blank-faced dolls in pale dresses, seated on the lid of a rattling pressure cooker, sucking on salted caramel sweets. They have kept her naïve. The world is filled with big fish which eat small fish and

33

big people who eat smaller people. How to change what happened, or how it feels? Take her anger at her own ignorance and make it experience. Avoid anyone who might consume her.

And that could be anyone at all. She'd half-liked that man, before he changed into something she couldn't recognise. Something monstrous. Something cruel.

Innocence and Ignorance can sit on their pressure cooker, bubbling whatever they want in the pan beneath their skirts. She hopes the metal burns their backsides. She won't let them hurt her again.

'Stop,' she whispers to her body. 'You know how to be cold. So, freeze.'

Each night Danu cartwheels, a painted clown face hiding her true expressions. After each show, she spends time at the periphery of the campfire, watching others singing and chattering together. Since the night she was trapped in that bathroom, she's more tongue-bound than ever. She doesn't want to talk to anyone, and has stopped mixing with the flatties.

Most people are more interested in themselves than her, and she's glad of it. There are individuals and their clusters: Gianto and his bedraggled authority, the clutch of young women her own age – Nadie, Posuma, Loretta. Boy clown's been kissing all of them and lying about it. They spend most nights bickering. Hattie's beard is curlier than ever, and she's taken to dyeing it black. The crystal reader never smiles at Danu. Her dad died at the same time as Danu's parents. The farrier and the tightrope walker always have a ready grin. Night after night, Danu waits for Mag and Sandy to go off to bed, gives them an hour or so alone, and goes quietly to her own.

During the daytimes, she stays in the caravan as much as possible. Many days are spent sitting on her single bed with the yellow curtain closed and her body wrapped in her purple coverlet. Mag and Sandy have noticed the quietness in her – she's overheard Mag murmur, *Best leave her to it.*

One morning Danu's sitting on her bed, hugging a cushion. Her body relives every unwanted touch it received from the flattie man like bad echoes. She can't remember the last time she asked Mag or Sandy for a hug. She opens her curtain and the caravan is filled with steam. There are shapes in warm fog, slow splashes and waves. She watches them move and thicken.

Mag and Sandy come in from outside. They're talking about landslides.

Mag yells, 'For flipsake, lass!' She rushes to turn off the kettle.

Sandy flaps the door to clear the air. He shakes his head at Danu. 'Coffee?'

She nods.

Mag gets a jar of sugar out of the cupboard and clunks it on the counter.

Danu carries her cushion over to the table, and sits hugging it to her chest.

Mag opens a window and rinses three mugs. She glances at Danu. 'Still gloomy, then.'

Danu asks, 'How did you two decide to be in love?'

Sandy steps past Mag to wash mud off his hands. 'It's not a deciding thing. Well, you decide when to say something, I suppose. It was me who first fell on top of Mag, not the other way round. Contortions take a while to get right.'

Mag puts the coffee jug and mugs on the table. 'I wish you'd keep a better eye on things, girl.' She gets a carton of milk from the fridge and sits down. 'It wasn't who fell on top of who. We neither of us had to try.' She pats her heart. 'There were others all around us, acting this, saying that, preening or sobbing heartbreak all over each other. We were just easy.'

Sandy nudges Mag. 'I've loved you since when you had your ankles—'

Mag pats his arm. 'Not now.' She turns to Danu. 'Have you fallen for someone? Tell me he's not a flattie.'

Danu says, 'I've not. And I won't.'

Sandy interrupts, 'Mag, it *was* when your ankles—'

Mag shushes him again.

Sandy laughs and says to Danu, 'You should hear about our first bash at escapology: there was this wardrobe and the back fell off, and—'

Mag puts both hands on the table. 'Sandy. Shut up. She's upset!'

Danu says, 'Don't worry about me—'

Mag shakes her head. 'You've been moping for a while.'

'Not moping, thinking.'

Sandy says, 'Well. Don't think for too long. It'll make you maudlin. Now, eggs.' He leans under the table and retrieves a small hardback book. He opens it on a page full of pictures of speckled eggs. 'Fascinating. There are so many colours and types—'

Mag says to Danu, 'It's only ever been me and himself. I love him. He loves me. It's simple.'

Sandy puts the book down, feigning shock. 'You've not said you love me for years!'

She slaps his wrist. 'You bugger. I tell you all the time.'

Danu says, 'I'm sorry if I worried you by leaving the camp alone at night.'

Mag says, 'You're not knocked up, are you?'

'Why does everyone always think quiet girls have nothing better to do than get knocked up? No! I'm just changing.'

Sandy slides the book across the table towards Danu. 'Well, that's as bad as thinking. Now, look at these.' He points at a page of blue eggs. 'They're the ones to look out for in the woods round here . . .' He launches into an explanation about exactly what height the nests containing these particular eggs will be in the trees, till Mag interrupts to tell him it's the wrong time of year to be looking for eggs at all.

Once Sandy's gone outside again, and Mag's dismantled a stack of washing-up, Danu asks, 'Were you scared of him, at first?'

'Who?'

'Sandy.'

She laughs. ''Course not.' She puts on her coat and rummages through the pockets. Spying her purse on the table, she picks it up and shoves it into her bag. 'Right, I'm off to the shops. Need to get some supplies in. Sandy's gotten through the cheddar. Bloody mouse.'

Turning a page in her notebook, Danu examines a pencil drawing of a rose she did a few days ago. It's intricate and detailed, and the leaves have smooth curves. She's written *who are you* over and over again to form a frame around the drawing. The thorns appear sharp but the petals are thickly shaded. Getting a rubber, she tries to lighten their edges to make them more delicate.

Mag comes back into the caravan, carrying a box of groceries.

Danu says, 'Mag, did my parents ever speak with you about someone called Rosa?'

'No, why?'

Danu closes her notebook and gets up to help Mag unpack the box. 'They occasionally mentioned her name. But they never told me who she was.'

'Well, what did they say about her?' Mag gets two cans of beans out of the box and hands them to Danu to put away.

'I think they'd have told me about her, eventually. She was

37

someone important. Just saying her name made them sad.' Danu watches Mag putting a pack of soaps under the sink. 'Are there any chores needing done?'

'You could bleach the tea towels. There's two in the washbasket, the others are in the drawer.'

Once the groceries are put away, Mag puts her hand on Danu's shoulder. 'Look, I know we're fuddies. But I hope there's someone you can talk to about all the things in your head.'

'I don't need to talk—'

She pats her shoulder. 'You do, pet.'

When Danu's alone in the caravan, she lies on her bed for hours staring at a frantic spider who's covering the ceiling with its web. The web's so fine it catches only the tiniest flies. She never sees the spider consume them.

If she stares without blinking for long enough, pictures of her parents' faces appear. These images are always of the moment of dying. The virus has turned into a black thing, like ink. She can't look away as blackness spreads and obliterates their faces. An ink-black illness and ink-black death.

Sometimes her mind replays the moments of them dying over and over again, and she forces herself to watch them. She imagines asking each of them questions. She tries to ask her mother if all men have a monster inside them, and she tries to ask her father if women have monsters too and is it all right to prefer to talk to animals rather than people. Sometimes she asks them who Rosa is. Sometimes she simply asks them to tell her all the things they were going to tell her when she was old enough to hear them.

But the images of death never change, no matter what she asks. They look as they did then, and say what they did then. There's the smell of tea. The texture of a surgical mask stretched over her face. It feels so strange to be able to change, to think, to be taller and wiser or more stupid than she was then, while her parents remain exactly as they were in such vivid detail. The marks on her mother's nightgown. Her father's eyes.

In her notebook she draws a picture of a girl made from oceans. Her hair is tangled seaweed and her heart is sealed inside a lobster pot. Danu can't talk to anyone about how she feels because she doesn't want to upset them. Everyone else seems fine. She needs them to remain fine. But all the same, her heart aches with silent hurt.

She waits till her heart is ready to speak to her.

In a quiet moment, it tells her: I need to learn something new, to patch up my holes.

If Danu doesn't listen to this, she'll be unlikely to survive. After all, if a heart is already broken by death, it is likely to be broken still more by life, and then surely it is only a matter of time till it stops.

She decides to obey her heart, and learn something new. Surrounded by people with a myriad of skills, she will choose someone to teach her, and become consumed in learning.

Danu wears a long purple tutu for Sandy and Mag's anniversary celebrations. For once, her dark hair is brushed, and it ripples over her shawl. By the campfire, she's playing minor chords on the squeezebox. She's sitting on a bale of hay, singing a song to a spider, from a fly:

> If you are to tangle my body,
> and twine me in threads which glisten,
> I'll wait for your moistening silks
> and ache as I watch your legs flicker;
> a slight stroke of loose strands,

tense and slacken, teasing out lines.
Sting and bind, pinch and wind.
Your thickening toughening silks
stretch out this tightening yearning.
Your deadening softening silks
draw me to you, shivering, burning.

As Danu sings the chorus, the key changes from minor to major, and as she repeats it, other people learn the simple tune and words. Their voices join hers:

If you're bound and tied, don't ever
    go dumb.
When you're caught in a web, your
    song's just a hum.
Flies hunger for spiders but spiders
    eat flies,
so break the tight silks, and let your
    wings rise.

Familiarity and singing are a heady mix, when there's a tune to carry it all along. These people all around her, *know* her. She won't have disappeared from their view in the same way she's not been able to see them. They'll have watched her movements. Talked about her. Singing the chorus a few extra times, she soaks in this feeling of companionship.

On the other side of the fire, flamelight dances across Mag's face as she strokes Sandy's arm. Beside them Gianto is packing his tarot cards away. Boy clown warms his hands at the fire. He's not really a boy any more, and won't be a clown for much longer. He's learning stilt walking.

Danu can finally see them clearly again.

TWO FOR LEARNING

Morrie is a tightrope walker who possesses glints in both of his eyes. He stands under a tree, not far from the campfire. He's watching Danu, and she notices the curled edges of his smile. With a little persuasion, he might teach her everything he knows. His dark hair is tied back in a ponytail and when performing, he always displays his muscular legs in tights and a pair of puffed shorts. He's about ten years older than Danu. He has a hunchback he is sensitive about, and often dons wings or cloaks as costumes, to disguise it. She used to wonder if he learned to tightrope walk to prove he could balance despite his hunchback. Many of the people in the circus are attracted to him – he's sometimes vivacious and sometimes subdued. He's known for his fast talk and sweet conversation. When alone with someone, they glow because he makes them feel bright.

Danu can see all this well enough, and resolves never to allow herself to be so mesmerised. Despite the myriad incestuous relationships and bickerings there are in the circus community, he's never tried it on with her. Never teased or had a bad word to say of her, nor she him.

Danu brushes mud from her skirt.

Morrie's still watching her.

She leaves the fireside and approaches him.

He rests his arm against the tree trunk.

She asks, 'Tightrope walking is dangerous, isn't it?'

He replies in his softest voice, 'Until you know how to balance, everything is.'

'And could you teach me to balance?'

His eyes explore hers. 'I'd teach you anything I could.'

Focus shines in his eyes. It would take that level of intensity to be able to kill someone. Has he ever murdered? She doesn't ask him, because his answer won't make any difference to her. She asks, 'Could you teach me about walking on wire – what's dangerous, and what's safe—'

'Ah, danger and safety. Those two roads.' He kicks a clump of mud off his boot, and raises his eyes to hers. 'I think you've already been travelling them with the flatties. Will you stop?'

She hugs her arms around herself. 'Don't tell me what to do.'

'I'm not. I'm asking if you're going to stop. I saw a bruise on you.'

Her cheeks burn. 'That was less than nothing, and I already have stopped. So will you teach me?'

Slowly he replies, 'If we have long enough together. Will we?'

Danu hears herself say, 'We might not.' She's confused at the words emerging before the thought which brought them. The light from the campfire flickers on the ridged bark of the tree. She says it again, testing the words. 'We might not.'

Morrie continues to speak softly. 'There's something else you're wanting to ask me?'

'Yes. If you teach me to tightrope walk, what would you want in return?'

'Just to be beside you.' His eyes don't flinch from her gaze. They look gentle now.

She says, 'There's no game?'

'Agreed. No game. I won't even ask you to trust me. You just will.'

Danu trusts Morrie to teach her, though doesn't know how or why. Within weeks, she's walking a slack wire, not too far off the ground, carrying a short pole with weighted ends. While Morrie instructs her, his focus is entirely on her slippered feet. He tightens and loosens the wire till the tension is right. He tells her to keep the balance coming from her hips, refers to her legs as a *base of support* but doesn't look too closely at them.

She's learning to balance. Each night she dreams of the tight-rope wire. Sometimes the wire changes into a bridge which leads to the land of the dead. It stretches ahead of her, over oceans, over mountains, across empty landscapes. No matter how far she walks, the dead are always in the distance. On other nights she dreams she's heavy. The wire is a thread through air and her feet are made of lead. She plummets herself awake. Sometimes she dreams she's light. The wind lifts her away from the wire and carries her too high. The wire is barbed, threaded through with torn ribbons. She can't land to it.

She asks Morrie if he ever dreams of the wire.

He tells her, 'I never remember my dreams.'

'Why not?'

He shrugs. 'I prefer real things.'

She smiles. 'Sometimes I dream I'm split in half. And even in those half-dreams, I try to dream of real things. I fall asleep thinking about trees, rocks, earth. Sometimes I think of you, telling me to balance. Steadying things. But the thing is with dreams—'

'They make real things unreal?'

'Yes. Like the wire – in a dream it becomes a line on a map, a skipping rope, a lasso . . .'

He says, 'For me, the wire is entirely about balance.'

'Well you're probably best off not dreaming.'

He grins. 'Dreaming's far too dangerous for me.'

She laughs. 'You're too honest for your own good.'

'Can anyone be too honest?'

'Perhaps.'

Within a few months, the wire has been raised. Morrie has been shouting *centre of mass* at her in every lesson, and he's now stopped.

When Danu and Morrie gather with the others to eat or talk, he's good at raising laughter. Sometimes he prefers to chatter quietly, sometimes he acts the scamp. Often he plays the bodhran and sings a new song of wildness; of distant places the tune leads him to, or the tales of some stranger he met along the road. When the song is spent, it vanishes from him as easily as it arrived.

He packs the drum away, wanders to the edge of the gathering and watches the interactions from afar.

One night, Danu leaves the others and sits next to him on a drystone wall. His eyes shine as he turns to her and says, 'Let's try having both of us on the wire.'

She replies, 'Has it been done before?'

He shrugs. 'I think *we* could do it.'

'Is it safe?'

'No.'

The following morning, they set up a low wire between two trees.

She falls first. He falls next. They both fall over and over again. He hums, and they both step in time to the rhythm of his tune. Their steps on the wire have to match with complete precision.

They practise stepping with him humming, and then both of them humming. They fall less often, but still fall.

Morrie says to her, 'Can you take them off, or loosen them?' He's looking at the bootlaces which are bound around her ankles. 'They're pinching. That'll affect your balance.'

Her throat feels choked. 'They were my father's. I'll not take them off till they drop off.'

He pauses before he replies. 'We should go for a walk one day. Talk about him and your mother. If you like.'

She can't speak. She wants him to read her mind as it shouts. *I can't talk about them. I'll break if I do.* She's not sure if he hears her thoughts or not, but is relieved when he changes the subject.

Morrie suggests using musical beats as a way to more precisely match their steps. They raise the wire higher from the ground. With the safety net in place, they both step onto the wire, eyes locked. Morrie sings a slow easy tune – a lullaby they've often heard sung as the campfire dies. They step forwards on the first syllable of each word. They step again.

He nods. 'This could work. But we need still more precision. As I sing, look at my eyes. When I narrow them, step.' The wire vibrates and throws them into the net.

Each day, they continue to practise and Morrie sings the same lullaby. They develop a language of blinks and the narrowing of eyelids to communicate even the slightest movement of their bodies. After a few weeks, Morrie stops singing.

They read the signs in one another's eyes to know precisely when to transfer the weight onto the foot. They have to consider each consecutive step: mutual balance, combined weight. Two bodies on one line.

The wire is raised higher and higher until the safety net is finally removed. They must never break eye contact or allow themselves any thought other than predicting how the other will move, and mirroring that movement with precision. They breathe in unison.

Danu writes a story from which they develop a basic act which focuses on them almost touching one another, but always out of reach. She rewrites the story into the lyrics for a song. Danu plays a moth opposite Morrie's donkey. The story they tell is simple: a tragic love between two creatures who can never lie together without the annihilation of one, and the grief of the other.

This act is added to the daybills and they perform it in front of a live audience. Enveloped in the walling of the circular performing tent, the audience erupts with applause and many have tears in their eyes when the act is over and the pair descend the ladders to take their bows.

Side by side on the circle of sand, they bow. Applause grows. The front three rows of the audience ripple to their feet, clapping with raised hands. Cheering comes in waves from the back rows.

Shaking his head and grinning, Morrie turns to Danu, grabs her hand, and shouts, 'Listen to them – this is euphoric! Danu, marry me!'

Danu's stomach clenches.

Morrie raises her hand, they beam at the audience, bow again, and straighten. Danu glances at him. He remains facing the audience. Drinking it in, he's avoiding looking at her.

She squeezes his hand as she leans into his ear. 'I can't marry anyone till I've fully found my centre of mass.'

He glances at her and grins, looking grateful she hasn't taken him seriously.

They take their final bow.

* * *

46

Danu rushes into Sandy and Mag's caravan, banging the door behind her. Crouching, she looks under her bed and drags out an old pair of wide trousers to cut up.

Sandy's voice says, 'There you are. Do you want some food, missy? I've made flatbreads and—'

Danu looks at him over her shoulder. His red apron is covered in flour. She replies, 'No thanks, I'm fine.'

'Can I have a word?'

She shakes the creases out of the trousers. 'For a moment—'

'Me and Mag think you might be best off moving in with Morrie. You're eighteen now. Most girls your age are either wedded or bedding down for it—'

She bites her lip. 'Are you wanting rid of me?'

'No, no. It's . . .' He scratches his cheek. 'Well you're there all the time. Seems mad for us to be taking so much of your wages still, though you're earning more. It feels unfair.'

'I'll not move in with Morrie. I've not fallen for him or anything.'

'But you're round there all the time. Look, we've set a little aside. Like your ma and da would have done for you. Everyone reckons you're on the verge of getting hitched, they're talking chemistry. So if you two—'

'There's no *you two* about it. It's the act. It needs all we've got – the pair of us. We've to trust each other more than we trust ourselves. Like he's the music and I'm the picture and he's the song and I'm the words of it all. And if there's *chemistry* crackling along a fine straight line suspended over a fall, we're only dancing with it.'

She's heard others mention chemistry. It's been said in front of them both, but they've never discussed it. Anything made from chemicals might be too easily blown up and destroyed.

Sandy says, 'Well you're keeping the audiences happy

47

with your non-explosions, I'll give you that. But if you and he ever—'

'We won't.' She glances at the door. 'I'm best off alone.'

'But you're not alone. You're off back to him now, aren't you? Not spending any hours with us.'

'We've new costumes to do, and not long to make them in. Do you *want* more hours off me? You and Mag are always so . . .'

'So, what?'

'Bound up in each other.'

Sandy goes to the counter, wiping his hands on a cloth. 'We loved your mam and dad. A lot. They each worked their socks off as well. Look, at least take these. For Morrie if not for yourself.' He hands her two steaming flatbreads.

Danu has learned that the wire is an axis. She understands rotational inertia, and how to be static. Her notebooks are filling with elaborate stories, song lyrics and drawings. She also writes lists:

A lion could so easily love a lamb to death. A lamb may only see the softness of the lion's mane.

The island of the pale fox is snow-soaked. The grey ocean is an island to the herring gull. Neither creature can settle in the landscape of the other.

A raven loves the mirror of itself which it finds in another raven.

Morrie listens to each tale as soon as she's written it. Sometimes he forgets an element of the tale – or the ending changes shape in his mind. The ones he likes, she rewrites over and over again, condensing them down to one page. Once she's rewritten the tale into a song, Morrie gives it a tune and the band set it to music. For the latest song, he's devising the choreography they'll perform on the wire – he will play the white fox and she will play the herring gull.

Most of Danu's tales are tragic. The original act she wrote – of the moth and the donkey – is the closest she's come to a comic tale. They still perform this as their most regular act. There is always something magical about the first act ever performed.

Danu and Morrie now have a sequence of acts, and perform three spots in each show. Word spreads between villages and towns. Many people travel a long way to see what becomes known as the best wire act in any circus. Each night on the wire above a crowd of observers, the two walkers face each other, eyes locked, steps matching with precision.

One morning in the early hours, Danu's in Morrie's caravan, sitting cross-legged on the floor while he rocks in his mother's old chair. Danu's drunk enough rum to loosen her tongue, and has her notebook open to show Morrie her drawings of a goat skull she found. She holds out her empty glass as she resumes talking. 'A jackdaw could easily fall in love with a goat, but a goat could never love a jackdaw.'

She frowns, thinking hard about it.

He asks, 'Why not?'

She points at her drawing. 'Horns. Might a goat with horns consider itself too dangerous to love anything at all? Horns are made to . . . To gouge. Gouge. It's what they do. All horned animals must be scared about the damage they could cause another creature, if they were to become affectionate.'

Morrie shakes his head.

But she can't stop talking. 'And without hands . . . well. No animal can lop its own horns off and make itself a softer, less

49

dangerous kind of beast entirely . . . do you think they ever want to?'

She looks at him, expecting him to be able to answer this.

He's laughing at her.

Grinning back, she shrugs. 'What?'

He refills both of their glasses. 'You're so animated when you're making up stuff. And when you're a bit drunk. I like hearing you. Look, you're here all the time anyway. Bring your things in, will you? I'll clear some space. Been meaning to get rid for a while.' He nods at a pile of boxes and empty jam jars in the corner. 'We're good, aren't we. Yes, it's the rum talking. But we are good.'

'We are. But I'll be bringing my own mattress.'

'Of course.'

'So clear me a bit of floor. And I'll need somewhere to hang my clothes so they don't crease. So you'd best move yours along. You've got far too many—'

'You're rumpled. You never hang anything up.'

'And you've to look away when I get undressed.'

'I'll look away.'

'Good. Ooh. That disappeared quick. Can I have another?' She holds her empty rum glass out to him.

The rest of the night ends up sunk in laughter and rum.

The morning after she's moved in, they're outside the caravan. Morrie is perched on a rickety stool, stirring salt through his porridge. Danu is sitting with her back against a wheel. She strokes the grass with her bare toes.

She says, 'Do you think flatties imagine themselves on the wire as they watch us? As if it's their own bodies which could fall, not ours? I'm sure they . . .' Danu's voice trails away.

Morrie says, 'What is it? You're ashen.'

There's a magpie on the roof of a nearby caravan. Danu knocks her porridge bowl over in the grass. Running towards the magpie, she claps her hands. 'Get off! Get away, get gone!'

She claps her hands again and the magpie croaks, leaps from the roof and flies off.

Danu covers her mouth with her hands.

Morrie's on his feet, shaking his head in bewilderment. 'What was that about?'

Danu goes into the caravan. She sits on his bed, sobs trapped in her throat.

A moment later, Morrie comes in and puts their breakfast bowls in the sink. He sits next to her and puts an arm around her shoulders. 'You're shivering. Do you want—'

'I want my parents back.'

'But they're dead.'

She punches his chest. He's too blunt. She values his honesty. Doesn't want it. Needs it.

He pulls her towards him. His body is warm, his arms hold her too tight but she doesn't want him to let go. A moment later she hates herself for wanting to be held so she pushes him away and stands up. 'I'll go for a walk. There's no room here.'

He glances around the caravan. 'There's plenty of room.'

'Not for me. All this is yours. Your mother's books. Even your childhood toys. I had to give all my parents' things away when they died. Look –' she waves at her two bags in the corner. 'That's all I've got left and you've not even thought to offer me a cupboard.'

'But your mattress takes—'

'Shall I move it out of your way?' She kicks her coverlet off and tries to roll the mattress up but can't make it bend . . .

Morrie lays a hand on her shoulder. 'Now stop it. Let's walk. Outside. Come on.'

51

'I've changed my mind. I'll not have anyone else see me crying, it's bad enough you're seeing.'

'Well, talk to me.'

'I am talking. There's no room for me here.'

''Course there's room. I'll move more of my stuff—'

'It's not my home. I lost mine. Everything got lost. All of it.'

Morrie opens a drawer and empties socks and scarves onto his bed. 'Here, have this one.'

'It's not about that.'

'It is.'

'You didn't bother clearing some room for me.'

'No, I didn't.'

'Well you could have.'

'I've not lived with anyone since Mum took off. I don't really know what to do.'

She looks at him closely. 'You weren't trying to tell me you didn't want me to move in?'

'No. I didn't think about what you'd want. I asked you to move in because I wanted you to.'

She shakes her head and looks at the closed door. 'Oh. Well. It's probably fine then. You're never anything but honest, are you . . .'

'Are you all right?'

Her expression clears as she returns her gaze to his face. 'I'm rattled about the magpie.'

'What was it about the magpie?'

'Their claws. The sound. When my parents were dying. Now, every time I see them I think they bring death. I hate them.'

'There are worse things to hate. Pilfering things which magpies are.' Laughter glints in his eyes. 'Thieves with wings. You should put them in one of those stories of yours. Give *them* a horrible death.' He empties another drawer and crams the contents into a box under his bed. What doesn't fit, he packs between other boxes. He indicates the empty drawers with a sweep of his hand as he glances at Danu. 'All yours. Now get your things put away tidy now, won't you. I'll go and check the snares.'

How can such a kind man kill so easily? His snares are made from a wire loop which strangles each rabbit as it struggles to escape. Danu touches her throat. What would that kind of death feel like?

He says lightly, 'I'll take my time.' He gets his knife and rummages in a cupboard for a hessian bag. Shoving these things in his coat pockets, he goes to the door, saying, 'Unpack,' as he closes it behind him.

She watches the back of the door for a while. What might the door feel, as his hands open and close it? What does the doorframe feel when his body passes through it? The air inside the caravan is heavier, now he's not breathing it, moving it around. She goes to Morrie's bed, picks up his pillow and smells the scent of his hair. She hugs the pillow to her chest. She closes her eyes and breathes. Smelling him, smelling him, smelling him.

She takes out her notebook and writes:

I want but can't have him. I want to be crushed against his body. About a week ago there was this moment. There were people all around us. I was upset about something and tears were threatening. He was there. He looked at me and opened his arms with a question in his face. I didn't speak aloud but my body said yes. His arms made me stop needing to cry. I can still feel the trace of the sensation of his flat chest against my right breast. I felt something bigger than we were pass between us. I pulled away and thanked him for the hug. Told him he was such a good friend to me.

Since then I've been imagining us surrounded by other people talking. He's always next to me. We're talking to some of these faceless people, not to each other. We're not even looking at one another at all but he's aware of me. I'm aware of him. From the corner of my eye I watch his hands move as he speaks. I want to turn and look at his hands, see the colours of his skin, the earth under his fingernails. But in this imagining, I don't. Someone else is speaking to me and I'm answering whatever it is they're saying but I want to turn to him and tell him I've felt the cold all my life, but he, well. He makes me feel warm.

I don't ever turn or speak.

If I did, I know what would happen. I would look at his hands. He'd reach one of them to me. I'd take it. My palm would feel as if it was touching a fire which didn't hurt. My other hand would touch his face. He'd turn to me and I'd look in his eyes. I'd see desire in them. For a second I'd wonder how long I'd wanted him and how long he'd wanted me. I'd kiss him and my lips would ache as he kissed me back. We'd soon be alone together. He would press his body against me again and this time I wouldn't draw away. I'd hold on for dear life. I'd tell him I loved him.

No. That's not what would happen at all.

What would happen is this: If we kissed, I'd be terrified of him. Now we live in the same place, I wouldn't be able to get away. He would press his body against me and I'd panic and draw away. My body would go numb and I'd feel powerless. He might look hurt, or he might smile and try to bring me back to him. But I would refuse to look at him in case he changed into a monster. I'd refuse to see any expression on his face, instead I'd hide the tears on mine. Soon I'd be alone on my own mattress, facing away from him, hoping that I could still trust him, still like him, and that he'd feel the same about me. But I'd feel naked under the cover, curled like a baby, not knowing who I was. The next day I'd begin to teach his eyes to see something ugly about me, and only ever let them see ugliness. Over time, he'd find himself someone else to love him as he needs to be loved.

Just beyond the outskirts of a small town called Clattering, Danu stands alone on a stone bridge. Along the banks of the river, silver birches transform into shadows of themselves at dusk. Their bare branches breathe in whispers and scrapes. On either side of the riverbanks, great rocks rise like fragments of cliffs – this is a muscular landscape. The few dead trees are ancient ones. They are bleached sculptural forms, as if every crack has been thoughtfully designed and drawn in pencil long before the tree died. Danu listens to the water as it surges around deeply embedded rocks.

She allows herself to think of her parents. Others saw them as a happy couple, but she's been trying hard to push her own memories of them away since they died. Her birthdays, and theirs, have been the hardest days.

Surrounded by the whispers of trees, she remembers how much their resentments terrified her. The quiet bickering over the small things: a burnt pan, an unintentional nudge, the lack of compliments, the frustration about who went to bed first and why they never went to bed at the same time any more.

A conversation between her parents surfaces in her memory, catching her unaware. They had been silent with one another for days. Danu was in a den made from a blanket and a small table. They didn't know she was listening. Her mother said, *So, should we kill it?* Her father asked, *Kill what?* Her mother replied, *Us.* Her father said, *No. Think of Danu.*

55

She was glue for them. A sticky substance which hardens as it bonds.

They were silent for a while, and in her den, Danu placed a yellow brick beside a black brick on the floorboards. Then Adelaide said, *Well, then. Tell me you forgive me. I didn't mean to blame you, not really. We made the decision together.* Her voice was muffled.

Over the years there were many half-heard conversations which Danu didn't understand. There was always something frightening about dramatic words being spoken quietly. She tried to keep them light, make them laugh, distract them. As she grew older she often felt that they were her children, rather than her parents.

She mines her memory for the ways they showed her love: alphabet lessons, songs and stories. Visits to libraries and galleries in all the towns they passed through. Hours spent trying to understand the magic within history books, classic stories and science texts. Hide-and-seek games in woods and cliff explorations.

They filled her mind with wonder about the natural world and a belief in the magic of imagination. These things are gifts.

As she grew older, the thickening quietness between them spanned hours or days, and as she grew older still, months and years. They forgot how to clear the air.

There's never enough air inside a caravan.

But there were clear signs that they loved each other too. They never spent a single night apart. They always celebrated their wedding anniversary. They watched and praised each other's performances.

What is the right way to remember them, when her memories tell her conflicted things?

They weren't meant to die so young. Not without taking her with them.

The setting sun illuminates the silver birch trunks. Danu's eyes spring with tears as beauty catches her breath. She wishes she believed in god, or a devil, or any kind of deity. God could make her stop missing her parents because she could believe in a reunion in heaven. A devil could stop her feeling guilty for seeing all of this beauty when they can't.

Without a deity with an artistic masterplan, where does this beauty come from – the filtering light of a sunset, this clear air, these temperamental waters? Surely something vast must have designed the world, for it to be so deeply beautiful. She searches the landscape. The waters crash over stones and the trees are clothed in dusk's shadows. Touching the stone bridge, she feels gravity's magnetic pull.

She stares into the river, longing for the emergence of something profound. A water spirit, who trickles and surges through rivers and streams, before gathering herself as a powerful ocean.

The sound of gushing water subsides. Light shifts. The river stills. Danu drifts into the clouds, reflected beneath her in water.

The campfire rages, and two children bicker over a thin piece of roasted duck. Danu warms herself by the fire as this night is a cold one. Gianto is on his feet, speaking with authority. He's explaining why the circus needs to move on tomorrow.

'There's not enough village flatties travelling into the small towns. A cold winter chases people indoors and keeps them in the warm.' He rubs his hands together. 'We've not done so well in the last month. I'm thinking we might need to head further north. We need a city.'

There's murmurings around the campfire, about *the city of circles*.

'Matryoshka.' Gianto nods. 'Aye. You're with me. A few weeks there would fill our pockets. Make up for fallow months. But it's a long hard road. I've sent word up to the Tober there. So while we're waiting to hear back, have yourselves a mull.'

After Gianto's done with talking, there's an eruption of chatter all around the fire. Excitement. Concern about the distance, but the volume of excitement is far louder than murmurs of worry.

Morrie draws Gianto aside and asks his advice about how best to mend a crack along one of the seams of the caravan. Gianto is the father or grandfather of many of the circus people. A distinctive mole on his cheek marks his kin with freckled echoes. Morrie doesn't carry any variation of this mark, but his mother Louisa never did name his dad. She raised Morrie alone – happier to let people gossip rather than interfere.

Gianto and Morrie walk off in the direction of the caravan.

When Gianto returns alone, Danu goes over to Morrie. He's running his thumb along the crack.

She asks, 'What'd he say to do?'

'Sand it down. Patch it in. Paint it. It's only surface.'

'Do you want a hand?'

'We'll do it tomorrow.'

'What do you think about us heading to Matryoshka?'

'It's a long way, but it'd keep us fed a while.'

Danu nods.

He rubs her shoulder. 'You'll not remember it at all. It'd be good for you to see it?'

She remembers once asking her parents if they'd ever go back to Matryoshka, and they responded with a silence so thick, she didn't break into it. But she feels excited and unsettled at the idea of seeing her birthplace. She changes the subject. 'You get on all right with Gianto, don't you?'

'Yes. He's fine. He . . .' Morrie shakes his head. 'Nosy, though.'

'I'm never sure of him. Of what he's thinking.'

Morrie's eyes soften. She can't tell what he's thinking either.

He kisses her.

She kisses him back.

Morrie takes her hand and leads her into the caravan. He shuts the door behind them.

Danu can't speak.

They sit on the edge of his bed. He releases her hand and places his palms on his knees.

Her fingers feel empty. She clenches them.

He says, 'I know you don't love me. You said that when you were so drunk you've probably forgot the whole conversation. You were yelling at me not to make you love me. It was almost funny. Apart from . . . you seemed really upset.'

She doesn't look at him.

He says, 'Don't worry, I never touched you. But you've just kissed me like you meant it and we've neither of us had a drop of booze.'

She wants to leave the caravan, to go somewhere cold. But she can't move.

He keeps talking. 'But I expect nothing from you other than you thinking – one day, you *might* love me.'

Still, he doesn't touch her.

Her body aches to run away. It also aches for him. This pull in two directions is paralysing. Her voice breaks from her. 'You shouldn't—'

He touches a finger to her lips, to silence her. He tells her, 'It's a risk I'm prepared to take. So let me take it.'

She takes his hand, strokes each fingertip with hers. She can't look at his eyes. She'll want to swallow him whole if she does. She'll want to run away.

'My risk,' he says. 'Not yours. I won't kiss you again unless you ask me to.'

She doesn't ask him to, but hearing his words makes her want to laugh and cry at the same time. She says, 'I trust you more than I trust anyone.' She shakes her head in confusion. 'When I'm near you, no matter what we're doing or talking about, I often feel your arms around me.'

He laughs and squeezes her hand. 'That sounds like love to me.'

She frowns at the floor. 'No, it's not.'

'Then what is it?'

'I don't know. I don't always like it, Morrie. I don't . . .' She bites her lip to stop herself talking and lets go of his hand. She turns to him, but doesn't meet his eyes. Bathroom tiles appear on the floor but she knows they're not real. She blinks them away as she thinks the words, *Don't change into a monster.*

'I'm sorry. Ignore me, Morrie. I'm just scared.'

Morrie rises and goes over to the sink. 'We'll have to be up early in the morning, if I'm to fix the crack before we leave.'

He's released her. Her mattress is near the door. The door isn't bolted. He's not looking at her as her nightgown goes on over her clothes. Clothes off from underneath, she gets into bed.

She stares at the wood-clad wall and listens.

The sounds of cutlery clanking in the sink. Sounds of crockery clinking. Footsteps. Water running. Toothbrush against teeth. Footsteps again. Boots and clothing being removed.

She pretends sleep, holding her breath.

A sigh. Creak of bed. Murmur of blankets.

And now he's still.

She tries not to listen to his rapid breathing but hears it anyway.

Finally, a small snore. He's asleep.

Now, she can breathe.

Part of her is in the air above him, floating on his breath. Part of her stands beside the door, preparing to run.

*   *   *

As the circus travels further north, the winter spreads wide and high. Stars shine coldness through dark blue nights. Frost glitters the grass and hail beats down on the caravan roof. Clouds smudge the frozen surfaces of lakes. The shortest day passes.

The sun rises and falls like a pale coin.

Catkin buds appear along the roadsides. The bases of tree trunks are buried in mists of blue petals. From the branches, blackbirds trill.

The circus camps up in a deserted warehouse ground on the edge of a town called Acherton. There's a dilapidated structure which could once have been the back end of a pier, but there's no water. The weather's clear, so Morrie gets busy. He applies sealant around the caravan windows, repairs the spokes on a wheel, stitches tarpaulin and helps Mag and Sandy rehang their door.

Though this winter lasted longer than the last one, and though it was snowless, something settles for Danu. Even the routine of irregular and ill-attended shows have their own rhythm. Morrie often hums to himself. Smiles at nothing at all. He must be made of music as he hears it all the time, even when no one else can.

Though they have a vast repertoire of acts, Danu's always trying to invent more. She wants to try writing about different characters rather than animals and birds. She starts a new story in her notebook:

This tale is about love and a tightrope wire. A woman is looking straight ahead, stumbling for steps. The woman understands nothing apart from all the risks of falling. She is trying to hum a tune she can't remember. A man who is made of music is singing at the other end of the tightrope. They aim to meet halfway. Just to know if when they're both in the middle

of the wire trying to balance, at least one of them might be
able to sing . . .

She can't finish this story because she can't imagine where it
will end.

Danu's been trying to remember how her parents described
Matryoshka to her. They mentioned bright colours. Timber
houses, or was it stone? They spoke of artisans, the maternity
ward's walls being painted yellow, violin music, and the streets
curving, rather than running in straight lines. Something about
smells? Maybe some scent they couldn't place. These memories
are like ancient stories.

Gianto's garnered support for his plan of *stockpiling*
Matryoshkan coinage. It didn't take much persuasion. They're
already heading north, and will perform in many small towns
along the way. If the Tober gets word back to them that there's
a slot free, they'll head further into the mountains, to Matryoshka.

The circus has camped up on the outskirts of a town called
Thriffield. Danu's outside the horses' enclosure with the farrier,
Tomas Bell. He always wears brass-rimmed spectacles which
make him appear as clever as he genuinely is. Without them, he
has a profound squint. He was originally from Matryoshka, but
left at the age of eighteen and travelled for a while before joining
the circus. She's been asking him what he remembers of it.

Danu says to Tomas, 'Is the whole city really built on top of
a volcano?'

'Oh yes.'

'Isn't everyone who lives there scared it'll erupt?'

'Most people rarely speak about the volcano beneath them
at all, preferring to view it with the attitude that the city,
therefore the mountain, therefore the volcano, is their home.

And,' he grins at her, 'when you do force these conversations to happen, you find there are mainly two opinion camps. The majority is formed of people who have the expectation that *home* will automatically be a motherly, nurturing type of place. A duality of belonging. They to it, it to them. As such, most Matryoshkans assume the volcano would never be thoughtless enough to erupt.'

'But how can they live on something which could kill them?'

He looks thoughtful. 'Denial. Lovely thing. Keeps them feeling safe when they're not. The other camp is in favour of the murderous mother idea: kiss, and kill before death genuinely hurts. I heard someone say, *Well if she blows, we'll be dead before we know we're dying. We'll just wake up dead.* It's probably a win-win situation, if you don't think about it too emotionally.'

She smiles at him. 'You don't think emotionally at all, do you?'

He shakes his head. 'I did briefly work as a lawyer. I respect facts.'

One of the jugglers swaggers past, high on something or other. He's overheard part of their conversation. He turns from them, drops his trousers, bends over and says his anus is a volcano. Danu leans away from the sight of it, laughing as she hides her face against Tomas's shoulder.

As the juggler buckles his trousers and lurches away, Tomas says, 'Here's another unemotional fact: people should always inspect their arse cheeks for pustules before airing them.'

Danu nods, unable to speak for laughing.

Adjacent to the horses' enclosure, the caravans are camped in a small field. In the clearing in the middle, Morrie is lighting the fire. She beckons him to come over.

He nods at her and lays another log on the fire.

The skyline on the other side of the horses' enclosure is layered with jagged-roofed factories and terraced houses. Everything is grey under a sky thick with coal smoke – these flatties work hard through days. The circus will fill their evenings with colour.

Tomas says, 'Could you do the mares – they like your touch better than mine?' He reaches into the bag he's hung on the fence and hands her a body brush and dandy comb. He gets another body brush and hoofpick and goes into the enclosure, holding the gate for her to follow. He begins with Totle – a brown gelding. Danu approaches a mud-speckled mare called Electra. Still thinking about Matryoshka, she remembers her father telling her that the circus camped up in the outer circle, but she was born in the second circle. She's wracking her brain to remember what else they told her about the city . . .

She calls to Tomas, 'How many circles does Matryoshka have?'

'Three. Outer, second and Inner Circle.'

She can't remember her parents mentioning the Inner Circle at all, so perhaps they didn't visit that part of the city. Adelaide must have been exhausted after her birth. As Danu's sweeping the brush across Electra's white back, she looks towards the campfire.

Morrie's gone. The fire is out. Sandy's crouching to relight it, striking match after match.

After brushing Electra, Danu brushes Camila and her charcoal-coloured sister Shewolf. She speaks the horses' names to each of them softly, to keep them calm while being handled. Tomas brushes Brute, Peddio, Salad and Maggot. As Danu finishes Beatrice, Mag and Sandy's black horse, she says to Tomas, 'You head off. I'll do Inferno.'

Inferno is Morrie's horse. He's a beautiful dappled creature, with a wildness in his eyes that makes some folks scared to go near him. If Morrie hadn't broken him in when he was a foal, he'd never have been biddable at all. Danu sings softly into Inferno's ears as she grooms him, and every time she thinks he can't really hear her, he proves her wrong by stamping along to the rhythm.

Once he's gleaming, Danu goes to Morrie's caravan.

Morrie is lying on his bed with his back facing her. She closes the door behind her.

She asks, 'What is it?'

No reply.

She pulls a chair from under the small table and sits next to his bed.

Still nothing.

She speaks softly, 'I can probably guess, if you'd rather I said it, not you.'

He sits up and looks at her, darkness filling his eyes. Still he doesn't speak.

Danu says, 'You were jealous. You saw me laughing with someone else, and you felt jealous. And now you don't speak because . . .'

His words release, 'Because I've no right to be jealous, have I?'

'You've the right to feel anything. But does anyone have the right to *be* it towards another person?'

He frowns. 'What does *that* bloody mean?'

'I mean *acting* jealous.'

'If you were my wife . . .'

She frowns. 'Do you really want a wife? What would you do with one?'

'It's not my fault I've fallen for you. You don't *choose* these things.'

'Why do people talk as if love has to involve a *fall*, like it's some cliff edge?' She bites her lip. She's speaking without considering his emotions. She says softly, 'I can't hurt you, as I've not promised you anything. So why are you jealous?'

His voice is sullen. 'I've not said I am.'

She folds her arms. 'Well, you look it. But you've no cause to be jealous when seeing me laughing with someone else.'

'So because you've made me no promises, I should deny my feelings?'

'No. You should know them well. Look at them while they're raging. But then let them go, and don't act on them unless you have to.'

He frowns and looks away.

She says, 'If people didn't get jealous, there'd be a lot less arguing. They'd know that when they saw the person they love laughing with someone else, they were seeing simply that.'

'Simply what?'

'The person they love, laughing.'

The next day, Morrie apologises and says he's been petulant. Over the following week he looks away when he sees Danu laughing with others, but doesn't sulk. So he's settled whatever storm it was he was feeling. She admires him for it.

The circus moves on, and moves on again. The road ahead narrows.

Whenever they're drinking, Danu's eyes spring tears if Morrie puts his arm around her, as her skin awakens yearning, but she freezes and forces her tears to stop. Morrie makes light, tells her she's fussing over a hug.

One night after a show, Morrie plays bodhran with a cluster of other musicians by the campfire. His drumbeats stop and all around Danu, many voices are still singing. They've eaten a pot of stew made from some kind of meat Danu couldn't identify. She goes over to Tomas and asks his advice about a sore on Inferno's leg.

When they've spoken about what needs to be done, she looks around.

The fiddles and guitars slow as they reach the end of the tune. Morrie's drum lies abandoned in the grass. He never leaves it lying around. His mother gave it to him the night she left the circus. Surely he's not jealous again about Tomas?

She takes the bodhran back to the caravan. Could Morrie be unsteady with some bad mix of alcohol? Danu goes into the caravan and puts the drum on his empty bed.

She looks outside again, scanning the fire-lit faces but Morrie's not there. She sits on the doorstep till the others have all gone to bed. The night air is cold. She makes two mugs of tea. She drinks hers and when Morrie's is cold, she tips it away. She tells herself that he's just gone for a walk and will be back when he's ready.

But Morrie never just leaves his bodhran lying around. This is the flea in Danu's thoughts.

It bites her. The campfire's a mound of glowing ash.

Danu leaves the camp and runs along the streets. She searches the backyards of silent factories and pubs, the alleyways between the brewery, the loading bays of shops, she calls Morrie's name in the parks, looks under empty benches. She scurries behind each headstone in the graveyard, behind railings, under bushes, down basement steps. She isn't in control of how she searches; she's made of eyes, her movements are dislocated from her thoughts. She even looks at the stars to see if he's climbed up there. Nothing.

She goes back to the circus camp and looks in all the dark places. Morrie's not under any caravans. There are no sinister piles of fresh soil. He's nowhere.

Back in the caravan, Danu washes the dishes, cleans the toilet and sink, the table and cupboard doors. She wipes the counter, descales the kettle, clears crockery away. She folds the pile of clothes beside her mattress and puts them in her drawer. She learns each whorl in the surface of the door.

Exhaustion aches her body, thoughts frazzle her mind. She has to sleep.

She opens the curtains so she'll wake with the light. She lies down to snatch a few hours of sleep not long before dawn.

When she wakes, Morrie's drum is on the chair beside the table. He's back in his bed.

Danu shakes him awake. His hair is wet and he smells of soap. Morrie shields his eyes though the curtains are now closed. Danu asks, 'Are you all right?'

He replies, 'I . . . don't know.'

'How can you not know? Are you sick? You don't look sick. You look pale.'

'No.'

'I was worried about you.'

'I'm fine.'

There's a damp towel on the floor beside his bed.

Danu shakes her head. 'When did you wash your hair?'

Morrie says, 'Can I sleep now?'

'But why would you have washed in the middle of the night?'

He won't look at her.

Danu says, 'Go back to sleep. I'm just glad you're safe, is all.'

Morrie's sleep is fitful. He frowns, wakes and asks for water, but is asleep again by the time Danu's run the tap.

When he finally wakes, Danu again asks if he's all right.

Morrie says, 'Can we leave off talking about it?'

He still won't speak about it the next day.

Over the following days, they're quiet together.

She stops asking. He'll talk when he's ready.

One night after a show, everyone's gathering for a communal meal. Danu's changed into a warm jumper and thick skirts but Morrie's still in his costume.

68

She says, 'I'm starving, so I'll head out. Are you coming soon?'

He's looking out of the window. He says quietly, 'It'll rain.'

'I'll bring you in some food, if you like.'

He's lost in his own thoughts.

Danu goes outside and bumps straight into boy clown who's now performing under his real name, Mario. Tonight he's performed a solo act for the first time. He juggled knives while stilt walking, and the act's climax was when he threw them at Loretta, who was strapped to a spinning wheel.

He grins at Danu. 'Hey! What did you think?'

Laughing, she says, 'You were bloody brilliant. Not a drop of blood.'

Mario glances at the caravan. He asks quietly, 'Is Morrie all right?'

'Why?'

'Loretta had a go at him earlier.'

'What about?'

'Gist of it was that he didn't know what was good for him. But she didn't say it as nice as that.'

'I'm sure he can handle Loretta.'

Mario nudges Danu's arm. 'Look at us, though. You on the wire and me on stilts. Who'd have thought clowns could rise so high!'

She smiles at him. 'Proud of you.'

He nods. 'And me, you. Come on, let's dispose of the evidence. Can't believe Sandy trapped a bloody turkey.'

After she's eaten her share of the roast beside the fire, Danu takes a plate of food in to Morrie.

He sits at the table and eats it slowly as she gets out her notebook and looks through some of her recent drawings. She's been sketching clouds and coils of mist. In one of these drawings, she drew the faces of two girls, emerging from fog.

Frowning at the drawing, she tries to remember what she was thinking when she drew it.

Morrie seems so low. He says, 'You're kind, Danu. You give too much and ask for nothing.'

Danu looks up at him as she says, 'I don't want anything in return.'

He tilts his head as he considers her. 'Never?'

'I don't think kindness works like that. I care about you, Morrie. I just do.'

He smiles to himself as he continues eating. 'Shame not everyone thinks like you, eh.'

But the next day, he's still down. She worries he's sickened and watches him too closely. Then she thinks she's annoying him by watching him. So she distracts herself by clattering around the caravan looking for ingredients.

She fries him a pancake made from butter, brown sugar, an egg, caraway seeds and rye flour. Even when she covers it in black cherry jam and bashed-up walnuts, it still looks terrible.

Morrie thanks her and doesn't eat more than a mouthful.

Later on, Danu sees him outside, sprinkling crumbs on the fence posts. He's feeding the rest of the pancake to sparrows.

One night after a show, Morrie gets straight into his bed but doesn't seem tired. He's propped up on pillows. He says, 'Do you never talk about your parents?'

Danu stares at him, startled by the mention of them.

Morrie says, 'I mean about their deaths. What you felt.'

Danu's mouth is crammed with impossible answers and her lips lock them in. She gets a bottle of elderberry wine and drinks three glasses of it too quick.

Morrie watches her in silence.

Finally, he says, 'You must miss them so much. To still not be able to speak of them . . .'

And now Danu head's spinning from the alcohol, she can speak.

'I was thinking, just this morning, about my father. About what he did when I had measles. Do you know how he distracted me from having horrible spots all over me?'

Morrie shakes his head.

'He played join the dots on my arms and while he did that, he told me about stars. About archers. About all the fish in the sky. Now whenever I see a blemish on my skin, I see a star. How can I live without someone who was as gentle as that?'

For a while, they both sit in silence.

Danu takes another slug of wine and tells Morrie, 'My heart's tied up in loss. Like these.' She points at her bound ankles and the locket chain choking her neck.

'I've always wondered what you keep in that locket.'

She sways, and rights herself. 'It's my mother's. It could be something horrible. What if she wrote some terrible secret – something fearful that once happened to her . . . what would I do with that? I'd want to mend her. But . . .'

His eyes widen. 'You've not opened it in all this time?'

She stares at the floor. 'It's my fault they're dead. I caught the virus first, and I even know the moment I caught it. Why didn't I die too? I can still hear that man's cough. They were buying me a birthday gift.'

Morrie says, 'That's not your fault.'

'I infected them.'

'What was the gift?'

'It doesn't even matter. They were dead before my birthday and when I sold the caravan, I just got rid of everything.'

'Trust me, you've nothing to feel guilty for.'

Danu says, 'I don't trust anyone.'

He asks, 'Trust them with what?'

The walls come close and recede. Danu presses her palms against her eyes. 'With me!'

He speaks gently. 'To get this drunk so you can talk freely, you must trust me.'

Danu glances upwards, eyes stinging. 'Oh . . . Morrie, can we stop speaking . . .' The floor is unstable and she wants her mattress. She crawls under her coverlet. There's two spiders on the ceiling but she knows there's really only the one and it's Danu's pet because she hasn't got a horse – apart from she's pretending Inferno is hers though he's not – and the pet spider's not a twin and she's called her Cleo. Or Dido. No, Cleo.

She closes her eyes.

Morrie's mumbling around the caravan. He's probably talking and those footsteps are his and they're near and . . . shift away. Danu mumbles back in drunk murmurs. 'Too much too quick . . . Stupid wine. I trust you mostly, Morrie. Not all of you. Most bits of you. Stupid mouth.' Her head spins one way and her body spins another till she falls into blank sleep.

The scattered towns and villages this far north are unfamiliar places, filled with their own customs and traditions. There are unusual weavings in the market stalls, playing cards are used to tell fortunes, and many of the women have blue patterns painted on their hands and cheeks. Along the roads between these places are deep lakes, tall mountains, wide skies. At dusk, tree trunks at the roadsides glow with an orange light, but distant trees glow blue. The north is a strange landscape at times. Danu is enchanted, and captures it in phrases inside her notebook:

The blackened ridge – coal cliffs loom over a basin of charcoal sand.

On a heath, red dogwood stems push through scorched heather.

The smoke village – each smallholding houses a burning brazier in its backyard.

A moor formed entirely of grey rock, black ice frozen in seams, eagles circling.

Deserted villages within a forest, webbed curtains, antique keys rusted into locks.

One early morning, Danu looks up from her mattress and Morrie's sitting up in bed awake, so she tells him her ideas for her next tales. These will be stories of trees, skies, branches, rocks, oceans, the sun and the moon. She's barely awake, and her mind scrambles and misunderstands the shapes of constellations as she speaks of the love triangles, messy hexagons and impossibly distant pairings of combinations of stars.

Morrie tells her, 'They'd be beautiful tales. But it sounds to me that you're searching for love for everything in the world, except for yourself.' He gets out of bed and puts on his worn dressing gown. 'I'll make some bread. I'll show you how to build an earth-oven, if you like.' He turns to her, eyebrows raised, almost childlike. 'You could plait dough. Yes, girls know how to plait.'

She nods. 'Yes. Girls do.'

He prepares the bread mix using flour, salt, water, yeast.

She makes three rolls of the yeast-scented dough, but it's tacky – her hands can't plait evenly.

Seeing the rolls thinning into strands, he tells her he'll need to even them out.

She watches her hands move over his and his over hers. He brushes egg white across the bumps in the dough.

She patterns them with sesame seeds and tries not to count how many of them stick.

Danu sits on a storm-torn branch next to the horses' enclosure. The sun is not long risen, and spreads pink across the horizon. She wears layers of woollens and her skirts are covered in splashes of clay-coloured earth. She runs a thumb through a tangle in her hair to loosen the strands. Finding a bigger tangle, she gives up and goes over to the fence.

She speaks to the horses. 'Last night, two barn owls kept me awake. They were calling to one another. Have you ever seen them? They look like ghosts of themselves.'

The horses are eating meal from tin buckets. She says, 'I've upset Morrie. He was crouched next to me when I woke and I don't like him too close when I'm bleary. But what . . .' She frowns at the horses who are absorbed in their food. They look like they've got buckets for heads.

She runs her thumb over a prong in the barbed wire fence. It's pointless, talking to horses when they're eating.

Camila, a brown and white mare, removes her head from an emptied bucket and tosses her mane. She approaches Danu and puts her nose, huffing, into her hand.

Danu says, 'Morrie didn't deserve to be snapped at.'

The mare snorts and bucks her head.

Danu leans on a fence post, resting her chin on her forearms.

Camila stamps a foot and is joined at the fence by Inferno.

'He said I should write a love story about my parents. I told him I'd never do that, because they weren't happily married. He said *Of course they were*. I got angry, because he'd said what everyone always thinks.'

Camila rubs her neck on the barbed-wire fence, scratching an itch. Danu strokes her from forehead to nose. 'He didn't even ask what I meant. He said he was glad to hear me speak of them, but why talk to anyone? Mining memories only surfaces fool's gold.'

Inferno nudges Camila's throat with his nose. She whinnies.

Picking flakes of skin from her lips, Danu says, 'My father's rags were remarkable colours but they became muddied. My mother's riches were cold gold. Then I made them so sick, they died. What kind of love story is that?'

Camila's ripping the grass with her enormous teeth as Inferno nudges Danu's hand. She strokes his neck.

Horses' answers always come in small sounds, huffs of breath, the shuffling of hooves. They have no sympathy for anyone at all. She likes their kind of listening.

Gianto is beside her at the fence so suddenly, it's as if he's appeared out of a fog. He leans in close, whispers to her ear, 'The Devil is your tarot card. You're using Morrie. His granddad was one of my cols. Old times' sake, looking out for him.'

She steps away from him as she replies, 'Me using or not using anyone has nothing to do with you.'

'Morrie's not getting any younger. He should be wed, having a babby of his own. In your head there's other fish, other seas for you, no doubt. But he's sticking with you. It's all wrong, if you'll not do the same.' He rubs his arms. 'Chilly today, isn't it?'

'It's always cold.'

'Get yourself heated up about something then, girl.' Gianto thrusts his long hands into deep pockets and walks away. He disappears between two caravans.

There's a devil sitting on Danu's back. She shakes it off.

A few days later, the circus has stopped further north at a small market town. Not many people live there, and they've requested just one show. It's unusual for the circus to assemble the

75

performing tent for only one night, but Gianto's been saying *any* income is better than none.

Loretta watches Danu from her caravan window. She's curvaceous, confident and blonde. She shares a caravan with her aunt, an even blonder crystal reader. When Loretta's not having knives hurled at her by Mario, she reads palms. She's been wearing her best waist-clinching dress of late. Danu ignores Loretta's scowl as she makes her way across the grass to the performance tent.

Gianto's voice again. 'The Lovers. Give and take. Cop, if you rokker the old jib. What are you giving Morrie, girl?'

Danu almost drops the coiled wire she's lugging on her shoulder. She swerves around. 'Will you stop sneaking up! Are you drawing tarot cards on me?'

'You never come and see me. Others do.' He glances at Loretta, who moves away from her window. Turning back to Danu, he says, 'You traished?' He always slips in old words of parlari to remind people he's the eldest by far and therefore wisest by assumption. He's the only one who knows the full language.

Danu understands some of the words. 'I'm not scared. If I wanted my cards read, I'd ask.'

He folds his arms. 'Complete picture in each card. If you stare a long while, you get knowing. For folks who don't ask for the knowing, I use major arcana. You're missing out on all the subtles. Why *don't* you ask?'

'So tarot can't tell you *everything*.' She matches the strength of his stare. 'Do you draw cards for yourself or only for others?'

'My own each day.'

'What do they tell you about yourself?'

Gianto grimaces. 'That the bevvy always leads to the karsi. Joking with you. They tell me I've to know everything that's going on.'

76

'I like to keep things to myself.' Could he predict her death with his cards? And would he tell her, if he saw it coming?

He considers her for a while and smirks. 'My cards this morning said not to make promises.'

The town names sound more foreign to Danu as they head further north, and local dialects vary in thickness. They're in a town called Epoh where they've been performing for three nights.

It's dawn and Morrie is outside stacking scaffold poles and bagging the props. Danu's been woken by the bangs and clatters. Clasping her mug, she inhales the smell of coffee as she sits on the caravan steps. She says to Morrie, 'I wish we could stay here a while longer.'

He glances at her. 'This isn't a good town.'

Danu says, 'I don't want to be back on the road yet. To be this constantly moving.'

'We've got to get to the fork in the road before night. Go north-east, we're on the right road. Go north-west, we're in hell. Or so Gianto says.' Morrie glances at the sky. 'He was asking about Inferno's name, but he'd already been named when I bought him. Apparently in the north-west mountains, there's an underground city . . .' A drop of rain lands in his eye and he wipes it away. 'The air's thickened.' He grins at her. 'I've always thought we should chase ahead of the weather, not behind it.' Spots of rain darken his shirt. Grabbing a bundle of scaffold poles, he carries them towards the wagons.

Danu gets the bag of props and takes it inside. She lifts the caravan window open to hear the rain against glass. As she uncrumples the sheet on her mattress and straightens her pillow, Gianto's voice says, 'You got The Chariot. You're scarpering.'

Though clothed, Danu covers her body with a blanket.

Gianto's silver-bearded face stares in through the window.

He smirks at the mattress on the floor and speaks slowly. 'You're not even sharing his bed.'

Danu slips into Gianto's fractured parlari, 'I'm nanti scarpering! Get yourself gone!'

He taps the window over his head. 'Just taking parni shelter. The day before, your card was The Wheel. Full circle. Going back to begin all over again.' His voice becomes sing-song. 'Where were you born, pretty donah, handsome donah, with your lovely olive skin, pretty donah?'

Danu pulls the blanket tighter around her body. 'I was born in Matryoshka. Go. Away.'

He nods at her, unsmiling. 'I know, pet. And to make good time on the road, we'll do no more shows between now and then.'

'We're definitely going, then?'

He nods. 'The last decent city in the north. Peter's just arrived back with the news. Tober-Omey there's booked us for four weeks. We might even get eight, if we're lucky. Good dinali. And if we're scarpering the Tober here, that'll be kushti.' He pats his liver-spotted hands on his shirt pocket, rattling coins. He looks again at the mattress and speaks quietly. 'You're going to leave us and join the flatties in Matryoshka.'

'I am not.'

Gianto says, 'Know why they're called flatties?' He rests an arm on the windowsill.

Danu does, but she's glad to let him be distracted from talking about her.

He continues, 'Because life without circus highs, the danger of your wire, the mood-lifts of the audience and the mirth in applause, is a flat one. A life on one level, have the flatties. Think it's a happy life, do you?' He watches her face. 'Your silence speaks loud, eh. You're not thinking of Matryoshka as your birthplace yet. And all that'll come at you, there. You will be. The lost cities in the northern mountain ranges are strange places. I'd not be surprised if your next card just might be The Tower.' He winks at her and leaves her alone.

As they travel along a potholed road, Danu stays inside the caravan with the curtains closed. Without even touching her, Gianto's pushing her body flat to the ground with his palm.

When the caravan stops, she looks outside. Flatlands of pink-grey bog span across to mountains stippled with thin fir trees. The sun sets in a glow. People emerge from caravans, stretching. They all look exhausted, but excited. Some of the youngest kids sit in the grass beside Mag and Sandy's caravan. They're making a volcano out of piles of spent matchsticks. Danu's palms sweat as she watches their hands move. She wipes them on her skirt and takes deep breaths to calm herself down. She's sure that her parents wouldn't have wanted to go back to Matryoshka, and this excitement or nervousness feels like a betrayal. But she wants to see her birthplace, at least once, as an adult.

From night through till dawn, Danu half-dreams of what gifts or curses Matryoshka might bring to her. She conjures pictures of the things she might be able to retaliate with. These dream-pictures are on cards which she keeps in her pockets. She draws them out one at a time and looks at their images. A burning sun, a flame-whip, a lake, a tin cup filled with stars, a burning matchbox, a jar filled with sea salt . . . Symbols of fire and water.

From a distance, the city of Matryoshka appears to rise on the horizon as one great mountain among many. Getting nearer, the skyline of domes and rooftops under yellow-tinted clouds give it a sense of mystery. It draws the eye to itself.

Leaning out of the side window as the caravan bumps along

79

the road, Danu tightens her shawl. The mountain air is freezing cold. So many clouds surround Matryoshka's summit, the top circle of the city is in the sky. Danu can hear calls of excitement from the caravans in front. *Nearly there now! Can you see the size of it!* Around the base of the city, there's a high wooden fence. There's a wide gap where a proud gate must once have stood.

Danu calls to Morrie, who's at the front porch of the caravan, 'Can we pull over, fall back?'

There's the click of the harness. The caravan slows but only a little. Morrie's voice yells, 'Road's too narrow here to let others pass – are you all right?'

Danu calls back, 'Feeling a bit sick!'

'Get some water down you. Not long now!'

She doesn't really feel sick. She just wants a moment of stillness before she meets the place in which she was born. Knowing she won't get this, she places her feet flat to the floorboards and tries to settle herself. She tries to pretend she's beside a stream in a wood, alone and calm, but everything is too loud. Wooden wheels turn on stone, the horse's footfall clatters outside, the stovepipe and cowl rattle. The chain which holds the water jack in place clinks rhythmically. There's the chinking of glass, clanging of pots and clanking of crockery.

Morrie calls, 'Sorry, got to go faster, they're speeding up ahead!'

A few moments later, his voice comes again. 'Danu?'

'Yes?'

'Can you hear that?'

'Hear what?'

'Music!'

Flutes. A tune is carried on the air. It's so hypnotic, it sounds like a troupe of pied pipers have already captured all of the children and all of the rats, and now lure the birds out of the sky.

Danu grips the window ledge and leans out further as the pace picks up. On the great fence which spans Matryoshka's outer circle, three flautists are seated on a scaffold platform. Their figures are clad in blue, red and green. Danu almost expects to see the flags of a medieval army waving above them. But there are no robes or feathers, no armour, no staffs or arrows. Just three people in bright-coloured clothing playing a tune in close harmony.

Nearing the entrance to the city, Inferno slows to a halt. Up ahead, Gianto will be seeking the Tober, checking on what area they're to camp in, where the performing tent is to be erected, and seeing what provision has been made for the horses. There's a thick smell of sulphur. Danu runs a glass of water and stares into it. It should surely become cloudy.

Morrie touches her shoulder. She jerks away, startled by his sudden presence.

He says, 'Are you all right now?'

'What do you mean?'

He frowns. 'You said you felt sick?'

'Oh. Yes.' She looks at him intently. 'It's so warm – do you feel it too, like your skin could melt?'

He grins, eyes sparkling with anticipation. 'Come and sit out front with me now, as we go into this great city.' He takes the glass from her hand, and sips.

A shout comes from the caravans in front, passed back, back and back. Morrie and Danu are seated on the front porch. Morrie grips Inferno's reins as they turn to holler at the caravans behind them.

All cry the same repeated word: *Shiftyon!*

The wagon in front bumps forward. Two clicks of the reins and Inferno jerks into movement, pulling them into the city. Rose petals fall like red snow as they pass through the wide gap in the fence.

Calls of *Circus! Circus!* come from pedestrians as they turn into the main street. Tall timber buildings flank both sides of the road. Some of the buildings are leaning against each other, and others are propped up with scaffolding. Many have been painted with murals of dancers, musicians and musical instruments. There's a painted face of a girl, whose terracotta cheeks are peeling. Above the shop awnings, open-shuttered windows punctuate the walls. What must it be like – to perch on one of those balconies and view this street from above? Or even higher, from one of those skyscrapers further up the mountain that disappear into clouds? Danu imagines herself somewhere in between, at tree-height, watching kingfishers flitting along a stream.

They're in the thick of crowds. People, movement, noise.

Danu has never seen so many different faces in one place. She stares at two women with hooked noses as they block half of the pavement with an argument. On a corner, two boys pass a paper bag of sweets back and forth. Three men growl at each other, but their expressions change as a woman with orange feathers in her hair joins them.

The people sitting outside the cafés have elaborate makeup, tattoos, pierced nostrils, stretched earlobes, dark eyebrows and multicoloured hair. They're dressed in bright skirts and silk dresses, or baggy-bottomed trousers in all the colours of fireworks. Danu glances at her long coat, noticing the splatters of mud.

Still, red petals fall from clouds to cobbles.

As they move further along the main street of the outer circle, the falling petals cease. This is a vibrant chaos – and Danu's eyes blur from seeing so many unfamiliar things all at once. Her nose compensates for her eyes and smells rush in – fried food, patchouli oil . . . and a hundred other scents. She closes her eyes and sniffs. Incense, beeswax, pipe smoke. As they move further along the street, music comes from all directions, and her ears are overwhelmed by clashing sounds. So she opens her eyes again.

There are buskers dotted along these pavements. A guitarist in a grim reaper outfit strums as he sings a nonsense song about posthumous limericks. He catches Danu's eye and nods his skull as they pass by. She wonders how old his face looks, without face paint. Would her parents have met any of these street entertainers while they were here, or do street performers change careers as they age?

On top of a letter box, a woman in a bee outfit made of pom-poms stands on her hands. She's playing a frantic tune on a mouth organ which is attached to her face with wires. On the next corner a magician stands on a high platform. He's reciting some poem about *explosion and explosion, a bang and a bomb and a gun*, while bashing cymbals between his knees. He conducts his coin-collections via the raising and lowering of a pointed hat on strings. A velvet-clad violinist walks a slack rope strung between two lamp posts. A stilt walker strides along next to them for a few lengthy paces, strumming a mandolin.

Now too many sounds merge together for Danu to pick out any one strain of music. Morrie's saying something and she shakes her head, pointing at her ears.

He leans closer and says loudly, 'Will we get the kind of audiences here which Gianto's been promised? Practically everyone's an entertainer . . .'

Danu's distracted by two street performers. There's a boy whose head is a little too big for his body. He's holding the hand

83

of a corseted girl who's dressed as a princess. In his other hand, he's carrying a copper birdcage. Inside the birdcage is an enormous toad. There's a shrieking noise, as the princess takes an eyeliner pencil from her pocket and draws a black X on her lips. The boy opens the cage door. The princess puckers as she leans towards the cage and the shrieking gets louder . . .

Danu points at the cage as she says to Morrie, 'Is the toad *screaming* in there?'

Morrie can't hear her. The boy, princess and toad are left behind as the caravan moves further along the curved main street.

A cloaked woman has a bowl of red apples and a carving knife. At her feet, a raven pecks at a basket of cores. She's carving faces into their skins, and on a table beside her are apple carvings, each one containing a candle. She looks about sixty. Perhaps Danu's parents might have bought some of her lanterns as a temporary souvenir. They didn't have room in the caravan for anything permanent. She imagines the lanterns flickering along a path in a thick forest of trees. Her parents linking hands, walking away . . . and Danu following them, deeper into the forest . . .

Morrie's speaking: '. . . the people who are shopping and watching the buskers, eating and drinking – by night they'll be ours. And there's the folks who live in the two other circles as well, who must surely come out to play. This circle is supposed to be the liveliest one – they probably provide the entire city's nightlife. But oh, I'm hot. Here, take these.' He gives the reins to Danu so his coat and jerkin can come off.

Danu says to Morrie, 'Do you think my mother would have been frightened to give birth among so many people . . .'

Morrie nods at a young woman who's staring at them, saucer-eyed, from the pavement as he pulls his braces back into place.

Another shout comes from the caravan they're following and

they pass it back. *Rounding, rounding to stall!* They're nearing the place where they'll set up camp.

And another shout, *Setiup for firstnight!*

They pass the shouts back to the caravans behind them. Morrie shakes his head. 'For tonight?' He takes the reins back as they turn into a narrow side street. 'That's not giving us much time. But if that's what Gianto's offered . . . You'd best settle your stomach.' He nudges Danu. 'Take it easy a short while.'

'Thanks. I'll still fix the wire though.'

They pass a small pub called Piglet Romantic which has a painted sign over the door of a pig wearing a top hat and cravat. At an outdoor table there's a huddle of women in purple wigs who are all wearing the same shade of bright pink lipstick. A yellow-veiled bride-to-be laughs as the others wrap her up in a tablecloth painted with a large chicken. The rattling of wheels on cobbles causes the women to look around as Inferno moves uphill towards another tight corner. One of the women eyes Morrie, and says something to the others. They all look at him and one of them hunches over. They erupt into laughter.

Morrie moves his shoulders awkwardly as he growls, 'What are they bloody laughing at?'

'A hen party, in Matryoshka?' Danu rubs his arm. 'I'd imagine they have high expectations of male strippers. Perhaps they want to watch you lay them an egg.'

They set up camp in three neighbouring squares along the side streets of the outer circle. Tomas and Danu tether the horses to railings to be brushed and cooled. They fill buckets of water from a water pump which stands on a built-up plinth. Deep in the pool of water which surrounds the pump, coins glint like small suns and moons. What do people wish for here, which blessings do they want to draw to them, which curses would they prefer to avoid?

Inferno is wild-eyed, and his head jerks as a baby's wail carries from somewhere in the surrounding buildings. He doesn't like sharp noises. Danu rests her head against his forehead and talks to him without speaking. This calms him, and also stills her own thoughts.

Once the horses are all inside their enclosed square, Danu goes back to the caravan and opens a window to let the air in. People skitter around outside. Closing the curtains, she shuts them away. Despite the sounds of excitement which crash in, she's not quite ready to meet this city. But from what she's already seen, it's magnificent. She will soon enough soak it in, hear the sounds of it, smell it, taste it, and absorb this air of excitement.

But not yet.

She was born here.

Her parents should be with her now.

Can she summon their ghosts? She's never been able to before. But now she's finally returned to her birthplace, would calling them make them come?

She sits cross-legged on the floor and remembers the story of her birth she often asked her parents to tell her. They'd described it well. The labour started in the caravan. Adelaide panted and screamed herself into wild sweats, and Clem willed Danu to be born healthy with whispers to gods he didn't believe in, whispers he didn't want Adelaide to hear. It had been a long labour, too long. A local midwife had been found and was there, sleeves rolled, talking calmly but unsure what to do. The baby was stuck. Adelaide was shaking and her eyes were wide with panic.

Danu whispers, 'Come back to me now. This is the place I first met you.'

Clem and the midwife managed to get Adelaide to the hospital in the second circle. The hospital midwife was more confident. She remained hopeful and steady. Clem was told to go away.

He paced the corridor.

Adelaide fainted.

But then the birth happened fast. Clem told Danu that he was called back into the room only moments later. *Your mother glowed; she was brimming with joy.*

Danu bows her head and opens her palms. 'I'm remembering you with a beckoning. Come to me now.'

Adelaide described holding Danu as holding something made of light, which warmed her.

'I beckon you now.'

When they spoke about her birth, it felt to Danu as if they were describing a dream. They'd look at their own arms, seeing her there, grown tiny again. Her mother would often cry after describing it. Sometimes she'd ask to be left alone and Clem would take Danu out for a walk. Does remembering childbirth make all women sad?

Danu half-remembers a sensation of soft fabric wrapped around her body. A heartbeat, booming against her. Air against skin, a breath . . . The feeling of sudden coldness. Is this memory, or imagination? It's a familiar coldness. An old feeling from when she was very small. Something is missing.

'Where are you?'

Nothing. Nothing but the sting in her ankles and the tightness at her throat.

The pain that her parents don't reply is bigger than the pain in her ankles which are swollen from heat. This pain is the wrong way around. She grabs her ankles and squeezes so the bootlace knots cut in deeper.

Fingering the curved metal of the locket, she wonders if she'll ever be able to open it. What did Adelaide treasure enough to keep on this chain which grips Danu's neck in a strangle-hold? Something of the body: strands of hair, a torn fingernail. Her mother's handwriting was miniscule. A poem, the lyrics of a song. An insect's wing, an ivy leaf, daisy petals . . . Nothing but a secret is ever kept inside a locket. Whatever Adelaide's secret was, it will have held a personal meaning Danu is unlikely to understand, and this unknowing of her mother will hurt.

Outside, the city bongs with clanging bells.

The sound jerks Danu back to the caravan, to the city outside, the first night's show, the wire.

Scents of cooking and spices thicken the air. The buildings around the caravans are bright-painted timber houses with decorated shutters and terracotta roof tiles. There are no trees to muffle any sound. People talk, shriek, call. Surges of laughter. Temple bells clang from all directions. Drumbeats and cymbal clashes dance in the air. Danu wants to swim anonymously in these sounds for a while. To walk the same streets that her parents walked all those years ago. But she has work to do first.

Getting the coil of wire and turnbuckles from the bellybox, she walks along cobbles to the next square. The performing tent has already been assembled. Inside, the circle of sand is laid and the ladders are fixed to the poles. Morrie and the others have worked fast. Two of the clowns are setting the chairs out, and three others are positioning the lighting. Danu climbs a ladder to one of the platforms. Running the wire through the barrel of the turnbuckle, she bends the wire, passes it through, and fixes it in place. She climbs the other ladder and uses her entire body weight to pull the wire taut. She's precise and cautious – it may expand in this heat.

When she finally leaves the performing tent through the wide entrance, Morrie is on the other side of the square, rearranging the placement of the ticketing stall. He's already in costume. She waves at him, and goes back to the caravan to get changed.

Inside, the caravan is oven hot. Danu shakes out her grey moth costume. The moth and donkey routine is still by far their most popular act. Once dressed, she hooks the door open to let in more air.

At the table, she props a small mirror against a milk jug. She wipes her face clean and pats it dry. She rummages in the box of stage makeup. The design of grey moth wings around her eyes always looks like a mask, face-painted night after night after night.

Danu hates looking in mirrors. She always sees someone who isn't really there.

She focuses on the makeup.

Sponge on a layer of white, and smudge the edges.

Load a wide paintbrush with pale grey for the wing shapes.

Thin brush adds darker greys, black detail and textures.

Highlight the design in fine white lines around the eyebrows.

The feeling of being watched is a strange one. Once noticed in a sudden rush of cold to the back of the neck, the skin spreads the sensation as the mind realises the watching could have been going on for some time. Danu turns away from the mirror to see a tall figure in the doorway.

Gianto silently watches her. He's holding a tarot card in his hand, showing her the picture.

The Tower.

Tunnel vision: a dark tower, falling. Flames licking crumbling foundations. Bodies fall from broken windows.

Gianto turns and leaves.

She rushes to the door, calling after his retreating figure, 'Let me alone, I'm not to be played with!'

Her hands shake.

The Tower symbol has pierced her too deep.

Sharp, black, jagged. Defences falling away. Invasion. Sudden change. Collapse. Destruction of everything which has been so carefully built.

This feels like the end of something.

She thinks about losing what's most precious to her, and bumps her head on the door to nudge these thoughts away. She says to herself, 'Me and Morrie have never begun. If it hasn't begun, it can't end.'

Her words sound like an impotent defence against The Tower.

She has to focus. There are three spots to perform tonight. She hangs her squirrel and peacock costumes from the curtain rail, and places a fur mask and blue and green stage makeup on the table. Attaching her moth wings to her back, she retrieves her grey slippers from the floor and goes to the performing tent.

The hurdy gurdy music is hypnotic as Danu climbs the ladder and steps onto the platform. Morrie frowns with concentration as he steps onto the platform opposite her. The air is thickly baked, high in the top. His fur jerkin and leggings will be sticking to his skin. His donkey headpiece must weigh too heavy because as he stands opposite her, about to step onto the wire, he takes a while to focus his gaze straight ahead and meet her eyes.

Her wings are light, constructed from fine wire and mesh. Stage makeup drips down her cheeks and her grey dress clings to her thighs.

They step onto the wire. The hurdy gurdy music surges, subsides, surges again. They dance, steps matching, towards one another. Their eyes are locked, the slight movement of eyelids expressing their code to the placement of the next step. In the centre of the wire, they reach their hands towards one another, to almost touch fingertips. Morrie's palms shine with sweat. His eyelids flicker as she moves hers, they step back simultaneously. They almost touch, and part. Almost collide, and withdraw. His eyes shine, his gaze is secure. The wire they tread links them, their bodies move along it and back, along it and together with precision.

The music changes from hypnotic sounds to a more rhythmic tune played by the fiddle, squeezebox and tambourine. Love is about to go wrong as both characters realise they can never lie together due to the vast difference in the size of their physical bodies. Their movements become more comedic as Morrie exaggerates his size and Danu shrinks, flits and flutters. The slow rhythmic song she wrote for this part of the act, 'Together and Apart' resonates from three bass voices in the band, singing in close harmony:

> If moth were together, but donkey was falling apart
> she still couldn't land in his cold and straggled fur
> heart
> for this slight touch, her flickering touch alone
> wouldn't put him together, or fill his heart warm.
>
> If donkey were together, but moth was falling apart
> he still couldn't land in her cold and fragile small
> heart
> for this weighty touch, his weighty touch alone
> would crumple her dead, leaving him to mourn.
>
> Chorus:
> When threat of annihilation fills your lover with dread
> if you're not the same size then you're ill-advised to wed
> the bed's a mile down when your wings get frantic
> and rushed
> never lie with a lover who's small enough to be
> crushed.

The final tableau is Danu moth-quivering, crouched, looking up at donkey-Morrie who's standing over her. His vast shadow looms on the canvas of the tent.

The audience erupts with applause as the music ends and Danu and Morrie spin to opposite ends of the wire.

On her way back to the caravan to get changed for their next spot, Danu is being watched again. This time, it's Loretta, who's perched on a wagon-step buckling her yellow shoes. She catches Danu's eye and smirks.

Danu approaches her. 'You'll get Morrie if and when he wants you back. He's his own, not mine. So you can stop it with the knife-eyes.'

Loretta hops off the step, determination in her eyes. 'So the ice queen's finally spoken. Let him go. Give someone else a chance. Someone who'll bed him. All men want to be bedded.'

'Not all women do.'

'That's not what I heard.' She looks Danu up and down, slowly.

'Are you calling me frigid or a whore? No one can be both. Set your mind straight, Loretta.'

Loretta's cheeks flush. 'I'm calling you a tease. How come you always get changed in Morrie's caravan when us lot strip off backstage?'

'I'm just private. Get lost, Loretta.' Danu goes back to the caravan and shuts the door. Leaning back against it, she looks at the ceiling. Her eyes sting. Gianto's clearly told Loretta that Danu's not sleeping in Morrie's bed, and Loretta's never been one to keep her gob shut. People want to see strings attached. Morrie's bound to get rattled by their talk, and demand some kind of strings soon enough.

Is this the approach of The Tower?

* * *

92

After their final performance of the opening night, Danu is back at the mirror in the caravan with sponges and a bowl of water on the table. Her cheeks and forehead smudge peacock greens and blues pale and paler, as her skin returns to its true tones.

Morrie has washed and changed. Danu watches him in the mirror as he attaches braces to his brown breeches. His posture is always vulnerable when changing. He doesn't like her to see his back. The slight curve of his spine which he calls his hump isn't as exaggerated as he thinks.

Between them is silence.

Danu speaks into it. 'Loretta said—'

Morrie interrupts. 'I'm not interested in what she'll have said.'

A knock at the door. Morrie shouts, 'Out in a moment!' He crams his wallet into his jacket pocket. 'Folks want to explore the outer circle's nightlife. Take in some new music.'

Danu turns to him and asks, 'What are you going to see?'

Morrie runs his fingers through his hair. 'A music tavern – they gave the band a flier claiming *unique percussion*. Strange instruments. Elastic bands, jelly moulds and kettles by the looks of the picture on it. I can tell the others to go on ahead – we can catch them up if you want to come?'

'I don't want to be in a crowded tavern. But enjoy yourself. Morrie . . .'

'What is it?'

'That night you disappeared. Ages ago. I was scared for you – I thought something was wrong.'

Morrie crouches to straighten a rug.

Danu continues, 'And you were so down, for ages afterwards. But if you want to disappear now . . . It's fine. You should have fun in Matryoshka. Dance like a devil. Kiss someone you've only just met, all of those things.'

Rising from the floor, Morrie frowns. 'Is that what *you* want to do here?'

'No.'

He searches her face for dishonesty, and on finding none, nods. 'Well, neither will I.'

Danu laughs a little, encouraging lightness. 'Go out and don't dare come back till you've kissed someone. Or if they're all flighty out there, pick two, or three . . .'

He shakes his head. 'I'm not listening.' Putting on his shoes, he squeezes her shoulder before he goes outside.

The night air is a warm breeze and Danu's skin glows. She hunts in her drawer for light clothing and draws out a striped scarlet vest and rose-embroidered circle skirt. Mismatched colours and patterns might suit the exuberance of this place well enough.

She slips her feet into unlaced boots that hide her swollen ankles, and hooks her money-purse to her belt. Her hair is in a mangled top-knot by the time she opens the caravan door. The smell of pastries comes from a nearby bakery, scenting the air with ginger and yeast. She walks along the square touching railings. Flecks of paint stick to her fingertips. Turning into an alley, she follows the sounds of music and laughter.

On finding herself in a crowded street, she leans against a wall to get her bearings. This is the main street which curves around the base of the city, and she vaguely remembers Adelaide saying it was possible to walk all the way around it and be back where you'd started. She never said how long it would take though.

The main street must be the hub of the outer circle. It looks to be a circle inhabited by rogues, entertainers and pleasure-seekers. Café tables are crowded with enthused and argumentative conversations. Thieves snatch and scarper, the drunken swagger, lovers kiss, and vagabonds plot in huddles on corners.

Under lanterns and streetlamps, the colours of clothes are like jewels. The people can't all be intoxicated, but there's something lurching about the way they move. A group of seven women pass her, reeling from one side of the pavement to the other. She looks across the road at a row of bars and cabaret venues. There are so many entertainment venues here, perhaps they *could* all be drunk.

She's seeing through a scented orange haze. There's a smell of sweet nutmeg – no, it's smoked paprika. Everything looks coloured in.

Even the cobblestones are ochre.

Ochre? They were slate-grey a moment ago.

Danu elbows her way to the edge of the pavement. Wiping a fingertip across a cobble, she makes a grey line of stone. She tastes her fingertip.

Spices.

People rush, push, stumble past. Their footprints smudge. All around her, everyone's so busy drinking, eating, dancing, crashing, playing, kissing, fighting, laughing, they're not even looking up.

In the glow of streetlamps, coloured dust swirls in red, orange, ochre, yellow, black, white . . . Mist descends through the night sky, magnified around the lights. She holds onto a lamp post with both hands, leans her head back and beams. Flavours and smells compete as colours dance. Allspice, cardamom, chilli . . . cinnamon, curry, pepper . . . cinnamon again, ginger . . . she's drunk with it. Her hair is coated, spices colour the sweat on her arms. She laughs again, again, again.

This is the weather of the outer circle. Spice mists.

The spice mist surrounds her as she stumbles onwards. A tall woman passes her, and her hair is a frizz of blue. Danu was hungry when she left the caravan, but now feels full. And very drunk. Has she got everything she left with? She pats the coin purse on her belt, and leans against a wall. Two men pass her, and their faces leer like grotesque masks. She's too lightheaded to feel safe among all these strange bodies, and wants to get back to the caravan.

Three women walk past her, and their faces look like feathered birds. Parrots or ostriches, chickens or budgerigars . . . or are they birds, dressed as women? Unsure of how real anything is, Danu pushes herself away from the wall and walks a few paces. She's not gone far from the camp, but can't recognise anything familiar. She turns back again and walks a few paces, turns again, changes direction.

Finally, she recognises an archway. Its walls are drenched in vine leaves and trickles of ivy. Her faltering steps lead her onwards, hand to railings.

Here is the square, the gate, the caravans cramped in. All of the windows are dark. How long has she been gone? She fumbles with the handle of the caravan door till it lets her in.

She shuts the door behind her. No light.

Morrie isn't back yet. Stumbling again, she feels intoxicated. Her clothes come off, her nightgown goes on. The darkness is thick, shifting around her. Did she drink? When did she drink?

She crashes into Morrie's bed and falls into softness. Her face is against his pillow. It smells of lemon shampoo.

The smell swallows her.

She dreams of looking into a mirror.

Her face is not quite her own face.

Danu whispers, 'I miss you.'

The reflection speaks. It says, 'You're closer than ever.'

Confused, Danu tries to reply but now her lips won't move. She touches the mirror. Glass transforms into metal. The face disappears, along with the dream.

Awake. It's still night. Morrie's raising the duvet of his bed. He is looking at her body. The smell of gin.

He murmurs, 'Ah, but I could use you.'

She closes her eyes. Her body is a stone.

The bed shifts. He lies beside her.

No part of his body touches her body.

A sensation of drowning as sleep drags her down.

Again, Danu opens her eyes. She's in Morrie's bed and he's lying beside her, facing away.

His back is bare. Dawn filters in, casting shadows across his spine. She wants to wake him, to tell him his hunchback exists because wings grow inside him, folded under his skin.

Her eyelids fall, closing him away.

Danu's eyelids rise.

Morrie watches her from his pillow. As he moves his head, stubble scrapes against cotton. There's warmth. From him, or her?

She speaks from a half-dream. 'You've not disappeared.'

There's a smile in his eyes. 'No.'

'You were meant to. This place is full of pretty girls.' Her voice sounds slurred. 'So many dreams. It's too hot. I'm my own imaginary twin. Which one's real?'

He draws a finger-line along her cheek and cups his palm against her neck.

So warm, she doesn't want him to stop. He could be anyone. He could be himself. But who is she? There's a small part of her which has woken and wants to be held. A breeze drifts in under the curtains. She gently removes his hand. 'Sorry, I didn't mean to say that. Another dream. Morrie, what am I doing in your bed?'

He grins at her. 'You were here when I came in last night. Curled up fast asleep. I wasn't going to sleep on your mattress. It's far too uncomfortable. Though, I didn't try.'

'Was I drunk? I don't remember drinking . . .'

'You'd not been drinking.' He laughs. 'You smelled of curry powder.'

She frowns and shifts her body further from his. 'Sorry. I'm in the wrong place. I don't want to give you false hope.'

He replies, 'I can hope all I like.'

She touches his cheek and her hand lingers before she realises what she's doing. And yet she can't take it away because his skin is so soft. 'You can hope. But I can't give it to you. If you have it, know it's yours and from yourself.'

'Well then. Hope's belonging and mine, and . . .' The mattress moves beneath them as he shifts a little. 'A fine thing to have. And I'd not be alive without it. One day you'll trust yourself as well as you do me. That's my hope. Oh, and don't worry.' He winks at her. 'I've not touched you.'

'You said you wouldn't unless I asked you to.'

He strokes her shoulder.

'I can't ask you to.' Danu stares at her hand, still resting on his cheek. 'People can seem to be a whole thing, and turn out to be only a half of it.'

'What do you mean?'

'Part of a dream that's disappearing. But what if I'm not who you think I am?'

'And who are you, other than the one I see every day?'

'I don't even know what you're seeing.'

'I'm seeing you.' His eyes darken.

Danu's body pulls away from his. 'Are you hungry? I'll make us porridge.' She gets out of his bed and is suddenly cold. Pulling a baggy jumper from her drawer, she puts it on over her nightgown.

Morrie's watching her. 'One day, will you tell me what exactly it is you think is so bad about yourself?'

She rolls up her sleeves and reaches for the thick-bottomed pan. 'Salt, or honey?'

'Salt today.'

She lights the flame under the trivet and stirs oats through water in a figure of eight. Should she design a tarot card and paint it on her face as a mask? Take her tarot card face to Gianto and tell him, 'Go on, explode your bloody Tower. And read me instead.' It would be a picture of a heart on a string-free kite. Suspended in clouds, blown by winds. Unbound. Unbinding. Unafraid.

And yet, she and Morrie share this caravan, sleep in this small space. Each night they dream their separate dreams into this air. She sometimes remembers hers, he never remembers his. But these memorable and forgettable dreams must still fill the air between them.

She stirs and stirs till the porridge huffs steaming holes in its surface. She pours porridge into two bowls, adds a sprinkle of salt to both, and clinks spoons onto the table.

Morrie is out of bed now, fully clothed in green trousers and a rumpled linen shirt. After he's splashed his face and tied his hair back, he says, 'I'll check on Inferno while breakfast cools. He'll need plenty of water in this heat.'

Danu nods, and he goes outside.

She smells her wrists. Morrie's right, she does smell of curry. And ginger.

But she shouldn't have slept in his bed.

When he comes back in, he's whistling an upbeat tune.

She asks, 'Were Inferno's eyes soft, or wild?'

'Soft. Everything's good today. I woke up with you.'

'Don't be happy, Morrie . . .' The words slip out too fast. She bites her lip, waiting to see hurt in his expression.

He grins at her. 'Just be quiet.'

'Oh. So you know all the things I want to say, and I don't need to say them?'

'Aye.' He's still grinning.

He glows when he's happy, even if it's misplaced. She should tell him she won't sleep in his bed for a second time.

He hums as he washes his hands. He's like a child when he's happy.

To hurt him would be to steal the song from his throat.

THREE FOR REFUSAL

After the subsequent night's performance the scents of spices beckon Danu away from the circus. Chasing a narrowing aroma of aniseed, she walks along side streets. The scent of cardamom lingers in the narrowest alleyways, while black pepper lurks in the twitterns and allspice creeps through the small squares. There's a heady mixture of cumin, garam masala and nutmeg whenever she nears the hubbub of the main street.

Chasing subtler scents, she turns corner after corner within the side streets. As her nostrils fill with paprika, her fingertips seek textures and temperatures. Even metal is warm, here. She clasps door handles without turning them. She runs her thumb along broken hinges, and picks up dropped nails and rusted screws from the pavements. As she walks, these small sharp things clink in her pockets.

Black pepper makes her sneeze, clearing her nostrils of a build-up of scents. Her eyes wake to the colours of thickly painted doors, illuminated under lamplight. Running her palms over the cracked layers of paint, each door of these houses becomes a history of colours. They began bright, there were many years of ochres followed by decades of paler hues. What colours would they have been when her parents were here? Now, they're bright colours again.

On the corner of a side street is a small curved building with a domed roof. It's painted in layers of different shades of blue. This is one of many temples which punctuate the streets. The temples often erupt with clanging bells, but Danu can't yet predict whether it's time or spontaneous enthusiasm that triggers the ringing. One bell starts somewhere in the distance, followed by bells ringing from all of them. Danu finds it comforting to hear them because bells are old things. Her parents would have heard the sounds of these very same bells.

She looks through the temple doorway. The air is cool, and smells of old books. An altar is in the centre of the room, and long curtains hide the walls away. Above the curtain rails, a mural of moon phases covers the pale blue walls. On the altar is a circular sculpture. It's lit from within, shining out punctured star constellations.

Turning away from the temple, the scent of turmeric coats her face like velvet. She follows the scent and it leads her, nose raised, through an archway and along a lengthy alleyway. It's so quiet in this narrow street flanked with houses. Some homes are well cared for, others are falling apart or show signs of half-hearted care. Decay can be so beautiful. So can the colours of rust, textures of erosion, flaws and cracks, these are like fault lines in buildings . . . She imagines them being patched up with gold, making lightning strikes in their surfaces . . .

As she exhales, her heart awakens. She imagines her parents are walking beside her and she's talking to them. *Look at the clashing colours of green moss against a red-painted wall.* She examines a set of elaborate brown keys on a hook beside a broken door and looks up at decorative window frames as if her parents can see these things through her eyes. She pauses to look at a broken facade with its internal timber exposed. Speaking to her parents in her mind feels deeply right, even though they don't reply. *When you were here, were all these buildings cared for, or were some already abandoned?* The scent of turmeric merges into chilli and Danu dances like a flame past blue ceramic pots containing tall ferns. This city in all the colours of fire and water catches at some buried spark inside her.

Somewhere between fire and water there must be something of air. Perhaps air carries echoes of footsteps. She is somehow certain that her parents walked the same route she treads tonight. There's a feeling of fate, or the trace of it. But where's it coming from?

Perhaps their ghosts really are beside her, for the first time.

She touches the locket.

Leaning against a window ledge, she undoes the tight chain. Her heartbeat pulses in her throat as she tries to click the catch open. It's rusted shut. She exhales, and her heartbeat slows. The locket doesn't want to be opened. She reattaches it to her neck and tells herself that she's been right all along: she shouldn't ever look inside.

What meaning can any small thing have, apart from to the person who claims it as a secret or as a wish?

Strands of hair. A duck feather. A dead ladybird.

She walks back the way she came.

An eyelash. The claw of a cat. A rose petal.

As she nears the main street, combinations of sweet and bitter spices thicken the air.

A postage stamp, a sunflower seed, a wasp sting.

When she creeps back into the caravan. Morrie is asleep. She slips off her boots and curls up on her mattress. Holding her palm to her face, she falls asleep thinking of small things as she inhales the fading scent of nutmeg.

* * *

In the morning, Danu gets up and looks out of the window. Morrie's outside, talking to Gianto beside a washing line strung with shirts. Gianto glances over at her, and nods without smiling. She moves away. Morrie's left half a loaf of fresh bread and a jar of bramble jam on the table.

Danu's wiping breadcrumbs from her plate when Morrie turns the handle, steps inside, and clicks the door shut. She stares into the sink. His eyes are on her. She feels surrounded.

His voice, close behind her.

He says her name.

She turns around.

He clasps her hand in his. He looks into her eyes, and his lips part to speak.

She says, 'Don't. Whatever it is. Don't.'

'Just say you're mine.'

She grips his hand. 'I can't.'

'It's only words.'

She says again, 'I can't.'

'I want to wed you. On your own terms. You don't even have to share my bed.'

'What exactly has Gianto just said to you, Morrie?'

His cheeks flush.

Danu says, 'Well don't tell me, then. I'm not bothered about talk.'

Morrie lets go of her hand. 'I'll always look after you—'

'You're not listening.'

There's a knock on the door.

Morrie calls, 'I'll only be a tick!' His voice lowers as he says, 'That'll be Tomas, and we'll be out for the day. We'll speak about this after tonight's show.'

'I've already said everything I can.'

'Your grief's gone on too long. I can't get close to you.' He pales a little and takes a deep breath. 'I'll tell you what happened that night I disappeared. I bedded Loretta. I was drunk and wanted to make you jealous. To make you feel *something*. But it felt like a betrayal of you, so I couldn't tell you of it.'

Danu speaks harshly: 'Well go with Loretta, if that's what you want.'

'You told *me* not to be jealous. And now *you* are.'

Danu's heart thuds in her throat. 'You're keeping Tomas waiting.'

Morrie shakes his head in disbelief. 'So I've finally told you what you wanted to know. But *you'll* be the one talking later because it's about bloody time you did.'

'I can't talk. I'll not do it.'

There's a sharpness to Morrie's gaze that Danu doesn't recognise. He says, 'I should've kept this guilt for myself, swallowed it up like the poison it is. Have you nothing to say of jealousy?'

Danu clenches her fists. 'Morrie, if I talk, I might crack. I mean break. No, I mean crack. Do we have to do this?'

'Yes. We do! I've never met anyone so bloody scared in my life.' He goes outside, slamming the door.

After he's gone, Danu wants to tear things to pieces, break glass, get violently drunk. This can't be jealousy. She's got nothing to feel jealous about. She won't act it. Instead, she busies herself. She takes bed linen out of a crammed cupboard, shakes out sheets, folds them, shakes them out, refolds and puts them away more creased than they were to begin with. She finds one of Morrie's socks which needs darning, darns it carefully, tests the stiches and breaks the threads with her fingers. She throws the sock on top of the potato peelings in the bin.

Morrie's always been kind to her. Always. They've developed a beautiful series of acts and he's always been interested in her thoughts. He's the best friend she's ever had. He never usually pushes her to do anything she doesn't want to do. If there is a monster inside him, he has it controlled. But he slept with Loretta. Did she see the monster? Is there also a monster in her?

She imagines them in bed together and wants to tear something to shreds.

Unable to stop moving, but not wanting to go outside, Danu looks around for useful things to do. Boiling the kettle, she fills the sink with hot water and washes all the pots and pans. The water thickens with fats, so they come out slimed. She washes them again with soap which leaves white streaks. She boils the kettle and washes them yet again. She wipes them with dry tea towels till they're gleaming and hangs them back on their hooks.

She empties the sink, and refills it with cold water. She washes her hands and arms with salt, scrubbing till it scratches, scraping till it stings. She sits on her mattress with her notebook and a black pen. She wants to cry. She won't let herself. Instead, she draws a picture of a veiled woman with magpie skulls attached to each curl of her long hair.

She writes the word *Morrigan*.

A phantom bride. A goddess of death.

Danu's mind fills with images of blood and bones and muscles and cells and tissues as she writes words around her picture: *what are we made from, from what are we made, what are we missing, from what are we missed* . . . she scrawls these words over and over and over again.

When she finally stops, she closes her notebook and looks at her reddened hands. She's cold, now. Freezing. She lies under her coverlet. Darkness eats her. She is bone thin, made of ice. She lets herself shiver and shiver and shiver until she stops.

Opposite Morrie on the wire, matching step to step, eye movement to eye movement, technically, they are faultless. But the act is mechanical. Danu is a puppet dressed as an insect, moving her arms, legs, feet, hands in all the right ways, but aside from the flickers from her eyes to Morrie's, her face is a mask.

At the end of the night, they're side by side in the centre of the sand circle. The front eight rows of the audience are on their feet. Cheering comes wave after wave.

Morrie doesn't take her hand or glance at her as he bows, and bows again. As she matches her curtseys to the pace of his bows, he is a shadow beside her.

Danu removes her costume and makeup, and puts on a long green dress. Quickly slipping on her boots, she opens the caravan door. The camp is quiet – she's hoping Morrie won't rush back to the caravan. He would usually remain for a short while in the small tent which functions as a changing room.

She scrawls a note and leaves it on his bed:

Morrie,
I can't speak about the things you want me to.
Don't know how. Please don't ask me to. Sorry.
I'm going out for a walk – don't worry, I'm fine.
Just losing and finding myself.
You know, like I have to sometimes.
Back later,
Danu

Danu can exhale now she's on the main street surrounded by strangers. She walks through crowds of pleasure-seekers without seeing their faces. Under streetlights, the sheens of vibrant clothing become a river of colour which smells of lavender perfume, musky sweat and jasmine hair oils.

A fine yellow mist swirls down through the air. Not as

thick and overwhelming as before, but she can taste its flavour – savoury, a little spicy, almost sweet . . . This is the flavour of the colour yellow. Purest lemongrass. She breathes it in.

Intoxicating, beguiling. Warming to the heart.

If the outer circle of Matryoshka wasn't part of a city, but something alive . . .

If the outer circle of Matryoshka was a person . . .

If the outer circle of Matryoshka was a person in love, it would whisper and kiss and surround the bodies which move through it. It would be a lover who warmed with flames because they wanted to be burned, a lover who soaked with waters because they wanted to be drowned. The outer circle pours colour into eyes, it pours sounds into ears, teases the mouth with flavours, flickers skin with warmth, fills nostrils with expanding and contracting scents. As a lover it could gain answer after answer after answer without ever asking any questions.

It offers nothing it doesn't want to give, makes no promises, asks for nothing in return . . . it floods.

Danu wants to flood back.

She'd give this city all of her breaths in return for the flavour of the colour yellow. She'd offer it the colour from her eyes in return for this lemongrass mist drawn from the sky . . .

On the first night she met this city, it overwhelmed her senses with its spice mists.

On the second night, it showed her the colours and textures of its alleyways. It let her walk where her parents had walked and made her feel as if they walked alongside her.

And tonight, it kisses her with a flavour.

Her lips are kissed, her eyes are kissed, her hands are kissed. She drifts.

A male voice speaks close to Danu's ear, 'Watch for me on the ether.'

Jerked from her reverie, she searches the faces around her to see who has spoken. No one is waiting for her to speak back. The faces are made from small petals and saffron strands stirred together.

She pushes herself away and leans back against a wall. Covering her nose, she tries not to inhale. Sounds are amplified. A whistle. A bass guitar. She looks around for ordinary things. Cutlery on a café table. Awnings swaying above open-doored bars. A musician strums a lute. A red-haired girl has broken the heel of her shoe and rubs her shin. Above the street, orange pillowcases sag along a clothes line strung between windows.

Danu fixes her eyes to the washing line and imagines hanging from it with pegged hands.

Conversations rattle, coins chink, a glass smashes. What generosity, for a city to be so full of sounds and yet demand no words.

She tells herself that the voice wasn't there.

Danu's beautifying Matryoshka – recasting it as a city painted with light. Gianto's tarot card and his previous words, *you're scarpering* creep into her thoughts. As she explores further, she tries to force herself to see the city's ugly side: searching for an underbelly covered in warts. But even the most shadowed alleys hold the promise of forbidden secrets.

She wanders for hours, imagining herself living in one of the narrow houses in these alleys, tucked away from the crowds. She pictures herself replacing cracked windowpanes and storing possessions that she no longer wants in the basements. She creeps down into the basement of a derelict house, and looks inside through a half-open door. There are vast rusted pipes along both ceiling and floor, and the sound of running water. In the corner, an industrial wheel slowly turns. It's too dark to see what it might be attached to. This basement goes far deeper beneath the house than she'd imagined. What would she use this space for, if this was her home?

Dismissing these odd fantasies, she goes to the square where the horses are kept. The moon reflects in the top layer of windows around the square. Inferno sniffs the air and catches her scent. He comes over to the railings to greet her. The gate's padlocked. She leans her head against the railings and lets Inferno huff his breath against her forehead. He's unusually tranquil.

After she's caught some of his calmness, she goes back to Morrie's caravan and closes the door behind her with a click.

Her eyes adjust to darkness. Morrie is sprawled face down across his bed. He's written a reply to her note and left it on her pillow.

D,
 I'm sorry. Gianto got to me. Forget I said anything. I'll not press you to wed me, and I'll not make you talk. Let's just be separate for a while if you want. Go and keep doing whatever it is you're doing in Matryoshka. And I'll do the same.
 We'll speak when you're ready.
 In the meantime, see you each night on the wire.
 M.

Word has rapidly spread about the circus, and by two o'clock each afternoon, tickets have sold out for that night. The audiences are enthusiastic and cheerful, and the atmosphere in the performing tent is buoyant. After the audience has left, the circus performers go out for entertainment themselves, or gather together to celebrate their success. As soon as Danu can slip away, she continues to explore Matryoshka alone. She wanders further and further away from the circus every night, and often doesn't return till just before dawn. Matryoshka draws her into its nocturnal world as if she's sleepwalking through a sensual dream.

Tonight, she's gone still further away, and she walks through a more rundown area of the outer circle. In a narrow alleyway, grapevines cascade from pots on roof terraces. A steep stone staircase interrupts the walls, leading up to what must be the second circle. The stairway is lit by white globe lights. Dust gathers in the cracks on the steps. The hospital in which she was born is somewhere in the second circle. It could be right at the top of this staircase.

As she climbs the stairs, she gets more of a sense of Matryoshka's great height. There are three circles, and this staircase alone takes an eternity to climb. She pauses every so often, and catches her breath. But when she gets within sight of the top, there's a wall blocking any entry to the second circle. Why would a staircase lead to a dead end? Above the wall, skyscrapers make angular puzzle shapes in the night sky.

Perhaps, like the voice last night, the wall isn't really there, and it's a hallucination brought on by the spice mists. She tries to guess what the hospital might look like, but can only imagine the doors. In her mind, they're black, heavy, and arched like gravestones. She climbs to the top of the staircase and feels the wall. It's solid thick stone. This is no dream. But as she presses her hands against it, something clicks. The wall moves slightly to the left. Not much, but enough to unsettle her. Walls are expected to be solid, sturdy things. She quickly descends the staircase, and emerges in the outer circle.

Passing houses, she glances up at open-shuttered windows and pictures the people who might live in the rooms behind them. For now these people are unknowable because, as always, she's just passing through.

She imagines remaining here and being still. As immobile as a stone wall should be.

Her future would become entirely dependent on who she spoke to, which person she met first, who they introduced her to, and the cause and effect of others. But to remain here alone she would need to be a different person entirely – more talkative, more able to grab chances, and far bolder.

Along the main street she looks in a shop window which advertises houses and flats to rent. They're hugely expensive compared to what she's used to earning. There are surely other ways of obtaining a home in this city other than renting from landlords. Dereliction in a warm city rather than a cold one wouldn't kill her. There are hidden rooms everywhere. Rooms no one cares about.

But how would she earn enough money to survive, here? She's a tightrope walker with few practical skills. Apart from performing, she enjoys drawing and writing stories, but no one gets paid to do those things. She couldn't surely earn enough as a street performer among so many others competing for coins. She couldn't even clean people's houses particularly well. She wouldn't know how to obtain any goods to sell, or understand which things people might want to buy. And even if one of the entertainment venues would consider employing a tightrope walker, she has never performed solo.

She thinks about being static, not constantly travelling from place to place. What might stillness do . . . who might she become? There is movement everywhere in this city which captivates her with mysteries: the intoxicating spices, echoes of voices and a staircase leading nowhere. It feels as if there's something just around the next corner, which she's fated to discover.

* * *

Over the following few days, possibility and impossibility pull Danu in two directions. Whenever she imagines living in Matryoshka, memories flash through her mind. Her mother, painting their caravan with new colours but keeping the same patterns. Gianto complaining that red and pink were unconventional, but at least it was good and bright. Loretta pinching Danu's neck when they were about four years old. Pinching Loretta's stomach in a carefully planned retaliation when they were about five. Hattie's beard when it was stubble, and then an inch, then two, and then suddenly curly. Her father, running a race against the other men, determined to win a bottle of perfume that had fallen from a flattie's handbag. He didn't win, as Gianto had been a sneak with a tripwire. Adelaide telling Gianto that she didn't want *that cheap scent* anyway. She remembers Sandy using stale bread as fishing bait and not catching anything. He went off fishing again the next day with a jar of innards and came back with three fish. Mario, aged seven, getting a kick to the backside off a farmer for being caught milking one of his cows into a tin bucket. Morrie watching her from his caravan steps the morning after the wake.

Would these memories gradually disappear if she wasn't with the people who'd helped make them? She remembers Mag and her mother repairing a tarpaulin with stitches and tape. She can't bear the idea of having no one around her who remembers her parents. At the same time, this city opens the possibility of a new future which is as strange as a foreign country.

There are horizons inside her.

No, she'd miss Morrie and the circus too much.

All the same, one night she pauses outside a tall mustard-coloured building with eight windows. Which window would be her room? She forces herself not to choose one of those green-shuttered windows, in case she batters in the door, climbs flights of stairs and finds an empty room awaiting her. She pretends to herself that she has always lived here in a strange parallel universe, and when she's left, part of her will remain here forever.

A middle-aged man steps out of the front door, carrying a small brown suitcase. He removes a key from his pocket and locks the door behind him.

Danu approaches him and asks, 'Is this a safe area to live in?'

He assesses her with a glance. 'For a single young woman?'

She nods.

'Not really,' he replies. 'There's too many beggars. Watch out for them – they're vicious.'

The main street's still crowded with people, though it must by now be the early hours of the morning. There's a piece of paper on the cobbles, and she picks it up. It's a rough-inked drawing of a tarot card. Looking around, there are drawings pinned to a board propped on the pavement – a variety of other tarot cards and rune symbols. Beside them is a cross-legged beggar with blind smoky eyes. Does someone guide his hand to draw them, or has he drawn from the memory of sight? All of the pictures are in black and white.

Is it possible to see without sight, have a view without viewing, to look without looking? Does he trace his fingers over the creased lines of his face, and try to guess what his expressions show?

The beggar doesn't look vicious. He looks overwhelmed. There's too much music, too many shouts, too much chatter, too many words from the mouths that pass by. Sounds must be amplified, without sight.

She approaches him and drops a few coins into his rumpled cap.

The clink of Danu's coins reaches his ears and he nods. She

114

crouches beside him and whispers into his ear, 'I want to tell you about a colour. Blue is skylight, the sea, eyes. Blue is lit brighter by the sun and deepened by the moon. Blue is what stars float in. Blue is calming, complete, cool, perfection, tranquil. Blue is flute music, tears, two shades in a rainbow. The smell of rain.'

His grins up at an imagined sky.

She whispers, 'It's my favourite colour,' and as she's about to walk away, she asks him, 'If you were thinking about renting a room, where would you avoid living?'

He says, 'Oh, avoid areas with lots of pubs. Especially Effanbee. The drunkards there are lascivious.'

She whispers, 'Think of blue,' and watches him smile again as she walks away.

The drawing in her hand is The Fool – a jester stepping jovially off the edge of a cliff. There is surely a glint in his eye. The Fool – the start of a new journey, not knowing whether the path will lead to a fatal drop, or whether clouds will appear and be solid enough to support the bold footfall of an idiot.

And she is an idiot. She is falling in love with a city.

Fingering the drawing, she resolves not to be a fool. She will find something about Matryoshka she can't love, so it will be easier when she leaves it behind.

The next night, once the show is over, Danu slips away from the camp and follows signs which lead her to the area called Effanbee.

In Effanbee, all the streets have an inordinate number of pubs, punctuated by dental surgeries, betting shops and fancy dress costumiers. Outside one of the pubs, a woman sits at a table, staring into her drink. Her hair is unravelling from its beehive shape, and one of her red stockings slumps in wrinkles around her knee. She looks a little lascivious, but alcohol has rendered her impotent. Danu approaches her and asks which areas aren't safe to live in.

The woman tries to focus her kohl-stained eyes. 'Oh, hello. Hello. I always avoid . . . Silkstone and Bleuette. Silkstone's three blocks along, Bleuette's three blocks more.'

'Where do the names of the areas come from?'

The woman slurs, 'They're named after dolls. Like Matryoshka itself.'

'Why should I avoid these two?'

'There's too many foreigners living there.' She sways in her chair.

As a foreigner to Matryoshka herself, Danu is bemused as to what danger she'd pose to this woman. She asks, 'What do foreigners do to you?'

The woman holds her head in both hands as if it might fall off. 'They insult me . . . Talking about me in all their languages . . .'

Danu asks her, 'Do you speak other languages?'

She shakes her head.

'Then how do you know what they're saying?'

Exhausted by the effort of speaking, the woman's head slumps onto her arms.

Fear can spread like an illness, but does it have to be contagious? Danu could follow a trail of fear around this whole city, and decide that everywhere is far too dangerous.

On another night, Danu explores an area called Sasha, which is quieter than Effanbee. All along the main street, there are several souvenir shops selling 'Sugared Curios'. She pauses to look at a window display of red silk roses coated in fine white grains, and pink fuchsias dripping amber syrup. A monocle sunk in a block of clear caramel catches her eye. On another shelf, there's a framed pink glove which is coated in strips of blue icing sugar.

She remembers souvenirs from seaside towns which were striped rock and oversized dummies. At the time, she'd wondered if tourists ate these sweets when they got home, or if they put them in the back of a larder and let sugars drip away in unseen bright colours. If seaside towns want to be remembered with a sticky nostalgia, Matryoshka wants to be remembered for an inedible and curious sweetness.

There's an information sheet pasted into the window. It reads:

Matryoshkan Spices.
The main export of Matryoshka is spices, and all visitors are enchanted by the variety of specialist Spice Shops scattered throughout the outer circle. Many Spice Factors roast their own blends, and the spice factories of the second circle mass produce many cost-effective varieties. For tastings, do visit an artisan shop. Or if you're here for a few days, you could attend a spice factory open day and see the historic machinery at work! The greenhouses of the Inner Circle produce all the plants, but unfortunately access to these is unavailable to visitors. At night time, walk the streets and inhale the mists — many Spice Factors roast in outdoor furnaces, adding to the scents from the factories. At certain times of year, the mists are so thick, some have reported feeling a delightful sense of intoxication. Enjoy the free smells, as well as the products available to purchase and take home as a lingering memento of your Matryoshkan experience.

Danu smiles to herself, as she's finally discovered the source of the spice mists. Leaving the main street, she enters a tunnelled labyrinth of streets. As she sits on the cobblestones in an arched passageway, a white cat appears, and hides in her shadow. The thin cat has caught himself a sparrow and is determined to eat it all in one go.

The cat tells her without speaking that he belongs to no one and his name is Ghost.

Danu can tell that Ghost doesn't want to be touched, so doesn't insult him by trying. She tells him, 'I'm lost, and in love with this city.'

Ghost pulls the innards out of the sparrow, and growls as he bites into its neck.

In a side street called Wringers Street, a terraced house slowly disintegrates. A cobweb stretches across its front door. Rusted metal numbers – one and nine are half hidden by the web. Danu crouches on the pavement on the opposite side of the street. She's been watching the dark windows for at least an hour.

On both sides of the street, a few other front doors are keyed open as people stagger home. Lights go on. There's a distant sound of a street sweeper brushing the cobbles of some other street. Danu listens to the sound till it's gone. She stares at number nineteen as the lights in other houses on Wringers Street are extinguished.

Still no sign of life.

The streetlamps go off. The light changes overhead. Dawn is coming.

Danu makes her way back to the circus, drinking in everything she sees on the way. Even the newspaper billboards are fascinating. There's one on the pavement which says, 'oversized pies RUIN pie-eating competition'. She imagines the scale of the pies which might be involved, and mentally compares them to the sizes of mouths. The spice mists have faded but she can still smell the lingering scents of cayenne and cardamom in her hair.

Sandy's pacing around outside when she arrives back at the camp. He beckons as he sees her, and she approaches him.

Danu says quietly, 'What're you doing up so early?'

'I'm too hot to sleep. What're you doing up so late?' He winks at her.

'I love this city at night, is all.'

He frowns. 'Are you and Morrie getting on all right?'

'Not really. I just need to not think about him for a time. We'll be fine again soon.'

'You can always stop over with me and Mag. Don't put yourself in danger for the sake of avoiding him.'

Sandy understands her far better than she'd realised. She bites her lip. 'No, it's not that. What do you make of this city?'

'It's quite a place.' He looks up at the brightening sky. 'Quite a place. Be careful, though. Mag wouldn't walk around Matryoshka alone after dark. All kinds of rogues about . . .'

She rubs his arm. 'Everyone here is having either fun or arguments with people they already know. They're not interested in me.' She grins. 'It feels like I'm a little bit magic, or a little bit invisible.'

'Well, just know that me and Mag care for you. Any trouble, you tell us.'

'Thanks Sandy. I will.' She knows she won't as soon as these words leave her lips. She hugs him for caring and wishes him goodnight.

One night when Danu faces Morrie on the wire, he has questions in his eyes. When she's back in the caravan getting changed, she makes sure his note is lying next to her notebook, to remind him of their agreement about being separate. She goes out before he returns from the performing tent, and goes back to the house on Wringers Street in order to check the cobweb is still in place. If it is, it means no one is opening or closing the front door.

She stares at the exterior of the house, imagining what it's like inside. She thinks about hidden rooms behind doors, ceilings over ceilings and floors beneath floors. She imagines the angles of its inner staircases. Houses must be made out of all kinds of things which can't be seen: bricks and stone, rubble, wood, tiles and rafters. Hundreds of nails. And what are foundations made from – enormous screws and bolts, or long planks of wood, like a ship?

She considers all these things while staring at number nineteen's intact cobweb. If no one but her cares about observing the web, surely *anyone* could claim ownership of this house. Perhaps number nineteen belongs to the spider, and it's protecting it with web-magic. Should she befriend the spider and offer to pay it fly-shaped rent?

A few people walk past, but no one glances at the house. Number nineteen Wringers Street might be a good home to have, because no one notices it at all.

Danu goes back to check the cobweb is in place every night for over a week. While visiting this house she feels faithless to every single person in the circus. She can't tell them what she's doing. They'd never understand why she needs to play out the whole fantasy of remaining here, before she feels able to leave. She doesn't fully understand it herself.

Since she arrived in Matryoshka, many of her half-remembered dreams involve seeing herself as if in a mirror. Last night a strange reflection said, 'Only metal divides us.' Danu woke from this dream feeling suddenly cold. Wanting something she couldn't name. The confusion about what this might mean has lingered all day. It's brought memories with it. She remembers as a very small child she often played alone underneath their caravan, talking constantly. This unnerved Adelaide, but Clem said he liked to hear her chattering away because he always knew where she was.

And under the caravan, taking shade from the sun or shelter from rain, Danu played with a rag doll, or picked petals off daisies with someone that she couldn't see. When she was very small, she was certain they were invisibly there.

As she grew older, she suspected that they weren't.

When she finally realised this for certain, she felt freezing cold and burst into tears.

Clem sat on the caravan steps, hugging her as she cried into his neck. Adelaide examined her knees and elbows for grazes. They wanted her to tell them what was wrong, but she had no words for it.

Does every birthplace create strange dreams and trigger memories? Or is this how Matryoshka entices people back who were born here, and claims ownership?

She's held by the arms of the city.

Whenever she's too near the circus camp, her heart pounds and her limbs tense, preparing to fight. There's a strange wildness inside her and she's afraid of its strength. Wildness always has claws of some kind or another.

The city beckons, drawing her away every night.

Time has passed quickly and they've already been in Matryoshka for over three weeks. But there was talk about staying for eight. Danu can't bear to ask anyone how soon they'll be leaving. When the time comes, she will leave with the circus and remember her time in Matryoshka as a beguiling dream. And yet the future now frightens her. It looks like cardboard and dust. Feeling too grey, she'd eventually agree to wed Morrie just to find some colour in a celebration. But there wouldn't really be any colour. This future looks like a silhouetted cut-out: of one dark monster tied to another dark monster, with their claws clipped blunt.

One night she goes back to number nineteen Wringers Street again, telling herself this will be the last time she allows herself to do so. The cobweb across the front door remains unbroken. For the first time, Danu explores the back of the house. At the end of Wringers Street, there's a cobbled alleyway where someone has dumped old doors and broken wardrobes. The terraced houses of Wringers Street all have backyards and a brick wall spans the length of the street. The crumbled bricks provide easy footholds. Danu creeps all the way along the wall, glancing into the backyards of the odd-numbered side. She counts houses till she finds number nineteen. The rear wall is three storeys high, and stained with damp shadows. The roof is broken. It looks like a carcass.

In the cluttered backyard, a crow topples the lid off an empty metal bin and flies away. The dark windows look like cracked empty eyes. She sits on the wall, watching for hidden signs of life. Unseen cats yowl at each other through the night.

Danu yowls back at them without making a sound.

One morning Morrie wakes Danu by clunking a strong coffee on the caravan floor beside her mattress. He hasn't shaved for a while.

She sits up. Thanks him for the coffee.

He says, 'Look, we need to talk. I stupidly thought you'd want to, sooner than this. I'm sorry. Didn't mean to pressure you. Gianto just got to me. He's simmered down. Everyone's been distracted by the fun they can have here, practically all night every night if they want it. We've made a fortune. Gianto's bought himself a silk jacket. Others go out in groups and pairs though, whereas you're too much the loner.'

'I only care if it bothers you.'

'The only thing bothering me is I've barely seen you. You've done the shows and headed off, not come back till I'm long abed, and slept the days away.'

She blinks, trying to force herself into wakefulness.

His eyes are fixed on hers. 'So, what've you been doing out there?'

She takes a gulp of coffee. 'I'm standing on the edge of a cliff not sure whether to jump or not. If I'll be caught if I do. If I'll fly, or fall into my own reflection.' She shakes her head. 'No, ignore me. I'm too sleepy to talk sense.'

He frowns. 'Sounds like sense to me, of a kind.'

She stares into coffee, imagining a black whirlpool.

After a while, Morrie says, 'Are you upset about me sleeping with Loretta?'

'No. You did what you wanted to do, and regretted it, by the looks of you. It's got nothing to do with me.'

'Have you met someone?'

She replies, 'You have to speak to people, to *meet* them.'

'And you clearly don't want to speak to me. But speak to someone. A cliff edge sounds like it needs to be talked about.' He looks sad but the sadness lightens as their eyes meet. He ruffles her hair and goes outside.

Danu puts her mug in the sink. There's a sealed envelope with Morrie's name on it on the cluttered table. She recognises Loretta's handwriting in the wide looped letters. There's a love heart inked around his name, drawn like a tattoo of barbed wire. His name looks fenced in.

She's still half asleep and even strong coffee hasn't helped. So she puts herself back to bed.

Danu wakes in the early afternoon. Morrie's left Danu a note on the floor beside her mattress:

D.

Hope you're all right. I've left out bread and cheese for you. I'm heading off with Gianto and Mag for food supplies. We're stocking up for the journey as we've to leave tomorrow, which is a bugger for us all. Gianto thought the next troupe were as good as cancelled, as the Tober hadn't had any word from them in ages. Pyrotechnicians, a tiger and seven acrobats and not one of them bothered to finalise their dates. But they've finally sent word, and they arrive here in three days. The Ringmaster's the Tober's bloody cousin, so he's gotten away with it. That all said, it was worth the journey. We've sold out again tonight and there's another picture in the local paper. This time it's of Hattie, Mario and all the clowns. They're all crowing. Try and see it if you get the chance.

Can you wash our linen?

See you later

M.

Leaving. She knew it would come, but hoped it wouldn't be so soon. Danu gets dressed quickly, opens the door and shields her eyes from the bright sun. She crosses the square and leaves the circus camp.

Two streets away, her eye is caught by a sculpture of a metal castle with lights shining from its windows. It's on display in a dimly lit gallery. She goes inside and looks at miniature oil paintings. She's drawn to a painting of a gate, in greys and white. The brushstrokes are delicate, depicting the gate's design in curves of leaf, petal and stem.

She asks the white-haired man at the counter what the rest of Matryoshka is like.

He replies in the tone of a salesman speaking to a wealthy customer. 'Madam, it's a city in three parts. Like an opera should be, but now it's being sung out of tune. Decay becomes a note in a song . . . if your ear is tuned well. Each concentric circle has a different tone, the further in you go.'

Danu says, 'By whose standards?'

'I'm sorry?' He adjusts his spectacles and looks closely at her.

She tilts her head. 'I've only seen this circle and it's intoxicating. I might not have liked the two others as much.'

He nods, slowly. 'This is true. Beauty is subjective. As is ugliness. Some people find the second circle too subtle, after the outer circle. Others find it far more stimulating. It's all about taste and tuning. Tuning of the eye, as much as of the ear.'

'I tried to go up to the second circle, but—'

'You encountered a wall?'

'Yes.'

'There are three staircases. It's all in the timing. Just walk round and try the next one along.'

She wants to ask him more questions, but his focus has returned to the paintings he wants to sell. 'This fine example,' he waves a hand at the oil painting she was looking at, 'is of the gate to the Inner Circle. A gate few people ever visit.'

'Why?'

'The gate is always locked.'

She turns to face him. 'So I couldn't have seen the Inner Circle anyway?'

He shakes his head.

'For what reason?'

He brushes flakes of dandruff from the shoulder of his crimson jacket as he responds. 'No one is entirely sure. There's much gossip, of course.'

'What do people say?'

'A variety of things. Some say the people who live there are greedy and want to keep their wealth to themselves. Others say they've formed an alternative religion . . . And there's something about possessiveness I've heard . . . or was it pacifism . . . no, poetry . . . Sorry. I once edited dictionaries. I may now sell art, but I miss the dictionaries. The words which fill my head, however, are highly useful for descriptions of paintings . . . used capriciously . . . would you like to see a catalogue?' He reaches for a leather-bound book.

'No, no thanks.' Danu goes outside and leans against a wall. Hugging herself, she looks up at the dizzying reflections of sky, sun and clouds in the skyscraper windows of the second circle. She doesn't have time to find all three staircases to see which one gives her access to the second circle, then find yet another staircase to see the locked gate of the Inner Circle. She wanted more time to explore Matryoshka slowly. Savour its gifts. Tune her ears to be able to hear each note the city hums. She clenches her hands and her nails bruise her palms.

She was so certain she'd meet someone purely by chance who she was fated to meet. Perhaps someone who'd met her parents and could tell her something she needs to hear, or someone who'd greatly influence her future. But is it possible to recognise fate in a stranger's face?

Attempting to resign herself to the fact that she's soon to be leaving, unfulfilled, she decides that this will be a beautiful ache to take with her. She will savour it. How wonderful to remember she loves her birthplace this much.

There's so little time.

Walking away from the wall, she goes to the main street, keeping her eyes on the doors of foodstores so she can get away quickly if she sees Morrie and the others. She wants as much time alone with Matryoshka as possible. She passes a shop with an A-board which announces 'Alternating Practices'. Its list of treatments includes 'toenail analysis' and 'arm extension prophecies'. She remembers seeing a fortune teller read palms outside this shop a few nights ago. Her head was attached to her body the wrong way around. She was seated at a velvet-covered table with a man who wore a ruby earring.

This picture of red fortunes and a backwards head feels more like a dream than a real memory. So does obsessing for so long about a cobweb over a door. But then again, there was cayenne pepper in the air on the night she saw the backwards head. It made her laugh at the time, but she's forgotten it till now.

Spice mists must have side effects. Obsession, distraction, hallucination, confusion.

She should go back to the circus. Do the bloody laundry. Pack up. Be useful. But the scents of orange zest and cloves curl through the air and wake her senses. Smiling, she inhales. Orange tints the sky and warms her lungs. Cloves turn the clouds brown and warm her lips. She is tempted. Beckoned.

She'll make each moment she's got left with Matryoshka, the best moment she's had.

Fragments of green glass sparkle between cobblestones. The scents of lime and chilli beckon. A bell rings, a trumpet blasts, and she wants to dance. So she dances as she walks, to any busker's melody which carries her along. On a corner, an old man plays guitar and a young boy beats a drum. They're listening to each other, matching rhythms.

Danu remembers her mother singing. Her pure, operatic voice. Her range. Her poise.

She approaches the buskers, and asks if she can sing along for a while.

The old man nods. 'Of course. I'll warn you when there's a chord change.' He strums a wild tune. Danu joins in, singing with no words. At first her voice is a stream on jagged rocks. But as the chords change from minor to major, the sound widens and deepens. She improvises with high soaring notes in a wild, gypsy style.

Passers-by throw money.

Her love for her mother floods through expelled sound. When she's got no more notes inside her, she bows to the buskers in thanks, and walks away as they play on. She'll remember singing with them. Her mother would probably have thought her tone was terrible, but this is a good memory to take with her, and she'll collect a few more before tonight's show.

Like some kind of fool, she feels reckless as she remembers her father's playfulness. He loved exploring places he wasn't meant to go. He ignored *no entry* signs and *staff only* and *private property* notices. He would climb over padlocked gates, just to find out what was behind them. If he got caught, he'd either act a little bit lost, or a little bit simple, or a little bit charming. He could get away with anything. Danu clambers rickety ladders and peeks into bathrooms and bedrooms. She searches for rats behind rows of bins. In a food market, she samples everything until she's had a whole meal of sour plums, apple jam, red curry and green stir fry, pickles and blue cheeses.

As the sun sets, she climbs to the top of a scaffolding tower which props up a house. Starlings whir through the sky as she takes off her boots. Gripping a scaffolding bar, she hangs in the air, kicking her bare feet through a cardamom mist.

Once their final show in Matryoshka is over, the circus sends fireworks into the night sky, lighting the outer circle red and orange. In the morning they will return to the cold mountains outside Matryoshka and head south again.

After the fireworks are spent, Danu secures glassware and crockery in the caravan, ensuring each cupboard door is firmly closed.

Morrie's sullen, probably because he's been preparing for the journey all day, and the one job he gave her hasn't been completed. Their unwashed laundry is still in the basket.

She apologises, but he says gruffly, 'Let's just get to bed. It'll be an early start.'

Danu wakes just before dawn and slips outside. The square is dimly lit by streetlamps. Sandy and Mario are already up, and they're crouched next to the railings rolling up a tent. She goes over to them, and asks if they need a hand.

Mario grins as he sees her. 'Not seen you of a morning for ages, night bird.'

She smiles back at him. 'Do you need a hand?'

Sandy says, 'We're fine. Better organised than usual. Did you get to see everything in Matryoshka you wanted to?'

'No. I should have at least visited the hospital where I was born.'

He frowns up at her. 'Aye. You should. Hope you've rested enough?'

Mario says, 'We're to keep going till we've found a well – it'll be a long day.'

Danu nods. 'I'll go for a short walk while there's still time.'

Mario says, 'Hey – did you see me in the paper?'

'No, sorry. I forgot.'

'I got a copy. I'll show you later. I look cross-eyed!'

Danu smiles at him. 'I bet you all look brilliant.'

Sandy says, 'You'd best go quick if you want to stretch your legs. Don't be too long.' He returns his attention to tying the rolled tent into its bindings.

Danu goes along to the square where the horses shuffle in their enclosure. Inferno nudges the head of Gianto's white mare with his nose. They are silent apart from the occasional sound of tongues slapping against trough-water.

She glances around, looking for Gianto, willing him to appear and tell her to remain here and let Morrie go.

But he doesn't.

She wills Mag to appear and tell her she belongs with the circus, and should never leave them.

But she doesn't appear either.

Surely there should be clear signs. Magpies descending from above and terrifying her into running away. A lightning bolt stopping her heartbeat. If she's to believe Gianto's Tower card, something immense should be happening to force this decision she can't make.

The horses are waiting. Waiting for the morning light on their backs, waiting to be fed the same feed yet again, waiting to be harnessed, waiting to drag caravans along roads. Danu imagines them free. Unshod, they would wander forests, lumber along mountain paths, canter across plains. Inferno whinnies. The sound makes Danu yearn to lead them all out of the city, loose them, and watch them gallop away . . .

And then the circus couldn't ever leave.

But horses are valuable things. They have all been saved for, worked for, fought for. And none of them belong to her.

She thinks about the gate to the Inner Circle. The lock on the gate. Its key.

She thinks about secrets.

About being born here, and returning.

About fate.

Ginger-scented air twists around her. As she inhales it, her thoughts sharpen.

Undoing the clasp of her locket, she removes the chain from her neck.

She returns to the circus camp with the locket clutched in her palm. It's still not yet light, but more people have got up early, and they're flustered and busy. Hattie's carrying a box into her caravan, and Loretta's talking animatedly with Gianto and Sandy. Mag and Tomas are hauling sacks of rubbish towards the gate. On seeing Danu, Mag calls, 'Where's Morrie?'

'Probably still asleep.'

'We're off at dawn. Just over an hour. Get him woke.'

Inside the caravan, Danu opens the curtains and sits on the edge of Morrie's bed.

Her thoughts are clear. 'Morrie. Wake up.'

'What's happening?'

Danu's hand trembles as she holds out the locket. 'I need you to help me open my mother's locket. Here. Where I was born. Before we leave.'

He sits up, frowning. 'You've still never looked?'

She shakes her head. 'It's rusted shut and I don't want to break it.'

'You should have asked me—'

'And . . . I've been too scared. I'll tell you what I think's inside it: it's my mother's hair, entwined with my father's, which proves they loved one another more than I thought they did. It's a poem to my mother from a lover I never knew she had. It's two ancient pictures of my mother's parents who I have never met. It's a secret she kept for her closest friend who is someone she never told me about. It's her deepest fear, written in black ink, which she never trusted me with. It's got nothing but air inside it. It's empty, because my mother was waiting her whole life to find something precious enough to hide inside it, but she never found anything worth keeping.

'That's what is inside this locket.

'It's all the things I don't know about her, but should have done.' Danu's tears stream. 'I'm sorry.'

He rubs her arm. 'Well we'd best open it then. That's far too many things to keep in one locket. And in your head.' He smiles at her and takes the locket. As he examines the rusted catch, he says, we can just ease it open with one of the tiny screwdrivers. There's a set in my toolbox.'

She gets them and sits down again. Taking the locket back from him, she says, 'I'd better do it. In case it breaks.'

He sits up straighter. 'Go on, then. Do it now. Like ripping off a scab.'

With the locket in her palm, she works a tiny screwdriver along the edge and eases it open without breaking the catch.

A strip of folded paper is brown-flecked with age.

Danu unfolds it, trying not to let it fall apart at the creases. She leans over her palm to read Adelaide's tiny handwriting, in fine black ink:

Judith Crown
15 Duffle Close
Inner Circle
Matryoshka

She frowns at Morrie. 'What's this supposed to mean?'

He looks at the piece of paper. 'She could be a distant relative?'

'Why carry her name in a locket? My mother had an address book. Not that she used it.'

'You might *never* know.'

'I've *got* to know!' Danu refolds the piece of paper, unfolds it again, and whispers, 'I've got to know.'

Morrie shakes his head. 'But we're leaving. Quickly – write her a letter—'

'And give her what address to write back to? We're never anywhere long enough.'

'Gianto might try to organise us coming back sometime, rather than getting slotted in because some other circus couldn't make it . . .'

'Gianto never thinks ahead.'

'I could ask him to—'

'When's he ever done something because he's been asked to?'

Morrie says nothing, because he can't argue with this.

Danu looks down at the piece of paper. 'My mother insisted I took this locket on her deathbed. It could be important. It could be nothing at all. Not knowing will be terrible.'

Silence thickens between them.

Danu breaks it. 'I'm going to stay here in Matryoshka.'

He eyes the piece of paper with suspicion.

Still watching him, she puts it back in the locket, and reattaches the chain to her neck.

He looks, blank-faced, at her hand reaching for his. Eventually he meets her gaze. He looks sad, but doesn't speak of sadness. 'Look, you've never promised me anything. I'm counting myself lucky to have had you with me this long.'

She squeezes his hand. 'No, you've been my luck, and I grabbed it. But listen, I was told to wake you – everyone else is up and nearly ready to set off.'

As Morrie gets washed and dressed, Danu bundles her possessions into two large leather bags. Clothing and costumes, soaps and candles, scraps of writings and notebooks, the money she's scrimped over the years, her bedding, the spare coiled metal wire, turnbuckle, clamps and ring bolts.

Morrie's beside the sink, wolfing down a stale pastry. He nods

133

at her sealed bags. 'Right then. Oh, don't forget your wages. They're on the table.'

She puts the brown envelope in her coat pocket. 'Hopefully this will last me a while.'

He says, 'Should do. So you're all done, then.'

'Would you do one more thing for me, and I'm sorry to ask it of you?'

He goes over to her and squeezes her hand. 'You've never asked me for anything. You're on a roll now. That's twice in under an hour.'

'I can't bear to speak any farewells. We'll leave last. You can drop me on the way out and I'll slip quietly away. It's hard enough to say goodbye to you. And if I just go, yes, they'll be shocked I've left, but they'll be more shocked for your sake. They'll rally round you and—'

Morrie glances at her bags again. His eyes are moist. 'Ah Danu. I wish—'

Danu has never seen him cry, or get this close to it. He shakes his head, and there's a rumour of a smile as he says, 'Enough of all this. I'll be all right. And so will you.'

She writes the address of the empty house at Wringers Street on a scrap of paper, and presses it into his palm. 'All being well, I'll live there. If you can, write me a letter. About any kind of nonsense, or about nothing at all.'

While the caravans move out through the gap in the city's fence, Morrie keeps Inferno walking. The horses up ahead break into a trot. When the rest of the circus is further ahead, he brings Inferno to a halt. The caravan wheels grind against stone, and stop.

Danu thuds her bags onto the roadside. Her throat is thick with barbs. How can she say the word goodbye when there are so many other trapped words which could be said?

At the front of the caravan, she strokes Inferno's mane. Morrie's eyes shine as he looks at her, but there's a smile at the edges of his lips.

He touches his heart, dips his head and says, 'Watch for me on the ether.'

'It was *your* voice in the crowd. How—'

He interrupts her. 'You're really staring at me.'

'I want to memorise your face. Every line, each crease. That stain on your skin. This bump, that flake of skin, each pore of your nose.'

He gets down from the front porch and takes her hands. He speaks softly, 'And you think this isn't love?'

'I do.'

'Still?'

'Still.' She kisses him. Tender and slow. She wants to give him something of herself, even if it is fleeting.

With her lips on his, she feels him let her go.

He climbs back up to his seat and grips the reins. As he fixes his gaze straight ahead, Danu steps back onto the verge. At his command, Inferno walks a few yards and breaks into a trot.

Danu watches as the shuddering caravan shrinks smaller and smaller along the road. Her heart quickens with anticipation; he's left her with a question rather than a goodbye. She doesn't know if the ether is something or nothing, but it probably meant the same as her kiss. Just something to think of from time to time, something to remember him by.

He is kind. He *was* kind.

The caravan becomes miniature. And so soon, disappears.

Oh, but now he's gone.

They're all gone. Everyone she knows. This is too sudden.

The image of The Tower crashes into her thoughts. The crumbling black rocks, the bodies falling from windows. Destruction.

Flames. Lightning bolts shearing through grey clouds. She banishes it by staring at the empty road – the grey uneven surface, the black ragged mountains on either side, the horizon which pulls at her with invisible threads.

Dawn sweeps pale. Her future has disappeared along this road. She hates the sight of it. She reminds herself it's a future she didn't want as a gale blows through her empty arms. Her body can shiver as much as it likes. It has heavy bags to carry back into Matryoshka. An abandoned house to quietly break into. A stranger to find. She puts one bag on her back and fills her arms with the other.

An empty road is no future. It is just an empty road.

Her future is in Matryoshka; the place in which she was born and held the arms of parents who loved her. She will now begin all over again with no arms around her at all.

Full circle.

So here Morrie is, reins in his hand, flicking them at the sodding horse, flacking them to the blasted road, watching the clouds ahead darken without Danu at his side. Ahead, the whistles of tuneless gales are picking up. There's a storm coming straight at them as they move fast away, away. On to the next town. Back to the wire, solo. Leave her behind. He's caught up with the caravans, he's got a whole circus of folks to follow. They'll keep him moving away. When they stop, when he tells them she's gone, they'll try to make him forget her.

But nothing that's said will make him forget her.

Aye, there were others before her. Like any man who's got hot blood in the veins, he's been caught by a fine set of ankles, nice pair of tits or a silken neck. Eyes are poachers of bodies and a body is sometimes a noose. Sometimes it's all bodies and sometimes it's bodies and minds, loving women. When it's just bodies, the noose grips and releases.

Skin and muscles, their flavours never taste rich for too long. He should never have loved Danu's mind.

When she was a child, he barely noticed her. She was awkward and knock-kneed though her hands swam like fishes whenever a tune filled the air. When she hit fifteen, she already had the body of a woman. She danced like a snake and told stories with her voice and her arms. He felt bad for noticing how fine she'd blossomed, but his eyes were drawn.

He bedded other circus women. They told him how gentle or rough their bodies liked it. Some got attached, asked him for things he couldn't give them. Still, he noticed Danu and sometimes wished she'd ask something of him. But she was a strange thing – never asked anyone for anything. She'd got more than enough filling that mind of hers to be going on with. Or that's what it looked like. Tight-knit group, her with her folks. Even at fifteen, she was always with one or the both of them. A good lass, she was. A light lass. She laughed a lot before her folks took ill and died.

She turned feral, he'd swear it. That body of hers had only just ripened and she shrivelled it thin. Not eating enough, like as not. Happen grief needed her hunger for a time. She'd fill out when hunger and grief got out of the bed they were sharing with her. And because she never asked anyone for anything, no one paid her attention. Mag and Sandy did their best, but they'd never had stray kittens, let alone kids. Didn't know what to do with her. Tooth and nail. Blood and bone. That's how she'd fight. He thought it whenever he looked on her. It was all there, tied in her silent tongue but free as loud madness if you looked in her eyes.

But Danu was feral gone, make no bones about it. There was anger in those eyes of hers once her folks died. She never raised her voice with it, but it was the worst type of anger. The dangerous kind, the kind that explodes and takes everything down.

Happen she never even knew she'd the rage burning in her. Happen she still doesn't know.

Men looked at Danu all the time and she either hated it or ignored it. Which likely made them look at her all the more. No, she never saw much around her.

Before Danu moved in with him, Morrie saw her slip away at night and followed her. He couldn't bear waiting outside as she went into some flattie party filled with boys pretending to be men. He hated not knowing what was going on behind those walls which locked her away, those walls thick as jails. Thought she'd end up dead or worse. Worse than dead? He's sure there's such a thing. After following her, he told himself to look away.

But he couldn't look away. He'd a heavy pounding in his heart for her, and it wasn't getting any lighter.

So on another night when he saw her sneak off, Morrie did what his mam taught him and followed her in a whole different way. He saw the light and dark of it all. Sent himself after her in the only way he knew how. Travelled a part of himself to her. A part. The rest of him stayed in the caravan alone.

He can't speak of what he felt, seeing her kiss someone else in a tiled bathroom. She was more innocent than he'd imagined her. All the same, he hated seeing her arms around anyone. And when that bastard turned on her he wasn't able to punch him and pull Danu away. It doesn't work like that – there's no body to punch with. But he was there all the same.

He'd felt angry. When he felt it, he was pulled back to the quiet of his flesh-and-bone body too soon. Eyes open, sitting still in the caravan, not even the flicker of a candle or the sounds of birds to give counsel. And buggered with exhaustion. His mam had said *You can be with anyone you love but, my. It stretches you thin at first*. And it did. Morrie felt thinned. Dog tired for days. Awake for three nights. It scared the shit out of him. The journey back was too much of a rush.

Morrie figured he'd to set aside his own feelings. He decided the next time, he'd do that. Then he'd be able to stay near her for longer. *Pure love lets you stay close*, his mam had said. *Feel for them, not for yourself. Then you're with them as long as you want to be.* But there wasn't a next time. Danu had come back bruised and frightened and never snuck off alone again.

Ether, his mam had called it. *A method of travel.* She'd told him a lot. She said, *You need a clear head and the will not to change anything. When it works, you're wherever they are, the person you love. Sometimes you see what's there, so clear. Sometimes you feel what the person's feeling but can't see too much. You know when they're safe and when they're in danger.*

Had Danu felt he'd been so near her? She'd looked at him the next day, as he was outside planing the edge of his door. He'd thought she'd seen into him, all the way through. But then her eyes blurred to blank.

Now he's sure she never did know he'd travelled the ether to her. She'd have said something while they lived together if she was ever going to say it. He was always waiting. Maybe she'd speak in her sleep and say she'd once felt him beside her when he wasn't there. He listened for it, ear to her mouth, catching murmurs when she'd never have let him close enough if she was awake. He'd hunch over her bed and look at her body shaping the covers. Aye, he was always waiting for her to talk but she never did.

Morrie's mam was a traveller of a woman, a traveller of all kinds. If she wasn't able to walk her real body to a place, she'd send out her *ether body*, she called it. She said folks were made of more than one body. One body that's the flesh and bone of it, and another body which can travel further than the roads it's on. *This*, she said, *this ether body, it's made of pure love. Some folks call it their soul, others call it their spirit.* She said it could travel using wind and light. *That's what the ether is made from – wind, and light.*

She told him: *This is how it's done. Close your eyes. Feel your love for the person you want to be with. How high, how wide, how deep is it? Next, make it grow. Build it vast enough to fill your flesh body, and let it flood through you. Shift in it till you feel your spirit separating from your body. Then look to see where they are. The room they're in or the field, the bed they're lying in, the washtub they're running . . . See the whole picture with them in it. Watch them a while. Who's with them, what are they saying, and most important – what are they feeling? Get your heart beating to the time of theirs if you can.*

See a line linking you to them. Don't look on it direct. Catch its light. Think of love pouring from you to them. Love bridges the gap between you.

There's a rush of a gale and your spirit leaves your body behind. It tunnels through light to where they are. Never look around to see what kind of wind you're travelling on, because no wind is a stable thing. Practise. Recover. What happens next, when you've finally got it right, is you're there with them. You can't change a thing. All you can do is watch and surround them. Might be different for you. But that's how it is for me.

Once Danu was living with Morrie, he didn't need the ether apart from that one time he followed her in Matryoshka. He liked sharing his caravan with her. She'd not care how messy he was, as she was the same. He liked joking around with her when they were both drunk. He liked the mad questions she'd ask him about her stories. He liked her quietness, and that she knew when to let him alone. He liked who he was with her, better than who he was without her. And all the while, he wanted her, too much perhaps. She couldn't ever be just a body. But his body wanted her body all the same. Some nights he'd lift her covers while she was sleeping sound, to look at her. Oh he wanted her, wanted her, wanted her. Those thighs, the curve of her waist, those dark-nippled breasts. Her long neck and smooth-skinned legs.

Danu's mam and da never knew of the ether, or if they did, they never taught Danu what they knew. Down to earth or grounded by earth. Rooted in, like most folks are. Morrie guesses his own mam knew she'd be running off sooner or later for love. She loved hard, his mam. Went after it like a pirate after treasure. She's still hovering around sometimes, so she's still alive. She still loves the bones of him. Bodies have their own free will. One day he'll know when she's dead, for there's no free will in dying and death stops all kinds of travelling.

Gianto knew something was coming. He'd been on at Morrie about Danu for a while. He said understanding comes from the pictures he turned in the cards. He told Morrie that if he took up with a secretive girl, he'd be best served to have a look in her head from time to time. So Morrie thought of Danu's mind and shuffled and each tarot spread was laid under a candle. Gianto'd have a bevvy and mutter to himself. He'd have another bevvy and point at each card. There was a queen and a knight and some other queen, but Morrie can't remember the meanings for these. Gianto was more definite about Death and The Devil, The Wheel and The Lovers. When fatally, The Tower appeared, Gianto told Morrie there was no arguing with The Tower. *Just take it*, he said. *Don't try to fight.*

And so here Morrie is. Danu's left him, no more able to love him than she was when he first kissed her and didn't kiss her again. Most women want more than one kiss once they've had the first taste. Not her. Most women wouldn't sleep on the floor when there's a bed with a man in it who's wanting them. Not her. Bunged up in her mind about love, she is. Got tunnels and drains in her head and they're none of them washing through.

A storm hits the road. In this wind which brings rain, even the weather's telling him it's wrong to leave her behind. The gale rises, blasting into his face. Gales know when things are being pulled apart when they should be bound together. The skies know. This lashing rain knows. Morrie wipes his eyes and it hits them again, cold, blind.

His body strains as he tells himself to keep going. Keep moving away. He's shivering now. The empty space where she should be sitting beside him, the gap's more chilling than the gale. That's the thing with flesh-and-bone bodies with all their meat and muscle, hair and hands – they don't like to wander too far from what they want. The head can chatter all it likes about any choice it's made – to keep moving, keep going, get away, but the body still feels the pull.

His head is winning.

Danu's got to miss him. He's never given her the chance to do this. Folks need to have time to miss each other, else they don't know what they've got. They get used to love, it gets to be so usual they can't even see it's there.

So he'll travel onwards along roads and roads till Danu's missing him. And she will. Danu loves him more than she loves herself – she just needs to know it. And when she's ready to say she loves him, to admit it to herself, then . . . he'll make her wait.

She's got no way to find him. To come after him. She'll not know where the circus is, where it's been, where it's left and arrived at. It'll break her heart if she lets herself feel it.

And what'll Danu do with heartbreak?

That's the rub. Heartbreak might send her into the beds of flatties, looking for something she's never found. It might make her drink herself into blackness. It might make her topple herself off the first high building she climbs, looking for a wire in the clouds which isn't there.

Who can say which way she'll blow? Love's all about risk.

As the wind howls in the gaps between boulders, he lashes the horse to push on through the storm. 'Faster, faster away. Don't stop. Because one day I'll run back. Make her mine.'

In Wringers Street most of the houses have been occupied for years, some with a succession of transients, others with families who've been there for generations. The one house which hasn't experienced these types of occupancy, is number nineteen.

When houses are persistently empty, they become introspective. And with so many rooms to introspect, intropomorphise and intromeditate on, the atmosphere of each house increases in strength with any duration of emptiness. Sealed windows, doors and letter boxes allow no air to enter. Rooms are lungs to houses. Unaired lungs contain all kinds of dusty tunnels.

Put simply, empty houses look inwards. They create and re-create their own atmospheres. Human habitation forms at least nine-tenths of any house's atmosphere. There is an invasive power in objects and personal possessions, and a sweeping claustrophobia surrounds births, deaths and thundering parties. All of these irritations spread echoes through rooms. Houses are further weakened by people calling them *homes* rather than the *houses* they know themselves as. Changing what something calls itself is usually an attempt to own it.

Houses know this, but with the pervasive occupancy of humans, many forget. Number nineteen has had a long time to consider what *home* means. It has learned to protect itself from new invasions, and yet, the memories it caresses in its air, the feeling of *fullness* it remembers so well, are all from a time of having been possessed.

Number nineteen is filled with memories. A woman, long ago, once lived inside it and loved it. She called it her *home* whenever she spoke of how she loved it to others who visited her. The house became what she wanted as it gained so much in return. Number nineteen remembers how being loved felt, and still misses her. It welcomed in anyone who'd loved her. It even welcomed her daughter, though retreated a little till the screaming baby had subsided into a small child. The woman had wanted her home to be happy, and number nineteen had surrendered. Even after the father of the child left, perhaps yet more so, it had felt her desire for happiness in every touch of her hands, each sweep of her brush, every wipe of her cloth. She filled it with the smells of candlewax, linseed oil and soap. Whenever she hung a picture, shelves or a mirror, she stroked its wall before the hammer's first bang.

Number nineteen felt a deep crack open within its foundations when she closed its front door for the last time.

The woman left most of her possessions behind. These are artefacts, mementos, relics. They belong to number nineteen now, they are treasured. Her cookbooks and magic books, her alchemy charts, candles and ornaments, pots and pans, her pictures and furniture are tokens of love. The house cloaks them in soft dust and its spiders decorate and redecorate them with perfectly engineered webs.

Since her, no one has lived in number nineteen, though a few people have come in through the front door. One pair attempted to move in but left as quickly as they arrived. They opened its front door with a visceral attitude of possession. Number nineteen doesn't tolerate bumps and tumbles, clumsy nudges, or anyone who brings too much physical baggage with them. The tenants brought their own possessions in boxes, and displayed a tangible intention to get rid of the relics. But their sensitivity to atmosphere meant they were easily frightened off.

No one expects a house to be able to evict people by itself. Number nineteen has a powerful atmosphere, which it has developed and fine-tuned over the long and empty years. As soon as the words 'all this stuff will have to go' echoed in its hallway, it set its atmosphere on them.

The tenants couldn't sleep. Too many unexplainable noises at night time. When people don't sleep, they do see odd things. Hallucinations, they call these. Atmosphere, is what these visions really are.

Pale-faced and goose-bumped, they removed themselves, unsure of exactly why they were leaving.

The other people who visit once a year wear suits and always come in pairs. They crawl on number nineteen's floorboards, prising. They exercise its doors. They press their thumbnails into its windowsills. They criticise its condensation, bad-mouth its sagging ceilings and swear about its damaged roof. They talk to each other, always discussing the dual notions of *repair* and *attractiveness for tenants*. The word *facelift* has been used.

They are offensive, but never stay for long. *Not enough funds*. They have said this phrase each time they've visited. Once these people have left, number nineteen celebrates by dropping another tile from its roof.

Number nineteen is dark and suspicious because today, there is a young woman half inside it. She's hanging her upper body through the kitchen window she's forced open from the backyard.

Scraping and clawing her way in, she drops herself onto its cracked floor tiles. With some creaking in the lock, she crunches its back-door key and wrenches open the door. Letting in a gulp of air, she drags two leather bags inside. Closing and locking the door behind her, she sighs and glances around the kitchen.

She speaks. 'Hello, house. I'm going to live in you.'

Number nineteen is unaccustomed to such directness. She intends to *live in*. None of the few others who've entered over its empty years have ever announced their intentions.

The girl should repair the crack she's made in its window frame. Though perhaps she doesn't have any glues in those bags, perhaps she has *not enough funds*, either. After all, someone rich would come striding through its front door. It is neglected, a little hurt, and doesn't want to shelter anyone who might need something from it. But it is being tolerant in not evicting her immediately. Almost . . . kind. No, not kind. Kindness isn't an admirable quality in anything which wants to retain its possessions. It is tolerating her, as it tolerates the woodworm in its skeleton and the birds who creep in and squawk out of the gaping holes in its roof.

This young woman is little more than a girl. There is something deeply lost about her own miniature atmosphere; as she wanders from the kitchen into the living room, a small wave follows her around. It's a lost and yet hopeful wave. There's a tentative euphoria in the splashes.

People are never aware of their atmospheres the way houses are. Though the girl can't see the wave swirling around her ankles, she appears to be constantly attempting to keep her balance. She climbs its stairs and looks in the bathroom. In the hallway, she shifts and kicks her legs, stands on her tiptoes, walks in straight lines with her feet planted so firmly on the gaps between floorboards she must be in constant fear of tripping.

People are so often scared of all the wrong things.

In its attic, the girl looks out through a beautifully shaped

146

hole in the roof. The girl hasn't yet touched any of the house's sacred relics. Perhaps she is in awe of their abundance as she has so few possessions of her own. Seeming overly determined in her crunching footfall, she goes downstairs again.

She drags her bags up its first flight of stairs, catches her breath, and continues up the next. She puts her bags in the middle of the attic room. She unbuckles the bags but doesn't remove her things. Now that is respectful: she doesn't expect them to be *housed*.

Number nineteen doesn't believe for a tick of the hallway clock that the girl will remain inside it for long. After all, she can never be the woman who strengthened its atmosphere with her magic, her love and her sorrow. It does, however, accept the woman will never return. It's waited for her for over a century. And now, it's far too late. People have such short lifespans.

Which is highly disappointing when houses spend quite so long waiting for them to come back.

The girl says, 'I've found myself a home which doesn't move between days and nights.'

This girl talks a lot, for someone who is inside a house which isn't convinced it wants her to stay. It gives her a little benign atmosphere to shut her mouth, and shifts the musty scent from the basement in her general direction. But the girl is oblivious as she descends its stairway, glancing in the master bedroom and child's playroom. She frowns at the collection of dolls houses, shakes her head, goes downstairs to the ground floor and circles its front room. She's humming, though there's no music to sing along to.

Again, she speaks. 'For the first time in my life, I can be still.'

Number nineteen sighs, and lets a little more atmosphere creep out of the floorboards. The girl steps over it. Doesn't even flinch. Her wave washes from her, spreading all the way to the skirting boards.

Is she completely insensitive?

The girl speaks yet again, her face raised as she speaks to its cracked ceiling. 'Some children dream of running away from home to join a travelling circus. I spent my childhood dreaming of running away from the circus to live in a home.' She exhales and her breath sends dust motes spinning.

She says, 'I had a dream of a home in this city. It was airy and light. One room had a mirror and my reflection came to life. That house wasn't like you at all.'

Her shoulders slump as she sits on the dusty sofa, staring at the mantelpiece where two ancient dried flowers drape over the rim of a beautifully cracked vase. She touches the necklace at her throat. Her wave retreats from the skirting boards, closing back in on her, lapping around her feet. Euphoria dissolves. The wave moves around her ankles in two directions.

She covers her face with her hands and whispers, 'What have I done? I feel homeless.'

The house retrieves its own atmosphere from the floorboards, as she's clearly going to ignore it. Homeless? What a useful thing to know. She's not claiming ownership, so won't be hard to evict – she's far more vulnerable than she looks if her mood can change this rapidly. Perhaps she needs some repairs to her own structure as well. People should build their own foundations more solidly than they ever do.

Number nineteen is a touch irritated, and more than a little intrigued. For a long time it has wanted to fully understand how human atmospheres work. The woman who loved it left such a complete absence on her departure. Number nineteen has never fully recovered. It needs to retreat into itself for now and consider the girl's atmosphere in peace, especially if she remains so determined to *talk*.

* * *

So far, Danu's spent most of the daylight hours indoors, sneaking in and out for food supplies at night. Uncertain of the laws in this city concerning the borrowing of empty houses, she's been leaving through the back door when most honest people will be sleeping. Last night she overheard a conversation outside a corner shop – the area Wringers Street is in is called Incassable, and she heard it described as *rough* by one woman, and *bohemian* by another. She's been browsing the headlines of newspapers, but not yet found any mention of squats or evictions. All the same, it is best to remain discreet.

The bakeries stay open past midnight, and Danu has survived so far on sugared pastries, apples, dried fruit and herb breads. Morrie slipped some extra money in her bag without her seeing. There was a ribbon tied around a roll of notes, and a scrap of paper on which he'd written, *When the time comes, get yourself a birthday gift. Might make this year's one better than last year*.

She found a discarded leather purse in the gutter two nights ago – any notes had been thieved, but the coins and some stamps remained. Last night those extra coins bought her coconut milk, a bag of dried tropical fruit and her new favourite: a cheap local delicacy of curry-pasted flatbread.

Each night she's been outside, when she returns, she hitches her skirt and ties it at her hips. She climbs the wall at the end of Wringers Street, crouches and runs along the wall. At number nineteen, she drops into the backyard which is scattered with rotten wood and broken chairs. Brown fungus grows inside a tin bucket and she can't bring herself to tip out the stagnant water.

She loves this city, but now she has decided to remain in its company, how she loves it has changed. Now, she wants something from it.

She wants both this house and this city to become her home.

She wants to know why Judith Crown's name hangs in the locket at her throat.

For the first time in her life, she has demands.

But inside this house, nothing responds to demands. Almost everything is broken and she asks herself what she expected – any derelict house would need work. Her practical inadequacies bring rushes of emotions: surges of euphoria about being completely free because she's alone, but intense grief as well. For the first time, she misses her parents' possessions. She remembers thinking it would hurt to keep her mother's box of old broken rings. She wishes she'd kept the leather roll which contained her father's tools and the greeny-black feathers he collected. Things they'd touched.

Tonight, the cracks in the windowpanes cast streetlight in fractured diamonds on the walls. Danu shields her candle so she's not seen from outside as she passes a ragged-curtained window on the stairway. The air smells of faded perfume, or cologne, or of drains and stagnant water. These are the smells of melancholia.

The attic door isn't attached to its frame. It leans against the wall out on the landing. Inside the attic, a sturdy wardrobe has its back against the wall. There's a large cot in the corner and in the middle of the room is a yellow and pink sofa with tall arms.

Danu lies on the sofa under the purple velvet coverlet she's owned all her life. When she was a small child, her parents folded it into thirds to tuck around her small body. She unfolded it as she grew, and it warmed her no matter what the season, even against the draughts which crept over the floor of Morrie's caravan. She'd wrapped Morrie in it the last time he was poorly. It was bitterly icy outside, too cold to even snow. He was looking drawn, and gave up on the day at noon. He came back into the caravan and lay on his bed.

Danu had closed the curtains to shut the cold outside and wrapped her coverlet around him. When he stirred to move, he said to her, *Our roof needs patching. I'll get the ladder.* He'd winked at her as he slung on his jacket. *Blanketlove. That's what you do. We need new words when there's none that fit right.* He went outside again. She thought about hermits and anchoresses living in lonely caves on mountains while she listened to the sound of hammering.

She buries her nose in the coverlet. The smell of Morrie's caravan fills her nostrils, familiar scents of tea leaves and boot polish . . . but there's no scent of him. She could have so easily taken one of his unwashed shirts. A pillowcase. A lock of his hair. But she didn't.

As she stares into the night sky between rafters, drums and cymbals bump and clash. What a sky it is – between clouds there are trails of light, twists of mist. The stars and moon appear and disappear and reappear. Seen through the spice mists, they are the colours of fireworks with all of the brightness, and none of the noise.

Her mind races and she can't get to sleep. Sitting up, she draws the candle closer. Tearing a page from one of her notebooks, she writes:

Dear Judith Crown,

My name is Danu Mock and I have not long arrived in Matryoshka. I intend to remain here. Your name and address were written on a scrap of paper in my mother's locket which she wore constantly. She and my father died, and I would like to know why she carried your name so close to her heart. Their names were Clem and Adelaide Mock and they were part of a travelling circus.

Could you shed any light on this mystery? You can write to me at 19 Wringers Street, Incassable, outer circle, Matryoshka. If you'd prefer to meet in person, do say any time, date and place, and I will be there.

Thank you.

Danu Mock

P.S. I don't believe in heaven so I need my answers down here on earth. If you believe in heaven and it turns out to be real, I hope you'll be rewarded there if you can set my mind at rest. It still feels like only yesterday they died.

Danu closes her eyes and half-dreams of a story she wrote about heaven. In one of Morrie's drawers, he kept a small pair of midnight blue boots. He told her about playing a childhood game where he imagined he was wading through swamp-clouds. After hearing this, Danu thought about clouds. About sharp things, cutting through them. She wrote a story about a jewelled devil who wore boots made from knives. The devil danced across a clouded heaven.

She'd read the story to Morrie:

The devil was valuable. The jewels were a part of his skin, like the scales of a dragon. He was made of amethysts, amber, moonstones and diamonds. He reflected every shade of blue there ever was. But the devil danced and he murdered the rain. This made heaven barren. He killed the sun and made heaven persistently night. He murdered the moon and left the clouds nothing to reflect. He fixed his eye on the stars . . . No matter what the devil murdered, no matter how evil he became, no matter how much destruction he caused with his boots made from knives, the blue-feathered angels who ruled this particular heaven would not let him fall.

Morrie interrupted her to ask, *But why didn't the angels get rid of the devil?* Danu replied, *They didn't want to.*

The angels felt desire collectively, not as individuals. They bound his tongue during a ceremony in which they all told him they loved him. The devil knew that what they really loved was what he was worth. They thought the angels in neighbouring heavens would think them special because they had something so valuable, so beautiful, as him. He hated them for this lie, he hated them for this vanity. He stabbed out the stars so it was dark throughout their heaven. His revenge on the angels was blindness. In the purest darkness, all jewels are invisible.

Morrie nodded, when she'd finished the telling of this tale. He looked sad, but she thoughtlessly didn't ask him why. A pang. What *was* he feeling? What if there were many things left unsaid?

He has this address. The circus will pass many letter boxes.

Picking up her candle, Danu descends the staircases to the ground floor, rubs her thumbnail along the edges of the rusted letter box and checks that it works. She imagines the clang it will make as Morrie's letter passes through.

Danu has to remain in this house if she ever wants to hear from him again.

She climbs the staircases back to the attic. Hope follows her like a dog she doesn't want.

She picks up her notebook, and writes an unsendable letter.

Dear Morrie,

I'll tell you of a night-time walk I trod two nights ago. Walks in Matryoshka are on pavements but I miss soil and rocks under my feet. I've been finding it tough here, since you're gone. Or is it me who's gone? Anyway. I was walking. I bought a half-bottle of cheap rum in a corner shop and sipped it along the way.

All the while I walked, I was thinking about being in the wrong time but in the right place or in the wrong place at the right time. A white feather on the pavement landed my eye to the ground. Picking it up, I stroked it. Fingertip to thumb-whorl it sounded like paper.

I once heard that at some other time and in some other country, deserters of war were handed white feathers and thus called cowards. So as I walked carrying this feather, it held the weight of a judgement. I thought of you and felt like a coward.

Why didn't you suggest that you stayed here with me? Why didn't I ask you to?

You'll never read this. But I wish caravans had letter boxes, or postmen went travelling off their pre-determined routes.

Danu

Danu closes her notebook and puts it back in her bag. She's keeping the few things she owns inside her bags, so she can leave quickly if anyone comes into the house. The sky is lightening towards dawn but she's more awake than she was before she wrote these two letters. Bundling up a pile of dirty underwear, she carries it downstairs to the bathroom. The bath cradles fragments of plaster which have fallen from the ceiling.

A bang in the hall.

She goes to the doorway. A jester hand puppet lies on the floor beside a bookshelf. It's glaring at her with one cracked glass eye and a hole where the other one was. She picks it up and places it back on the gap in the dust on a shelf.

Something is watching her. Her heartbeat is too loud, and she barely breathes. She half-expects the appearance of some angry spirit, a spirit which could curse her spiralling into a grey madness.

Where is the puppet's missing eye?

She hunts for it urgently, moving objects along the hallway shelves. The puppet has a grin painted on its hook-nosed face. Was it smiling before?

Back inside the bathroom, she bolts herself in. Planting her feet on cold tiles, she takes a deep breath and remembers Morrie in training, demanding that she find her centre of mass. She stands on one leg. Alters her posture. Centre of mass over base of support. Balance imagination. Level away fear.

This isn't working. There are so many empty rooms surrounding her. She imagines the hallway doors opening and closing like mouths. Staring at the bolted bathroom door, tunnel vision closes in. Her vision focuses on the keyhole.

She crouches, listening. At first she hears nothing.

A small noise intensifies: the sound of a marble rolling across floorboards.

A marble, or a puppet's missing eye.

FOUR FOR YEARNING

Danu can't stay indoors waiting for the sound of the letter box every morning. It's pouring with rain, and she wants to feel it on her skin. Through quiet streets, she lets herself get soaked. Her skin wakes, her mind wakes. Telling herself that she's walking in the rain is different to telling herself she's getting wet. She is here, this moment is now, it's not what's been lost, it's not what's yet to come.

Beside an alleyway she hasn't noticed before, a sign on the wall reads: The Smallest Museum in Matryoshka.

She walks along the alleyway which leads to a square formed of crumbling buildings. There are many hidden places in the outer circle, and this one looks forgotten. Ivy grows between gaps in the timber.

The museum door is propped open, so she goes inside. A Welcome Board appears to replace the need for staff, as it indicates what can be found behind four closed doors. One room is about geothermal energy and electricity production in the city. Another is about the local geology. Another is about mountain wildlife.

The fourth room is about Matryoshka's history, and this is the one which most interests her. It's a small windowless room where text is printed in a handwritten font all over the white walls. Within the quietness of this empty room she reads:

The Story of Matryoshka's Birth.

Centuries ago, an architect set off on his travels without a map or a compass. He crossed a continent at the widest part and upon reaching the north, he climbed the highest range of mountains he could discover without crossing an ocean. He was prone to seasickness, so would never travel by boat. In this mountain range, he found many people living in hamlets and villages which were scattered within a vast forest. Many of these people were hospitable to him, offering him straw beds to sleep in and hot stews to warm him. He thought they'd perhaps appreciate living more closely together, as they often spoke of loneliness.

He was good company for them. He was interested in their houses because some were so ancient. They listened rapt as he opened their attics and examined the rafters, tapped the window-sills and doorsteps and enlightened them about mantelpieces and lintels. He described their homes to them in archaeological terms. When they asked about him, he told them he was a rootless architect with an overly active imagination, a healthy ego, a great sense of style, and an inordinately wealthy sponsor who suffered from unrequited love.

The architect finally stopped travelling when he discovered a strange mountain.

He didn't see a mountain, he saw a city. He saw the city it could become.

He would name this city Matryoshka, after the wooden dolls who live inside one another's stomachs. As a child, he'd been given a set of these dolls as a silencing device by a particularly punishing nanny. His initial terror of her had made him tough while still young. As an adolescent, toughness became resilience, which in adulthood transformed itself into determination.

He stared with curiosity at his imagined city, which was

temporarily still a mountain. He didn't even want to scale it yet. He wanted to draw it. The shape of the mountain was like a squashed version of one of these Matryoshka dolls. It looked to the architect as if someone had smashed their collective heads and revealed the circles within them. This was how the idea of the city of Matryoshka came to be first conceived. The architect camped at the base of the mountain, and extracted a roll of thick paper from the buckles of his canvas bag.

He first drew the city in pencil, with bright paints for decoration.

Now the city existed outside his mind, he looked at the drawing. It was exquisitely beautiful.

The structure of the city was to be three concentric circles, each one self-contained, each one smaller than the last as it rose with the mountain to meet the sky.

He had been born with no sense of smell, and was unaware of the foul scents in the soil. Living so alone meant he had time to fill his mind with immense possibilities and extravagant ideas. He measured the whole mountain and produced many sketches of each of the three concentric circles. Once they were complete, he called in workers to lay the foundations. Word spread fast as the sounds of digging, thudding and hammering echoed through the quiet country. Many people were keen to live in the proposed city as the climate in the mountain range was cold, while this particular mountain was always warm.

Masons and blemmeres, cafenders and hilliers, moulders and joyners with a myriad of apprentices arrived to begin the great task of city-building. They all commented on the smell. The architect was also curious about the high temperature and textures of the soil. While the structural work commenced, he called in a blentonist and a dowser. They told him there was far too much water inside the mountain. They also, being well travelled, recognised the mountain's scent as sulphur, and suspected the high temperature may be due to volcanic activity.

Many people would have turned back, but the architect's great determination won against fear in a brief internal battle. He called in geologists who measured the mountain's inner mixture of water and gases. It was deemed to be unlikely to ever erupt, if the water was extracted, cleansed, and utilised to provide the city's water supply. Unlikely, though not impossible.

The architect, who often looked to the heavens for answers to creative problems, also consulted a weatherspy. She calculated the precise astrological chart which the city could have if it was deemed 'born' when the last stone was laid. She examined the angles of planets for a variety of dates and times. They explored the trines, sextiles, squares and oppositions. They discussed in particular the inner nature of the mountain, and how the city could be born with characteristics which would ensure its survival. After exploring various combinations, the architect and weatherspy decided the city should be born at a time which gave it a Leo sun, Cancer rising and moon in Libra. Fire, water and air in harmony. Which should, in theory, suggest eruptions were unlikely as they arose, surely, from disharmony. And in terms of the city's personality, it would be outgoing and vivacious, capable of providing warm and sensitive homes, and be constantly striving for aesthetic behaviour and agreement.

The concentric circles were constructed, different materials and styles of architecture in each one, and after a number of years, the city was finally inhabited. However, the last of the building work was running late. When the overdue work was finished and the final stone was ready to be put in place, the new inhabitants of the city gathered in the streets for a jubilant ceremony, with offerings to burn and paintings to be unveiled in celebration of the lion, the crab and the scales.

On a copper-coated wall at the pinnacle of the city, the architect and weatherspy stood shoulder to shoulder. The weatherspy clasped a watch in one hand and a stopwatch in the other.

The last stone was fixed.

She shook her head. It had been born late.

One of the chosen planets had danced away.

Bells clanged.

The weatherspy announced through a reverberating cone, 'Though the city has not been gifted its chosen astral personality, all things ever born choose their time themselves. For reasons humans cannot comprehend, any birth can quicken or slow. The stars watch. The planets transit. They make contact and dance away. Leo still roars, Cancer still walks sideways, but the unintentional moon sign is Scorpio rather than Libra.' Her shoulders sagged.

The weatherspy continued. 'A Scorpio moon sign will add intensity and passion rather than aestheticism and rational analysis. It will mean the city has difficulty in accepting the need for change. Possessiveness and control may surface. After a late birth, albeit due to delays in building work, we now need to keep this city safe from the sting of the Scorpio influence. To overcome the new combination of the elements of fire, water and water, when more water is not optimistic for a city built on a volcano, you must turn your spiritual attentions and faith . . . to the wisdom of the moon.'

After the weatherspy spoke, she disappeared in a cloud of thwarted predictions.

The architect looked to the horizon. As the celebrations began, he slipped away, seeking the next landscape which would spark his imagination. The architect left his initial drawing behind. It was so beautiful the inhabitants framed it in gold filigree and hung it in the main hall of the library.

Over the years which were to follow, though other architects came and went, though all areas of the city suffered decay, no one altered any part of the city from the original design, as it became known as a work of great art.

This city was born after a long labour filled with passion and determination. Danu loves Matryoshka more than ever as she leaves this room, though there's something creepy about a museum with no other visitors and no staff. She resolves to make herself go outside each day and explore more of Matryoshka. This will distract her from thinking about when she'll get a letter from either Judith Crown or Morrie. There will be many things which will spark her curiosity as she gradually learns how to make her house into a home.

The girl has lightened number nineteen's hallway walls with insipid yellow paint. She hasn't *mended* the cracks in its walls; she has simply *moisturised* them with gloopy layers.

In its kitchen, the girl washes paint off a brush. Her hands stain all she touches yellow. Number nineteen remembers the woman it loved once telling her child a story called 'The Midas Touch'. It tries to feel golden as the girl leaves smears on its draining board, but the smell of paint cuts through all its glorious scents of mildew.

The girl lifts a large paper bag from the floor and places it on its kitchen table. She glances at the dresser, at the dusty ornaments and cookbooks which *aren't hers*.

The house is concerned about the thoughts behind glances. The girl touches the relics occasionally. She is particularly concerned with the effigies which people call *dolls*. The woman who used to live in number nineteen all those years ago made several rag effigies: she stitched them in anger after the man went away.

One night she stuck pins in one of them.

On another night she sewed a mouth up.

But she made a few for her child that weren't part of any ritual.

The man shouldn't have tried to hurt her. But he did try, and did succeed. It was a drunken night, and he black-eyed her through misplaced jealousy. Though number nineteen rattled and shook to the foundations, it was the woman who got him outside.

The woman looked at the man through its open front door. Her expression was that of someone seeing a stranger. He stood on one side of the threshold and she stood on the other. She cried words about innocence and the breaking of trust.

Finally he was silent, swaying with drink, but silent.

She took a ring off her finger and put it into his hand. Clenching his fingers around it, she banished him by closing him away on the other side of the front door. His fist pounded, but eventually his footsteps retreated.

He remained gone for a long time. Her friends visited her. A celebration. A birthday, and another. For all of this time, the woman soothed fears away from her tearful child – she cradled it as it grew. She was big while it was awake. She was small while it slept and she had time to cry for herself.

For a while, she performed small rituals. She drew rings of salt on its floorboards, lit candles and sang to the ghosts of her dead ancestors to protect her. What she might have sensed, but couldn't see, was that there were no ghosts around her at all. But during these rituals there were many atmospheres which made visitations, and moved the air particles around her, thickening and thinning, circling and fading.

Time passed, and the man tried to return. He banged on the front door, shouted through the letter box, banged on the door again, night after night . . . The woman tried to keep his shouted claims of ownership from her child's ears but he kept coming back, and back, and back. So early one morning, she took the child and three bags of possessions, and evicted herself.

The woman was gone, she is gone, and now she will always be gone.

In its kitchen, the girl is still looking at the dresser. The house drops a shadow across it which carries an atmosphere that prickles the air: *Don't touch. Don't touch. Don't touch.*

This atmosphere is made of sharpened air particles. These clump around the dresser and a small group become solid enough to knock a cookbook out of its place. The atmosphere thins and the air particles become blunt as the book bangs onto the floor.

The girl jumps at the sound. She looks at the book and shakes her head, dismissing some ghastly thought. She sits on a chair and empties her purse into her palm. Counting notes and coins, she clinks them back into her purse and puts it away. She unpacks the contents of the paper bag and spreads them across the table. Wiping her brow, she appears to contemplate the yards of cheap velvet fabric and matching thread reels, tape, coils of curtain cord and packets of pins and needles. This girl will never have the Midas touch. The colour of the fabric is gold-gone-wrong. Like the paint, it's *yellow*.

Again, the girl looks at the fallen cookbook. She places it back on the shelf. Turning around, she frowns at the fabric on the table. She rolls up her sleeves.

Gripping a pair of rusty scissors, she advances towards the fabric.

Snip. Tear. Snip. Tear. Rip.

She is going to make soft furnishings.

Badly.

All through number nineteen's stairways, woodworm bore

tiny holes. These are itchy, irritating things. The house sighs, as deeply as all broken things sigh, when their surfaces are given attention but the damage is still there underneath.

In the hours of dark and many shadows, the girl sleeps. While she sleeps, number nineteen watches the atmospheres which surround her.

Her wave is there all the time. It's about ten inches tall at its wildest. When she's awake, it swirls around her feet and ankles wherever she walks. When she lies down, it bubbles foam through her tangled hair. As she sleeps, it pools beneath her.

It's intriguing, but tonight something else is happening which is far more interesting.

Beside her, there is a thickening of air. Clumped particles. It swirls around her shoulders. Someone else's atmosphere has followed her here.

This atmosphere appears as a pale shadow, close to the girl. She rolls onto her side. It sinks to the floor beside her as she continues to sleep.

The atmosphere thickens as the girl's chest rises and falls. It gathers its own strength and becomes more of itself. The figure of a human body, a little larger than life.

It waits.

It grabs her.

It disappears.

Whenever Morrie's on the wire, there's faces below and nothing above. The lights shine bright from the edge of the ring. Danu's steps steadied him more than they threw his balance, though when they were learning and she got it wrong, he was often hurled down to the net.

It's been nearly two months now, since she left.

Happen she could always balance better than him. Happen he never told her so.

He can still walk, he can still balance, but there's nothing to want at the other end of the wire. During each show, he thinks of nothing but how to balance himself without her. But it's quickly time to bow, dismount, bow again. Each night he eats with the others, he tries not to think about Danu though others often talk of her.

Gianto's not mentioned her name, not even once. Instead, he's been on at Morrie about Loretta. *Talk to the girl. You'll find her sweet. You need a new flavour. Nothing so bitter as what you had before.*

Morrie responded that he'd never met anyone who'd want to eat Loretta, but if Gianto was that keen on her sugars, he should have her himself.

Gianto bristled. *I can't. We're too close-related.*

At the campfire, Loretta's sat herself beside Morrie yet again. Words sound shrill from her gob. Childlike, she nudges him with her shoulder. 'I just keep finding myself beside you, Morrie. Like my body is guided to yours. Have you noticed?'

He doesn't reply.

She says, 'Forget Danu. She forced men to love her, then took off.'

He speaks quietly: 'You understand less than nothing. Don't speak of her.'

She folds her arms. 'Tomas was always half in love with her. And Mario, when they was younger and clowning together.'

'Well, it was my caravan she bedded herself down in.'

'Who's loving her now, do you think about that?'

He doesn't even look at her as he murmurs, 'No one.'

'You don't know that.' She puts a nail-painted hand on his wrist. 'She'll have been with half the flatties in Matryoshka by now . . .'

He moves his hand away. 'Get lost, Loretta.'

Crestfallen, she rises, throws her shawl around her shoulders, and stalks off.

He looks into a bowl of grey rabbit stew he's not got the stomach for. It's been in his hand for so long it's cold now. He puts the bowl in the grass.

Loretta's talking to Gianto on the other side of the fire. They glance over at Morrie.

He looks away.

The next afternoon, Gianto raps the door, opens it and comes into Morrie's caravan. He sets himself down at the table. 'You got a dram for me?'

While Morrie pours him a whisky, Gianto takes his pack of tarot cards out of his pocket. He shuffles them, hands them to Morrie, and knocks back his drink.

Morrie shuffles them, eyeing Gianto silently. He passes them back.

Watching Morrie's face, Gianto turns over the cards.

Morrie watches for some sleight to his hand. He doesn't see it, but somehow Gianto's made damn certain there's the picture of some blonde queen right next to Morrie's significator – The Hierophant.

Gianto says to Morrie, 'You should train Loretta as walker, wife or both.' He points at the blonde queen and, tapping her face, says, 'She's pliable, despite the gob she's got on her. Stop hankering for what's gone.'

Morrie nods, and puts the whisky bottle back in the cupboard. 'Can you let me alone now, I've things that need seeing to.'

'As you wish.' Gianto gives him a knowing look as he rises from his chair. At the caravan door, he murmurs, 'But mull it over, lad. Mull it over.'

* * *

Late afternoon, there's another knock on the caravan door.

Morrie's found one of Danu's old scarves under his bed. He's holding it in his hand as he opens the door, wanting some miracle to have happened to make it be Danu who's knocking.

It's Loretta with a simper-smile on her face. She's dyed her hair coal black.

She says, 'D'you like it?' She twirls a curl round her finger. 'Left the dye on too long, but it'll fade to dark brown, the kind of hair you like the best, after it's washed a few times.'

Morrie turns away. 'You'll never be the spit of anyone else. You shouldn't even try.' He shuts the door on her and the daylight.

Loretta calls, 'You'll take to it. I've had a good natter with my mirror, and it's best with dark eye-makeup. I look mysterious. See you later, sweetheart.'

There's no offending Loretta, no matter what he does. Without wanting to, he's starting to admire her persistence.

Sitting on his bed, he looks at the pulled warp and weft of the scarf in his hands. It's well worn, though he never saw Danu wearing it. Should he have noticed her clothes more, admired them? That seems to be what women want, but Danu never seemed bothered about compliments. He'll burn this scarf in the campfire after tonight's show.

Danu left too many of her things behind her. It wrenches him each time he finds some reminder. He's been burning each thing, just quietly, as he finds them. Her wooden hairbrush. A small box of dried autumn leaves. He even burnt a pair of her knickers. He considered bundling these things up and posting them to her, but she'd not want them. She never cared enough for what was hers.

He unpicks the strands at the edge of Danu's scarf. He holds it to his nose, closes his eyes, and tries to find the scent of her. There's only dust.

Morrie's travelled the ether to her just once since she left the circus. After the tunnel of wind and light, there was an attic. An old door, propped against a wall, and Morrie was with her. But then something darkened around her. There were waves and Danu was buried in currents. All Morrie could do was to move through darkness to find her and make himself as strong as he could.

He got too close.

Even without the flesh-and-bone body, want turns to need. He couldn't help but touch what he wanted but couldn't have. He grabbed her and held her. He was sent back to his own body, so fast it was dizzying.

No one is meant to touch anyone else, not while travelling the ether. His mam had been clear on that. But it was so dark, it took all Morrie's strength to get close enough to see her. And once he was so close, there was the smell of her. Morrie wanted to feel her. Taste her. Touch her.

Opening his eyes to the caravan without her felt desperate. He was filled with yearning. He was hungered. And he's still hungered, now.

There's an anger in his body now Danu's gone. It wanted her, and was denied. He controlled his lust when they lived together, so Danu wouldn't flit off. Happen that he shouldn't have controlled it so long. Happen that hunger builds to starvation when it's not satisfied.

He drops Danu's unravelling scarf on the floor. It lies like a sickened snake.

Folks are talking outside but he stoppers his ears.

Lying on his bed, Morrie thinks about making love to Danu in every way he's wanted to. Gripping her wild hair, fucking her hard, then stroking her tenderly.

His mam said the ether was made of pure love. It wasn't ever to be travelled while feeling anger or lust, or to seek revenge. She said if those things were felt, it would darken. Danu was always so scared – didn't like to be touched too often or hugged too hard. Happen that she was right to be scared. Happen that she saw something in Morrie which he'd never known was there.

The setting sun glints on the metal pans by the sink. They're too clean. Everything that shines is too clean.

Since he travelled the ether, he's found it hard to eat. He tries to kid himself that the ether is something his mam only invented. That he's only imagined he was with Danu. But for the symptoms of his body, he could believe this.

Morrie's flesh-and-bone body has got thinner, and too quick. He's subdued, wants to sleep all the time, and doesn't want to talk. He can't raise a laugh, can't sing, can't drum, and the caravan's got a mouse which scurries loud as a rat half the nights. What little he eats goes straight through him. He wants Danu more than ever, now he's lost her.

Someone knocks the door. Loretta again? Morrie gets up and bolts it, loud.

Sandy's voice calls, 'Well, that's pleasant. I only wanted to give you some seedcake from Mag.'

Morrie shouts, 'I'm not eating bloody seeds,' and lies back on his bed.

He'll stay indoors till the sun sinks, and someone knocks the door to send him onto the wire once it's dark. If this lack of appetite keeps up, he'll thin too fast. But then again, bodies thin evenly, no one side shrinks more than the other. Doesn't matter how light or how heavy he becomes. Not to the wire.

Men die in the hunting of women. Spears and swords, fists and fights. He can't let himself turn hunter and touch her again. But all the same, touching her was as heady as a night filled with drunken drumbeats.

There's love in him, but there's darkness as well. Unless he can change how he feels, when he next travels the ether to Danu, he'll return to himself unspent and starved.

He's often heard it said that men can die for love. Is this how?

Danu wakes remembering a poem her mother once read to her. It was about a Lady who was *half sick of shadows*. The Lady was trapped inside a room filled with shadows all day and all night. She spoke to no one. With bright threads, she tried to capture the daylight in pictures. Her pictures must not have been bright enough, once complete, because the Lady became full sick of shadows, and ended up dead in a river. What made her lie down in a boat, close her eyes, and float downstream knowing she was dying? Why didn't she fight or speak? Had shadows entirely filled her?

There was a mirror in the Lady's room. Perhaps she looked at herself and saw something else. Perhaps she saw shadows swimming inside her eyes. Perhaps she thought that the shadows were death, consuming her from within, and these thoughts led her outside to the coffin she made from a boat.

Outside, the sky is white. Today is Danu's birthday. It has arrived, as birthdays always do, year in, year out, whether they're wanted or not. She rolls onto her side and stares at the pink and yellow fabric on the back of the sofa. She traces a pattern of a leaf with her thumb, and lets her hand lie where it falls.

She's wanted to avoid her birthday since her parents died and now she finally can, because no one is looking.

What a gift she gave them: a virus in exchange for a birthday present she didn't even receive.

She wonders if it was a book of poems.

Each year after they died the people in the circus insisted Danu was at least toasted, which led to most people getting drunk. She wore the mask of a grin when they laughed, but during the celebration she'd pretend to be too tired or too drunk, so she could go somewhere quiet, alone. She'd flex her bootlace-bound ankles so they pinched. She'd end each of her birthdays clutching the silver locket till her hand went numb.

The evening of Danu's last birthday was spent in the caravan with Morrie. After they'd eaten the meal he'd prepared, he kissed her forehead and said, *happy birthday*. Only a friendly kiss, but she felt he wanted something else from her. As he took their plates to the sink, an uneasy feeling surrounded her and prickled across the surface of her skin. He wiped a plate clean. He wasn't even looking at her. She thought he wanted her to go to him, put her arms around him. Thank him for the meal with more than words. But then he glanced at her and the feeling left. He'd controlled it.

Fully clothed, she'd gone to bed early and pretended to be asleep. Morrie shut himself in the toilet cubicle and was in there a while. She tried not to hear, but heard all the same. Rhythmic breathing. An intake of breath. Taps running. Hands washed. The brushing of teeth.

When Morrie was in his bed and his breathing was steady, she crept off her mattress. Grabbing a shawl, she left the caravan and wandered barefoot into a frosted field. She stood numb, staring into the night. The clouds were black. Between the clouds were inches of sky in a deep forgettable blue. No moon. No stars. After a time, Morrie was beside her. He told her *it's dawn, come back in*. She could still only see black clouds. She looked down. Her frozen feet had turned dark. He took her hand and led her inside.

It took blankets and blankets and blankets to warm her.

Morrie will remember this. Perhaps he might have sent her a birthday card.

She goes downstairs and waits at the window, watching for the postman. Eventually he passes the house without stopping.

In the early afternoon, Danu splashes cold water on her red eyes, takes a deep breath and finally ventures outside. She slowly wanders the streets of the outer circle. Strangers hand her fliers for cabaret shows. She looks at a few of these fliers before shoving them in her bag. They're not all for cabaret venues. They offer promises:

Startling coffee and surprising cakes.
A bone-crunching hug from a man-bear: feel good about your inner jelly.
Public Lecture: God-given or Devil-taken – the seven heavens of Sin.
Visit Tox, who will flatten your wrinkles with poisonwood.
Heavenly Raptures! A sun/moon tandem ride towards your new inner vision.
Be a painted Goddess: Make Up or Break Down.

Any of these things, on any other day, would at least spark her curiosity. But today even the ceramics, crafts and paintings in small art galleries are washed out. She can't think of a single thing to buy which might cheer her or give her pleasure. She should want the things on offer because clearly everyone else does, but she doesn't. This thought makes her feel out of place, but she doesn't know where she might go, to feel *in place*.

Not looking where she's going, she bashes against a man using crutches. He swears at her.

She's too numb to even speak the word *sorry*.

Nothing is kind.

She looks without seeing, steps without feeling, and remembers her childhood birthdays. Her parents would each sing her a song they'd invent on the spot. Her mother would sing un-rhyming words brilliantly. Her father would sing rhyming ones terribly.

And there was always a toast, whatever they were drinking, which was usually sweetened tea.

After toasting Danu, her mother would quietly say, *and to Rosa*.

All three of them would chink mugs and take another sip, and her parents would be silent.

At first, Danu used to ask who Rosa was. But their sadness when they said the name Rosa made her tongue-bound as a child. When Danu was about eight, she'd assumed that Rosa was an aunt, or another member of her mother's family who'd disowned her. Adelaide hated talking of her past, and the rare times she mentioned her own mother, she referred to her as *that vain narcissist*. For a few years Danu stopped asking, and just toasted Rosa with them on each birthday. She asked who Rosa was again when she turned thirteen. They said that they'd tell her when she was sixteen. Or maybe it was eighteen they'd said.

Danu wishes now that she'd pushed them harder for an answer.

There were a few other times she heard them say the name Rosa. Usually in whispers or during their quiet arguments. These memories flash through her mind like pictures and sounds but before she's able to see or hear them clearly, each one flashes away.

This birthday is a day to be travelled away from, she will travel herself away within it.

She learns throughout the rest of the afternoon how to make herself feel *gone*:

Walk, don't eat, don't drink, don't rest or stop moving.

Don't make eye contact. Don't look at anyone, don't see.

Imagine sleepwalking, evict all sounds from the ears till the world becomes a song with no notes.

Think in fat and thin thoughts:

everything's too big, it's too small, too wide, too narrow, too tall, too short . . .

in fact, everything is broken.

If something appears unbroken, it will be secretly cracked on the inside. Touch will break it.

So don't touch anything.

Keep all of these thoughts as a tight juggle of rules in the mind.

A temple bell clangs through Danu's thoughts. And another. Another. The sun is brighter than it was a moment ago. Her feet follow the sound of the nearest bell, seeking darkness and the flickers of candles.

As she reaches a temple and steps through the doorway, the bells cease. Unusually, there are people inside this one. A click, behind her. A low gate is placed across the doorway by a teenage boy wearing a robe embroidered with stars. He hooks it closed, sweeps his fingers through his long fringe and clasps his hands together.

Danu looks around at the people who have gathered. What do they want from this building, from each other? Perhaps something from above or below, some heaven or hell, god or devil will speak through them. An intense experience felt by others might lift her out of numb. After all, belief can be infectious, even if its influence is temporary.

Six drummers and singers stand on a raised platform in front of a gathering of fifteen people. They chant in an unidentifiable language. *Yenom, doof, evol, sdneirf, ytreporp* . . . The temple walls are painted dark blue, and hanging from the domed ceiling is a small circular cage in which candles flicker.

The chanting increases in volume. Two women wearing purple robes and white beads approach an altar. The chanting grows louder. *Tuo thgin suocuar a, tug yppah a. Sdeb fo tsetfos eht no llor a dna evol dna xes. Tnaw I tahw.* One of these women looks directly at Danu with some silent question in her brown eyes.

She's beautiful, in an unusual way. Perhaps it's her nose, which has clearly been broken at some stage in her life and never set right. Danu wants to approach the woman, take her hands, draw her away from the others and ask her own questions – *What brings all these people together? Without a translation, any chant becomes meaningless.*

And more than anything, she wants to ask, *Can you say something which will wake me from numb? You don't have to mean it, but say it anyway.*

But the woman looks upwards and her face becomes an expressionless mask. Her mouth barely moves as she recites the chant. She's her own ventriloquist.

The shadows of flickering candles look like shrouded figures dancing in a blue heaven. Danu wishes she could invent a heaven with a kind custodian, and believe her parents into it. She could give them a god with dawn shining from his smile, or a goddess wearing a crown made of twilight. But the moment she imagines these deities, they disperse like mist. Perhaps all gods who are imagined into existence want to remain invisible.

People are beaming at each other as they sing. It hurts to see their expressions of happiness, relief, companionship, euphoria, hope. These are all light things, but her heart is too heavy. A piece of writing in a long frame hangs on the curved wall beside the doorway. The paper is parchment, the blue calligraphy ink is smudged at the edges.

She walks towards it, and reads:

The Story of Moons.

Once upon a time, there were twenty-eight moons. They each took turns to rise into the night sky, circle the blue and green world they all wanted to look down on, and sink back into the ocean of night in which they lived.

One of these moons was the widest, the roundest. Its surface was sheened by salt mists and peppers of dust. It was impatient while waiting for its next turn to look down at the world, for its eyes were always hungry.

One of these moons was invisible. It was the wildest, the darkest. It wanted to be able to look, and look away. It had many other invisible things to watch out for, which lived inside the blackness of the night sky.

And all of the silver moons in between wanted different things from the world which swam with mists of blue oceans and green landscapes.

The people who lived on this world loved seeing each moon because they all shone so beautifully. But some of these people were afraid of them. The moons never spoke, and people felt observed and suspicious. Some of them talked and talked louder, till all the others listened. They had decided that the twenty-eight moons must be only one moon, which was only ever changed by their world's shadow.

These people invented telescopes and science and religions to try to capture the twenty-eight moons into one thing. The idea of one moon was written into many languages, it was measured and drawn into books containing fine equations, variable distances and secure facts.

This was easier than trying to understand the conflicting hopes, motivations and dreams of twenty-eight silent moons.

The trees grew taller during the nights. They grew and grew, stretching their leaf-whispers as far as they could reach, so the wind could take their sounds and carry them upwards.

The people of the world told the story of one moon to themselves over and over again, in all kinds of ways. Over time, most of them continued to believe it, but some did not. They argued. One person killed another person in order to prove that a dead body can no longer see either one moon or many. A group of people retaliated, and killed another group of people who lost all their opinions on their last breaths.

Inside the night, when it was not their turn to shine, all of the other moons were buried in darkness. Within silence, pieces of themselves that they didn't want would drift away in shining fragments.

People couldn't understand why either the moon or the moons would give anything away, and this made them more fearful. There were further disagreements about these shining fragments, which caused a great war which was never won or lost. The war was said to have ended when people drew these bright fragments as marks on a map and called them stars. They made a map of constellations which mirrored the things around them which were familiar: lions, dogs and bulls, eagles, harps and swans.

If there are other things in our heavens, those things have decided to remain invisible to the people of our world. But the moons care nothing for peace, or fear, or anything we fight for.

Each moon listens, instead, to the remarkable stories that the trees are telling them.

So these people aren't revering a god or a devil, this is moon-worship. A religion revering something as fluctuating as the moon must have to incorporate change. And yet most religions have ritual. Repetition. Commitment. Ceremony. The flowers of harvest, the blood of martyrs, the rings which encircle fingers: these rituals must have been originally designed to feel like arms around each believer, holding them steady. When people first invented these rituals, did they ever imagine they might cause wars? No one in this temple is fighting. Bodies sway, lips chant, hands clap. There's joy in these faces. Collective joy is a bubble. Easily punctured by someone who doesn't feel it.

Danu unlatches the temple gate and slips outside.

The teenage boy in the starry robe follows her into the street. He hands her a flier on pale blue paper. 'If you're going, take one of these. Someone's left a whole pile of them to be handed out to as many people as possible.' His wide green eyes look a little sleepy and downy fuzz covers his top lip.

Danu hasn't spoken at all today. Her voice cracks as she asks, 'Why's the temple full this evening when it's usually empty?'

He replies, 'The full moon's been getting fat and fatter – it'll be obese tonight. A cotton moon. Hope you're going out to celebrate?'

'I didn't know about it.'

'The dancehalls are the best places. The energy is high. Cotton moon obesity brings people out to dance for whatever they're wanting to fatten their lives with.'

The voices from inside the temple become louder. She asks, 'What language is the chanting in?'

'Oh, ours. But backwards.'

'Why backwards?'

Still smiling, he rolls his eyes. 'Oh, politics. If we're honest.'

She looks at him blankly.

He elaborates. 'The priests and priestesses of the second circle have recently let slip that they think *we've* got it all wrong in the outer circle. One of them was being interviewed for the paper

178

and he said, *they're seeing the moons through a mirror.* It was quoted. And no one's retracted it.'

'What does it mean?'

He sighs. 'It means we've taken offence. And now we're proving the point – whatever way around anyone sees things, *we* can still worship better than them.' He raises his eyes to the sky. 'Of *course* the moons don't care whether words are chanted forwards or backwards as long as it's heartfelt. But this seems new to you?'

Danu nods.

'It's not new to me. My mother's the priestess of this temple. When she feels like it. Which is usually when the priests and priestesses of the second circle are being *offensive*.' He leans closer to Danu. 'Why anyone in one colour of robe cares so much about the opinions of someone in a different-coloured robe, I'll never understand. But disagreements are always good for getting more people to come into the temples . . . People want to be seen on the high-minded side of any argument. I saw you read the story of moons—'

Danu says, 'I think it's partly about constancy. Look at what's going on between the moons and the trees.'

He nods. 'It's also a warning against listening to loud opinions while knowing bugger all about quieter ones. And of course, the futility of violence.' Indicating the temple, he says, 'Do come here again. You might find something you need. Sorry, I am repeating what I've been told to say. Loyalty to Mum. And the moons are good things to believe in.'

Danu tilts her head. 'In what way?'

He replies, 'I ask them for things, though they can't hear me. Purely from speaking my thoughts aloud, I understand what I want.' He looks thoughtfully at Danu. 'What do you want?'

She shoves the blue flier he gave her into her bag with all the others.

'I want to know how long it takes someone in the Inner Circle to reply to a letter.'

He grins. 'As long as this: *in their own good time*. I should go back in. I'm in training to become a priest.' He disappears back into the temple.

Danu wanders away, imagining him in a few years' time – older, wiser and shining. Perhaps he's gained something from having faith in something he can see. His faith isn't blind, it's distant.

Three side streets along from Wringers Street, there's a dancehall called Wide Night. Danu is drinking her third glass of gin at a table beneath red-brick archways. Hanging candelabras drip wax onto white tablecloths. Above a stage, midnight ticks away on a huge clock with curved hands.

Danu raises her glass and murmurs, 'To next year's birthday not lasting as long as this one. To not being in bed at midnight. To people who chant for the things they want, and to the wise horses I used to love talking to. To silent letter boxes and their sealed metal lips.'

Black and white lines criss-cross the dance floor, which is filled with dancers of all ages: teenagers swing one another around, and ninety-year-olds dance and flirt in hold. The scent of rose-water fills the vast room.

Looking at the empty chair opposite her, she sips from her glass and raises it again. 'To my parents, and the gap beside me.'

The music surges and Danu's attention is grabbed by the swing band, who wear matching white waistcoats. One of them raises a glass and shouts, 'Here's to the obesity of the cotton moon! Eat up all your merriness, drink down your laughter and spew it out again, fatten up your joy!' Their next tune is lively, and lifts everyone up to dance. Glass-bead necklaces and flowing skirts swing as women grip hands with partners, and long hair whips through the air.

Danu is rapidly drunk, and all these people look incredibly beautiful. She steps onto the dance floor. Half-closing her eyes, she dances to gypsy swing music which holds her heartbeat in place. She is a flamenco dancer and a tap dancer.

Apart from when she returns to her table and drinks another glass of gin.

She is a ballerina and a ballroom dancer.

Apart from when she sits on the floor under a column, trying to make friends with three women with blue eyelashes by talking about their matching crimson shoes.

She is a whirling dervish and a ceilidh dancer.

Apart from when she hides in a dark corner kissing one of these women and her spindly boyfriend. They take turns with her lips; they want to share her.

She's outside now, staggering along the main street, arm in arm with this amorous pair. A procession of people in white robes carry candles, and chant, eyes raised to the sky. Danu wants to stop and look at them, but the pair draw her into a side street. They enter a terraced house through a black front door and climb flights of worn stairs.

In a bedroom, the girlfriend lights candles. Fringed shawls cover the walls.

Danu's asking for more music as she slumps down onto a velvet floor cushion. She's handed a penny whistle so she blows into it before her fingers find the holes and she tries to pick out a folk tune she once knew . . . such a long time ago . . . her fingers can't find the notes.

The boyfriend passes her a smoke of something pungent.

It tastes of old lace so she passes it back.

The girlfriend takes the penny whistle away and gives Danu

a bottle which shines silver-blue. Danu eyes the bottle as she asks, 'Is this the cure for numb? I'll take anything for fixing it.' She takes a swig. Cinnamon and pomegranate flavours fizz through alcohol.

The boyfriend smiles at her. He looks a few years younger than the girlfriend. 'No, kisses are cures.'

Danu leans towards him. 'You're ridiculously sweet . . .'

She can't tell what the expression on his face means.

The girlfriend says, 'Sex is a cure for heartbreak. If you make sure you feel it.' Her hand is on Danu's thigh. She arches her back and her voice sounds low, almost tired. 'Have you got heartbreak in you, Danu? You look like you do. Something about the eyes.'

The boyfriend moves a cushion to clear a space on the floor, 'Shall we spin the bottle when you're done drinking from it?'

The bottle is still in Danu's hand. She swigs from it. Sparkles of flavour, like the pips of fruit, bursting.

The boyfriend is still talking. 'Let's make the bottle a compass. Decide the direction. High or Chill. Sex or Magic. The bottle chooses. Or we could use the knife.' He glances at the woman.

Holding the bottle to her chest, Danu searches their hands for a knife.

They told her their names but she doesn't remember them. Is it rude to ask? Her eyes blur their faces, and she swigs from the bottle again. The pair are playing some private game. Associating words on lips, back-forth-back in a game she doesn't understand.

'Bong?'

'Kiss.'

They kiss each other.

Danu takes another swig from the bottle and holds it out, 'Please, take this away.'

The boyfriend takes it, swigs, and locks eyes with the woman again.

Danu says, 'Is it still my birthday or is it gone? I didn't toast Rosa—'

She looks at the closed door and can't feel her legs. She lurches forward to rub sensation into them.

The couple are still talking, passing one word each, back-forth-back.

They are locked in word-speak, 'dot,'

'join,'

'Kiss.'

'Which?'

The boyfriend kisses Danu. Her head spins and she might be sick so she twists away. She says, 'No, I've got to go. The horses are bolting.' She staggers to her feet, the walls shift, she falls.

Footfall, to floorboards. People, not horses.

Her body is lifted and dropped. Is this smooth-soft-cold-satin a bed, or a silk ocean?

Sink into something silver.

Dance in this liquid.

It's mercury.

Trickle down walls.

A streetlamp's glow filters into the room through a torn curtain. Danu wakes, fully clothed, on a satin-covered bed between a skinny man in a chocolate-coloured loincloth and a woman in a black slip. Kohl makeup darkens their eyelids.

It's night, but what time? She can't see a clock. Her wrist aches. She examines it. A cut. Not deep.

She lifts the woman's arm. She also has a small cut on her wrist, as does the man. Danu shuffles down the bed. Her boots are under a cushion. She slips them on and retrieves her coat from beneath a wooden chair.

Beside the window, a lamp glows on the dressing table. On a granite slab, there's a silver knife. It's old, but recently polished. She examines the handle which has an enamelled black dot inside a silver circle. A small glass bottle contains dark liquid. Tracks of light move across her vision as she holds the bottle over the lamp and examines its contents.

Blood.

Danu crosses the room and opens the bedroom door. Out in the hallway, she looks down curved banisters, checking how easy it will be to get outside.

From the doorway, she says, 'Wake up.'

The woman raises herself on an elbow.

'What's this?' Danu points to the cut on her wrist.

The woman replies, 'You didn't mind at the time.'

'Was I unconscious?' Danu's lips crackle with pins and needles.

A green line twists around the woman's face. She sees Danu's confusion and says, 'It'll wear off when you're more awake . . . This happens sometimes, after.' The woman gets out of bed and takes Danu's wrist in both hands. As she leans over the cut, her black hair slides across Danu's fingertips.

Danu pulls her hand away.

The woman narrows her eyes. 'You were sweeter earlier, when you told both of us you couldn't possibly love us. You didn't listen at all when we said we didn't want you to.'

'And this?' Again, Danu indicates her wrist.

'You woke, but didn't want to be physically touched. So we each took a hallucinogen, and as I remember it,' she frowns, ' . . . decided to mix our blood. At the time, we all fervently believed blood was made from passion, though . . .' She wrinkles her nose.

'I didn't cut us deep enough. Though that's hallucinogens for you. I thought our skin was petal thin. His suggestion, I think.' She jerks her head in the direction of her sleeping boyfriend, who rolls into a foetal position. Her face softens. 'Look at him. Sweetie. He's washed himself out.' She approaches the dressing table. 'You joined us in a Scorpionist ritual. He was stern and gorgeous.'

'What kind of ritual?'

The woman thumbs the knife blade. 'Evocation of passion. It didn't work for *you*. We shouldn't really have used the twenty-ninth moon for something so trifling.'

She sees Danu's question before she asks it. 'The twenty-ninth moon appears after the exact minute the moon is full, but only for a few seconds. A black spot, slightly off-centre. The symbol's used in dark rituals. None of the clanging clappers in the moon temples want any part of it. And their names for the full moons – cotton moon, tin moon, glitter moon – that's just superstition. All spiritual Matryoshkans, no matter which worship they vaguely adhere to, are still, after generations, hell-bent on trying to dissolve Scorpio on hanging metal scales. As if any creature possessing a sting would ever allow itself to be *weighed*.'

She fingers the tip of the knife. 'Blood is used for cursing and passion. Bodily fluids are the sting in the tail of all Scorpionist rituals.'

Danu has a vague memory of drops of blood falling like rubies. She goes over to the dressing table and picks up the bottle of blood. 'I'm not leaving anything here you could curse me with.'

She shrugs. 'So pour it away. The bathroom's downstairs. To want to curse you, we'd have to either love or hate you. We've only just met you.'

'You're not going to meet me again.' Danu goes to the bedroom door.

'Before you go . . .'

Danu turns to face her.

The woman lights a fringed lamp. 'Who's Morrie?'

Danu freezes. 'Why?'

'Because you may have told us you couldn't love us, but you spent at least half an hour over there,' she nods at a high-backed chair in the corner, 'saying over and over again that you loved him. You spoke as if he was there. You were trying to talk to him, crying when he wouldn't answer. I wondered if he was dead. Is he?'

'You shouldn't have listened.'

'You're in our room!'

'I suppose you've got a point.'

Dark-eyed, the woman approaches Danu. 'You need to get in touch with your heart. The heart you're denying when you're so out of it you tell strangers you can't love anyone. Because I heard what you said while you were sobbing . . .' Her mouth is dark red, smudged with lipstick. She whispers into Danu's ear, 'Can I speak to you as an unwanted friend? Last night you spoke of love in ways that made me realise I've never felt it.'

Danu grips the bottle of blood in her palm.

'You love Morrie,' the woman glances at her boyfriend, 'more than most people have ever loved anyone.'

FIVE FOR AN ELEMENT

Morrie's relieved the circus has finally pitched up. It's not long till dawn, but they had to travel onwards till they found another well. There're not enough landmarks on this road heading south, and sometimes stopping is all about water, if the land's dry.

Mag walks past Morrie's caravan and makes a sharp point of glancing in the window. He doesn't rise to it. She was mad-angry after Danu took off, and anyone who knows Danu would think of her around her birthday. They'd all made a fuss of the teenage orphan she once was. Danu barely noticed the cheer or small kindnesses. All the same, Morrie liked Danu all the more for ignoring the attention of others. He thought she'd be a faithful lover because of how she never wanted anyone's eyes to linger on her.

But now Morrie thinks she wasn't ignoring the attention, she just had her mind elsewhere. Likely as not, all she wanted was for her folks to come back from the dead. Now that would have been some fearful gift. Especially if they'd come back grave-fresh – rotten and missing her. He shudders at the thought of the stench.

The field's quiet outside, with everyone likely grateful to at last be in bed.

Morrie sits himself down and lights a half-burned candle.

The dirty soup bowl beside him on the table fades away as his eyes fix to the flame.

And he thinks of Danu. Her face and neck. Her shoulders.

Tingling to the skin. Flickers of lust.

Banish lust. The ether is love. Light and its lines lead from him to her.

Eyes closed and he can see the tunnel glowing. The entry point is narrowed by dark edges. Open the tunnel by feeling love. At first he only imagines seeing Danu at the other end. Her eyes, hair, lips. Her voice. Her wild dreams and stories, her hands as they draw pencil marks on paper. The way she moves her hips when she dances . . . No, banish lust. Think of her mind, her heart. Grow the feeling of love, and spread it like a bridge through the tunnel, towards her.

And now he sees her. In the distance. Inside the same attic room as before, curled asleep on the sofa.

The bridge becomes a burning line through the tunnel which leads from him to her. Light threads, lit white as the hottest fire. Strands and strands of it all. He feels love all through himself, and sends it along the line. Enough love to fill the tunnel, enough love to find her with.

It floods from his heart, not his loins.

The entrance to the tunnel opens wider.

A rush of air and light and his spirit leaves his flesh-and-bone body at the table in the caravan where it's sitting. The ether is a wide bright tunnel, and he's travelling it so fast he's blurring. He disappears, reappears, and disappears from himself. He looks only ahead, sees Danu asleep, sees the sofa she sleeps on, smells the damp of the house she's in. He moves towards her in a rush of wind. Faster than light, faster than sound.

A sudden gust pushes him into the place where she lies. Her olive skin is pale. His spirit hovers next to her, trying to see her face clearer. She frowns in her sleep and moves her arm across her chest.

And now he's looking down at her, he could so easily forget love and light and feel lust, demand weight to inhabit his spirit. Desire builds. If his spirit was thickened enough, he could lie with her.

His mother said, *If there is so much as one shadow, something is wrong. Go back to your flesh body, before you're forced to.*

But all around him, the room darkens with shadows. They're falling away from him. From what he wants. His spirit thickens as he looks down at Danu's parted lips.

It thickens still more as he gets closer to her.

Desire is a hungry creature. Starve it or feed it.

His arms are gleaming coal. If he wanted to, he'd be able to possess her.

But he looks at her face.

The trust there is in it, while sleeping.

He can't hurt her.

But there's a pulling sensation, and he's drawn to her. He wants to feel what she feels from inside her body, just once.

He touches her shoulder and his hand darkens.

There's booze on her breath. The scent of burnt roses.

His spirit lies on top of her, and he sinks himself inside her, a storm inside a cloud.

Her real lungs fit around his shadow lungs, his shadow heart is inside her real heart, he pushes his shadow tongue into her real tongue. He occupies her. Feels her. Is her.

As he speaks into Danu's mind, she murmurs his words, *We are two halves making a whole.* He twists inside her, occupying her real liver with his shadow liver, her brain with his brain, her spine twists as his vertebrae shift into place inside it.

And now he can feel what she feels from the inside.

All of her guilt. All of her hope. All of her patience.

All of her grief. It feels lifelong. And there's something of fear.

It's infected her body and frozen all the way through, like ice.

So cold. No wonder she never asked him to touch her. He was burning for her. He'd have thawed her too fast and left her with nothing of herself.

An interruption – a sliver of sound like a knife being drawn. He raises his face out of Danu's face, trying to see the room around them, but the darkness is thick as deep currents.

Something thuds through his head.

He yowls, thins and slides out of Danu.

Too dark to see much, too dark to see enough? But there's something else here – a pale figure is standing between him and Danu. It's shifting. It changes from a human shape into a swirl of fireflies forming the shape of a shield. The shield flickers and settles into the shape of a bright wall which blocks Danu away behind it.

The ether is a route made of love, for love, by love.

No one else should love her. But someone does. Someone who's protecting her.

Morrie's spirit roars as he charges at the wall and as his hands make contact with light . . . he burns. He springs away, repelled.

Back in the caravan, Morrie's eyes open.

He's sitting at the table where the candle flame flickers. His palms sting burnt red, but as he looks at them, they're corpse-pale.

Morrie knocks plates smashing to the floor, upturns his chair as he staggers like some drunk. He's dizzied with the rush of being sent back here too fast. He's got a storm of curses in his gob and he's hurling them. As his cursing subsides, his body falters and shakes. A rash rises hot on his arms. He rolls up his shirt sleeves to look but his arms are wax-white. His cheeks are aflame with humiliation.

He catches sight of himself reflected in a window.

Thinner than ever. Hollow cheeks. A touch to the skin and it's freezing, though inside his body, he's burning with pulses and blood.

He rushes to the sink and throws up on top of dirtied pans. And again and again. There's acid in the soup he swallowed earlier, ale mixed with bread, bread mixed with bile, he retches, retches . . .

Slumping over the sink, sweat drips from his scalp. His body is a wrong thing. Some phantom, some ghoul. He fills a glass of water. Gulps it down.

But who else would travel to Danu? Who would have blocked him? Someone who recalls Danu's birthday . . . Half the circus folk would know that, but none talk of the ether. Who else travels it, who taught it to them, isn't it secret to most?

He hurls water. Retches again. Spits. Swallows the rest.

With trembling hands, he undoes the salt cellar and pours salt in his palms. He rubs his fingers, the backs of his hands, his wrists. Not enough. He gets a box of salt from the cupboard and pours more of it, scrubbing his hands clean over and over again.

He puts himself to bed and shakes without sleep. He'll not travel the ether again till he knows who blocked him. He vows this all the way through his mind and two bodies – flesh and bone, light and shadow – the ether is a killing thing, when used wrong.

Under the blankets his body spasms. His voice groans, 'Am I dying, now?'

He covers his ears so he won't hear the answer to this question.

* * *

191

Late at night, Danu's walking along Wringers Street looking into the front windows to catch glimpses of the people she's secretly living beside. Grass grows between the paving stones. It's dark, and spitting with rain. Towards the far end of Wringers Street, a man emerges from a gap between two houses. He's wearing dark green pyjamas and his thinning hair is a frazzled nest.

He approaches Danu, speaking urgently. 'No one ever stops to listen!'

She speaks calmly, as he's so agitated. 'I'll listen. Where do you live?'

'Right here!' He draws her into the gap between houses and waves at an open door in a side wall. 'I've to tell someone!'

'Well, tell me.' Danu guides him in through the door, and extracts an old wooden chair from a cluster of wooden boxes. She places it at the foot of the stairs and sits on a step. Patting the seat, she says, 'Come on. Sit.'

He does so with some difficulty. 'There's this dog . . . name of Badger. He's the dog of my best friend. Black and white, the cleverest thing – understands all kinds of commands . . .'

Danu asks gently, 'What about the dog?'

'It was some dispute. Badger had gone for some other farmer's chickens. My friend had been ordered to shoot him. Couldn't leave his farm for the sake of a dog. Doesn't work like that, not in the country. We were in a field. Badger was playing with a ball. Usually runs at you with it and makes you throw it. But Badger saw my friend getting the gun off his trailer. The dog came rushing to me. He knew about the gun. What guns mean. The dog put his snout in my hand and waves of fear came juddering off him. My friend wouldn't shoot unless he had a clear shot. I put my arms round Badger, and he said *don't let me be shot*. And I heard those words as loud as if he'd spoke them. I didn't believe a dog could be talking but I hung on to

192

him tight. He said again, *don't let me be shot*. I rubbed his head and thought how I could save him from the bullet. I've no room in my flat. I thought Mam and Dad could take him for a while. At that point I remembered they died near on thirty years ago.'

Danu strokes the man's arm.

His eyes brim with tears. 'But I love the dog. I don't know how best to look after him, or where. I have to save him. If there were no guns, there'd be no bullets . . . That moment of shooting's too quick. You don't have to think, but death needs to be thought about . . .'

The man grabs Danu's hand in both of his. There is relief in his face as if he's evicted a great anxiety. 'Oh.' He gives her a watery smile. 'I'm so sorry pet. A dream, isn't it?'

'It sounds like one.'

He looks down at his pyjamas. 'I'm undressed. I'll go back up . . .' He eases himself upright.

'Can I help you upstairs?'

'No, pet. My flat's not fit for a dog, so it's not fit for a visitor.'

He moves awkwardly, clinging to the banister as he climbs.

Danu calls, 'What's your name?'

'Mr Habbard. I was a shopkeeper, then a landowner, then a shopkeeper . . . now I'm a blasted dodderer . . .'

She calls, 'Can I ask you something, because you were once a shopkeeper?'

He pauses. 'As you like.'

'I might have a terrible sense of direction, but why can't I ever find the same shops twice?'

He reaches the top of the stairs and turns to face her, twirling a long finger in the air. 'Oh, they move. Round and round.'

'Do you mean the shopkeepers move their wares into other shops?'

'No, the circles move round! Bloody overambitious architect.'

'They rotate?'

'Of course. They're clunky now though. Slow. And there's cogs for some of the smaller streets. But time and damp . . . Time and damp . . .'

'When I climbed one of the staircases to the second circle, there was a wall. Is the wall always there?'

'Sometimes it's there, sometimes it's not. Goodnight missy.' He turns to the left and disappears behind a wall. There's the click of a door, closing.

Danu listens for a moment and as all is quiet, she goes back outside. Cold rain hits warm air, making a thick mist along the rooftops.

She goes along to the main street and scrutinises the surface of the road. Faded red paint-marks run across the pavements and cobblestones. These lines must once have been some kind of marker. There are narrow gaps between the paving stones about once every thirty paces. With her back against a wall to avoid people bumping into her, she removes her boots and plants her soles flat on the pavement. She waits for movement, a shift, motion.

A slight nudge against the balls of her feet. She waits for another . . .

It doesn't come.

The circles must rotate extremely slowly. Each curved section must be made from many small pieces laid close together, like a maze or a jigsaw puzzle.

Slipping her boots back on, she crouches and tries to visualise the shape of the underground mechanisms. A city architecturally designed in three circles is already unusual. But to have the three circles rotating as well, and on such a grand scale? As well as naming Matryoshka after a set of dolls, and the areas as types of dolls, the whole city is designed like a vast mechanical toy. The architect must have been obsessed with childhood objects. She remembers the story she read about him in the museum. This obsession might be a result of him having had such a punishing nanny. Painful memories, transformed into something beautiful.

She shakes her head, wondering at the sheer scope of imagination, engineering and passion that this vision must have involved.

Morrie's been able to eat nothing but soaked oats and bran. This is horse food. It's painful to swallow though it's only one small bite at a time. He examines the muscles of his arms. How did he get this thin, so fast? He'd hang his head from having using the ether so wrong, but what's the point of guilt? His punishment's already been delivered.

Building up a weakened body takes time, and right now, time is sands stuck in the narrowest part of a glass. Everything has to happen slow, else it doesn't happen at all. Even with his watch ticking and ticking on, he's no sense of the hour.

He rummages in the pockets of his coat and draws out a scrap of paper.

19 Wringers Street.

Weak as a grain, he drags himself over to Mag and Sandy's caravan. Morrie's mam always liked Mag but never said why. And apart from him, they knew Danu the best. Planting a foot on their steps, he knocks the half-open door and leans in.

Mag's arm-deep in a sinkful of dishes.

'What's up?' She looks at him bright-faced.

He steps inside. 'Is Sandy not around?'

'Hardware store.'

Morrie perches on the edge of their bed. 'I want to sound

you out.' He shows her the slip of paper with Danu's address. 'Danu told me where she'd be living.'

She looks closely at it. 'You'd never go . . .'

'I might, one day. I want to wed her. Do you think—'

Mag stares at him wide-eyed. 'Are you sick in the head? If she'd not wed you when she was living with you, she'll never wed you, lad.'

He slips the address back in his pocket and leans his arms on his knees. 'I'm no lad.'

'Sorry, pet. Turn of phrase. You're younger than me. And . . .' She frowns. '. . . a fair whack older than her. There's bright lights and a thousand handsome faces in Matryoshka. She'll have had her head turned by now. If she's not, then she's no one's.'

'If she'd not have me, she'll not have them.'

Mag wipes her hands on a tea towel. 'I've been thinking that girl would have been best placed in a convent if she'd had religion in her blood. Somewhere she'd be always quiet and learning, somewhere in safe company. She never wanted a sweetheart of her own, not like the rest of us . . . Curious about it, mind, but didn't need it.'

He looks at the floorboards. 'She loved me. It's just she wouldn't admit it.' Even to his own ears, there's a sulk to his voice he can't hide. 'She was angry and it never came out. Angry with her folks for dying and leaving her alone. Wild with rage on the inside.' He glances at Mag.

Mag looks unconvinced. 'And you think you'd be the one to tame it?'

'Aye. I would.'

'But Morrie, did she ever get angry?' She drops the tea towel on the table, comes over and sits next to him. The mattress creaks.

'No. She snapped at me sometimes.'

'Every bugger in the world snaps at folks sometimes. Folks

who bottle up rage have explosions from time to time. She never did.'

He looks at her. 'I lived with her a long while.'

Mag glances at him. 'Not as long as we did. No, *you're* angry. Don't make it hers.'

'She *was* angry. For being left alone.'

Mag shakes her head. 'She was never alone. She had us.'

'She blamed herself for her folks dying.'

Mag looks sad for a moment. 'I suppose there is that.' She rubs at a stain on her skirt. 'And how would you make her love you, when she wouldn't before?'

'I'd make her feel how much she needs me.'

She nudges him with an elbow. 'Ha! You can't *make* her feel anything. You've got to give any woman choices, she'll not do what you want without them.'

He shakes his head. 'You're not making bloody sense.'

'No one ever makes sense if you're listening to them proper. But hear this, pet. You can't hang on to her. You've already proved it.'

Morrie says, 'You couldn't keep her with us either.'

Mag's tone of voice becomes harsh. 'She was gone before I knew she was going. *You* should have said something.' She frowns at him. 'What's a girl like Danu going to do in a place the size of Matryoshka? If she gets herself into one of her maudlin states, there's no one to help her out of it.'

'It's what she wanted.'

'Aye pet, but *you* should've known better.' She gets up and takes a tube of hand cream out of a cluttered bowl on the table. She squeezes out a gob of white cream and rubs it in. Her hands sound like paper.

She throws the tube back into the bowl. 'I'll make a brew.' She fills the kettle. 'Sandy'll be back with the rope soon.'

'What rope?'

'New act. Escapology trick. Needs thinner rope than what we've got.' She sets the kettle to boil and spoons tea leaves into a cracked yellow teapot. 'Have you thought about fresh blood to work with? Train one of the older clowns up for the wire. Sheila's sprouting a good pair of legs, and the rest . . .'

Morrie watches the steam rise from the kettle.

Mag sits beside him again and puts her hand on his arm. 'Danu loved you in her own way. But not enough.'

He thinks of the ice he felt in Danu when his spirit occupied her body. He replies, 'She's froze herself cold.'

Mag looks at him so close, he'd swear she's reading his mind. She says, 'The truth hurts but it's not as sore as lying. Let her go. From in here.' She taps her heart. 'I miss her as well.'

'If I tried to get her back, it would be my risk. Not yours.'

Mag nods, and pats his shoulder. She sees to the boiling kettle and rinses out the teapot. 'Aye, lad. A risk is the right word for it. Now stop thinking like this. It'll do you in. Do you want an egg and black pud sandwich? You're looking sick as a drowning crow.' She spoons in tea leaves, pours water and clinks on the lid.

Morrie shrugs. 'If Danu was here, she'd say a crow wouldn't ever eat black pudding. She'd say it would only eat straw because it was in love with a straw-eating goat.'

'It's local bought. The butcher here's a good one.' As she opens the fridge, the smell of ripe cheese fills the caravan as she stoops to reach inside.

Morrie puts his hand over his mouth and swallows.

The package of meat fills her palm like a stone; Mag smirks at it and there's a look on her face he's not seen before. She looks smug as a witch. No, he's mistook that look. She's got too much of earth in her to be witching. Mag looks at him with a frown. 'What?'

'Can't stomach much by way of food.'

Her expression changes to a kinder one. 'Well I'll do you just an egg then. But listen to me. Crows can't eat anything when they've been half drowned *in something they shouldn't have gotten into*, pet.'

She knows he's been up to something which has made him sicken. A touch of psychic, no doubt. But perhaps she's one of those who don't pay it heed. She turns away, wipes her frying pan with a dry cloth and clatters jars in and out of her herb rack. Probably she doesn't even realise what she's just said. Aye, she's of earth. Bread, butter, oil, offal and eggs. Her mind's on them now.

She asks, 'Sunny side up?'

'Aye. Ta. I will try an egg.' Morrie kicks off his boots and goes over to take a seat at the table.

As she's sizzling the pan, she says over her shoulder, 'I promised her mother. Danu's under my protection. Lifelong. Hers or mine. It was agreed. It's not right, what you did.'

'What are you talking about?'

Her voice is quiet. 'The ether, Morrie. Don't *act* with me.'

'Did *you* sicken me—'

She lifts an egg dripping fat from the pan. 'Aye, I did. And I'd do it again. But you were lucky. Some folks who travel the ether protect it far harder than me.'

'Who?'

'I don't know. But I heard about one woman getting sent back to her body by a whole storm of other folks' spirits. Right enough, she'd travelled the ether to her ex-lover, and was trying to do him a damage. She ended up locked inside her body, and it was months before she could even speak.'

'All I wanted was to—'

'I don't care what you wanted. *Never* touch anyone's flesh

body. Their spirit gets unsettled when feelings or senses get sparked for no reason they can understand.' She shakes her head. 'Your mammy will have taught you all that, for it was me who taught her, and she – make no bones about this – she understood.'

Morrie looks into Mag's tunnelling stare. She's an eagle. She nods, seeing she's hit home. 'Now, I've had words, so you've been told.' She slops the fried egg onto a plate. 'Looks a bit naked. Can I fry you some bread or do you want mushrooms?' She hands him a knife and fork.

'This'll do me.' Aye, she's a witch for sure, of one kind or another. She might play it down but she knows what she's doing.

The fried egg on his plate looks like a sickened eye. He slices a clean line through the yolk. It runs yellow over white.

Mag's watching him close. 'You going to eat that or play with it?'

Sometimes he thinks every man only ever eats because some woman says he should. But there's as much power in eating as there's power in feeding. He spears the egg with the fork and shoves the whole thing in his gob. It slips down his gullet and too late, he tastes its bitter flavour.

Mag smirks. 'Good. That'll put you back to your bed for some time yet. I don't trust you one inch.' She looks at his eyes without blinking.

His lips prickle with pin-pricks. It spreads fast, and his whole mouth is numb, too numb to speak. His stomach clenches from whatever she's poisoned him with.

She passes him a tin bucket to spew in. 'Leave. Danu. Alone.'

Danu sips strong coffee as she peers out of the front window at Wringers Street. The postman walks along the opposite side putting letters through other people's doors. She empties her bag seeking stray notes or coins and pulls out a handful of pens, scrap paper and fliers.

A blue flier catches her eye.

She reads its black print:

> PUBLIC LECTURE: (Department of Cultural Studies)
> Professor I. Jemica
> **Ether Talk**
> **the fifth element**
>
> *There are other worlds all around us, telescopic and micro-scopic, hidden and exposed, expansive, expanding, contracting and narrow. In interacting with other people's emotional worlds, we are simultaneously close and far away.*
> *What if emotions last for longer than we feel them?*
> *We are, each one of us, one world within worlds.*

Danu thinks of Morrie's parting words to her as she reads the small print. The lecture is at the university, which is in the second circle. It's at noon tomorrow. Wringers Street isn't far from the staircase which led up to a wall. She'll try that one again first, but will need to get up early to allow time to walk around the main street and find one of the other two staircases if it's blocked. She places the flier on the kitchen table.

Back at the front window, the postman has disappeared from view. She knows his routine, and this means he's crossed to the odd-numbered side of the street. A few minutes later, he reappears and pauses on the pavement outside number nineteen.

Danu's heartbeat is too fast.

Extracting a letter from his bag, he approaches the front door.

She steps back from the window and holds her breath.

The letter box squeaks open. Slams shut.

An envelope lies on the floor.

She rushes to pick it up.

It's her own letter to Judith Crown, with the name and address crossed out. The Wringers Street address is scrawled on the front and the envelope has been re-sealed with tape.

Written across the top of the envelope, the words read:

Please return to sender.

Tears flood. She's waited so long to hear nothing.

Halfway up the mountain, Matryoshka is an entirely different city. The buildings in the second circle are built from limestone, sandstone, marble and granite. Danu has just reached the top of the staircase, and this time the wall isn't here. She almost expects to see some kind of border, or bag-search or ticketing office, but she emerges onto a pavement. So no one minds who comes and goes between these two circles.

Opposite her is a prison, which has carvings of swallows around its gables. She's got at least three hours before the Ether Talk, so there's plenty of time to explore a little and find out where the university is. Just along from the prison is a large bookstore with stained-glass windows depicting mathematical equations and alchemy symbols. She walks a little further along the main street and goes into the entranceway of the City Hall. She peeks through internal windows at a room with a high ceiling and tall windows. Beneath a large triangular table, the pink-threaded marble floor is cracked as a result of years upon years of the shifting of chairs.

Staff are arriving to begin their working day so she moves away from the doors. She explores a few of the nearest side streets, which are mainly residential. They are punctuated with tall archways and in the centre of many small squares, leaded statues of kingfishers and eagles are set with semi-precious stones. As she leaves them behind and walks along the main street again, she passes a row of shops with bright windows displaying gleaming kitchens and housewares. She's handed business cards as well as fliers. These cards advertise exclusive clubs and bars which offer 'discreet delights', 'culinary lessons', and 'pamper rooms'. The second circle temples are hexagonal buildings containing marble columns carved with lunar symbols.

The internal walls of public buildings have been covered and recovered in plaster over the years. These walls are decorated with murals painted with natural pigments – browned scenes of rivers, lakes and oceans. Parts of the oldest murals have been preserved, while other sections have been repainted, thus creating a patchwork effect of different landscapes.

Danu can tell which people are locals within the second circle because as they walk along the main street, they all look straight ahead. Most of them wear muted suits or tailored dresses. People from the outer circle, or visitors to the city all have raised faces because they're looking in awe at the dramatically high office buildings. Granite skyscrapers catch silver light in hundreds of windows. Fire escapes zigzag from basements to heavens.

As Danu walks, she uses peripheral vision to sense other bodies, so she can keep looking upwards. She feels vibrations under the pavement. There are walkways and sewers beneath the roads. This part of the city has a basement. Today it's raining lightly. Steam rises in curls from the warm pavement.

Danu goes into a hotel through a set of revolving doors. In a vast entrance hall, a grand reception desk hosts one member of staff in a blue uniform. She wears crimson lipstick and a poppy-coloured beret. Two elevators made from glass and matt metal rise and fall slowly. Miniature oak and willow trees are trapped inside vast stone pots.

Danu approaches the reception desk and asks, 'Do you have a map of the second circle?'

'Of course.' The receptionist wears a well-practised smile. Her diamante earrings catch the light as she reaches under the counter and slides a folded map towards Danu. 'Where are you from?'

'I'm living in the outer circle.'

The receptionist glances over at a side door where a vast luggage trolley is being wheeled in by a man in a blue peaked cap. She follows his progress across the lobby as she says to Danu, 'Well, have a wonderful stay at the Majestico, madam.'

Danu asks quietly, 'Is he yours?'

'What?'

'The man you're gazing at.'

'Erm. No.' She leans on the counter so she's closer to Danu and lowers her voice. 'Sorry, I wasn't listening properly. Are you a guest?'

'No, I was just passing.'

She glances around to check she's not being overheard. 'It's complicated.' She indicates the empty third finger of her left hand.

'You're married?'

The receptionist shakes her head.

'*He's* married?'

'Not happily.'

They both glance over at the man, who's grinning at the receptionist while wheeling the trolley towards an elevator. Danu says, 'He looks happy right now.'

The receptionist blushes and lowers her eyes. 'Yes. He does, doesn't he?' She watches him push the button to call the elevator. 'These things take time. I've got time. Most people rush into things, as if the world could end in a moment. But there is *always* so much time.'

The man disappears behind sliding doors.

The receptionist straightens up. 'Sorry, don't listen to me. It throws me whenever I see him.' She pats her heart. 'I can't speak about this to my friends – they wouldn't understand. Or not till he's left her. I'm no good at lying.' She looks almost accusingly at Danu. 'And I do hate questions. Yours was very direct.' She nods at the map as she unfolds it on the counter. 'You can have this, but give me some idea of the kind of places you're after?' She unlids a pen.

'I've got to be at the university for noon.'

She looks up at her. 'Are you a student?'

'No, I'm a tightrope walker. There's a public lecture I want to hear.'

She laughs. 'I'm a tightrope walker too. No, I'm joking. It just feels like that sometimes.' She bites her lip. 'I'll mark all the main places for you.' She circles the museum, art galleries, libraries, university and art college.

Danu says, 'When the second circle moves around, where will I find these places?'

'The second circle is different to the outer circle in that all our side streets are fixed. Only the main street rotates. But extremely slowly. See these arrows?' She points the nib of her pen at the map. 'That's the direction.'

Danu leans over the map and examines the detail – the main street is drawn in a black and white circle which spans the whole page. She can't see the hospital, but she'll find it later so she can be sure to avoid it until she's ready. Arrows span the circumference of the map, pointing in a clockwise direction.

The receptionist says, 'The staircases move with the outer circle. If you mainly use the same staircase, you'll need to know the second circle landmarks. When it's not blocked, you could arrive anywhere.'

She folds the map and passes it to Danu. 'Ever seen a map of the outer circle?'

'No.'

'No one's ever made a completely accurate one. The cogs are too complex. No room for all the necessary arrows or possible directions. Nightmare. I can't tell left from right. And I never remember which way to go when I'm confronted with exit doors.'

'I love maps. I should try to draw one of the outer circle—'

The receptionist shakes her head vehemently. 'No one would believe you.'

An old man shuffles in through the swing doors and stops in the lobby. He puffs, drops a small carpet bag onto the floor, glances at the desk, and waits. The receptionist rings a bell on the desk, and a boy wearing a red cap rushes to him and picks up his bag.

The receptionist returns her attention to Danu. She speaks quietly, 'Mr Bracken practically lives here. Apart from when he goes out into the mountains looking for kestrels. He says he's studying their wingspans. But he'd have to catch them to measure them, surely . . . and why would he carry his tent in a carpet bag, not a backpack?'

Seeing Danu's raised eyebrows, she laughs. 'I'm suspicious of other people's secrets as I've got too many of my own. I've never seen a kestrel. For all I know, they like being caught in carpet bags and measured.'

Danu says, 'A bird of prey would tear their way out of any bag. But perhaps they hop in willingly if he carries vermin lures.'

She laughs. 'You think too much.'

'I like stories.'

'Which explains why you wanted me to talk about my man. Assuming this is confidential, would you like to ask me any more direct questions?' She has a glint in her eye.

Danu asks, 'When did you realise you were in love with him?'

'Not long after I first started working here. He nudged me in the elevator. He got my funny bone and I said I wanted to hit him round the head with a wet fish. He asked me, *Do you think fish know they're wet?* That was the exact moment I fell for him.'

'Why?'

Her eyes are sad. 'No one but me thinks like that.' She taps her forehead with a manicured nail. 'Well, it's how it began. Thinking the same. My ex talked in monologues. He only seemed interested in me after I'd left him. That's not love, that's stalking.'

'And is your married man more interested in you?'

'Yes, when he's got time off from being so very, very married. I'm not naturally jealous, though he tells me his wife is. But he loves me more than her, or says he does.'

Danu asks, 'Do you trust him?' She thinks of Morrie opposite her on the wire. He could have made her plummet to injury or death with the slightest movement of his foot.

Looking thoughtful, the receptionist says, 'Not entirely. And I might only love him because we think in similar ways. He got me a fish tank for my birthday. We've been trying to work out what fish *do* know. I wish . . .' She seems far away. 'Perhaps love *should* emerge in captivity. Then it can be examined brutally.' She shakes herself and says to Danu, 'Anyway. It's worth the risk.'

Danu replies quietly, 'You're far braver than I was.'

The receptionist tilts her head as she looks at Danu, examining her face with interest.

Danu smiles at her. 'What is it?'

'I was thinking I'd seen you before. But now I know what it is. I've seen a *painting* of you.'

Danu shakes her head. 'It can't have been me.'

The receptionist says, 'No, I'm sure of it. You look familiar, but I couldn't place you. In the portrait you were blue.'

Danu laughs. 'You can see I'm not blue. Where did you see it?'

She frowns. 'I wish I could remember. It'll have been somewhere in the second circle. One of the galleries. Maybe the museum.'

'Really, you're mistaken. I've never been painted.' Danu thanks her for the map and leaves through the revolving doors.

As Danu walks along the main street of the second circle in the direction of the university, a boy of about thirteen walks alongside her. He has a face sharp with thoughts. He's frowning at the deep-scored lines which span from the pavements all the way across the road.

Danu catches his eye and smiles.

He fidgets with the rim of his felted hat which doesn't match the smartness of his purple school uniform, and looks at the lines again.

He says, 'They mark the clicking points for the calendars.' His voice sounds gritty, as if he's not spoken for some time.

'The calendars?'

As they walk side by side, he restarts his voice with a cough. 'There's a different calendar for each circle. The second circle calendar's called The Vague Year.' He takes a pocketwatch from his waistcoat and frowns at it. 'The Vague Year has beautiful numbers. Three hundred and sixty-five days in a year, eighteen months of twenty days each and five unlucky days left over. Do you know how clever the number three hundred and sixty-five is?' He frowns as he walks, and loosens the buckle on his satchel.

Danu has no interest in the cleverness of numbers, but the boy is now distracted by his watch.

She says, 'Why would a city have more than one calendar?'

'Independence of subcultures, according to Dad, who is know-ledgeable despite the fact that he claims not to be. I think that's a lie, but he says it's modesty.'

Danu asks, 'What calendar is in use for the Inner Circle?'

'It's probably a long counting one but we've forgotten its proper name because no one wrote it down and kept it in a good no-holes pocket. It might have days, or months. But I think it's more likely that it might count years. Years before what, and after what? I haven't decided yet. Time measured by what? I've got a lot of ideas about that and there will be three and a half more new ideas soon.'

'What's your favourite idea so far?'

He frowns with intense concentration. 'They measure units of time with this. Wait for it . . .'

Danu tries not to laugh at his serious expression.

He says dramatically, 'They measure units of time with how long it takes them to see what every single person in the world who isn't them, is doing.' He nods emphatically. 'I thought of that idea because I once saw a telescope at the window of one of their highest buildings. They'd have a supremely slow calendar, if that's their way of measuring units of time, wouldn't they? *Supremely* slow.'

They walk past a post box. Danu says, 'They certainly took bloody ages to return a letter.'

The boy's eyes shine. 'It's exciting. One of our years might last for one of their hours.' He puts his watch back in his pocket, stops walking and turns to her. 'I have to go to school – up there.' He waves at a side street. 'I've been to the dentist and I'm really late.'

She says, 'Can I ask you just a couple of things before you go?'

He nods.

'Do you know anyone who's ever been into the Inner Circle?'

'Most people say no one goes in and no one comes out. But that's not entirely true. My friend Gladys went in after her mum died, because her dad lives there.'

'Could I meet her?'

'No. She's still there, and isn't allowed out. As in *never*. On any calendar, *Never* has got to be the longest month.'

'If her dad's from the Inner Circle, and presumably her mum wasn't, how did her parents meet?'

'He was allowed out to do field trips. He's an expert geographer.'

'Have you ever met him?'

He shakes his head. 'No. He didn't come out very often. I'd better get to school.' Though he's still right next to her, he waves as if this is a polite thing to do on parting company. He takes his felt hat off and shoves it into his satchel as he walks away up the side street.

The university building has star constellations carved into its stonework. Beside small-paned windows, rusted metal shutters are decorated with scythes, swords and flames. Danu goes in through the main doors. She's in an immense corridor with floor-to-ceiling windows looking out onto a courtyard. The Department of Cultural Studies appears on an arrowed list of departments. As Danu turns corners and pushes through swinging doors, copies of the flier advertising the Ether Talk are masking-taped along the walls.

The door to the lecture room is open, so she goes in and sits in the second row of tiered seating. About thirty other people are already seated. The atmosphere is one of anticipation.

A woman in a cerise trouser suit approaches the lectern. She nods at a student who's standing beside the exit. As he turns off the main lights, she puts on a pair of red-framed glasses.

In the front row, a man in a green velvet suit rises. He turns and announces, 'It is my great pleasure to welcome Professor Irena Jemica who is developing *quite* a reputation in a sub-field of Philosophy known as Ethereal Studies.'

The professor nods at him, and he returns to his seat.

A slide appears on the screen behind her. It shows an image of golden stars in a deep blue sky.

She speaks. 'We have scientifically proven that stars exist. We therefore believe in them even when they disappear behind clouds, or when our eyes become blind to them.'

Glancing around, she continues, 'Today, I encourage everyone to think beyond scientific proof. Consider what you inherently know. As children, we thought magically – but in adulthood, our magic is in science. We dismiss incomprehensible things as ethereal, as fey. We have allowed our sense of magic to be tamed.'

The image on the screen is a picture of the tarot card: The Magician. The expression on his face is one of indecision. She points to the section of the card which shows a figure of eight and a selection of symbols and tools.

She says, 'To tame the incomprehensible, we believe that we have to divide it. We speak of many elements and use them as concepts: earth, air, fire, water. Maruama proposed the following: *The fifth element, known as ether, has been scientifically searched for but remains elusive. It is seen by many as the material which forms all that is above and beyond what we can see.* Hopari described it as *our universe*, and Blemmen described it as being *a container of our universe*. A sea of energies, or the container of energies?'

Murmurs from the back row. She frowns, which silences them, and resumes speaking. 'But the facts are that we can't see the ether and it hasn't yet been measured. We also don't know what it does.

'Some possibilities. It could propagate light waves or sound waves and transmit forces. We have solid, liquid, gas, plasma. We have energy, magnetism, light, heat and motion. But what of energy and matter's interactions – imagine witnessing colliding matter particles disappearing in showers of radiant energy. What would the scientific "tying down" of the ether do to us individually – how would it benefit us if we were able to trace it?

'Have a look at this next slide. A diagram, from Fellows – you will see his concept of the ether involved it being weighted to the left. There is no proof for this. In fact, some other diagrams produced by Lightbody et al have weighted it entirely to the right. Personally I can't see how this can be substantiated. Anyway. I digress.

'Certain waves of different frequencies do or do not interact with one another. The infinite spectrum of energy gives rise to infinite grades of matter. These can pass through one another with or without interaction. Our universe, which we understand as colossal, could be one wave in an infinite spectrum of matter and energy.

'Is our world constantly interpenetrated by other worlds, beyond what we are capable of sensing?'

The next slide is blank. The professor is silent for a moment, staring at the slide. Then she says, 'The bleakness of empty space.'

She turns back to face the listeners. 'As Sharpe originally suggested, the structure of our universe could be embedded in an *etherosphere*. If we move through a stationary ether, we should be able to prove the closer presence of an ether wind. Despite, most recently, Ishida and Rosso failing to prove the existence of the ether, they also failed to prove the *non*-existence of the ether.

'If there is an ether wind blowing over our world, producing slight variations in the speed of light in different directions, why haven't we yet been able to trace it?'

She pauses, and when she speaks again, the tone of her voice is excited. The words want to rush out of her but she's trying to speak them slowly enough to be understood:

'I would like you to consider the possibility that the ether is a substance.

'And furthermore, it is a substance that can sense when it is being looked for.

'And yet more significantly: because the ether doesn't want to be examined or divided in order to be understood, when it's looked for, it moves away.'

The next three slides on the screen, in quick succession, are a black and white drawing of a white rabbit in a field, the same rabbit running towards a rabbit hole, and then the rabbit hole.

The professor's eyes shine. 'I would like you to consider this: the reason no one has been able to prove it is there, is that the ether won't allow itself to be seen.

'My findings thus far, tend to substantiate this proposition.'

She goes on to say that she will continue to explore both sound waves and emotional waves, in order to gain a deeper understanding of the ether. 'What if emotional waves continue to undulate once they have been released from us? What if our emotions feed into the ether, and strengthen it? I will leave you with that thought. And this one.

'As Ribinaccio once said, *Are the worlds beyond what we know far too beautiful, indeed, too ethereal, to be understood?*'

The initial image of stars reappears on the screen as the professor says, 'Look to the stars, try to remember the magic you felt when you saw them as a child. How would you prefer to *think*? How would you prefer to *feel*? Your answer should be different to mine, because it must be your own.'

As the professor removes her glasses, the man in the green suit advances to the front. 'I'm sure we'd all like to thank the professor for such an illuminating lecture, and wish her all the best with her ongoing investigations.' Danu joins in the applause as the professor takes a seat on the platform.

As the clapping subsides, the man sits beside the professor. He says, 'I will now open the floor to questions. Yes. Third row?'

A young man behind Danu says, 'I've recently re-read Beucamp's theory in which she states that the ether is a chimera. In my own investigations, there's a place for illusions which have logic, but research proposals need to include something that is measurable . . .' His voice trails away.

The man in green turns to the professor.

'I'm sorry,' she looks directly at the young man, 'was there a question in there?'

The young man tries again: 'What specifically, with regard to the ether, can I write in my proposal which shows that the ether is scientifically measureable?'

'Ah. Thank you for clarifying. Initially, you might suggest that auditory sensation may enable us to directly perceive a vibratory movement. You might also suggest that you wish to discover if the ether has a determined central point.'

There's another question from someone in the front row. 'Are you considering fluctuations when measuring human emotions?'

She responds, 'I don't intend to *change* the wave frequencies of any initial emotion. I intend to *follow* the wave frequencies. I want to see where these waves travel to. How far they go, and how long they last.'

Danu says, 'Is the ether a place that exists beside us, like a parallel world? Or is it more like a vast envelope and our world is inside it?'

The professor replies, 'In haste, so we can move on, but opinions are mixed. Myriade described the ether as a *route*. Nonoplis described it as *a universal grid containing many directions – covering both past, present, future*.'

Danu says, 'I'm sorry, but I don't understand if there's an answer in what you've said?'

The professor's eyes scan the front few rows as she asks, 'Next question please?'

The next questioner has a sarcastic voice. 'If the ether doesn't want to be seen, it's elusive. And if something is elusive, surely you have to have a supreme belief in yourself in order to even consider you might be the one person who could ever find it?'

The professor retaliates, 'Belief is a many-pronged fork. Don't scratch me with yours.'

The questioner speaks again, 'Who are you citing?'

The professor smirks. 'Myself.'

Danu asks, 'If the ether is a route or a universal grid, can it be travelled?'

Someone behind her laughs.

The velvet-suited man says, 'Please raise your hand if you have a question, but also, please wait until other questions have been answered.'

'Sorry.' Danu bites her lip. 'I don't know all your rules. I only really have one question and then I'll keep my gob shut. Someone said to me, *watch for me on the ether*. What did he mean?'

The professor holds Danu's gaze for a moment. 'I would say that the person making this statement was linking the ether to the concept of astral light. Astral light is reported to produce visions if the will to *see* is strong enough within a psychically sensitive individual. Clearly, his desire to provoke your curiosity has been effective.' Her eyes trail over the other faces within the lecture room.

She returns her intense gaze to Danu. 'Be wary of charisma.'

Danu responds, 'I am.'

Laughter comes from every direction.

As it subsides, the professor resumes talking. 'Now . . . returning to *your* question . . .' She gestures at the previous questioner, 'I assume you're drawing on Nevertell's *Sardonsemantics* – his theory that a *purist* belief in oneself must inevitably involve a *sullied* belief in other selves?'

Feeling out of her depth, Danu shuffles past a couple of seated students and emerges from the end of her row. As she closes the lecture-hall door behind her, she realises she's possibly broken another rule about when people are allowed to leave lectures – she's being scowled at by the whole of the front row and most of the second.

If only she could be more receptive, capable of hearing or seeing things which are just out of sight. The corner-of-the-eye things, which disappear when looked at directly. What if Morrie is trying to psychically communicate with her? The idea of him shouting, talking, whispering into her ears and remaining unheard makes her feel desperately sad.

When she returns to Wringers Street, she writes another unsendable letter in her notebook:

Dear Morrie,

If you are trying to talk to me in some way, I can't hear you.

In order to make a new life for myself here, I'm exploring Matryoshka, and I'll need to try and find a job soon. My letter to Judith Crown was returned, so I can only assume she's moved house. How can I find out more about the Inner Circle, or get through their locked gate, to look for her? You probably hate her name, or have already forgotten it, because she is the reason we are parted.

I'm trying to avoid thoughts of all the things I've lost, but I can't hide them from myself all the time. Why has this become so hard? When we were first here together, this city felt enchanted. It still does in many ways. Magic must be made of layers.

Though it's tough at times, it feels deeply right that I'm here. The other day, I found myself talking nonsense to a blackbird. I felt more fondness for that bird than any human in this vast city. Is that terrible? But it saddens me that as I think of you now, my memory of your face is no longer clear. I picture you in darkness, asleep. This scares me, in case you are becoming a forgotten thing.

Everything new I discover here fills my heart to bursting. I don't want the new things to push all the old things away. But perhaps this is what happens, when everything changes, and so suddenly.

Please, just write me one letter. Something real that you've touched, which I can hold on to.

Danu

SIX FOR SOLD

At lunchtime, Danu goes outside and along the main street of the outer circle. Sitting on a low wall in one of the squares, she looks around. People cluster near small cafés. Most of them must work in this area as they're carrying little with them other than purses and wallets. She studies their faces. Pieces of old pain are etched in wrinkles, enthusiasm radiates from eyes, and smooth foreheads suggest youth or few worries . . . Mouths with tight lips might hide too many secrets . . . but look away from individual faces, and they're a crowd again.

She once saw a farmer separate a sick sheep from a flock. The sheep was afraid of the farmer and his rope. Its cries sounded human. After tar was applied to seal its wound, it returned to the flock as if nothing had happened. Perhaps in its mind, nothing had. It rejoined its own kind.

How do people find other people who are their own kind?

Two apron-clad waitresses sit on a bench, eating cakes with plastic forks. They are easy with each other, laughing as they spoon cream and crumbs into their mouths.

Smiling, Danu rises with the intention of approaching them. But one wipes her apron with a napkin as the other takes their rubbish to the bin by the tables. Their break is over. They disappear back into a café.

Crossing the square, Danu weaves slowly between clumps of people having small picnics on the grass. She tries to guess if a red-haired woman is related to an auburn-haired one, or if their friendship sparked while having conversations about hair. Is the tall man over there the boss of the short man, or is it the other way around?

A woman with pink hair glances at Danu's feet as she passes her. 'Like your boots!'

Danu calls, 'Like your hair!'

The woman glances back. 'Thanks!' She waves as she walks away.

Danu looks at her likeable boots. Kicks them a little. The deep brown leather is cracked. She smiles at them. Likes them a little more.

Approaching a food stall, Danu scans a glass cabinet filled with pastries and pies. Labels in purple ink display a variety of flavoursome pairings – red wine and aubergine, lentil and cardamom, venison and fennel. She orders a sweet pastry – apricot and chilli-chocolate. The seller wraps it in a red napkin and hands it over. Danu counts small change from her purse into his palm. Her funds are depleted. If she can gain a job soon, it will earn her money, and possibly some friends.

While Danu sits eating on a bench, the flavours of the pastry mingle as the chocolate melts and the chilli kicks in. Her body is trained for the precision of the wire, her mind is trained in what to think to stop herself falling. She's seen a few cabaret bar posters advertising open auditions. She will find a way to tightrope walk in this city.

Danu has auditioned for a slot at two cabaret bars in the outer circle. For these auditions, she set up the wire and displayed her acrobatic and dance skills: the flips, spins and twists she can perform to any musical accompaniment. She kept her routines simple and precise.

Walking the wire without Morrie made her stomach clench. She felt as if she was blanking him out of the world. And she didn't even mention his name when she spoke of their previous acts, in case the managers thought she was no good on her own. It felt like a lie, to talk of their acts without saying that he trained her, and that the acts were developed together. Lying is a shrinking thing – it made her also play down her other circus skills and all the stories and songs she carries in her mind.

Today, she's at a third audition. She likes this venue, which is called Kasabar. It is a rundown yet popular place less than an hour's walk from Wringers Street. The internal walls are painted gloss black, and the lighting is mainly at stage level, so there would be the potential to work with shadows if she can have any influence in the design – additional lights could be angled upwards. Around the auditorium the walls are covered with shelves containing pink glass vases filled with red and green flowers which look like dragons.

She particularly likes the manager, who has gentle eyes and a determined frown. When she arrived an hour ago, he introduced himself with the nickname of Bo, but wouldn't tell her his real name as *nobody but the wrong kinds of people ever use it*. He is chaotic in terms of organising anything, enthusiastic in his ideas for developing new acts, and self-conscious about the roundness of his belly. Covering it with one hand, he eats cakes with the other from a three-tiered stand during an afternoon of auditions.

'Lovely,' he says, when she's finished her audition. 'I'll be in touch.' He jots something down in his notebook, claps three times, and turns to the others who are still waiting to audition: 'Break for half an hour.' He glances around till he catches Danu's eye. 'You can dismantle your wire while the stage is free.'

*　　*　　*

Danu hasn't yet had a letter from any of the places she's auditioned at, and it's been over a week. Her funds are running low. She decides to go and get their decisions in person. She walks around the main street towards Kasabar. The sun shines directly from above. The front door is locked so she goes round the side and knocks on the stage door.

Bo answers it himself. He glances anxiously along the side street. His hair looks unwashed, and a grey curl covers one of his eyes. As he smooths it away he says, 'Sorry, expecting an unwelcome visitor. Didn't see anyone in red, did you?'

'No . . .'

He exhales. 'Danu, isn't it? The tightroper?'

He remembers her. This must be a good sign. 'Tightrope walker. I want to save you the cost of a stamp. Have you decided about me yet?'

'Oh, yes yes. I'm just bogged down with other things. In you come.' He beckons her in, closing and double-bolting the door behind them. 'What's the old word for tightrope walkers?'

'Funambulists.' As Danu follows him along a dingy corridor lined with crammed clothes rails, she brushes past costumes made from feathers, satin and net.

As they enter his cluttered office, he tells her, 'I've never worked with a tightrope walker.' He follows her gaze and mutters, 'And yes. I'm appalling at paperwork.' He places a page with five columns of numbers next to a bottle of green ink. 'I worked two years in accounts, years ago. Burnt out, but not before I'd wrecked some good people's financial worlds. Now numbers make me fearful.' Beads of sweat form on his temples. 'I don't suppose you – no no.' He moves a pile of papers from one side of his desk to the other, frowns at them, and moves them back again. 'Of course not. Entertainment, it's all about entertainment.' He murmurs something about tightrope walkers and balance sheets and raises his eyes to meet hers, expectantly.

She laughs politely, though she's missed the joke.

He wipes his brow with a patterned handkerchief and gets a bottle labelled *watermelon liquor* from a shelf. He pours it into two small shot glasses and perches on a theatrical throne carved with an embossed crown. He waves Danu into the smaller chair opposite him.

He frowns at their pink drinks. 'No freezer in here. Sorry, I can pop to the kitchens for ice . . .'

'Don't worry, it's fine. Perfect.'

Bo relaxes into his throne. 'Right. I like the *idea* of a tightrope walker. I like how you look. Are you open to working closely with me to develop your act to fit our audience, perhaps adapting it again at a later date?' He knocks back his drink and straightens his bow tie.

Danu takes a sip of warm liquor. 'Of course.'

'I have extremely good ideas.' His eyes glaze a little. 'Visions, some say.'

'In the audition I fixed the wire low. But can I ask about the height available on stage?'

'If you use the dome area, potentially, it's *really* high. But do you think health and safety . . . oh no matter. If it comes to it, we'll say we did an assessment of risks, and as with everything in life, there *are* some.' He rummages in his desk drawer and presents her with a floorplan and measurements of the performance space. 'See, not as cack-handed as I look, am I? I can find *some* things in here.'

Danu calculates how she'd be able to set up and dismantle her wire. 'I'd want to use a tightwire, rather than slack.' She draws a quick sketch on the back of the floorplan, illustrating the height she'd like to have the wire at. 'Can you light this area?'

He smiles. 'There's a ring of lamps in the dome. I've always wanted to use it more – it's dramatic as a setting – all those windows . . .'

Danu nods. 'It is. And the night sky overhead . . . Have you got access to scaffold poles, wood for small platforms, and a long ladder we can keep fixed in place?'

'Oh, yes yes.' Bo becomes animated as their conversation transforms into a monologue.

He talks about his ideas for her act. Jumping from one image to another, he considers themes of crime, heartbreak, joy and punishment. He describes a whole range of costumes – a rail of them hangs in his mind. He flicks along them: from fetish all the way to bedraggled.

Once his vision is complete and she's agreed to his suggestions, he exhales and says, 'Perfection. I can see it already.' He makes notes for the costume-maker, set designer, musicians and lighting engineer. He says, 'These are mainly volunteers – art and theatre students. It's good experience for them. Front of house, band, acts, and refreshments staff are all on the payroll.' He glances up at her. 'And you'll accept whatever stage name I come up with?'

She laughs. 'As long as it's not insulting.'

Bo leans over the desk and shakes her hand with a firm grip. 'I like you. I like you a lot. So, welcome to Kasabar. Can you start rehearsals next week?'

Danu signs a one-page contract. The contract ties her to perform a short spot in consecutive shows for six nights out of seven. She will earn enough to eat and have a little left over.

She's found herself a job.

Morrie's in his bed, blankets shaken off, pulled back on, shaken off again. Acid sweat coats his skin. Water comes in a glass to his lips not often enough. He's got a thirst something desperate, but can't move his mouth to speak for it.

A glass is finally held to his lips again and he leans forward, dry lips seeking moisture, but is this salt? It doesn't taste right, even the air is poison. A sip. Another. Water spills over his chin. His chin is wiped. Whose hand is this? His eyes won't open, they're stuck with gunk or glue. The water's gone. Something cold wipes his forehead. Wipes his nose. His eyes. He retches, jerking forward. A bucket's held under his mouth. He spits, barely seeing what liquid's coming out of him. The bucket is gone. He sags, head to pillows, and falls into black.

Again, he's awake. Blankets are pulled off. His clothes stick to him as someone pulls his trousers down. He can't move his hands to stop them. A sponge rubs his knees, calves, feet. Thighs. The bed shifts and his shirt is half off. A woman's voice. 'Sit up, come on Morrie. Help me out. Sit up.'

Strong hands under his arms, pulling. He strains to raise himself and hears the voice say, 'Good, that's good.' He's upright, slouched forward.

His shirt is pulled at again so it's half over his head, sticking to his back. Another pull and he's naked. His back is being washed. Cold water, the smell of soap. It's far too dark.

He whispers, 'Open the curtains.'

'What did you say?'

His voice is louder. 'It's too dark.'

His back is held firm, one hand to the centre. Her other hand runs the sponge back and forth over his chest. The woman has long dark hair. Her voice says, 'It's night.'

Half-dreaming it's Danu come back to him, he whispers, 'Is it you?'

'It's me.' That's not Danu's voice.

The hand leaves his back too quickly and he thuds back onto pillows like a stone. Footsteps. A sheet lands on his naked legs and torso and sticks to damp skin. His eyes adjust and he can

224

make out the woman getting a candle from the table. Her eyesight's far better than his.

She sits next to him again. A match strikes and a candle is lit. She's wearing a thin green dressing gown. She turns her face and looks at him.

It's Loretta.

She wears a thick lipstick smile. 'Hello, Morrie. I've been nursing you. Are you feeling better yet?' She holds the candle towards him and he blinks and looks away from the glare.

His head thumps. 'How long?'

'How long, what?'

'Have I been ill?'

'Don't fret, I've been taking good care of you.' She looks at the candle and back at him. 'You ate something bad. Frightful food poisoning.'

He remembers a fried egg and nearly retches again. 'Mag tell you that, did she?'

'Aye, of course. She said she'd been sick too, but she only ate a tiny bit of the same stew. She recovered far quicker than you have.'

'I bet she did.'

'I'll feed you whatever you want. I'm a good little cook. We all know how proud you are. But you need help.'

Morrie tries to move his arm, and it's so weak he can barely lift it.

She touches his hand. 'I'm going to love you back to health again, whether you like it or not.'

There's a lace nightie hanging on the back of the door. He asks, 'Have you been sleeping here?'

'I've been right by your side this whole time. Sometimes you put your arms around me while you're asleep. Till you got too hot and threw all the covers off again . . . I landed on the floor all tangled in them last night.'

'Did I kick you out of bed, then?'

She slaps his arm gently. 'Aye, you did, Morrie. But you can't lie when you're asleep and you've put your hands all over me. So you're halfway to loving me, and by the time I've gotten you well again, you'll love me through and through. You've not yet tried my cooking. And you know what you're getting . . .' she glances at him, 'for you've already had me.'

Morrie touches her hand and speaks as soft as he can. 'Loretta, what would you do for me?'

'Anything.'

'So you'd help me till I'm strong enough to take care of myself again?'

'I'll do anything you need.'

'Would you post a letter for me?'

'Who to?'

'To Danu.'

Silence.

'Well?'

'I bloody would not.'

'Oh, forget it.' He rolls away from her. It takes all the strength he's got to get onto his side. 'Get out. Just go.'

Putting her hand on his shoulder, she says, 'But Morrie, you *need* me.'

She's bloody right. But what's she going to want in return?

The external facade of Kasabar is painted crimson and black. Inside, a small entrance hall is flanked by plastic plants. A gold door opens into the main auditorium where a wide circular stage is surrounded by tables. There's a long bar with swing doors behind it which lead to a kitchen.

For the first few days, Danu arrives early for rehearsals, so she can talk with the two refreshments staff. These aproned men spend most afternoons preparing food and drinks, and setting up the auditorium for the evening. Danu sits on a high stool at the bar and watches them shaking and stirring strange combinations of brandies with cinnamon liquor and pineapple juice, coconut rum, cold tea and spiced wine. These are the house specials, which they serve pre-mixed, in wide-lipped jugs.

She discovers that the easiest way to make new people like her is to ask them as many questions as possible.

As this busy pair rattle ice and liquid through shakers, she finds out:

Their nicknames as teenagers were Beetle and Creeper and the names stuck. These nicknames were given due to hair colour – black – and texture – heavily oiled – for Beetle, and for Creeper, the nickname was due to his preference for rubber-soled shoes, his sense of naughtiness and lanky physique.

They have always lived in the outer circle and first met each other at secondary school.

They were both desperately shy when it came to any hint of romance. They would never have kissed each other at all if they'd not been drunk.

They were drunk when they first kissed, and can't remember much about it. They remained drunk, to combat their shyness, for the first three months of their relationship.

Once they sobered up again, they weren't shy any more. They are now in their late thirties and got married last year.

Bo's recently had a visit about unpaid taxes and now has to pack in the audiences more than ever before.

Performers come and go rapidly – not everyone likes the way Bo works with them. He is single-minded about his ideas, and a sure way to get fired is to develop an act of your own making.

She must watch out for the stilt walker because she has tall poppy syndrome and is brutal in her criticism of others; the strongman because he can't keep his gob shut about anything; and the octopus woman because she has wandering hands.

Kasabar is popular with the punters because the entry fee is minimal, no one cares how much anyone drinks and no pockets or bags are searched at the door.

No one who is anyone in Matryoshka talks about the volcano underneath the city.

Everyone who is no one talks about the volcano all the time.

After learning all of this, Danu decides to abide by Bo's status quo regardless of her own opinions about her act because now she has this job, she wants to keep it.

After the first few days, Beetle and Creeper ask questions of Danu. They find out from her:

She has no family.

She claims not to remember the name of the street she lives in.

She isn't 'on the market' for their well-intentioned matchmaking.

She's not eating enough because she hasn't got much money left and is waiting for Bo to pay her. He is refusing to do so until she's performed in a live show for at least a week.

She doesn't speak about herself unless asked direct questions.

After learning all of this, they place a bowl of chilli peanuts next to each coffee she buys. A few days later, they tell her not to bother paying for her coffees any more. 'On the house.'

The performance area is a circular stage under a high dome ceiling. The audience capacity is for about fifty, seated at tables with red paper tablecloths. On each table there is a throwaway bill with timings and names of the acts in the show: The Snakers, the Kissergirls, Cry-Ocean Singers, Magician Supposition and Psychic Tsunami, the Big-Bummed-Benders, the Thunder Sisters and the Paw Yellow Rabbit . . . None of the acts last more than four minutes each.

'Down below' is what Beetle and Creeper call the communal dressing rooms. It's underneath the stage in the basement, and smells faintly of sulphur. It's a place of archways, too many chairs and a wall of lightbulb-lit mirrors.

Each performer ascends to the centre of the stage through a trapdoor which works via a complex pulley system. Looking at the tangle of wiring and wheels involved, Danu's relieved it only requires the pull of one lever to operate. Her act has developed well during the rehearsals: under Bo's strict and jovial direction, she's to perform a tightwire sequence that combines acrobatics, mime and dance. She will have musical accompaniment from the calliope – a steam-powered pipe organ.

When Danu is on the wire, she is in complete control of her body. She is aware of its every movement, its balance, its shape, of when she wants it to be admired, desired, or feared for. Acting feels like a lie, but it's a lie that is familiar. Danu doesn't like being looked at, so as a performer, she's always pretended she's someone who wants to be observed. Even in rehearsals, she commands an imaginary audience in her mind: *Audience – eyes up. Here is a figure on a wire. The figure is balanced and endangered. It is beautified with costumes and makeup and adornments. It can seduce you with a hand gesture or the slight tilt of a hip. Any figure which balances such a fine line at a great height may fall. This is magic. A dream, shared only with you. Eyes, be dazzled. And when the performance is over: mouths, beam; hands, applaud.*

Danu thinks all this while walking the wire, swathed in light.

Danu is about to perform her solo act in front of a live audience for the first time. As she stands on the lowered platform in the dressing room and adopts a coquettish pose, she is announced onto the stage at Kasabar by a disembodied voice:

'Please welcome ... drumroll please! The Balancing TimTamTremulous!'

Drums thunder as the trapdoor mechanism whirrs and lifts her up to the stage. A click beneath her feet, and she's in position. The spotlight shines on her as she extends one arm and takes a bow. She extends the other, and curtseys. Crossing the stage, the spotlight follows her footfall. She indicates the height of the wire by pointing both hands as the lights come on to illuminate the dome. She mimes an expression of fear. The audience laughs. The ladder on the scaffold tower is lit from below. Drumbeats which mimic the sound of a heartbeat thud through the auditorium. She climbs the ladder, pausing and pretending fear after each set of drumbeats. As she gets higher on the ladder, the audience murmurs. On the small platform, she extends one foot over the wire, and snatches it back. She covers her eyes with both hands.

The audience gasps as she steps forward, blind. She focuses on the wire beneath her slippered feet. The calliope organ music begins as drumbeats quicken, and she moves her body to the rhythm. She keeps her weight on her back leg when both feet are on the wire. She walks slowly along the wire to the other platform, uncovers her eyes and extends her arms. A burst of applause. She balances on one leg and swivels on the ball of her foot to turn and face in the other direction.

The volume of the organ and drumbeats rise. She launches herself into the dance routine. Two sides of her, one gracious and coquettish when walking in one direction, one strutting and flirtatious when facing the other. She is precise with her steps, facing ever forward. She dances along the wire and back again, back again and along the wire. She cartwheels without faltering and the audience cheers. After the final flip, she is back on the scaffold platform. She extends her arms as she looks up at her reflections in the windows of the dome.

She can't hear how loudly the audience is applauding as the organ is still playing and the higher notes squeal out of tune. As she bows and curtseys, curtseys and bows, she looks at the tables nearest the stage. There's chatter in the audience, but many eyes are still on her and she witnesses appreciative nods. The hands are still clapping. Behind the bar, Beetle raises a thumb and grins at her.

Even without Morrie, she can raise applause.

However, when the trapdoor lowers her into the dressing room, Bo is waiting beside her chair at the mirrors. He doesn't return her smile.

Danu asks, 'What's wrong?'

He shakes his head. 'I'm disappointed. The audience response was limp. I'm changing the lighting, first off.' He sighs over-dramatically. 'The audience needs more danger – perhaps we should make it look like you *could* fall . . . To . . . certain injury, if not death.' He taps his forehead. 'We could add something on the stage below the wire – a bed of nails or a wheel of knives?' He looks at her without seeing her. 'No. I don't want them *baying* . . . I am fond of you.' His face clears and becomes more certain. He nods. 'We'll change the act and explore *sentiment*. The danger of sentiment, to an audience, is to experience real emotion but not know where it comes from. Let's give their heartstrings a yank around. Right. For starters, I'm going to change the music.'

'But I like this costume. Your . . . vision.'

'I can have a new vision whenever I want.'

Danu says quickly, 'Of course you can. But can you give this act more of a chance first? You can't abandon it after just one night.'

He studies her intently. 'Well you've worked hard, and you look bloody good.'

Danu's features are masked with greasepaint: half male and half female. Danu's costume is half of a man's suit, and half of a woman's dress. She is both Tim and Tam. 'Yes, I have worked hard.' She holds a plea in her eyes.

He softens. 'All right. While I have a think, you've got one week to persuade me to keep this act, and I'll expect you to convince the audience to respond with higher tempo.' He pats her shoulder and goes off to talk to the strongman who's beckoning him over to a running rail.

She's heard a few performers gossiping about her being Bo's new favourite. It's not helping her make friends. He hugged her a couple of times in rehearsals and nearly squeezed the breath from her lungs. The girls in snakeskin body paint were clearly his protégés before Danu. They are generous with their hissing glares.

A frothy comedienne approaches Danu. 'Meet Tittytania with the Tremendous Tash!' Belly-laughing at her own joke, she attaches a curled moustache to Danu's upper lip.

Danu likes the moustache, so leaves it on. The Antisocial Tricksters who wear black masks are more aware of her presence than usual, and one of them bats his elongated lashes at her. He comes over and says, 'I saw a beautiful portrait of you a few weeks ago. Remind me – who was the artist?'

Remembering that the receptionist at a hotel in the second circle also mentioned a painting, Danu asks, 'Where was this?'

'One of the larger second circle galleries. I think I've got a postcard of it at home.'

'Could you bring it in to show me?'

'I'll hunt it out.'

Baffled, Danu says, 'Please do. Because I've never been painted by anyone. And certainly not in Matryoshka. Unless someone in the circus painted me without my knowledge and sold it here without telling me a thing about it . . .'

He frowns. 'That's odd.' He wanders back to the other Antisocial Trickster and whispers to him in the corner.

Before the next performance of the evening, Bo comes into the dressing room.

He sees her curled moustache and approaches her. 'No no no, too much male and not enough female. Balance such as yours needs to remain fluid.' His voice becomes overly dramatic. 'We want all genders to desire you.' He whips the moustache off, leaving her upper lip tingling and numb.

As he turns away, she murmurs, 'They already do. It doesn't mean I have to desire them back.'

Loretta's footfall echoes around the caravan as Morrie wakes. He says, 'Loretta, can you drive a horse?'

She replies, 'You've woke up in time to go to bed again. It's night. That last stew wiped you out.'

'Aye, but *can* you drive a horse?'

'Sandy drove us here, he'll help out again . . .'

He rolls over to face her. 'I want to get away.'

She's standing beside the sink, towel drying her hair. 'We're only going where everyone else is going—'

'Won't you run off with me?'

'Where would we run to, Morrie?' She places the towel over the back of a chair.

He hates the way she blinks at him, all feigned innocence in her eyes. He wants to get away from Mag. He can't have her interfering again with her poisoning or protection or whatever the witch would call what she's done to him.

Loretta wears a pink nightie and a sly smile. She's a faker and a flirt.

And he's turning into a liar because he's so weak that he bloody needs her.

He tries to soften his voice. 'I think we could find a good life together.'

'Oh Morrie, but you're lovely. I knew you'd come round.' She comes over to the bed and hugs him to her breasts till he can barely breathe.

Morrie gives her a peck on the cheek and she sighs as deep and long as if he's kissing her throat. She takes off her slippers and gets into bed with him. 'Budge up. I'll not leave the circus, Morrie. When you're well, you'll not want to leave, either.' Her breath is hot on his neck. She smells of honey.

Her hand clasps his flaccid cock. 'You're stirring for me, Morrie. Must be getting better already. I'm a good nurse, aren't I?'

His cock's not stirring, but from the sound of her quickened breath, she's convinced herself otherwise.

She murmurs, 'I knew you'd want me again, when you finally came round.'

He hardens to the grip of her palm. Has she been practising making him hard while he's been asleep?

Taking off her nightie, she pushes him onto his back and straddles his thighs. Leaning over him, she flicks her tongue around his ear. She expertly grips his cock again, and pushes it inside herself. He's weak, he'll not keep it up for long. Will she talk it all around the circus if he softens too quick?

'Fuck me,' she whispers, with a deepness to her voice which strengthens him. 'Fuck me.'

His cock hardens still more now it's cunt-deep. She's wet, pulsing, ready. She gasps like she's fit to come at the first weak thrust of his thighs. It'll not take much effort to get her there.

He closes his eyes, and imagines she's Danu.

It's the final performance of Danu's first week at Kasabar – her last chance to impress the audience and Bo. She places her foot on the wire and is simultaneously herself and someone else. She is an alchemist because she is the lights, the music, the costume, the illusion. She is both of these painted faces which hide her own face.

Half of a man, and half of a woman.

To Danu, these two halves are characters who have met, become friends, walked along holding hands, have clumsily made love, and are now telling the whole world that they are a couple.

This is the truth of acting anything you are not: to believe in a lie is to make it the truth. Temporarily.

Danu steps onto the wire as a strutting stereotype of a man.

At the end of the wire, Danu turns. She walks as a wiggling stereotype of a woman.

And now the two halves become inseparable.

One of these characters is lying. One of them is truthful. She can't tell which way around it is.

Danu balances, extends her arms, tumbles, flips and amid gasps from the audience, stands on her hands at the edge of the platform, her legs scissoring in the warm air. She drops her legs, stands, extends her arms above her head as beneath her feet, the wire vibrates.

Love as a tightrope wire. Two people trying not to fall. Merging. And still being their individual and confused selves.

A strange movement in the air all around her.

Morrie's face appears in her mind. Clearer than it's been for some time. Sweating and gasping, as if in pain.

Her palms break into a sweat as his face disappears.

She looks down.

The auditorium spins. Danu almost loses balance, her feet aren't firm enough on the wire. She moves back towards the platform and steps onto it.

She's safe.

Exhaling, she extends her arms, pretending that this step onto the platform is part of the act. The faces of the audience are still raised, watching to see what she will do next. The music surges.

Bo's frowning up at her from beside the bar. He knows the routine as well as she does. Stopping at this point isn't anything he's asked her to do. Beetle leans over the bar and says something to him.

The music builds to its crescendo. Final chance to impress Bo.

And she's back on the wire. She flows, she is graceful, she twists and releases her body. She struts the length of the wire as a man, sways back again as a woman, arms outstretched, hands flapping in time to the drum, smiling her widest grin as she listens to the whistles of the calliope organ. She flips, the audience gasps. She cartwheels. They cheer. She flips again and the people at the tables nearest the stage are already applauding.

As she focuses on extending grace from arms through to finger-tips, applause rises. She widens her beam. The applause rises higher.

Bo is still there at the bar, talking to Beetle while watching the faces of the crowd.

Danu descends from the stage into the dressing room.

Bo has come down the back stairs, and approaches her.

She says, 'Well?'

'Good, but still not enough applause. You can do better.'

'Sorry, I stalled—'

Bo shakes his head. 'The blip you had. A slight falter. It made me realise what I need you to be. You'll stagger, almost fall, and fly. Land, to ascend yet again. They'll all fall in love with you. Vulnerability. Temptation. Frailty. Femininity. You'll croon like the dawn chorus balancing on a telegraph wire. You'll wear white. A dove costume. A dove filling the clearest blue sky with her song.' He illustrates the sky with a sweep of his hand and a wistful expression. 'Like it or not, you're going to have to learn to sing.'

Danu is about to say she already can sing, but Bo puts his

palms on her cheeks and kisses her forehead. He tells her, 'Forget your day off – rehearsals for your dove act will start tomorrow.'

'But they're empty-headed things. Can doves even sing?'

'Of course they can.'

'Couldn't I be a raven, or a parrot, or even a goose?'

He turns away and she steps to block his exit. 'Bo, are you going to pay me?'

'We'll take this act off the listings – I want you focused on the new one. You're on board, girl.' He hugs her.

She exhales with relief because the hug is paternal.

Bo laughs as he releases her. 'I'll pay you tonight. Eat. Properly. Don't spin out again.'

Danu goes into the red-tiled washrooms to change out of her costume.

She's going to need a strong voice to fill the vacant spaces in the mind and breast of a dove. Danu's mother could have performed as any bird with a trilling song in its breast, and she would have invented new songs for all the silent birds. Sugar sweet, sour-grape bitter, nectar dark. That was her mother's voice, in song.

She hangs her outfit on the back of the cubicle door and puts on her clothes.

Her mother had never wanted to do anything other than sing, and sing as herself. She wasn't interested in pretending to be anyone she wasn't. She wore black for each performance, a floor-length and wrist-deep and neck-height thick dress. She wasn't interested in people looking at her or finding her attractive, though she was beautiful. She said it was her voice people paid to hear, so that's all they were entitled to. If she could have performed in the dark, or with her back to the audience, she would have chosen to do so.

Danu lowers the toilet lid and sits down to lace up her boots.

What would Adelaide and Clem have thought of this cheap cabaret bar?

They wouldn't be proud of her.

Leaving the cubicle, she slings on her jacket and goes back to the dressing room. Will the Antisocial Trickster have remembered to bring the postcard of the blue painting yet? They're brothers whose mime act focuses on tricking, trapping and ignoring each other. She'll have to talk to them when they're together, as she can't yet tell them apart. But they're not here. They must have already gone upstairs or home. She won't see them for a while if she's only coming in for the afternoon rehearsals. The painting is probably only a passing resemblance, but she'd still like to see it.

She goes up to the auditorium but they're not there either. She waits at the bar for her pay packet.

Beetle passes her a drink. He says, 'You had a weird moment up there—'

She speaks without thought. 'Morrie's fine now.' Shaking her head, she corrects herself. 'I mean, I'm fine.' Is there some link between them, that she knows this, even if she can't hear him? Over the years, she's heard many people talk of *just knowing something's wrong* without being beside one another.

Beetle's still talking. 'I told Bo you were hungry. I said unless he paid you, next time you'd plummet from low blood sugar.'

She frowns, trying not to think about Morrie. 'Thanks Beetle. Did the audience like it?'

'They always like you. Don't listen to Bo. It was a good crowd tonight.' Creeper looks thoughtful. 'There was a group of students from the second circle, as well as the regulars and tourists. They were celebrating the opening of their graduate exhibition. There was woman with them from the Inner Circle.'

Danu raises her eyebrows. 'Did you talk to her?'

Beetle says, 'There's no point. I heard if they're asked the kinds of questions I'd want to ask, they fall completely silent.'

Danu asks, 'How could you tell where she was from – was it something about her appearance?'

Creeper replies, 'The students kept coming to the bar in pairs and gossiping about her. But to me, she looked just like anyone else.'

After two weeks of rehearsals, Danu is back on the wire again. Costumed as a dove, she sings with the melancholic accompaniment of a calliope organ. She points her toes as she steps along the wire, extends white-feathered arms and lengthens her neck. In the centre of the wire, her arms arched over her head, she extends one leg into the air in the posture of a ballerina. She clutches her hands together over the downy feathers on her chest as she slowly sings the last chorus,

> . . . I thought he worshipped me with white feathers,
> and she adored me with softest black,
> but when I sent them my heart with this love song . . .
> they took to the skies and never came back.

As her act ends, she curtseys, mid wire. The audience cheers. She pirouettes along the wire and steps onto the platform. The audience watches her with their clapping hands held high. Her sweetest smile is a sugared mask.

Once the act is over, the trapdoor mechanism whirrs Danu down into the dressing room.

The applause continues as Bo emerges from the back stairway and joins her. 'You're divine! They love you! Our dove and her unending love!'

Danu's gut clenches at the fluttery compliment.

He pats her back. 'Beautiful voice. Beautiful you.' He turns away from her, claps his hands and announces, 'Our new explosion will soon be drawing crowds. So step up your game and let's get Kasabar on the map. It's working well, appreciating all of your efforts so far. Entertainment. It's all about entertainment. I'll crack open a few bottles. Fizz-bubbles. We need fizz-bubbles.'

Danu goes over to the mirrors. She gathers cotton wool from a box filled with useful detritus – clips and hairpins and ribbons all bundled together. She dunks the cotton wool in moisturiser and wipes off her makeup.

Black lipstick and white feathers disappear from Danu's face as she watches the others in the mirrors. Skin emerges as costumes and masks are removed. Everyone is brightly lit on this side of the dressing room while the other side is filled with shadows transforming from vamps into women and lady-killers into men.

They're speaking about how much fun they've been having, mentioning the names of people she doesn't know; they're chatting about some nightclub they went to three nights ago . . . how wild, how loud, how happy, how high . . .

Who can she trust, when everyone is still acting?

The snake girls pop the corks from three green bottles. Two jugglers rattle in with a tray of shot glasses. What else in their lives are they juggling when no one can see them? The octopus woman removes her tentacles and hangs the costume from a hook on the wall. Her tiny fingers move frantically as she unties her corset. What does she grab when she's away from the stage – does she steal purses or squeeze confidences?

Danu's peripheral vision blurs. She's surrounded by birds with dark feathers and darting amber eyes.

She removes her white headdress. Performing to Bo's visions makes her realise how generous Morrie was in accepting her ideas. How generous she was in accepting his. She wishes more than ever she'd said goodbye to the other people in the circus but she'd been blindsided by Matryoshka. She'd thought the only farewell that mattered was the one she'd had with Morrie.

It still matters. Morrie's goodbye.

It now seems so final. But no matter how far Morrie's travelled, he is still beneath the same sky as her. The sunlight may change, the dark clouds blow in or bluster away, there may be stars, moon or sun. They share nothing now but the landscape above them.

Mikka the strongman appears beside her. He says, 'Right. So you're the favourite. I need a chat if you've got Bo's ear.'

'I don't have his—'

Mikka continues, 'He's wanting to change my act yet again. Don't know if I can do what he wants. I mean, the costume could be heavier than the weights . . .' He sits next to her and the chair creaks. 'I'm to dress as a bloody rhino. He thinks he's a blasted visionary.'

She shrugs. 'He's all right.'

'He's not. He wants me to have rhino hands. What are they even called – feet or hooves? How am I meant to grip the weights?' He sighs and continues, 'He should have an act of his own – so he can feel what dying on stage is like.'

Bo walks past, whistling the tune to Danu's dove song.

Mikka says, 'Your song's bloody terrible. Love and feathers. Heard it all before.'

She lowers her voice. 'I know. Sentiment is genuine feeling. Sentimental is . . . pink and glitterish. All the same, the audience seems convinced.'

'People have no taste.'

'Well, thank you.'

'Oh *you're* fine. Dovetailing your sweet cheeks up there. You look good.'

'I feel like I've sold myself. Just for the sake of earning money.

241

I used to love developing acts, inventing them from scratch, and I'd care so much about everything – the imagery, style and meanings – but this—'

'Everybody who earns money sells something of themselves.' Mikka looks at her meaningfully and she can't read the glint in his eye. 'I still like you.'

He frowns at the snake girls who are smirking at Danu. Turning back, he says, 'Don't listen to the gossip about yourself.'

'I don't.'

'Well, there's two new acts being rehearsed next week. Maybe he'll be swayed by some other pretty girl. No one's ever jealous of me. When people first meet me they're usually frightened. Which fades fairly quickly if I can be bothered to make them laugh. Anyways, you've got a lovely voice in you.' He looks at her intently. 'Look, will you talk to Bo for me?'

Danu removes her hairnet and shakes her hair out of its coil. She glances in the mirror to see where Bo is and calls, 'Bo?'

Mikka nudges her. 'Not while I'm bloody *here*.'

'Well I don't spend time *alone* with him.'

'We all thought you must do.' He winks at her.

So that's what he meant about selling herself.

The trapdoor whirrs as it descends and the Kissergirls step onto it, their outfits bejewelled with fringes of false rubies. One crouches, clutching the thighs of the other, who extends her arms above her head. The mechanism whirrs and rises them in this tableau. From above, the timpani announces their emergence to the stage.

Bo comes back over to Danu. 'What is it, poppet?'

Danu says, 'Mikka doesn't want rhino hands.'

His mouth is set in a straight tight line. 'Adaptation is always for the greater good.' He turns and addresses the whole room. 'Look at Danu here.'

She flushes, wishing she still had white makeup smeared across her cheeks.

Bo continues, 'Now she's changed her act, it's better, and everyone's happy. Leaf out of her book.' He pats Mikka's shoulder and says again, 'Leaf out of her book.' He wanders off and disappears into a storeroom.

The dressing room hisses with glares.

Thuds from the stage as the Kissergirls chase each other around. The sound of cartwheeling, a crash, and silence. Catcalls from the audience as they kiss.

Mikka stands. 'Thanks for bloody nothing.' He goes over to the clowns and joins in with their low patter, casting Danu an irritated glance.

Beside her, one of the dancers wriggles into a tight green vest. Danu slings her clothes over her arm and goes towards the washrooms. Seeing the Antisocial Tricksters tying their laces in the corner, she approaches them.

'Did you find the postcard of that painting?'

One of them looks up at her. 'I did. It was *very* like you.'

'Who painted it?'

'I can't remember. I did bring it in, but you've not been here nights.'

'Could you bring it in again?'

'Goodness knows where I've put it. I'll try.'

Danu goes into the toilet cubicles. Two of the doors are locked.

Over the sound of pissing, the snake girls are talking to each other. One is saying, '. . . and she won't just strip off.'

The other one replies, 'Danu's got amber titties . . . reckons she's got to keep them hid or we'll all want to grab them. Hey, what do you think she's got in that locket she's always wearing?'

'A key to the chastity belt that protects her virginity?'

Laughter. So no one can decide if she's frigid or sleeping with

Bo. This reminds her far too much of her brief conversations with Loretta.

Their conversation continues. 'If she's a virgin at her age, she'll be poisoned by now.'

'Poisoned?'

'I read this book in the library. A whole section in it about the Widow's Disease.'

'What's that?'

'It's a disease which happens inside women who don't orgasm. Female semen, when unspent, turns to venom.'

'Now I can't piss. What book was this?'

'A history of medicine. I was looking up hysteria.'

'Why?'

'I can't stop laughing whenever I come. It's embarrassing.'

A toilet flushes.

Danu goes into an empty cubicle and bolts herself in.

Silence and a pause.

A cubicle door creaks open. Another flush.

Over the sound of taps running, one of them says in a low voice, 'Bugger. Did she hear?'

Paper towels shush across hands. Footsteps retreat, followed by laughter.

Danu slips out of her costume and puts it on the cistern. As she puts on her tunic and trousers, she decides not to stay for Bo's fizz-bubbles, euphoric as they sound, tonight.

A few nights later, Danu drinks sloe gin with the remaining performers who haven't left for the night. The Antisocial Tricksters are heading off as quietly as they always do, but tonight Danu spots them just before they leave.

She goes towards the doorway and calls, 'Did you bring the postcard?'

They turn around. The one on the right says, 'I haven't found it yet.'

The other says, 'Our home's been chaos . . . we're both hoarders. We had a huge clear-out last weekend. We threw out a load of books, old newspapers, paperwork.'

The first one chimes in again, 'And now we can't even find our birth certificates.'

Danu asks, 'Do you remember where you saw the painting?'

He frowns. 'It would have been in the Pignog Gallery – that exhibition was entirely painting. I went to quite a few other galleries in the second circle – spent a whole day looking at high art, low art, live art, dead art . . . Should have done it all at a far slower pace, but I love the headrush I get, seeing so many ideas all at once.'

'I'll go and see it at the Pignog Gallery. Whereabouts is it?'

He shakes his head. 'You can't – Pignog's changed hands. It's going to have a grand reopening and renaming ceremony. You're new in Matryoshka, aren't you? Have you seen a renaming ceremony yet?'

Danu shakes her head.

'They're gorgeous celebrations. The moon signs of the new owners are made into fire sculptures and carried on platforms in a procession. Lots of rumbling percussion.'

'When will the Pignog reopen?'

'In about three months, I think. I went on the last day of their final exhibition. Lots of artists were displayed – it was a retrospective for the work of the curator, rather than an individual artist. There were some really gentle and thoughtful portraits. Shame you couldn't have seen it. Oh.' He claps a hand to his head. 'The postcard will be in my *other* bag. I'll just need to find it . . . Sorry. I'll sort my things out properly this weekend. You can have the postcard as a gift.'

'Please. I'd love to see it.'

They wish her goodnight and disappear through the exit.

The other performers have gathered in the dressing room in a circle around a cluttered coffee table. Danu returns to them, takes a seat and pours herself a large drink. Holding up her glass, she leans back and squints at the others through red liquid. Ice cubes crack and knock. How beautiful they all are, seen through red. They're distorted creatures, black-eyed and swimming.

Lowering her glass, she continues to observe them. The disguises are gone, but the performances aren't finished. Among all the shouting and strong opinions she admires the jokers who speak in anecdotes. They're now playing a game, and Danu is passed a blank scrap of paper. She takes a pen from a tub on the table. A juggler announces how to play: *What's on your mind? Draw it, and we'll guess your psychology.* Danu stares at her blank slip of paper.

Scarlet, one of the singers, is beside her. She holds up her drawing.

Someone calls, 'Is that a vagina?'

Scarlet laughs. 'My psychology is vaginal?' She speaks in an exasperated tone, 'This is a boat made of metal. It's a boat for a lava-flow river. I had a dream last night that the volcano erupted—'

She's interrupted by Mikka's resonating voice, 'Look, look at mine!' He's drawn a picture of an elephant wearing a bow tie.

The octopus woman glances at his picture and says, 'Narcissist.'

A juggler has drawn a self-portrait with a sad mouth, juggling a plate, a kettle and a spoon.

Scarlet calls out, 'Sadness in domesticity.'

The juggler shrugs, and tears spring in his eyes.

No one notices, as they're showing their own pictures.

The comedienne and two of the dancers have drawn pictures of themselves as well. And now the others are talking about *selfish portraits*.

Danu takes another sip of sloe gin and quickly draws a picture on her slip of paper.

As she holds it up, the octopus woman frowns at it. 'Is that a cage?'

Danu says, 'No, it's a locked gate with secrets behind it.'

The octopus woman says, 'Is your psychology locked?'

Danu replies, 'Have any of you ever met someone from the Inner Circle?'

Scarlet says, 'I met a man from there. He was nice.'

Danu asks, 'How could you tell where he was from?'

She laughs. 'Because he *wouldn't* tell me where he was from. He was a something-or-other kind of doctor. But I met him in a bar.'

'Are you still in touch with him?'

She shakes her head. 'I only met him once.'

'I hear so many different things about the Inner Circle . . . Is there a directory of names and addresses kept anywhere?'

Scarlet shakes her head again. 'Not as far as I know. I think they sneak out from time to time and plant rumours to confuse us all. Most people think they're reclusive. But I think they're sinister. Imagine living in the centre of a city and never talking to everyone all around you.' She shivers. 'They could be pulling all kinds of strings we don't know about. We're told that the Cabinet is in charge, but what if it's them?'

'Where is the Cabinet based?'

'Second circle. But they don't even consult properly. Have you ever seen them circulate a questionnaire? I think they're a front for the Inner Circle's secret society of political puppeteers. But then again, I've always liked a good conspiracy theory.' She smiles at Mikka, who's talking loudly.

With nothing of their own to add to this conversation, the others have slipped into reminiscences about a couple of feather dancers who'd locked themselves in a store cupboard and were caught *in flagrante delicto* by Bo.

The octopus woman cries, 'Yes – I remember. About a year ago. Adriane and Nicholas!'

Danu asks, 'Where are they now?'

Scarlet says, 'A *better* cabaret bar.' She bites her lip and glances around.

A moment of silence.

The juggler says, 'What precise kind of sex can be had using only one feather?' He conjures a pink ostrich feather from nowhere and twirls it between his fingertips.

Mikka takes it from him. 'Shall I demonstrate the possibilities?' He runs the feather around his neck, tickles his own nipples, and lowers it slowly to his belt buckle.

Danu looks away, laughing. Her glass is empty so she refills it from the bottle which crowns the small coffee table.

Scarlet nudges her, holding her own glass out to be filled. She leans closer to Danu. 'Like your skirt. Makes you look like a gyppo though.'

'Does it?' Danu looks down at the rose-embroidered fabric.

'Hand-done, is it?'

Danu picks at the uneven stitches. Mag gave her this skirt. She should sew in the unravelling threads. Look after it better.

Laughter erupts from every direction as the juggler grabs the feather back. Scarlet covers her mouth as she watches him unbuckle Mikka's belt.

Above the laughter surrounding the table, someone says, 'Let's go dancing!'

Scarlet says to Danu, 'You should come. You've never come out with us.' She knocks back her drink, goes over to a dressing table and rifles through an assortment of eyeshadow palettes.

There is talk about being sure to have a mad or maddening

night, where to go, what bands are on, who else might come out to play. Danu goes over to the hooks to retrieve her coat and head back to Wringers Street. She turns and looks at them all, talking, still laughing. Lines of conversations criss-cross the dressing room. Mouth to ear to mouth . . . She's a bit drunk.

Should she go back to the quiet darkness of Wringers Street to spin her light head around empty rooms and think about an improbable blue portrait?

Madness and dancing might be bright things, tonight.

At the door to The Lagoon, the ticketer prods the back of Danu's hand with a forefinger dipped in blue ink. Scarlet and Mikka are behind her as they move down the narrow stairs into the basement.

It's a cavernous venue, lit blue and green. Pipes, vertical ladders and ancient industrial cogs and wheels entirely cover the back wall behind the stage. A band formed of musicians playing double bass, violin, guitars and a set of kettle drums are amplified through distant tunnels. Slow drumbeats resonate in the air as the strings throb in a minor key.

Sweaty bodies press against her. Someone grabs her backside, she swings an arm without thought and her elbow bashes into something.

Turning around, she faces one of the purple-uniformed staff, his face flushed with anger as blood runs from his nostril. Scarlet is near the bar, talking to the octopus woman and Mikka. They glance over at Danu as the man grabs her arm, storms her back upstairs and evicts her from the building.

Out in the street Danu sits on a low wall opposite the dancehall and tries to stop her head spinning. She watches the door to see if any of the others follow her out.

They don't.

She's shivering but it isn't cold.

At the café tables nearby, paper plates containing swirls of half-eaten food are taken away by pink-uniformed waiters. The leftovers are slopped into a bin. Sweet puddings arrive, and plastic spoons are raised. Danu's eyes blur as she watches mouths spilling conversations through sugars.

Her feet look so far away. She moves them in time to the café music and the knots in her father's bootlaces graze her ankles.

She whispers to herself, *Keep searching. Don't care about people who don't care about you. Stay curious. Sooner or later, you'll understand why you're here.*

A warm breeze blows across her face. She exhales and rises from the wall. Going against the the flow of pedestrians, she walks back towards Wringers Street. As she passes an alleyway, a tin can rattles along cobblestones. It's the kind of sound stars might make if they'd fallen loose, and dropped to roll along an ordinary street.

Pausing for a while, she listens to the sound of metal against stone.

She thinks of stars turning like keys and opening the heavens, the mechanisms inside locks.

She thinks about the strength of metal,

the lightness of air as it passes through the gaps in a gate.

She thinks about eyes.

About periscopes and telescopes and microscopes, magnifying glasses, spyholes and keyholes.

SEVEN FOR SECRETS,
NEVER TO BE TOLD

Danu climbs the narrow staircase which leads all the way up to the Inner Circle gate. The wrought-iron banisters are shaped like ivy, vines and passion flowers. She pauses often, to still her breathing and rest from the steep climb. She examines patterns and twists of metal which are beautifully carved, but stained by time and moisture and weather.

At the summit, the intricate silver gate comes into view. There's a large letter box embedded in the wall beside it. The wall which surrounds the Inner Circle is high, and its surface is smooth polished metal which tilts outwards slightly at the top. It would be impossible to scale.

She puts her eye to a gap between metal leaves. On the other side of the gate is a narrow staircase coated in copper. High above the staircase there are tall green turrets and minarets. A mist pours down, hiding this view away.

She listens.

There's such stillness, here. Peace. She traces the silver leaves with her thumb. They're edged with gold.

Silence.

Light comes in a warm glow from the moon. The edges of the high buildings flicker, disappearing and reappearing.

A white ball bounces down the stairway and lands next to the gate. Out of the mist, a girl in unruly blonde pigtails and a cream-coloured nightdress emerges. She approaches the gate, picks up the ball, and whispers, 'What are you doing out there?'

Danu doesn't want to frighten her, so speaks quietly. 'Can you let me in?'

The girl comes closer to the gate and tilts her head, eyeing Danu closely. She says, 'No. You're not who I thought.' Moonlight gleams on her escaping curls, giving her the appearance of an undersized angel.

A golden child.

'Who did you think I was?'

'Oh.' The girl pales as she kicks one sandalled foot against the other. 'Not meant to speak to you. Bad me. Bad.' She stamps her foot hard, eyeing Danu with curiosity.

Danu says, 'Do you know Judith Crown?'

'Artist lady, yes.' She waves her fingertips into the steam which piles up around her. It smells thickly of a combination of smells. Mainly sulphur, disinfectant and lavender.

Danu lowers her voice. 'She's an artist?'

The girl nods. 'She paints lots of things in blue. Fat geese, the singing lady, library rooms.'

'Some people have said there's a painting of me, in blue. Perhaps she painted it. I'm sure she'd like to meet me. Can you get her to come to the gate?'

'I don't know where she is.'

Danu says, 'You look like a clever little girl. I bet you know if there's a secret way to get in.'

The girl tilts her head. She obviously likes the idea of secrets, but there's honesty in her face as she replies, 'No. Any cracks in the wall get fixed.' She stands taller, as if reciting. 'We have all we need, right here.' She looks down at her feet. 'I'm going home now or my little brother will tell on me for being outside at night. I might have to hit him. I don't want to. But I might have to.'

'What do you all do in here?'

The girl's eyes fill with tears which make her look even more angelic. She glances around her, and lowers her voice. 'I'm not allowed to talk to you but I'm also not allowed to do lying!' She kicks off one of her sandals. 'If I lie to you I'll have to do another dot!'

She crouches and holds up her bare foot, showing Danu the sole. The pale skin is tattooed in angry black splodges. Someone's told her she'll get black spots on the soul from lying, and she's taken this literally.

Danu asks, 'Why are you shut away from the world?'

'We're not shut away. We're everywhere.'

'What do you mean?'

'We know some of you think we're bothering gods or bothering devils . . .' She pinches at a particularly dark spot on her foot, and grimaces. 'I feel bleach-sick from talking when I shouldn't.' A tear runs over her freckled cheek. She swipes it away. '*You* made me sick.' She glares up at Danu.

'I'm sorry. I won't say a word to anyone. But can I check Judith's address with you – she used to live at Duffle Close?'

'She still does, but she's not there now.'

'Where is she?'

'Probably doing art.'

'Could you get a message to her from me?'

'I told you, I don't know where she is! Go away and don't come back. No one will let you in.' Slipping her foot back into her sandal, she rises. Steam pours down the stairs as the girl ascends them and disappears.

❊   ❊   ❊

253

Morrie lies tangled in white bedsheets, silently cursing as the caravan jerks and stops moving yet again. Loretta's out the front, trying to control Inferno but he's bumping, starting and stopping along a rough road. He's not well enough yet to take to the reins, but Loretta's shown willing and learned all the commands. He can't hear the footfall of the horses up ahead – they must have fallen behind the others.

Her shrill voice, *gettiup!*

Inferno starts forward again, but without the pace he needs for the steepness of this road.

Speaking the right words to a horse does nothing if there's no strength to the calling.

Tomas calls from the caravan behind them, 'You're all right Loretta, just keep on at him!'

Morrie props himself on pillows and tries to hold his tongue. Loretta will make more of an effort to control Inferno if she thinks she's in charge.

Another jerk and they're moving slowly and painfully uphill. Morrie shifts against the mattress which today is too thin. Everything is too thin. The sheets, the pillows, the blankets. He feels every stone as the wheels bump and turn. He feels the road.

Another yell from out front, which sounds like Sandy's voice. They're moving only a little faster. Morrie rolls onto his side, takes an apple from a basket under the bed, and eats it while the caravan rocks and bumps, moving onwards. Once he's finished, he pushes the apple core under the mattress. Reaching into the basket again, he pulls out a bag of hazelnuts and eats a handful.

Though Morrie's stronger each day, he's pretending to Loretta he's weaker than he is. He wants to see how much she's prepared to do in exchange for what he's doing for her. Most nights, she climbs on top of him when she comes to bed.

Through silent gulps, Morrie tells himself, *remember Danu*. Though it takes little time to bring Loretta to gasping, it's sapping him more than it should. This doesn't bother Loretta. She's a taker, not a giver.

A keen worker though, Loretta's able and willing. She cooked yesterday, washed linens and scrubbed while Morrie sat by an open window letting fresh air clear his head. She's got the face of a fool at any mention of hammering or any kind of glue or repairs, but there's nothing of urgency. She keeps herself clean and perfumed, even paints her lips on each day. She sings to herself, though her voice is a plughole and she only likes bawdy songs. A guttural tongue, she's got, and a mind like a drain. Clearly, she's thinking herself happy. Morrie had best *keep* her thinking herself happy while he still needs her help.

When the circus finally camps up for the night, Loretta's doe-eyed and blushing as she cooks beef stew for them both. She sits on the edge of the bed to eat her meal, and watches to make sure Morrie clears his plate.

She says, 'It's you for me, Morrie. And soon you'll know, for you, it's me. Danu was just you not thinking straight.'

Loretta always takes silence as agreement.

When the meal's done with, she nuzzles his neck and takes off her nightie, but he's exhausted from eating red meat for the first time in ages. As his eyelids close, Loretta curses under her breath. She finishes herself off with her own fingers. She cries out, lies flat on her back beside him, and breaks into snoring.

Morrie smiles into darkness, liking Loretta a little more because she hasn't even asked to be held. She's bold, brash, knows what she wants and takes it. From her own hands if nothing else is available. Loretta won't be hurt when he nudges her out of his bed. She'll flail for a time and then sneak into someone else's. Aye, Loretta's easy enough.

She rolls away from him and lies on her side. He looks at her dyed hair and pretends it's Danu who's lying beside him. If it was, he'd grip her hair and twist its wild tangles. He'd kiss her neck till she turned and gripped him with her arms or her thighs. Absence might make a heart grow fonder, but the body is made fonder by distance.

His heart's a drumbeat, and his body's a gut string, stretching thinner as it gets pulled further away from her.

It's been too long since he's been able to travel the ether and now Loretta's here all the time, even if he was stronger, he can't even try. This thought makes him want to go and throttle Mag for what she's done to him. If he could talk to Danu with his head, like some psychic ranter, he'd tell her *talk back, don't stop talking*. But she only ever talked when drink freed her lips. Even then, it was only in brief flailings of words which she stoppered up fast. Aye, Danu would never talk proper about anything which hurt her. She was always on alert, but about all the wrong things. She was never settled, not with Mag and Sandy, not in this caravan, not with the circus.

She'd figure out her head by being quiet, or scribbling in those notebooks of hers. Thought she didn't need anyone else, like as not, or didn't trust them enough. Happen that's from being an only child. But he remembers her once saying she'd always thought her folks should have had another baby. She was head-spinning from wine, and she must have been cold as she wrapped her shawl around herself. He'd said, *But you liked having them to yourself, didn't you?* She'd shrugged and said, *I wasn't enough, not on my own.* After that she drew a picture of some zodiac sign. She was disappointed when she sat back and looked at it. She said, *The two faces were meant to match* but she was probably too drunk to draw well. She tore it out of her notebook and gave it to him. She said, *Only keep it if you want to. If not, burn it.*

He probably shoved it in a drawer. What sign has two faces? The picture was drawn by the same hand that wrote stories of mismatched creatures. He smiles, thinking that Danu might have sketched a bull and a virgin and tried to give them the same features.

Loretta's breathing is regular. Slipping out of bed, Morrie creeps to his drawers to see if he can find where he buried Danu's drawing.

Hand deep in the middle drawer, under fabrics he feels paper. He lights a candle and takes out receipts for wood and varnish. A handwritten invoice for paint. At the bottom of the drawer, he finds the drawing. It looks like two curved fish, but they've got human faces. Danu's tangled their hair together, and got them facing each other. Both faces have the full lips of girls, but one's fairer than the other. It's a rough sketch, and their bodies aren't fully formed. She's written *Pisces* along the edge of the paper, then scratched it out again and written *Gemini*.

Loretta's voice comes from behind him, 'What's that you're looking at?'

He shoves the drawing back in the drawer.

She's leaning on one elbow, watching him from the bed.

He says, 'Didn't mean to wake you.'

'What've you just hid?'

'I was looking for something.'

'Feeling better, are you?' She sits up and swings her feet onto the floor. Pulling the sheet away from her bare breasts, she looks up at him.

'I might sit up for a while. I've been in bed too long.'

'It's the middle of the bloody night.' Her voice softens as she says, 'If you're restless, come here. I'll make you pass out soon enough.' Holding his gaze, she strokes her neck.

'I'm not up to it. Go back to sleep.'

She glares at him. 'Look, Morrie. I can't be arsed with games. Let's be honest about this. I might be using you, but you're using me right back.'

He gets a glass of water and sits down at the table.

'Well you're much better, and that's my doing.' She folds her arms. 'If you're not going to fuck me, at least show me what you've hid in that drawer, otherwise you've woke me for no good reason.'

'It's one of Danu's drawings.'

'Bloody always bloody Danu.'

He speaks softly, 'Aye, it is. Sorry.'

She plumps up the pillow and lies facing away from him. 'No, you're not. But do me one favour.'

'What?'

'Tell Tomas *and* Mario I'm good in the sack.'

'All right, I will.' Morrie smiles, knowing he won't.

'Blow out the candle and don't wake me again. Beauty needs sleep.'

Since the girl has shown no sign of interfering with number nineteen's relics or attempting any evictions of the woman's possessions, number nineteen has kept its own atmosphere to itself. The girl appears to have abandoned the idea of forcing it to change. Her attempts at yellow curtains lie in ripped heaps on two of its kitchen chairs. She'd got all the measurements wrong, and couldn't work out what to do with curtain hooks. She let the paint brushes go hard in its sink, and only managed to paint half of its hallway walls.

Because of this laziness or hopelessness, number nineteen has decided the girl is benign. It remains intrigued by her, because through her presence it is learning about human atmospheres.

The girl places a postcard on the floorboards. She wraps herself in a shawl, lights a candle and sits cross-legged on the floor as she watches the flame.

Her waves rise, flooding out of her.

Speaking in a low voice, she says, 'You just vanished. Most people say the dead aren't gone: they live on in our hearts, love is stronger than death. Many people continue to talk to the dead, in temples and churches, in gardens, or in their imaginations. But what no one says is this: the dead don't talk back.

'If you would only speak, even once, even a word with no meaning . . . I could believe you still exist in some form. Speak. I've been listening for you for all this time. I still am.'

She covers her eyelids with her palms.

After a long time she whispers, 'So you can't, then. Even if I show you this picture?' Reaching for the postcard, she holds it up. 'It's me, isn't it? Can you still not speak, even if I tell you that the artist's name is printed on the back? Judith Crown. Portrait in Blue number 39. You know who she is. You know I've never met her.'

Silence.

'How would she know what I look like, to have painted me? Is she psychic? Is this something to do with the ether?'

Silence.

'So you can't reply. Or won't. What about you, Morrie? You could have told me about the ether. Help me to understand. Speak now. I'm listening with not only my ears, but my whole body.'

Eventually, her shoulders slump and she removes her hands from her eyes. As she cries, her atmosphere fills the attic and she's lost in deep currents.

Though she's clearly trying to summon the dead, there have never been any ghosts around her. Ghosts are different to human atmospheres. They are confused things, which spread coldness. Number nineteen has only ever witnessed one ghost – a man who once wandered in through an adjoining wall and stood freezing the air in the living room. He stamped his feet, spreading ice through floorboards. His glassy eyes looked around as they assessed where he was. As he moved into the downstairs hallway and passed away into the house next door, a few bricks froze and cracked. While terraced houses have entirely different atmospheres to each other, and often don't even like one another, their layouts are similar. To the newly dead, who no longer value the purpose of doors, this must be confusing.

Number nineteen used to creak and groan after the woman who loved it left, trying to call her back. It missed her atmosphere, which was made of white textured fabric which changed shape. When she was playing with her child, the atmosphere was shaped as small doilies which dotted the floor like snowflakes. Sometimes it was wrapped all around her like a lace wedding dress which throttled her. At other times it lay over her as she slept, as a shroud. Whenever she was happy, it puffed up and danced around her as a ballgown, even when her body was still.

In number nineteen's attic, the girl's waves wash and lap around her legs. As her tears cease, she sits there, staring at nothing.

Above her, an atmosphere of pale fireflies appears. These fireflies visit her most nights. Tonight, they form a flickering swarm, before they drop and circle her face. They hover for a few moments, and drift away through a hole in the roof. In between doing other far more important things, they're flitting in to check the girl is still breathing.

Number nineteen is certain the waves belong to the girl, as

her emotions so clearly affect their movements, currents and depth. People's atmospheres must be formed entirely from their straying emotions. But what do waves mean? The girl talks to the dead and the waves rise. When she cries, she is underwater. She must be in danger of drowning in grief.

So if people's atmospheres are made from stray emotions, the atmospheres that have visited the girl must have escaped from other people. These could be people who are looking for her, or merely thinking of her. From observing the atmospheres which have been present around the girl, number nineteen has ascertained:

The atmosphere which grabbed her was from someone who wants to possess the girl.

The atmosphere of fireflies is from someone who drifts in to check she is all right, night after night, never staying for long.

And there's been a new one, recently.

A third atmosphere.

As the girl gets ready for bed, she sings a sad tune to herself. As she sings, number nineteen's floorboards sigh, remembering the footfall of the woman it loved, so long, long ago.

The girl's waves spread in ripples across the floorboards, rushing from her, breaking at the base of the wardrobe, drawing back to her. The girl tries to change the tune to something happier but returns to minor notes. Her voice echoes in the stairway even after she stops singing.

She unties and reties the laces around her bruise-striped ankles, pulling them tight, snapping strands, tying extra knots to hold them in place.

When she lies down, her waves subside and lap gently in a pool under the sofa.

After she's been asleep for a while, the newest atmosphere appears again.

This third atmosphere is in the shape of a smaller, brighter version of the girl. Its edges are golden and blurred. It sits on top of the wardrobe, watching the girl from a distance. After a while, it changes into the shape of a small sun and floods light. The girl is still asleep but she rolls onto her back and pushes her blanket away from her shoulders as sunrays spread towards her, as if part of her feels warmth.

People are thinking about this girl. She's deeply loved, even if the people these atmospheres belong to are far away.

The girl has served her purpose – through her presence, number nineteen has gained a deeper understanding of human atmospheres. Number nineteen always wanted the woman who loved it to return, in any form. It is deeply hurt that the woman's atmosphere never, not even for a moment, visited it during her lifespan.

She just didn't love it enough.

One of its rafters creaks.

A doorframe drops seventeen splinters.

A crack opens deep in its foundations.

And she has never sent her ghost to haunt it.

Its cellar's dry rot mingles with wet rot.

A seam splits in one of the basement stairs.

Its woodlice scatter as if a small earthquake has juddered them out of place.

Number nineteen would have loved to have been a haunted house, but never was.

It needs to ensure its deep cracks don't fully break. It will sink into itself and ponder the sad changes within its own atmosphere. This girl is as transient as a fly. Time, when houses retreat into themselves, passes rapidly for houses but slowly for the occupants.

The house sighs its goodbye to the girl with a whisper of fading atmosphere: *from the home I could never be.*

* * *

Something bites Morrie's shoulder. He lashes out and sits up in bed.

Loretta jerks away from him. 'What's wrong?'

He rubs his shoulder. 'Do you have to bite me awake?'

'I thought you *were* awake!' She swings her legs out of bed and stands up. 'The bloody moment's gone.'

He tries to smile. 'Was there a moment? I must've slept through it.'

She gathers her clothes up and gets dressed. 'You bastard.' As she shoves her feet into her shoes, she scowls at him.

He says, 'What?'

'I'm off back to my own caravan.'

Was he meant to know this, or has she only just decided? She's waiting for an answer but he's not got one she'll like.

Shaking her head, she says, 'Thanks, Loretta, for taking care of me, for keeping me company, for fucking me. You're welcome, Morrie.'

Before he can reply, she says, 'Don't bloody bother if it doesn't come natural.' She storms over to his drawers, and takes out Danu's drawing. Holding it out, she says, 'I can't bloody compete with the ice queen, can I? Best thing she ever did, leaving you. Now she's frozen perfect in your head.'

He says, 'Put that down.'

She eyes him as she tears it in half and drops it on the table. She gets a carrier bag from under the sink and grabs her washbag, curses as she drops her hairbrush, picks up her nightie and bundles all her things into the bag.

When she finally looks at him again, he says, 'Thanks for everything you've done while I've been sick. And I do mean that.'

From the look on her face, this isn't enough gratitude. She says, 'You're not going to stop me going, then? Do I mean so little?'

'No. You can do whatever you want.'

'Bastard.' She grips her possessions to her chest as she unbolts the door. She says, 'I'll bloody get revenge. You've hurt me without thought.'

As the door slams behind her, Morrie leans back and exhales.

She's right. He doesn't think she's hurt, so if she is, he *has* done so without thought.

He gets dressed, strips the bed and opens a window to let the storm out, and the air in.

Sitting at the table, he tapes Danu's drawing back together.

One of the black and white faces looks so like Danu's it makes him heartsore. The other is a distorted version of the same face, as if she'd drawn one face with her right hand, and the other with the left. If the left-handed face was a real person, what a sight it would be. Especially with that fish-like body. She'd be a sideshow. There's something disturbing about the two faces. Something about how similar they are, and how different. He folds the picture in half and slips it into a box under his bed.

That night, Morrie prepares himself to travel the ether by sitting quiet and clearing his mind. But it's hard to be still, for his body keeps distracting him. First he's interrupted by thirst, then by hunger and then by the need to piss.

Even when he's dealt with all the demands of his body, his mind won't settle. Tonight he's no more than a body with its spirit trapped in the blood, trapped in the bones. It's as if he's never travelled the ether before. He sits still for a long time, but his mind flits to Mag's poisoning, to Loretta's anger, to his own confusion about all that's happened since Danu left him. He can't see a bright line, or a corridor, he can't even picture Danu's face.

And there's a strange feeling to his body, like threads tightening over his skin. He looks at his arms, but there's nothing there.

Someone's interfering.

He knows a little of witching from his mother. She was open as a palm to him – if she was making a smoke-flavoured brew or a bitter chutney to give someone trouble, if she was hell-bent on making one person love another, or breaking two people apart, she'd do it all in front of him, usually at the table. In between drying the dishes and putting them away, she'd laugh to herself as some bugger who'd annoyed her limped past the caravan window with a sudden gout.

Many folks often had a sudden gout, when his mother was in a prickled mood.

There's a feeling all around him that something's holding him in place, just when he's finally free of Loretta.

He tries to feel the air around him. Particles and movement. Shift and free himself . . .

But he's bound, spirit to body.

It can only be Mag who's done this to him. She must know he's well again now. Witch.

But he's got to be able to travel the ether. If Danu's fallen deep into someone else's bed, he wants to know. If she's surrounded by twittering flatties, he wants to know. If she's dancing like a devil each night in the arms of many, he wants to know. He thuds his fist to the table, closes his eyes again and wills himself to see beyond his own eyelids.

He feels bindings wound around his head like bandages. They're stopping his spirit moving away from his flesh-and-bone body, for he can't get beyond it. He'd send curses up to the rainclouds if he thought Mag would catch his frustration and just set him loose.

Blocker. Poisoner. Binder.

Morrie once saw his mother bind a poppet with string – head to foot, and that must be what Mag's done to him. Who teaches

265

women to be witches, and why don't men demand to know it as well? But he'd never trust a woman who promised to teach him to hex. He'd think they had their own interests at heart, and were tricking him to be under their control. Perhaps if he wasn't so untrusting of women's witching clouts, he'd have something of his own to bargain with. But he knows too little to hex Mag in return for this binding.

He recalls his mother's words in a half-heard memory. *Bind you from harming yourself. Bind you from harming others.* There should be some rule against binding the kin of another witch. But with witching, every woman's loyal to her own self, and her enemies can be kin, friend or rival.

Mag will have some poppet hid in her caravan. She'll have made it with a hair from his head. A nail clipping. A scraping from his skin. Bloody thief. She'll have taken something from his body when she poisoned him.

He'll have to make Mag unbind the poppet. He'll charm her with good intentions. And if that doesn't work, he'll charm her with meekness. Tell her he's good now, and bow in subservience as if she's some octogenarian minx with a cat-o'-nine-tails. But even with the sickness she's caused him, even with this binding spell, he admires her devotion to Danu. It's a shame Danu never knew how well Mag protects her. Happen Mag never spoke of it, or Danu never felt it enough.

He closes his eyes again, and tries one final time to travel the ether.

Think of Danu.

Flickers of light. No more than glitter.

Where is she?

Darkness.

There's nothing to feel but ropes, threads, rags, whatever substance Mag's wound tight around the poppet's eyes.

He's angry with Mag, too angry to bloody bow or plead. He wants to take off now, just to get away from her. But if he harnessed Inferno and left without Mag's blessing, she could easily smack a stone to the poppet's hip and give Morrie a throbbing ache. She could tie the poppet's wrists so Morrie couldn't use his hands to hold the reins. She could give him a pain in the head that's needle sharp and blinding.

Just as Mag's bound his spirit, she could make it bloody hard for his flesh-and-bone body to go anywhere. He's got to win back her trust, or steal the poppet she's made in his image and unbind it himself.

There's a rundown area in the second circle in which the markets and shops sell everything off cheaply for a period of one month. This is known as 'the Rummage'. It's mid-morning, and Danu advances from a graffiti wall she's been leaning against. Street sellers try to persuade her that the objects that will enhance her life can be easily obtained: ants trapped in clear resin, belly-dancing chains, leather bags with haphazard letters printed on their labels.

But she's not here to buy life-enhancing things. Since she was given the postcard of the painting by Judith Crown, she's been deeply confused. Somehow Judith's original painting and the postcard reproduction found their way out of the Inner Circle and into a second circle gallery. And since talking to the little girl at the gate, she now knows that Judith still lives at the same address, so why was her letter returned?

Danu's mind races, jumping from one possibility to another. Is her returned letter a rejection, or a mistake, or a denial of some kind? Is the painting a coincidence, a red herring, some strange distortion of reality? She's spent hours staring at the image on the postcard, as if there's some kind of clue in the brushstrokes. But it scares her. How can Judith Crown possibly know what she looks like? Could it be some kind of dark magic that's performed in the Inner Circle, or is Judith Crown someone she's already met? Someone who's secretly escaped the Inner Circle and been close enough to Danu to memorise her face? Or could an artist get this close a likeness from seeing a sly photograph?

She draws the postcard from her bag and looks at it again. In the image, Danu is seated in a comfortable chair, reading a book beside a tall bookshelf. Her body is painted slightly smaller than it should be, but the face is strikingly similar. Brushstrokes suggest titles on the spines of hardback books, but there are no words. Pale blues form the skin tones, and the eyes are focused and deep. Midnight blue coils make her hair. She's wearing a simple dress and buckled shoes. But there's no locket around her neck. No bootlaces around her bare ankles.

If Danu hunts through every street in the second circle, night and day, what might she find?

She turns the postcard over. The date of the painting is three years ago.

Long before Danu was ever in Matryoshka.

Nothing makes sense about this. Putting the postcard back in her bag, Danu tries to consider what to do next. Her mind brims with questions. As her painting was displayed in a gallery in the second circle, Judith Crown must surely have been here at some point. Should Danu be looking through the stalls of the Rummage for thrown-away clues: an object, old letters, or a locket which matches her mother's? Perhaps she will find a copy of another painting by Judith Crown.

She might be looking for something that's too hidden to be found.

The Rummage is halfway through its month, and queues stripe

the streets of this area. Some people have slept overnight on rubbish-strewn pavements outside the gridded doors of the indoor markets. Visitors have come in flocks from afar, and several of them wheel empty barrows which they clearly intend to pile high with the items they purchase.

Danu goes into the middle of one of the main market streets. It's been cordoned off with lines of flickering bunting, presumably to avoid adding delivery wagons into the throng. Overhead, electricity wires make a web of the sky. All along the street, people are crammed shoulder to shoulder around rows of trestle tables overloaded with jumbles of household goods.

Shuffling forward along a row of trestle tables, the people in front of her pick up carved figurines. They turn them over and over in their hands, examining each cut in the wood, the curve of the lines, the craftsperson's stamp in the base. There is a delicate figurine of a tawny owl perched on top of a pile of boxes; a carving in rosewood.

Wisdom is the plight of owls. The carving is a good one, created by a skilled pair of hands.

Perhaps today, Danu needs a talisman rather than a clue. She's had many bad dreams lately. Magpies with drops of blood hidden under their tongues. Each night they increase in number, as if stalking her. An owl could be a wise guardian, to watch over her and chase them from her dreams.

Danu tries to reach for the figurine, but the broad back of the man in front of her isn't yet moving forward. She stares at the owl, thinking about moving some of the dust-cloaked vases off the mantelpiece in the front room at Wringers Street. She could throw away the dead flowers and place the owl in the middle, pride of place. She'd look after it, clean it regularly, so the grain in the wood continued to glow. She'd move the sagging sofa to face it. The streetlights from outside would reflect watery shadows across its grained surface. Perhaps she might sleep better in that room than the attic.

But someone else's hand reaches towards the owl. Their bangled wrist rattles as they pick it up. Danu watches for the hand to return the owl to its empty perch.

The same hand reaches in, a blue note between finger and thumb. The spectacled seller shakes her head. She wants change. None comes. She takes the note, reaches into a coin belt, muttering. She clinks coins into the waiting hand.

The owl has been sold.

Bereft, Danu focuses on the next stall. There's a display of mobiles made from beads, bones and feathers.

Danu glances back at the figurines as the queue inches forward. The owl has reappeared. As soon as she's near enough to reach, she picks it up.

The seller holds out a hand for money.

About to take her coin purse from her bag, Danu stops. She leans towards the seller, indicating the owl. 'Did she not want it after all?'

'Did who not want it, missy?'

'I thought you'd sold it.'

'No, look!' The seller reaches under the table and extracts a box of identical rosewood owls. 'Got plenty more. So you're lucky, eh? I'll do you three for the price of two?'

Danu replies, 'What would I do with three whole owls?'

The seller looks baffled.

Danu changes her question. 'Why would the carver make so many of the same thing?'

'These aren't from a Matryoshkan carver. You'll have to fork out a lot more for them as they want their time paid by the hour. A woman from the mountains made these owls. She brings me a stack of carvings each year. You want pricey local carvings,

270

you'll have to go three streets along. But these,' she indicates the owl, 'are as good. My supplier doesn't mind making the same thing over and over, if that's what I'll buy. Last summer, everyone wanted her owls. By winter they didn't want them no more. For next summer, and I've wrote and told her, she'd better be bringing me tigers.'

The owl doesn't look wise any more. Danu places it back on the table.

Danu climbs a staircase to the second circle at night time. The circle has moved around, and she emerges from the staircase in an area she's unfamiliar with. The buildings are five storeys tall. Stone stains itself over time, clothing itself in patterns of damp.

She looks through the windows of a large wine bar and watches groups of people talking and laughing together. In the second circle, ready-made groups of friends go to bars. Families and couples go to theatres and restaurants. Where would artists go at night time? Someone in the same profession as Judith Crown may know her. They don't have uniforms, so how does anyone recognise them?

As Danu walks along the main street, she looks through restaurant windows. The eateries speak of refined and expensive tastes. Bubbles fizz in tall glasses and long-stemmed flowers adorn candlelit tables. Smartly dressed couples dine together, and she imagines proposals, sharp diamond rings, anniversary celebrations. She reads the menus of many restaurants she can't afford to eat in. Trojan Badger has a small menu, mainly formed of black and white foods. A few doors away, Epicurean Minotaur serves only steak and ribs. In the next street along, the expansive menu of Cyclopsia's Culinary Delights includes a starter of eyeball soup.

On many street corners, there are beggars. They wear their

personal tragedies on cardboard signs hung around their necks like albatrosses:

Left husband's violence – no home.
Child died, wife sick – please help.
Lost everything when marriage ended. Including tongue.

Danu doesn't know if these words are true or not. All the same, she parts with a few coins because the bravery it must take to ask strangers for money must surely be worth something. She asks one of the beggars where he's from.

He replies, 'I live in the outer circle. But I lost my job three months ago and I've not found another. I'm half starved and my flat's falling down around me.'

'Why do you beg in the second circle?'

'There's too much competition between the beggars down there. We get into fights for territories. But that said, poorer people part with more coins than rich folks do. And at least we get spoken to in the outer circle. Most folks here won't meet my eye. I'm still thinking . . . where's best . . .'

'Is there a place in the second circle where artists gather?'

He shrugs. 'It's probably too expensive. All the artists I've met have less money than I do.'

Most of the beggars are outside the shopping malls. Bright-lit windows display sparkling buttons and gold baubles, but don't show the prices of these treasures. There's a large store called Little Bo, Peeps. It only sells silk lingerie.

In the second circle, rich people are extremely rich. Poor people are extremely poor.

Danu can almost feel the motion of the pavement between her, and is sure it's moving faster – as she's never felt it before. She goes back to where she thinks the staircase should be, but there's a row of office buildings. The top of the staircase must be blocked by a wall again.

It's a long walk to get round to another staircase and back to Wringers Street. She's thirsty and tired. Going into a small restaurant, Danu asks the waiter if she might buy a hot chocolate but no meal. He reluctantly nods and disappears behind the counter. Steam shrieks from a small machine.

Amid crowded tables, Danu seats herself at the smallest, which has only one chair. A sugar bowl and a clutch of paper napkins are arranged on the table. She unfolds a napkin and writes on it:

Dear Morrie,
I don't know what I'm doing.
I'm searching for something I can't find.
Danu

It's a clear-skied night as Morrie approaches Mag and Sandy's caravan. The windows are dark but the curtains are open. They're probably at the campfire with the others. Their door is padlocked. This must mean the poppet's in there somewhere – Mag's not carrying it on her person.

A chicken and mushroom stew's being eaten at the campfire as he wanders towards the centre of the field. The circus has finally camped up for a few weeks in one place, so most folks have gathered together to eat, though a few have already gone off to bed.

There's light falling across thick grass from caravan windows. A fiddle's playing. It's Tomas, wandering along the fence, playing a slow tune he learned from a flattie girl who came by when they arrived here several hours ago. Morrie had hung out his washing, and was keeping an eye out for rain. Each time he looked out of his window, Tomas was still talking with her. As

Morrie went outside to bring his laundry in, she'd got a flute out of her schoolbag and was playing a sweet tune over and over again. She's not long gone home. She was too young for Tomas, but she's left him with a sad song for his strings all the same.

Mag's on the other side of the campfire. Seen through smoke, she's part of the fire. Taking a deep breath, Morrie walks around the edge of the gathering. He sets himself down in the damp grass beside her.

He waits, wanting her to speak first so she thinks she's got the upper hand. There's a thick mood between them, and he can't tell if it's his anger towards her, or hers towards him.

Everyone else is talking quiet to whoever's next to them. Hattie glances at Morrie, and looks away like she's not seen him. Come to think of it, no one is looking at him, and this is the first time in ages he's been outside with them all. Then again, it's been a long day on the road and everyone's buggered with exhaustion. Morrie will be back on the wire when the show opens tomorrow night, after being stuck too long on the ground.

Mag scans his face as she says, 'What've you to say for yourself, then?'

Morrie looks up at the stars. 'What have I to do, to make you trust me?'

Loretta comes out of her caravan and approaches the campfire.

Mag says, 'This isn't the time to talk of trust.'

Loretta flushes as she sees Morrie, and halts as if about to turn around and go back inside again. Mario calls her name and holds his hand out, wanting his palm read. She walks to him slowly and sits down.

Mag says quietly, 'Loretta's been talking rough about you.'

Morrie says, 'Well, she's no reason to.'

Mag stares into the fire as she speaks softly. 'Flames ignite, they burn bright, and in all the wrong colours if they're burning anything poisonous. But they eventually go out.'

Morrie presses her: 'No part of me would ever harm Danu. I've only ever wanted to take care of her—'

Mag says firmly, 'We'll not speak of Danu now.' He waits for her to say more, but she picks up a twig and leans forward. She rakes lines in the ashes at the edge of the fire in the shape of a bird's footprint. It's some rune symbol, but he's unsure of the meaning.

He should speak something that'll win her over, but what words will say enough, not too much? She's got too much power over him already.

Mag turns away from him. Sandy's sitting in the shadows beside her, engrossed in a book. He's holding it at an angle so the firelight falls on the page. She cranes over his shoulder and asks, 'What're you reading?'

He rests the book on his knee. 'It's about volcanoes. I was thinking of Danu – wondering if she'd get warning—' Noticing Morrie's there, he changes the subject. 'Ah, it's nothing. You all right then, Morrie?'

'I've been better.'

On the other side of the fire, Tomas's fiddle is being plucked at by one of the clowns. Loretta's moved away from Mario and is sitting next to Tomas. Clasping a mug to her chest, she leans against his shoulder. She's whispering to him.

Tomas looks over at Morrie. There's anger in his face, which isn't like him. He puts an arm round Loretta, and drops his gaze. He's frowning, uncertain of something.

Morrie leans towards Mag and says softly, 'What's Loretta said?'

Mag's jaw tenses as her eyes fall on Loretta and Tomas.

'Oh, bugger it,' she says, pushing herself upright. 'We need to talk. Come on.'

How often does a man go pale when any woman says *we need to talk*? Morrie gets to his feet and stretches, taking his time, making sure Mag thinks he's untroubled.

As they get to the door of Mag's caravan, she draws a key from her pocket and unlocks the padlock, catching his eye as she does it. He follows her inside.

She lights an oil lamp on the table, opens a bottle of red wine and pours them both a glass. She tells him to sit down.

He takes the chair opposite the one she's gripping and looks up at her. She's bursting to say something or other, but hesitating.

He'll get in there first now he's finally got her ear. He says, 'Mag, I'm torn. Half of me's mad as hell with you, and half of me feels bloody swaddled. Which is it? Are you set on harming, or mothering me? Because whichever one it is, I'm done in from it. If that's what you wanted, it's worked.'

She sits down and takes a slug of wine from her glass. 'Are you finished talking yet?'

He snaps too harsh at her. 'No.'

She sighs. 'Well get on with it, then.'

He tells her why she can trust him:

He tells her about how many times he wanted Danu but didn't ever try to push her.

He says he wants to see Danu laughing like she means it. The kind of laugh that creases lines round her eyes.

He tells her that he loves the way Danu thinks – her kindness towards him and all the lovesick creatures she carries in her head.

He tells Mag that he feels like a wrong thing, without Danu at his side.

He says he knows Mag's got him under a binding hex.

He asks her to let him go.

Leaning on the table, Mag says, 'Are you finished talking *now*, then?'

'Aye,' he says. 'I am.'

'I know you'd never hurt Danu deliberately. And I know you love her.'

Morrie exhales with relief.

Mag says, 'Well, drink up.' She nods at his glass. 'You're going to need it.'

He smiles. 'Poisoned it, have you?'

She raises her eyebrows. 'You *saw* me open a new bottle.'

He takes a gulp. 'So then,' he says. 'Talk back.'

She pauses. 'Right. First thing. *I've* not hexed you.'

He looks at her face for the traces of a lie, but can't find them. He says, 'So why're you locking your door, if you're not hiding some poppet?'

'Because Sandy's got cash hid in a shoebox and I only found it recent. He claims he's been collecting it for years but I don't feel safe now I know it's there. Some of it's Danu's wages he'd saved for her. But that's by the by. I might have blocked you on the ether, and aye, I did poison you to get you to be still for a time and come to your senses, but I've not hexed you.'

'So who has?'

She looks at him as if he's stupid. 'Who've you upset of late, Morrie?'

'Only Loretta.'

Silence.

Morrie raises his eyes to the ceiling. 'Loretta.'

'Well, then.'

He exhales with frustration. 'So she's hexed me, and now I've got to talk *her* round? Mag. You'd have been easier.'

'You need to hear this.' She nods at his glass. 'Drink up.'

He laughs. 'What do I need a dram to hear?'

She doesn't laugh.

He drinks half his glass down and she tops it up quick.

She says, 'There's no easy way. So I'll just say it. Loretta told me that you can't take no for an answer. She's saying you took advantage.'

Morrie freezes, glass half raised to his lips.

Mag continues, 'Now, she's not said *that* word yet, but if you rile her more than you already have, she might. I once spoke out against a man who'd hurt me more than I can talk of. I'll never speak that word again, as not one single person believed me. I was seventeen but I was no liar.' As she says this, she's got the eyes of a trapped rabbit that knows it's about to be clubbed.

Morrie reaches to take her hand but she's startled by it and snatches her hand away. 'Sorry,' she whispers. 'I can't talk of this well.'

Morrie's voice chokes out of him. 'I'd never hurt a woman.'

She looks at the floor. 'Aye. I know she's lying.'

He exhales. 'You're so certain, and I'm glad of it. But how do you tell a liar?'

'When she spoke to me earlier, I couldn't reply. I just grabbed her and held her and her body was a tense thing. What little she said reminded me too much of my own hurt. But then I took a deep breath and set my feelings aside. I lifted her chin, and looked in her eyes.'

'And what did you see?'

'Nothing.'

Morrie shakes his head, not understanding what this means.

Her voice is strained thin as she says, 'I know she was lying because I saw *nothing*. When you've been hurt deep yourself, you understand hurt in others. I've known many folks be silent from the shame of something that's been done to them which was never their fault. Even when they don't speak of it, I can always see it. Especially in other women.'

She stares at the ceiling. 'Loretta probably thinks I believed her. But if she says more, or talk spreads, if I have to . . .' She shakes her head. 'The only reason I didn't call her a liar there and then is because what if she'd pushed me and I'd blurted out talk of what happened to me? I don't trust her to keep anyone's secrets, and talking about my own does me in. I'm sorry I didn't shut her up straight away, Morrie. But I couldn't.'

He says gently, 'I'm just glad you believe me.'

'When folks lie about men's crimes, they tear holes in those of us who never spoke, or who did speak and were never listened to.' She looks closely at him. 'When violence is kept secret, it never goes away. It's like a poison – an illness of the heart.'

Her eyes glaze as she scratches the back of one of her hands and keeps scratching, not noticing the red marks, rising.

Morrie touches her fingers to stop her. 'I'm so sorry.'

Mag's quiet now, staring at nothing Morrie can see. She's tunnelled into herself and there's no way out.

After a while, Morrie tries to bring her back. He says, 'I have to talk to Loretta.'

Mag shakes herself and looks directly at him. Her voice is a stone. 'Don't you go near her. If she's riled, anything could come out of her gob.'

His knuckles are white. 'I don't understand why she'd say what she has.'

'Did you sleep with her?'

He looks at the floor. 'Aye. I did, and there's nothing can undo that. I wasn't thinking right.'

Mag shakes her head. 'And she knows that despite her *charms*, you're in love with Danu?'

'I can't lie to anyone about how I feel for Danu.'

'Well you're a bloody fool not to have done. Loretta's wanted you a long time and her seeing herself as a woman scorned was always going to get dirty.'

Morrie wants to curse with anger. 'She's not scorned. She'll be bedding someone else soon enough – she even asked me to tell—'

'That's what she *wants* you to think, Morrie. But no matter what she said to save her pride, right now she wants drama. Sympathy.'

He lowers his voice. 'I'll not call her a liar in front of all the others – but I'll not be accused—'

Mag says, 'She's predictable. So *think*, Morrie. If you go out to that campfire right now, she'll act fearful of you. She'll mouth off in front of everyone and say whatever comes into her head. Your name'll be blackened.'

'But they must know I'd never—'

'You know I check on how everyone's doing all the time?'

'Aye.'

'I *have* to do that. It's because no one was looking out for me when I most needed it. The circus was different back then. Times were different. These are good people, Morrie. So they'll look out for her first and ask questions later. You'd be the same.'

'Hattie wouldn't look at me tonight, and there's Tomas. I should talk to them.'

Mag gives him a stern look, and sits up straight. 'Now, stop this. You're going to finish this bottle with me,' she tops up their glasses, 'and head quietly off to your bed.'

'And then what?'

'You let *me* decide the best way to deal with this. Loretta's not watching me, but your molehills are her volcanoes. If she's talked to anyone besides me, I can have quiet words in ears.'

Morrie shakes his head. 'I can't believe she'd speak of me like this.'

'Aye. Well, I can, though it hurts me more than it's hurting you. Keep your feet on the ground.' She grips his arm as she says, 'And don't suddenly disappear, as absence means guilt. Say *nothing*. Otherwise I might end up being the only friend you've got left.'

'Till tonight, I've thought you my enemy.'

She nudges his arm. 'Well, I'm the best enemy you've got. I'm watching your back, not stabbing it.'

Danu is trapped inside a nightmare.

In a hall of mirrors, she looks at the surface of the mirrors but not their reflections.

She finds a glass door, and opens it. She steps through.

Thick smoke, red, turning to brown. She thins it, makes it disperse.

There's a desolate landscape. Carcasses of trees, burnt stumps in a bleached wilderness. The smell of dampened flames. She runs, cutting her feet on stones, blackening her ankles in charcoal. She's hunting in this wasteland. She stops running and crouches. She parts charcoal rushes with greying hands, seeking small things, anything living beneath the scorched vegetation which reaches to the horizon. She finds a burnt feather, a charred seedpod, an apple baked black.

Everything is still.

And now there is sound. Crunching. Splintering.

She scans the flat horizon.

Crunch. Crack.

Somewhere, something is moving.

Crack. Smash.

Nearby.

She steps through sharp rushes towards a lump of charcoal which was once the trunk of a tree. It's hollow inside.

Crunch. Crack.

The sounds come from within it. She lies on her belly like a snake.

Inside the trunk, surrounded by broken eggshells, are two white birds. They're breaking, cracking, crunching a hoard of bones. Their beaks are the bills of ducks but inside, there are rows of sharp teeth.

White birds with white teeth eating white bones.

She whispers, 'Bone-eaters,' and the birds ignore her. Crunch crack. Crack crunch.

What will they do, if they see her?

They won't see her. They have white-clouded eyes. Blind things eating dead things.

They're eating larger bone versions of themselves.

The bone-eaters are two skeletal chicks, emerged murderous from their shells.

From an upstairs window, Danu looks down into Wringers Street. Details become illuminated as she focuses on one object at a time. A scratched front door, a patch of light on the cobblestones. The sky, layered with thickening clouds. A black lamp post with copper stains threaded through thick gloss paint.

Many years ago, Danu met an Anchoress, and she remembers her now. The Anchoress was a wise woman who'd lived in a mountain cave for many years. She was brittle-thin and limping. She'd walked barefoot from her mountain to the field where the circus had pitched up for the night. She'd followed the smell of their cooking pot because she wanted to taste what bubbled inside.

Danu was about nine years old. She gave the Anchoress a bowl of mutton and leek stew, and asked her, *Are you lonely?*

The Anchoress looked closely at Danu as she replied,

Loneliness is felt most painfully when you're beside others. Especially those who say they love you, but don't. People climb mountains to talk to people like me about their own particular kinds of loneliness. I've been listening for some time. And as for myself, as long as I'm still curious, I don't mind loneliness. I've deeply considered all the types of loneliness that there are, and invented some new words.

Danu remembers the excitement she felt on hearing that new words could be invented. Her mother had recently been teaching her grammar rules, and the lessons were dull.

The Anchoress clearly saw a spark in her, as she eyed Danu closely. She said, *I'll show you my words, if you get me a pen and paper.*

Under the shelter of a tree, the Anchoress ate her fill of stew, sitting cross-legged in the grass. Once she placed the bowl down, her creased hands wrote a list.

Danu still has the list all these years later, because she pressed it like a flower.

Ascending the stairs to the attic, Danu draws an old notebook from her bag. She extracts the age-stained piece of paper from between pages:

15 Words for Loneliness

Ignornly – *The kind of loneliness which other people comment on – as in 'I think he's lonely' and their expression shows sympathy, but also a little wariness, as if loneliness could be contagious.*

Youache – *Where a specific person is missed, and only their physical presence will cure the ache of missing them.*

Idealone – *A hankering for an imagined scenario – where it's the idea of the situation that causes the loneliness. For example, the 'ideal' of the perfect friend sitting opposite on the* sofa, laughing over wine and confessions and saying all the right things.

Disampty – Where the immediate environment is problematic – in practical ways. The rubbish spilt all over the floor, an employer is waiting, the clock is ticking, it's lashing with rain and there's no one else around to ask for help.

Lonmyth – The belief no one cares/is interested, without any effort to allow people to care or show they're interested.

Crowdsad – Felt while around many other people. Crying while walking along streets crammed with strangers, feeling unable to speak during a burbling conversation in which others are talking loudly and not leaving any gaps.

Solilone – A type of melancholia experienced while gazing at a wide-skied landscape. A longing for strangeness, for the unreal or the surreal to appear.

Xiley – The loneliness of ears: usually during unexpected silence. For example, when music ceases to play.

Feartrap – When alone, overactive fears producing images of other people becoming monstrous.

Despane – The loneliness of feeling misunderstood, unloved or unheard by someone who used to understand, love or listen.

Uncharm – When you realise no matter where you go, everywhere and everyone looks almost exactly the same.

Starn – Craving something or someone to be there but knowing it's/they're not. Wanting to bite something.

Priclash – Keeping emotions or secrets private while desperately wanting to let them out.

Upwrench – The rational side – loneliness needs to be felt and solitude is needed even if it's not always comfortable. Letting loneliness come, but giving it a time limit: not wallowing.

Yorch – The final kick before you're about to be reunited with the person/people who you've missed.

Danu read and re-read this list once the Anchoress had finished writing it. The Anchoress asked her if she'd ever felt one of these kinds of loneliness.

Danu remembers replying without thought, *I've got youache for a person who's like me.*

The Anchoress said, *And who could that be for someone so young, apart from a growing ache to become yourself?*

Danu replied, *I don't know.*

They sat in silence for some time, and then the Anchoress said, *I don't understand what you're feeling. I'm sorry. But keep the list if you like. Put it somewhere safe.*

She rose to her feet and limped back to the road, stumbled through a field, and climbed all the way back to her lonely mountain cave.

Danu re-reads the list again now, and she reads it as a warning. She doesn't want this city to become her own lonely mountain, and this house her own lonely cave.

She forces herself to think of good things: her job is secure and she is never without food, she is sometimes lonely but can survive without having close friends or horses to talk to. Will she ever find out why Judith Crown's name is in her mother's locket? Part of her still believes that here in Matryoshka, if she keeps searching she'll find the one thing that will tell her why she felt so fated to leave the circus and remain here.

Sometimes she feels as if it's close by. Watching her. Waiting for her to see it, but just out of sight.

She looks through her notebooks. Stories and lists are interrupted by sketches of skulls, flowers, faces and gnarled trees, animals and birds. She's drawn many human faces in her notebooks over the years. These were all from her imagination: she never drew real people. What if, like Judith Crown's painting, her own drawings are of people who exist elsewhere? Or people who are soon to die without leaving any reminder of themselves in the world?

Doubt creeps into her mind about fate, and the reason she's here. Perhaps it's not fate which has kept her here. Perhaps something else has lured her back to the place she was born in.

Birth and death are, after all, two sides of the same coin.

It must be the early hours of the morning but yet again Morrie's wakeful, staring into dark. He's done what Mag's asked of him, and not gone near Loretta, and he's stayed away from them all whenever they've gathered at the campfire.

If Mag's doing anything, she's not yet told him of it. When he's had moments of doubt in her, he's remembered the scared rabbit he saw in her eyes. No one could see her that raw, that truthful and afraid, and not believe what she says. When he can think blade-clear, he understands that a truthful woman might be the only person who could get a scorned woman to swallow any lies she's got squirming on her tongue.

There's no winning this game. There's just two choices: the playing, or the refusal to play.

So far he's refusing, though he can't bear that he's unable to speak. The worst thing is knowing Loretta's got a binding hex on him. He still can't travel the ether and whenever he takes the time to sit quiet and still, his skin's tight and pinched.

Aye, he's been bound by Loretta in all ways. Everything's gone wrong for him since Danu left. Much of that's his own fault, and if he could push back time and start again, he'd do many things different. That storm that was pushing against him as he left Danu behind in Matryoshka had the right idea. He should've taken courage from the gale, turned and let that storm drive him back to her then. That was Gianto's doing – getting in his ear and telling him just to take whatever The

Tower brought. He should never have trusted a card more than his own gut.

He's not been able to travel the ether for so long that during the darkest nights he can't quite believe Danu still exists. If she was here, he'd not have been such a fool as to sleep with Loretta. But sometimes his body remembers how real Loretta's body felt, and he thinks he made Danu up. Her mattress is still rolled up and belted in the corner. Aye, that's real enough. Under shadows, it looks like a bound body.

It's his love for Danu that makes him get out of bed each day, wash himself, eat well, and keep busy in any way he can. It's his love for Danu that makes him high for a few moments while he's walking the wire and the audience is cheering him on, but still, it's a high that dips away when the clapping is over and he realises it was only for him. And closing his curtains after the show's done with each night is a relief. Everyone's shut out, and he doesn't have to hold his head high any more. It's the hope that one day he'll be with Danu again that keeps him keeping on. Aye, though his body used to hunger for her when she first left, missing her is an ache that's spread. It's all through his spine, heart and guts. It's the night times it's the worst, when it whirrs in his brain, spinning strange tricks.

They've been apart too long.

What's she thinking, what's she feeling, is she joyous or angered or sad?

Dawn crawls in through the curtains and rain splutters against the roof.

He gets up and kicks his boots and costume out of the way so there's a space cleared on the floor. He unfastens the two belts on Danu's mattress. Laying it down, it curls at the edges. He lies face down, making an imprint of his body where her body once slept.

* * *

Someone's knocking, hand to wood.

Morrie wakes and lifts his head. He's freezing cold, waking on Danu's mattress in the whirl of a draught. Was she this cold, sleeping here? The knock comes again, and the handle rattles.

Mag's voice says, 'It's me, open up.'

He unbolts the door.

Cold air comes in as Mag leans on the doorframe and scrapes her muddy boots on the ledge.

Slinging his coat round his shoulders, Morrie says, 'What hour is it?'

She steps inside and shuts the door. 'Too early for anyone else to be risen. Put the kettle on and we'll talk. Oh, but first, here.' She rummages in the pocket of her cardigan and draws out a small fabric doll. 'You'll be needing to do something or other with that.' She hands it to him carefully and rubs her hands to warm them.

In the palm of his hand is a small doll stuffed with straw, bound head to feet with grubby yellow wool. Loretta's poppet. She's given it a hump in the upper back. 'It's foul,' he says, looking at its bound face. 'Do I unwind the wool and that's the hex undone? Or are there words needing said?'

Mag says, 'I don't bloody know.' Sighing, she strides over to his kettle and fills it. 'Where's your teabags, or will coffee wake your ears up faster?'

He stares at the poppet. Its arse is too curved and there's a bulge in its groin. Should he be looking inside the bindings for the part of it that came from his body? A hair, a nail clipping? He asks Mag, 'Have you got a magnifying glass?'

She clanks two mugs onto his table. 'You can deal with it later. She can't harm you with it if it's safe in your hands. So, put it away.'

He slips it into his coat pocket. 'How did you get it?'

As Mag rinses out mugs and finds his teabags, she says, 'She'd hid it under her pillow of all places. Been having trouble sleeping, have you?'

'Aye.'

'Well, her head's been flattening you. I slipped a little something in her wine last night. She'll not wake for another couple of hours. She'll be rested, though might have a clanging head.'

'And what's she been saying of me, Mag?'

She opens the fridge. 'No more than she already has, so you've done the right thing, keeping your gob shut. If she gets in the sack with some other bugger, that would be for the best. I've given a couple of the lads a nod in her direction. Where's your milk?' She leaves the fridge door open and gets a teaspoon.

He goes over to her. 'I'd have a blackened name if it weren't for you.' He rubs her thin shoulder.

'When she realises you've gone, she might kick off again, but I'll deal with it.'

He smiles. 'Where am I going?'

She nudges him away. 'That's what we're talking about! Milk?'

He gets the milk jug from the top shelf of the fridge. 'Are we? And where's that?'

'To Danu! I travelled the ether just after I stole that . . . thing . . . from Loretta.' It's thrown me off kilter. I've been fretting about Danu for a while. And now I'm far more than fretting. You've got to go to her, Morrie. Now. Food for the journey. For starters, I've got a box of veg you can take, and a bag of tatties. Oh, there's also a chicken . . .'

His hands are freezing. 'What's wrong with Danu?'

She pours water in their mugs and spoons three sugars into hers. Glancing around, she picks up the salt cellar and adds a pinch of salt. 'This'll sort me out.' She points the spoon at him.

'Go straight there. Sleep as little as you can. Don't use the ether – you'll need all your energy for the road.'

He says again, 'What's wrong with her?'

She pauses. 'There's a Double.'

A draught runs up his spine. 'What's a Double?'

'A mirror thing. It's been faint but it's growing stronger. I couldn't see it clearly at first, but when it shone bright enough, it looked like Danu but with a slightly different shape. Danu was asleep with her arms wrapped tight around herself. It was beside her. Watching. I don't know if it's a doppelgänger, or someone who's travelled to her on the ether and they're mimicking her, or if it's part of her own spirit that's fractured. If it's from her, she may be splitting away from herself, like some kind of breaking.' She rubs her heart. 'I can't make sense of it. But the ether shows what's true. And that's the feeling and the picture of it all.'

Morrie's nauseous, and can feel his face turning pale. If he could be blown to Matryoshka on the winds, he'd run outside now, spread his arms and holler up a gale to take him there.

Mag takes a slug of tea and continues talking. 'Danu's lost so much, and she's trying to keep strong. But when folks are too much alone, they start to see things they shouldn't. She could *sense* the Double even in her sleep. I saw her reach her hand towards it. What'll happen to her mind if she *sees* it?'

'What d'you think could happen?'

'It depends what it is. Doubles often look like demons or fearful things, to those they mirror. It's the mind's tricks and fears. Imagine seeing yourself, but it's not quite yourself.' She shivers. 'Folks are right to be afraid of doppelgängers. I don't know what her Double means. But believe me, it was there.'

Morrie stares at Danu's mattress, imagining her lying there, asleep, safe.

Mag's looking at him closely. 'She needs to know she's loved.'

He lowers his head and stares at nothing.

Mag's words cut through. 'Loved by you, and by us all. Sandy knows I'm telling you to go to her. He'll give you Danu's wages that he kept back, to help out with the journey. And he'll leave marks on the trees and posts by all the crossroads from here onwards to show you which way we've gone. Go and get her, Morrie. Bring her back to us.'

Danu's been having nightmares each night for the past few weeks. The most recent ones have been about bones and death and magpies. Her mind is thick with images she fears, but doesn't understand. Under daylight, she tries to be strengthened by the things all around her which are beautiful and alive. The curve of a bud under sunlight, the stray cat stalking a chaffinch along a brick wall. Her evenings are spent mimicking a white bird on the wire, but for so long her daylight hours have been spent looking for clues to a puzzle she can't solve. So many parts of it are missing that it might be broken beyond repair.

If anything could halt frantic nightmares, it should surely be stillness. Silence and beauty. But it's not working. They're getting worse every night.

One morning on waking, Danu writes a dream into her notebook:

I am made of magpies. They are far smaller than most other magpies. They flock in me, assembling me. They are my body. There are hundreds of them, fluttering and squalling wherever I walk. Days pass and nights flit over and I feel lonely that no one else can see the magpies. The magpies call Death towards me.

And so soon, she is here. Beside me, Death walks. She is an evil thing, a monster, a demon.

Death is ink black and terrible. Her heart is made from claws. Her eyes see more colours than ordinary eyes. She wears the sharp beak of a raven. She holds my hand and won't let it go. She passes through every person I brush past on these pavements, and yet pays them no heed, for she wants the heads of my magpies.

Death wears the skulls of birds as jewellery. Sometimes I hear these foul beads rattling beside me as she walks. Whenever she speaks, I close my ears to her words because a thousand flames dance in her mouth. But sometimes I want Death to execute all these magpies I am made from so I can eternally hang, bone-thin and rattling, from her delicate neck.

Writing a dream from her mind onto paper helps to evict it. But she should be braver, and do something which will force these nightmares to stop.

Death has been stalking her since her parents died.

She was ill with the same virus that killed them. Why was she spared?

All her heartbeats beat through borrowed time.

A starved magpie with bloodshot eyes. A ticking clock.

Half-dreaming again, she forces herself back into wakefulness. She needs to face her grief, and stop running from it.

EIGHT FOR HEAVEN

When waking from a nightmare about the sharpness of broken eggshells, everything real seems broken. The chipped cup Danu drinks coffee from, the rip in the rug, the cracks in the dirty windowpanes. Even the floorboards spike splinters into the soles of her feet.

She lets all these broken things drive her outside.

But the outside world is no less broken. The back wall drops a brick as she climbs it, the cobblestones at the end of the street shift under her feet, and the sky? The sky has cracked in fine shatters, but keeps its breakage a secret. Thickly glued clouds hide all the cracks.

Danu goes back up to the second circle. Today, she seeks nothing but her own bravery, and knows exactly where she will find it.

At the top of the staircase, the circles have moved yet again. She has arrived in an area lined with stern limestone buildings. People are dressed smartly, move purposefully, and disappear into offices. As she walks, the sky changes. It's peppered with flecks.

Danu's fingertips sweep along a ridged stone wall surrounding one of the primary schools. Children shriek behind it. A bell clangs, once, twice. A door creaks, children's voices chatter. A whistle sounds. The door slams.

Silence spreads along the school wall. Ridged stone. Bumps of time. Pairs of initials are carved inside love hearts. Danu reaches the school gate and looks through the gaps at the mosaic-tiled surface of the playground. These tiles are arranged in bright coloured triangles, with loose pieces scattered around the edges. She's seen a few school playgrounds in the second circle, decorated with these loose mosaic tiles which the children gather and rearrange. Some of the surfaces must have been repaired under the supervision of artistic teachers, as the tiles have been fixed back into all kinds of pictures: proud dragons merge into curling snakes, lions become stars, clocks glow like candles.

Turning away from the school, she follows her feet as they walk onwards.

Along the pavement, the next man who passes Danu is pale. Gaunt. Rushing.

She says to him, 'I'm looking for the hospital – is this the right direction?'

The word hospital halts him. He stabs the air with his finger in the direction she is already walking. 'Keep going – you've got the right direction. Look for three columns. Sorry, sorry! Got to . . .' He hurries away.

Today is the day she's finally ready to see the place she was born. To remember and honour her parents.

She buys an enormous bouquet of bright pink and white lilies from a flower shop, and continues towards the hospital. The scent of flowers is as thick as boiled sugar.

It isn't long till three columns appear on the other side of the main street.

Clutching the flowers to her chest, she turns to face the hospital.

She remains static, staring. This must be bravery, because there's fear within it.

The hospital is built from blocks of sandstone. The edges of the individual blocks have eroded, but the sunflowers carved beneath the windows retain their sharp lines. The main doors are made of sliding glass.

A magpie circles in the mist above the hospital roof.

Though the air is warm, Danu shivers as she wills the magpie to move on.

The clean windows catch the flickers of a white sun through grey clouds. Inside the windows, people in orange uniforms rush past. These must be the doctors, nurses, midwives and specialists who flit like butterflies as they care for the sick, the dying, the hypochondriacs, the newborns.

Her body is numb, she is made of eyes.

On the edge of the hospital roof, the magpie lands. It hops, flaps its wings, and pecks at something in the gutter.

The magpies which kept landing on the caravan roof while her parents were dying were harbingers of death.

There were three magpies, not two.

Two magpies took her parents.

One magpie left her behind.

She should have told that magpie to be as black as its shadow, and begged it to claw her away.

The magpie didn't want her.

Not then.

But all the nightmares she's been having make her think that Death will come back for her.

Today, it's up on the roof.

But Danu is not here to die. She is here to honour her parents. So she faces the place where they first held her in their arms. She imagines them talking softly to her, wrapping her in a blanket, looking into her newborn eyes.

Glancing down at the flowers in her hands, she considers

whether to leave them on the steps of the hospital. Could remembrance be as simple as this?

She bites her lip. She must do something more than laying lilies on steps.

On the hospital roof, the magpie is a statue.

Beside her on the pavement, a young woman pauses, rummages in her bag, and hands Danu a flier.

The woman's looking at her expectantly, as if she's just asked her a question.

But Danu shoves the flier in her pocket as her eyes are drawn back to the hospital doors.

She could go inside and see if there's some kind of temple in which sad people leave bright flowers.

A man goes in through the front doors, which close behind him. They slide open again as a woman steps outside, walks down the pristine marble steps, and away. It looks so easy for them to walk in and out of the door. Going inside and placing flowers in some temple or chapel room her parents never even went into can't possibly honour them. It might even remove them from the places they now live inside her mind. They're safe there within their own landscapes. Clem lights fires along the edges of a forest path. Adelaide sings an everlasting song into the night.

The young woman's gone, now.

Danu doesn't know which room, or which section of which maternity ward her parents would have been in. She can't touch anything they've touched. It will all have been disinfected.

Her hands shake as they grip the bouquet. The lily petals blur into fragments. She wipes tears away but there's pollen on her fingertips and everything is yellow and stinging.

She wants to walk away, but she has to do something with these flowers.

On the roof, the magpie squawks and hops. Gripping the flowers, Danu goes up the steps and the doors slide open.

Inside, she walks past the queue for the reception desk and along a corridor. She locates an elevator and pushes the button.

A loud ping, and the door opens. Inside, a man who doesn't appear old enough to be as sick as he looks sits in a wheelchair. Danu steps back as a woman wheels him awkwardly through the sliding doors and pauses to examine the brakes on the wheels. She clicks one with a foot and pushes him forwards a little to check the wheel is free. She grips the handles, but doesn't move him yet. She's barely breathing.

The woman has dark hair and red lips. Her skin is plaster-white. She says, 'It's too sudden, Dad.'

Her father smiles. 'It can be, sometimes.' His eyes are watery and green. There's a light in them that Danu recognises from her own parents, when their deaths were near. She doesn't want them to notice her, but can't look away.

The daughter says, 'I can't believe it. Did they say you've got weeks left, or months?'

'Weeks or days.'

'I thought someone mentioned months. The consultant. What was her name? I don't remember her name.'

Her father says, 'I'm not scared of dying. Does that help?'

Danu wants to hug him. Her own parents were so afraid.

Frowning, the daughter says, 'Yes . . . yes it does sort of help.'

The elevator doors close, and Danu quickly pushes the button to open them again. Too late, the elevator is already ascending. She steps back and waits.

The man in the wheelchair clasps his daughter's hand. He says, 'I'm going to have the time of my life. I want your siblings home too. We need to play some music, and there's a painting

297

I want to do. And I'll want to see my friends . . . and hug your mother a lot . . .'

'You're being incredible . . .' Her voice chokes and decreases in volume. 'So beautiful.'

He smiles. 'No one's described me as beautiful before. Listen. Love doesn't go away when someone dies.'

'I should be trying to reassure *you*.' She rubs her father's shoulder and they fall into silence as they look at each other. In this private moment, for them there is no hospital, no smell of antiseptic, no girl with perfumed lilies waiting to get into the elevator.

The man breaks the silence as he says, 'Get me home. Those tests were horrible – I need a bath.'

They move away towards the front doors of the hospital, and are gone.

It's heartbreaking to have overheard this conversation. The daughter won't easily be able to bear it when he dies, whether within weeks or days or hours.

The elevator door opens and a nurse wheels out a woman who's attached by tubes to a bleeping machine.

Danu steps in and pushes the top button. She blinks away tears as the elevator jerks and ascends.

On the top floor, a stairway leads up to a fire exit. The corridor is deserted. As Danu climbs the stairway, the elevator shrieks as it descends. She pushes open the fire door. Three escape ladders curve over the edges of the building. As Danu steps into the wind which ripples the puddles on the flat roof, she startles the magpie.

It flies away.

She advances to a low railing which spans the roof. Her hair is blown across her face as she calls after the magpie, 'Go, then. Take no one today!'

A petal blows off one of the white lilies and the wind carries it up.

She picks another white petal off and throws it. It flies on the wind and is gone.

A baby wails, somewhere below.

She throws another white petal.

In rooms beneath her feet, people are being born at the same time as people are dying.

She rips off another petal and watches it spiral away.

These clouds are a heaven she can't believe in.

But this is as close to heaven as she can reach.

First she remembers her mother: Adelaide often said to Danu, in the quiet moments they had together, *I didn't think I'd ever have a child of my own, but here you are. My gift from life.*

Before Danu was born, they'd tried to have a child for years. Nothing had happened so Adelaide read medical books in libraries and decided she was infertile. A result of a gland going wrong in her brain, she'd thought. She hated doctors, and the circus moved on so often, she had an excuse not to get herself looked at. She decided that some of her hormones flooded too much, but her ovaries didn't work properly and so other hormones didn't flood enough. She said to Danu, *How can you learn a vocabulary for things you never see? I came to think of my insides as being stormy. After all, I've seen more storms than ovaries.*

Adelaide often laughed when perhaps she really wanted to cry. She'd said, *The fast hormones swam through my veins and arteries. The slow hormones were locked in a stone gland in my brain. I believed I had a misguided ocean inside my body, sending my hormones this way and that. But then . . .*

Danu knew this story so well, she always joined in at this point. *You believed you'd never have a baby. So you gave up hope.*

Adelaide would say, *And the moment I gave up hope was the moment hope returned. And there you were. A treasured golden egg hidden at the bottom of the sea. I never saw a doctor in all that time of travelling roads and mountains with you inside me. And you grew so big till the time came for you to be fished out and I could—*

Danu would interrupt, *cuddle me forever and never let me be washed away.* This was always the moment between them which Danu loved best, where Adelaide squeezed her so tightly they'd be red-faced from hugging.

Her mother would say, *Only you. That's all I believed in, for nine whole months.*

Danu never quite believed this story, as the words were exactly the same each time it was told, as if it had been memorised. She liked hearing it all the same. She liked her mother's arms.

With yellow fingertips, Danu throws another white petal into the sky. And another and another till all the white lilies are stripped. She watches them spiral into distant grey clouds.

She separates a pink petal from a stem and throws it into the air as she remembers her father.

Clem often said his favourite thing in the world was to fly a kite with his daughter. When the circus was near any coastline, he'd wake Danu early in the morning at any hint of a gale blowing in from the sea. He'd bundle her into layers of warm clothes and give her paper-wrapped sandwiches to put in her pocket. He'd fill a flask with water and they'd head out to the nearest cliffs. She'd carry their red and white kite. When they got there, they'd fly the kite into figures of eight, star shapes and diamonds and hearts.

Clem was never aware of time when he was doing something he loved. Danu saw the hours passing from where the sun was in the sky. Whenever she suggested they go back, her father said,

Just a little longer, there's a rising gust coming next, let's get it higher, eh . . . His eyes creased like lines in sand when he smiled. When they eventually wound up the kite string, Clem would carry Danu on his back. When they arrived at their caravan, Adelaide would scold Clem for the late hour of their return, tell him how worried she'd been about Danu getting cold, or wet, or tired . . .

He'd tell Adelaide she worried too much, and that Danu was strong. Her father often described her as strong. Her mother was always silent whenever he did, but Clem never seemed to notice. After the scolding was done with, he'd sit quietly with Danu.

He was always good to sit quietly with.

But a gale sometimes blew through Danu, when either of her parents were silent for long. With silence came a cold feeling she often had, but as a child, couldn't articulate. That sense of something missing. The incompleteness of herself, or a gap between her parents?

An overheard conversation blows into her mind. Adelaide looked guilty when she murmured to Clem, *I don't think we did the right thing.* Clem replied, *It might always feel wrong for us, but it was right for Rosa. She was so sickly.*

Another memory. Rosa. No more than a name, toasted each year. No more than a name, whispered about. Perhaps she was some elderly relative who'd helped Adelaide escape her family. Or perhaps she'd given them some money which helped buy the horse but then she died before they were able to repay her. But who would have told her parents she was dead? They were always moving on. Place to place to place, and though Adelaide had an address book in the bottom of a drawer, Danu never saw her write a letter.

Danu had always thought she'd find out who Rosa was, over time. Now all she can do is make up stories in her mind.

Death steals all the answers to unasked questions.

Danu stares into clouds as she takes a deep breath.

The man in the wheelchair said that love doesn't go away when someone dies. So Danu gathers all of her love for her parents. She sends it into the sky.

She throws another pink petal into the wind, and another, and another. When they're all gone, she drops the empty stems, leaves and stamens onto the roof. Pink petals spiral: small kites into grey.

Five geese pass over, honking. Part of her travels behind them through the warp and weft of clouds. On this rooftop-heaven, there is space for grief to move, even fly, at sky-height. Is it wing-envy which makes her watch these birds with her arms wrapped tightly around her chest?

Climb up to a roof.

Grieving was impossible because sound travels.

Climb up to a roof and throw.

Grieving was impossible because there was no empty space.

Climb up to a roof and throw love upwards.

Grieving will never stop until love thrown upwards doesn't fall down.

And here is the road, the concrete and stone of it all and the layers of grit under tar, or tar over grit, but what does any traveller know of roadbuilding? Gathering speed after a month on the road with the wind blowing against him, Morrie's racing against the last of the light from the west. His gaze is fixed to the hills on the distant horizon. He's had so little sleep that he now feels like a sand-twister of a thing which sees without eyes. Beyond those hills the road will turn in a thousand directions he'll not see in the dark, but he'll still feel the pull to the north.

Ever onwards, so he can gather Danu up if she's fallen, put

her together if she's broken, and whatever state she's in, give her enough love to keep her safe in this world. But as thin trees rush past on both sides of the road, flickering the sunset across the back of the horse, all thoughts of the future are false. He's no real idea what he'll find when he reaches her. And this journey of nights and days without count is made of road, skies and rains. He's missing her more now he's rushing towards her. All he can think of is ignoring the pains of the body, giving attention to the sweats of the horse, and the constant sounds of hooves against road.

The future is over those hills and the mountains beyond them. It's hanging at cloud-height, and is not to be guessed at. Guessing the future's a sure route to madness when there's so little sleep to be had.

Time moves backwards as he passes it, like this, over his shoulder. Away.

And just as it was when he left her to drown in a city with fire burning beneath it, there's a storm coming up behind him. Picking up wails, the wind blows against the back of the caravan, forcing Inferno to run at gale's pace. Each time he falters, Morrie lashes the reins and shouts, *Don't stop yet to sleep, don't stop yet to breathe, keep running while the wind's at our tail!* He lashes the reins, and as that doesn't speed him enough, he lashes again with the whip. The back of a horse is far stronger than any mule or man.

As the sun sinks faster than the moon rising and slower than the tearing clouds, minutes last seconds, weeks are days, and all days on this road have only lasted hours. But tonight the moon's full. He'll get further north while moonlight stretches light to the road.

The trees disappear as a valley comes into view. Shadowed bushes spike around a pale lake, and Inferno's faltering. Morrie draws him to a halt, unshackles him and leads him down the hill to drink.

Ankle-deep in water, Inferno jerks his head, breathing heavy between gulps. How long does a horse take to fill with water? Though they're still, Morrie's mind races. A phrase, repeating. *This is taking too long.*

This is taking too long, as he leads Inferno out of the lake onto frosted grass and watches him eat.

This is taking too long and this stone-earth is filled with slow layers and seams.

This is taking too long, the crunching of pebbles as he pisses at the edge of the road.

In his mind, Morrie bids Inferno, *Be ready to run for as long as there's light to see by.*

Morrie's back on the front porch of the caravan, swallowing torn bread, knocking back water, and gripping the reins.

Taking off again, the horse races, the wheels of the caravan race and Morrie's heart races with thudding beats.

And through this bright night, the gale keeps blowing them onwards and the land around them darkens as the moon dips into clouds. And still Morrie forces the horse on, and on, and up narrow tracks, and around a curve in the road, still heading north, as the moon comes out bright again and passes over in an arch. At the edge of the sky it will lay itself down in those thick clouds, and it'll be dark for a good few hours before the sun rises opposite.

The horse sweats hard and Morrie is dry-cheeked and mind-reeling. There's no salt in the gale, but this is a bitter wind. It's changing direction in stinging gusts . . . how much water does a brain need to think itself onwards? All he touches is sand-dry, the leather of reins, wood against his arse, the water jar that's rattling empty in chains.

Wheels shudder over potholes filled with gravel. The gale brings rain. Morrie tips his head back to catch water in his mouth as the horse's footfall slaps in widening puddles. Gusts blast northwards again. Through Morrie's dripping eyelids the horse is half-drowning, half-flying.

How many miles is it to the next well?

Thirst-many miles.

How many miles are there, between him and her?

Storm-many miles.

This is what it feels like to chase what you most want.

At the end of Wringers Street, Danu passes a young woman with blonde dreadlocks as she goes towards the back wall. She recognises her from somewhere, and turns, thinking she should have said hello. But she can't place her. The young woman quickens her pace, and has soon disappeared into the main street.

Inside number nineteen, there's something on the doormat behind the front door. Hopeful that it's a letter from Morrie, Danu rushes to pick it up. It's a flier for a graduate exhibition at the art college.

Thinking of the young woman she saw outside in the street, Danu has a strange feeling that she's deliberately delivered the flier to this address. But why? And where has she seen her before? She goes into the kitchen and puts the flier on the table.

Danu takes her underwear out of the kitchen sink where she left it to soak. She washes and wrings out her knickers and hangs them over the chair-backs.

The front of this house looks so derelict, there's never been any junk mail or fliers pushed through the letter box before.

The feeling of fate that Danu had when she first arrived in Matryoshka returns.

Judith Crown is an artist and her painting of Danu was in

the second circle. The art college is also in the second circle. Could there be a connection?

Her hand reaches for the flier. The image that advertises the show is of a silvery sun and bronze moon. A gold line twists between them in a figure of eight. The curve of infinity? Her heartbeat resonates through her as if these symbols hold some deep meaning she doesn't yet understand.

As she examines the printed details, ink spreads from her damp fingerprints. The last day of the exhibition is tomorrow.

Is she being summoned?

Danu whispers to herself, *All right then. I've not entirely given up yet. Tomorrow. I'll be there.*

At the graduate exhibition, Danu walks around free-standing sculptures of gods made from tin stars. The doors open as three students leave. A moment later, two older men come in and go straight to a large drawing of an eagle transforming into a tree. Danu walks along a wall of abstract paintings of moons.

Most of the artworks being shown are skilfully made, and some are beautiful, especially the paintings of a sickle moon parade. She returns to these images and examines the brush-strokes. Candlelight has been painted as reflections in people's eyes. But she can't focus for long because every time someone comes in or leaves the exhibition, her attention is drawn to the swinging doors. Is she meant to meet someone, or overhear something? She's been in these warm rooms for at least an hour, and has seen everything on display. Pausing under a papier-mâché sculpture of red birds which hangs from the centre of the ceiling, she wonders if they'd turn to mulch if they were hung outside in the rain.

She's too hot. As she takes her coat off and slings it over her arm, she glances around. The few other people who are visiting the exhibition are absorbed in the work. Beside the doors, a student talks with her parents. Her mother is asking her why her framed drawings are the smallest things in this exhibition. *I like minutiae*, she says. *Small things are interesting.*

Not if you're short-sighted, her father murmurs.

Danu does a final circuit of the whole exhibition, making sure she's seen by everyone who's there. But no one attempts to talk to her. She looks at all the images and sculptures, including their titles, descriptions and the names of the student artists. Nothing resonates as significant. What did she expect to find? Even without her coat, the high temperature in the exhibition makes her foggy-headed. She's getting too overheated to notice anything.

Outside in the art college courtyard, the sun is bright. Danu gets an iced chai tea from a stall. Sitting on a bench, she tries to cool down but the air is humid. Several students are clustered in groups seated on the grass.

She'll stay here for a while. Just to see if anything happens. Even if she only imagined the feeling of fate, it's good to be outside and in a new environment. Focusing on other people, the things they do and talk about, helps to distract her from the nightmares she's still having. She'd thought that visiting the hospital would shock her out of these dreams, and force her mind to take another direction. Perhaps Morrie was right and she should have talked about her parents more when they died. Cried more. She could have shouted and kicked and screamed, but she didn't let herself. Her grief must have got stuck inside her mind, and twisted itself into a dark, strange thing.

A nearby group of students are discussing Matryoshkan politics. One of these students, a man with orange hair, has taken on the role of teaching the others. He speaks of the past, 'Initially, there were Circle Representatives, but these were replaced by a self-appointed High Minister who established a Cabinet of thirty politicians, elected via public vote.'

Danu catches her breath as the young woman with blonde dreadlocks comes into the courtyard through one of the glass doors. She's clearly an art student, as she's carrying a sketchbook. Pausing at a bin, she rummages in her bag, and throws away a handful of exhibition fliers.

So it must have been her who delivered the flier to Wringers Street. The art student crosses the grass and joins the other students. She says hello to them, but they're absorbed in a conversation. Finally Danu remembers where she's seen her before – she handed her a flier outside the hospital. Danu was distracted at the time, and now realises she must have seemed rude. Picking up her coat from beside her on the bench, she rummages in the pockets. Inside there's a crumpled piece of paper. But it wasn't a flier she was given. It's an advert.

Life model required.
Please present yourself for consideration between 2 and 6pm any afternoon this week.
Block A, at the art college.
You have been specially selected by a student to receive this invitation. Please bring it with you and state your name at reception when you arrive.

Danu watches the art student as she sits down in the grass with the group who are discussing politics. So she'd wanted Danu to apply to be a life model, but that was a while ago. She's probably got someone by now. Is it a coincidence that she also put the flier through the letter box last night? Or was she simply trying to get as many people as possible to attend the graduate exhibition before it closed?

The male student is still talking. Appearing determined to teach the others as rapidly as possible, he doesn't even glance at the newcomer. She rummages in her bag and gets out a sandwich.

While the art student eats her lunch, the male student tells the others that the system of public voting briefly worked in Matryoshka, till the public decided they didn't like any of the people who put themselves up for election. The High Minister stepped down when the majority of people stopped voting for anyone. Once the voting entirely ceased, the Cabinet was unobserved. The students' conversation shifts as they discuss Matryoshkan attitudes to the current political system. The outer circle is dismissed as 'too pleasure-seeking to care about anything involving delayed gratification', the second circle is described as 'well intentioned but without impetus' and the Inner Circle is described as 'mysteriously elitist and possibly bourgeois'.

Danu hears him go on to say that the Cabinet has recently introduced a private voting system involving only itself. There are still only thirty people in the Cabinet, who will now canvass each other, give rousing internal speeches, and re-elect one another every five years.

He says, 'Right – presentation notes. Let's get on to the main topics.' The students have a large blank piece of paper lying on the grass next to them. They discuss the notion that what politicians called apathy, with regard to public votes, was in fact despair.

The art student has finished eating. She says, 'I'll scribe for you if you want.' She unlids a pen and draws a bullet point on their piece of paper. She writes the words: *apathy vs despair*.

A voice is raised as another student mentions ghostwriters and the narcissism of politicians.

The art student smirks. She says, 'Bullet points, or do you want a visual of a ghost and a narcissus?'

One of the young men turns to her: 'Give us a few more minutes.'

She responds, 'You're on my turf, politicoboy. Use the university café.'

One of them murmurs, 'It's quieter here.'

The art student gets some pencils out of her bag. As she opens her sketchbook and hunches over a page, the students keep their discussion flowing until they come to a shared conclusion. One of them writes a summary on the sheet of paper:

In an ideal society, expertise in any chosen field, wisdom, fairness, resolve, compassion and curiosity are the best personality traits for politicians to have.

'But unfortunately,' one of the quieter students concludes, 'most people who possess those admirable traits wouldn't want to be politicians.'

One of the others says, 'Should we jot that down as well?'

The male student who's done most of the talking flicks his orange fringe off his brow. 'No. We'll deliver this one verbally. We have to ram it home with sincerity. Trustworthy smiles please.'

The art student looks up at him from her sketchbook. She says, 'Who made you the king?'

He glares at her. 'Meaning?'

'I was just noticing you think you're in charge.'

He glances around at the others, who are gathering up their things and getting ready to go. 'I was appointed as the leader for this session. The conclusive statement is a group opinion.' He lowers his voice, 'Not mine. I don't even believe in it.'

She tilts her head. 'If, instead of the Cabinet, just one person was in charge of Matryoshka, what would that be like?'

He glances at the others, who are already leaving the court-yard. 'Well, first they'd gather their family and close allies.'

She shows him the sketch she's been drawing. 'A king or queen and their royal family. Ruling a hive of bees . . .'

'Similar. But in my view, an aggressive dictatorship might motivate apathetic Matryoshkans to be more actively interested in politics.'

'So if you were Mr King Dictator, would your policies be to intentionally annoy the bees, and get them riled up?'

He smirks. 'If they were busy stinging each other, I could get on with the things I'd really want to do.'

She closes her sketchbook. 'That sounds like being a bully, to me. And a sneak. And a cheat. Do we all only pretend we're grown up, but secretly remain eternal children?'

'You don't know anything about politics.' He follows the others out of the courtyard.

She calls after him, 'Of course I do. I'm an artist.'

The air is so thick, it feels like there's a storm coming. If the art student had any special message for Danu, or wanted her here for a particular reason, she'd have spoken to her by now. She's putting her sketchbook in her bag, and hasn't given Danu a second glance.

Disappointed, Danu tells herself she's imagining connections where there are none. She rises from the bench and goes back inside the art college. She walks along chalky floorboards towards the main door. In the shadows cast from pillars between tall leaded windows, it's far cooler than outside. Her head thuds as she steps through sunshine and shadows.

Rapid footsteps echo behind her and a female voice says, 'Wait a moment.'

She turns to face the art student. Her face is sweet, with wide blue eyes and full lips. 'I only noticed you in the courtyard when you left. Isn't it interesting how we don't see the things which are right in front of us, till they change. Do you often sit still for long periods of time?'

Danu shakes her head, smiling. 'No, I usually pace. Why?'

The student has a tattoo of a unicorn on her forearm. She says, 'There's a visiting artist, she's good. No, not merely good. Exceptional. She's on a residency at the art college – her portraiture work is stunning. She did this amazing talk . . . but anyway. She's looking for the right life model.'

'You gave me an advert a while ago—'

She shakes her head. 'None of the models who turned up were right. She's been more specific now. She particularly wants a young woman with olivey skin and dark hair. A gypsy look. Would you do it? And tell her I sent you? We're all in awe of her. She usually paints in blue hues but she's doing an exciting new series—'

Danu can barely breathe. 'What's her name?'

'Judith Crown. Say you will, and she'll crit my portfolio because I've done her a favour . . .'

'I want to meet her as soon as possible.'

The student looks at Danu expectantly. 'Tomorrow?'

'Where?'

'She's based in Block A. Just up the street. Sorry – I haven't even introduced myself. My name's Intarsia.' She shakes Danu's hand. 'Can I give her your name and say what time you'll be there?'

'Danu Mock.'

Intarsia claps her hands. 'I knew it. Perfect!'

Danu's heart thuds. 'Why is my name perfect?'

She flushes. 'I'm convinced you're what she wants.'

'Can't I go and meet her now?'

'No, she's out somewhere. I'm not stalking her. Or not much.' Her already pink cheeks deepen in colour.

'I'll be there. At eleven?'

'Brilliant.' Intarsia frowns. '*Promise* me?'

'I'll be there.'

Intarsia beams and rubs Danu's arm. 'Mention my name over and over again if you can – Intarsia Salter. You're exactly what she's looking for. Intarsia Salter. Shall I write it down for you?'

'I'll remember your name. Have you been stalking *me*?'

'I'm not a stalker! I was at Kasabar a few nights ago and your name was on the listings. So I kind of . . . followed you. I lost sight of you at the turnoff into Wringers Street. So I put a flier through each letter box on that street yesterday night in the hope you would come here today.'

'If you noticed my name on the listings, Judith Crown must have told you it. Otherwise why would it even be relevant?'

Intarsia scrunches up her face. 'Oh bloody hell. Look, I was told to find you and discreetly get you to meet her to talk about modelling. That's all. I agree it's strange, but she's secretive. She's from the Inner Circle, but you *mustn't* ask her about it. That's the first thing she told us. Of course, we're all dying to ask. But she's someone they call *Trusted*.'

'What does *trusted* mean?'

'She told us that experts in any field are allowed to come out to share knowledge, as long as they were born there. I think that's quite telling.'

'They're trusted to be experts?'

Intarsia laughs. 'No, that tells us that whatever else the Inner Circle believe in, they respect education. *Trusted* means that they keep their mouths firmly shut whenever stupid people ask them questions. My friend Max asked her a few days ago if the Inner Circle inhabitants were a sex cult. I can't believe he said that out loud. To her! But she just laughed and rolled her eyes. Do you know, I don't think she cares what we all say about them. There are so many rumours – about sex, or religion, or politics. Half the time I get the impression she thinks we're all ridiculous . . . Sorry. I'm gabbling. I've got a group seminar in . . .' She glances at her watch. 'Oh bugger. Now. I'd better go. I'm just so glad you've agreed to meet her. But please don't tell her I let slip that she asked for you by name.'

'I've got other things to talk to her about, so don't worry.'

At eleven in the morning, Danu approaches Block A of the art college. Now she's finally about to meet Judith Crown, her heart thuds.

The man at a small reception desk looks up as soon as she comes in and says, 'Danu Mock?'

'Yes.' Danu didn't realise this was such a formal appointment.

'She's expecting you.' He walks her along a corridor and waves towards an exit. 'Go outside – it's the studio with the green door.'

Danu emerges in a yard. The buildings look like houses, rather than anything as grand-sounding as a studio. Someone's pegged a row of blue carrier bags on a washing line which cuts across the yard. The bags drip crimson paint onto slate-grey paving slabs.

As Danu slowly approaches the green door, it swings open and a woman comes raging out. Her pinked cheeks are darkening. As she sweeps back her hair, sunlight catches its frazzled strands. She turns and shouts through the door she is leaving.

The conversation is one-sided, and though her anger is boiling, it sounds on the verge of bubbling itself out. ' . . . how bloody dare you, when you're sleeping with someone else as well! You're faithless, you kept me believing I was the only one for all of, what? Three weeks? It took me that long to fall for you, well let's see how long it takes me to fly at you, if the kind of cheating game you're . . .' Her voice trails off as she becomes aware of Danu's presence.

She looks her up and down. 'Are you Jude's latest mid-life crisis?'

Danu says, 'Not as far as I know . . .'

'She's blasted insatiable. Well if I were you, I wouldn't bother. Unless you don't expect to be made love to gently, tenderly, as a woman should, but prefer her to be rough like a man!' She pushes the door. It bumps against the doorframe as she walks away.

Barely breathing, Danu approaches the swaying front door. Inside there's a hallway which is lit from the back by a long window. In silhouette, a figure leans against the wall, knee bent and head raised.

There's something unreal about this whole scenario. Danu steps inside, trying to see the tall figure more clearly. 'Are you Judith Crown? Intarsia Salter sent me.'

The figure approaches Danu. Her sleek auburn hair and dark brown eyes are striking against her pale skin. She says, 'Call me Jude, not Judith.'

Her eyes search Danu's face without blinking. Is she already translating her into paint?

Unnerved by this intensity, Danu tries to lighten things. She says, 'And was she right?'

'Who?' Jude tilts her head, frowning as she examines Danu's hairline.

Danu closes the door behind her. 'Your spurned lover. Are you really as rough as a man?'

'Ha!' Jude's laugh is a loud crack, and Danu warms to her. 'She's not been genuinely spurned, as such. She's overdramatic. But as to me being rough . . . it all depends on who's in my bed and what they want while they're there.' She pauses. 'And

Miriam,' she nods at the door, 'in fact *did* want me to be rough. She's married, hurt and trying to teach her husband a lesson. Apparently, the lesson was me. But I'm far too discreet for her purposes.'

Danu appreciates Jude's frankness. 'And were you, as accused, faithless?'

Jude laughs again. 'I left a particularly feminine pair of knickers in my bed for her to find. Not the kind of fluff she might have expected me to wear . . . though I have, on occasion.'

Jude's white silk blouse makes her appear timelessly elegant. She shakes Danu's hand. 'Well, good to meet you.'

Danu's palm is sweaty. She lets go of Jude's hand and wipes it on her trousers. 'Sorry, I'm a bit nervous.'

Jude ignores this. 'I'm glad we've got my sexuality out of the way and you're unperturbed. And just to get this out of the way as well – you're *far* too young for me.' She walks along the corridor and opens a door on the left. She calls, 'You're nice to look at. Come on, come in. I've got a couple of hours if you're free now?'

Danu follows Jude into a large studio which smells of turpentine. Jude seems awkward, and slightly on edge. Should Danu play along with whatever game this is? If she keeps their interactions as simple as possible, she's got a better chance of finding out about the locket.

Three long windows fill the studio with daylight. One wall is entirely covered in shelves crammed with an assortment of pots and brushes, half-squeezed tubes of paint and rolls of paper. There are two deep metal sinks; one is empty and gleaming, and the other contains floating green-stained cloths. They look like sea creatures.

In the centre of the studio there is an arrangement of furniture; a narrow gold vase of dried willow branches stands on the edge of a table which is half hidden beneath a bundle of cheese-cloth. On the floor, there's a faded trunk with an engraved copper padlock. Stacked on top of the trunk are three ribboned tambou-rines. Dusty-pink fabric hangs in thick folds from a pole suspended from the high ceiling.

Jude removes her hands from the pockets of her wide blue trousers, goes over to a set of hooks, selects a paint-spattered smock and slips it on.

There's something compelling about the combination of her elegance and awkwardness. She's on edge, yet whenever she speaks, she sounds earnest. Could one of Danu's parents have had an affair with her? She can't yet bring herself to ask anything. But if she models for her, they'll be quiet together. She exhales a little. She'll have time to consider how best to phrase her ques-tions.

Danu looks at the easel. The canvas is painted black, and a few faint chalk lines mark out the shapes of furniture and fabrics.

Jude says, 'This could either be a life study or a portrait, if you'd prefer to be clothed. *Not* what you're wearing now.'

The red of Danu's tunic clashes with her green trousers. The arrangement in the middle of the room is like a set design in muted tones. If she is to be part of this tableau, the only colours which won't jolt against these colours are pale clothes, or the tones of bare skin. Danu goes to a chair in the corner and undresses. Her vest and knickers are dark blue and she wishes she'd worn lighter ones as she could at least have kept these on.

It feels surprisingly easy to remove her clothes in front of Jude. She's an artist, so will look at her in a different way. Brushing dust from her knees, she asks, 'Do you like my body?'

An expression of fleeting concern crosses Jude's face.

Danu straightens up. 'I mean, will I do for your painting?'

Jude's eyes shine. 'Oh yes. You'll more than do. You're

beautiful. Keep those on.' She indicates the frayed bootlaces binding Danu's ankles. 'I like their connotations.'

'You've already done a painting of me.'

Jude frowns. 'I haven't.'

'Then how do you explain this?' Danu rummages in her bag, but can't find the postcard. 'I must have left it on the table. I've got a postcard of one of your paintings.'

'Which one?'

'The one of me!'

'It must be a coincidence. Or a premonition.' Jude smiles. She seems so unperturbed that without the postcard, Danu feels unable to press her any further. She retreats into herself, silenced.

Jude arranges brown cushions so Danu can be seated on the floor, leaning against the padlocked trunk. She instructs Danu to place her feet flat and keep her knees together. One of Danu's hands lies palm-up beside her thigh, the other rests on her collarbone. Her head is tilted so light falls on her face from the window.

Once she's arranged Danu's position, Jude steps back and nods. 'Close your eyes. If you could give me a few brushstrokes warning before you need to move, and not leave it till the moment you have to, I'd be grateful.'

Danu closes her eyes and feels herself being closely observed. As her body warms, the locket's chain pinches her throat, and the bootlaces' sting spreads up her legs. Pain has become another layer of her body. For a moment Danu longs for Jude to speak her name, softly, into her ear. Not as a lover, but as if she's comforting a child.

She is here to ask questions but can't yet speak.

Jude's gaze warms each area of her skin as she seeks out its colours. But she lingers more on her face than anywhere else.

Danu waits for the sound of a paintbrush.

The scrapes of a palette knife. Soft footsteps. Liquid being poured. Footsteps again. A cloth, moist against a dry surface.

Finally, a brushstroke. And another.

These sounds touch Danu's skin. She can feel the paintbrush stroke her waist, her neck, her scalp. And her face. Again, and again, her face.

After unceasing brushstrokes, an exhalation of breath.

Jude says, 'Could you take off your locket?'

Danu still can't speak.

Eventually, Jude's voice comes again: 'All right. Slide it behind your neck. It's far too chunky.'

Without opening her eyes, Danu moves the locket out of Jude's sight.

Brushstrokes resume. The paintbrush strokes her collarbone, her shoulder, her neck.

After a while, Jude says, 'Keep your eyes closed, but can you tell me a little about your life? I want to imply a romantic narrative within this image, but it needs to feel true.'

There's something about the softness of Jude's voice which makes Danu feel that she can only speak the truth. Her own voice sounds choked as she replies, 'I love a man called Morrie.'

There's a smile in Jude's voice as she says, 'I don't just mean your love life.'

'My family's dead.'

'I'm so sorry. Close friends?'

'These days I like animals and birds more than people.'

'And your profession?'

'Tightrope walker.'

'Always?'

'Previously, clown.'

A low laugh. 'My daughter would love that.'

'How old's your daughter?'

'Sorry, can we talk later? For now, I need to focus.'

As Danu puts her underwear back on, Jude looks at her face, not her body.

Danu says, 'If I'd known you were in the second circle, I'd have sought you out sooner than this. I should tell you why.'

Jude's wiping a paintbrush clean. She turns away. 'Only if you want to.'

That's an odd response.

Jude's posture is tense as she says quickly, 'Most models want to see how I've painted them.'

Danu says, 'I don't care what I look like. I have to show you what's in my locket. I don't want anything from you, it's just . . . I need to know.' Her throat tightens. Even if Intarsia hadn't let slip that Jude asked for her by name, there's something staged about this whole situation. She wonders if the spurned lover, and perhaps even Jude herself, are actors.

But Jude looks at her so compassionately, surely no one could feign such a genuine expression. She replies, 'I've another visitor arriving soon, so we may be interrupted, but yes. Of course.' Pulling a plaster-spattered chair from under a table, she drags it over and sits next to Danu.

Danu undoes the clasp of the chain around her neck. She opens the locket and shows her the piece of paper. Nerves crack her voice as she says, 'This was my mother's. What does it mean that your name is inside?'

Jude frowns as she reads Adelaide's tiny handwriting. 'That's me, and I live at fifteen Duffle Close. But I don't know why it's in this locket.'

'I wrote to you. The letter was sent back.' Danu watches Jude closely.

'Post is unreliable.' Jude examines the note. 'I'm sorry.'

'What's that meant to mean?'

Jude pales and shifts her posture. 'It's not about me.'

Silence thickens.

The doorbell clangs.

Looking relieved, Jude rises to her feet. 'My visitor.'

Folding the piece of paper, Danu silently puts it back in the locket.

Jude glances at Danu's clothes which are tangled together on the dusty floor. 'You'd better finish getting dressed. Your payment's in there. Help yourself.' She waves at a small bag and leaves the studio.

This is too convenient an interruption.

Danu eyes the bag, listening to Jude's disappearing footsteps. She gets up quickly and removes a sealed white envelope with *model's fee* written on it. She explores the remaining contents of the bag, seeking anything personal which will tell her more about Jude. There's little of interest: drawing pens, a pocketful of coins and notes, tissues, a notebook containing lists of artists' materials and comments about art students' work. At the bottom of the bag there's a crumpled leaflet. Glancing at the leaflet, she takes it out and slips it into her own bag.

A few moments later, Jude's footsteps sound in the corridor. She reappears at the door as Danu's pulling on her tunic.

Jude says, 'Can you come back at the same time next week?'

Danu laces her boots in silence, waiting to see how much Jude wants her to return.

Jude comes into the studio as she says, 'The curator wants me to go to the gallery with her now. I can work from what I've started today, but I really need you to model for me again. Your skin tones are exquisite.'

She is keen to see Danu again, for reasons she's not yet prepared to say. If Danu doesn't push her too hard, what might she persuade her to speak of?

Danu says, 'All right. I'll see you next week.'

'See yourself out whenever you're ready.' Jude grabs her bag and disappears again, and there's the sound of low voices in the hallway, followed by the front door closing, and silence.

Danu reads the stolen leaflet:

Refresher briefing for those not present at the recent community meeting:

(Remember that any concerns can be reported to the next community meeting, or for more urgent matters, please discuss any issues with a member of the Trusted Committee.)

The ether *spreads vast waves of energy which span beyond distance, beyond time, beyond imagination. All energy is vulnerable, whether its origin is within tissues or waves, bloods or emotions, matter or sounds. People produce a variety of energy waves. When our spirits travel the ether, we strengthen it, because we flood our purest energies into it.*

The ether is everywhere. It is everything. It is infinite and vast. Some of us call it consciousness, some refer to it as god or the universe. Some of us call it a route, or a map containing infinite directions. Others imagine the ether as a container: within it is everything we have ever known or imagined. We do not need to argue among ourselves about what we believe it to be, because however we individually describe it, we are united within our common purpose:

Our role, as we see it, remains that of Caretakers. We keep our energies pure while travelling. We eliminate any darkness introduced to the ether by non-Caretakers by using our own energy to transform darkness into ether light.

'Darkness cannot drive out darkness. Only light can do that.'
(MLK – from another world)

Though this leaflet tells her nothing about the relationship of Jude to her parents, Danu now understands what goes on in the Inner Circle. Jude is part of a private community which is bound by a shared purpose: to travel the ether, and protect it.

For the first time in Morrie's life, he wakes remembering a dream. He's confused, as if he's slept through a storm, and waking is the clearing of air. Inside the caravan, there are real things to wake his mind to. The colours of wood, the texture of dirty sheets, the lumps in the pillow.

In the dream, he'd arrived in a mountain village, not unlike one he passed through about a week ago. He stopped at a wide river winding between houses. A great storm came down from a mountain and swept him into the river. As he entered it, he found that the river wasn't made of water. It was made of lily petals. They choked him and drowned him, his lungs breathed them in and his mouth spat them out. They tasted of salt, and blood, and sweat. As he was about to drown in them, he cried one single sob, and that sob blew the petals out of him, and he pushed himself upwards and was back on the riverbank. The people from the village gathered beside him, and they were small, whether child, adult or ancient. They all had blue eyes. The brightest blue. Too bright. Those blue eyes stared into him. They told him without speaking, *This is the second storm. Go back. Wake.*

If this is what dreaming is, he's glad to have not remembered any before. He's woken shivering, with a ragged mind. What is the second storm?

The real storm, the first storm, the one that darkened the sky so he couldn't see further as it hid the moon and forced him to stop till daylight came, is now dying down outside. He looks out of the window. Inferno is grazing, tethered in the shelter of a small copse. Beyond the copse, black mountains shrug their shoulders through white clouds.

His body still doesn't feel right. There's pinchings and pressures around his limbs, but nothing there to see. The poppet's wrapped in tissue paper and stored in a drawer. He opens the drawer, and without looking too closely at its grotesque form, unwraps the tissue.

He gets a white plate and places the foul yellow effigy in its centre. Seating himself before it at the table, he tries to recall what he saw his mam do when she was witching. He remembers there were candles, and lights one. She spoke words as well, and she spoke them with intent. But what were those words? Or was her intent more important? Sometimes she pricked her finger and bled it, sometimes she breathed a low song. Other times there was something of stone or bone, metal or water or leaf in her hands. She was instinctive. He saw her messing with human hair and the claws of a dead bird. But she never taught it to him.

He doesn't recall seeing her breaking a spell. Only making them. She often smiled as she did so. To her, witching was a joke or a gift, wrapped up in her mischief.

He's got to break this binding hex, for though Loretta's no longer able to stick pins in this poppet and hurt him, or keep him within the circus or his caravan, his body still feels bound when he lets himself feel it. Strings bind his head, his arms, his legs. His whole torso, neck, feet. He can see his leg move as he kicks it, so it can kick. But the sensation is pinched.

There must be some sense to it. To break a binding, unbind.

He gets a knife and makes a rip in the wool. Finding an end,

324

he unravels the poppet, seeking something from his body inside packed straw. There's a hair tied in with the binding. He separates it as he winds the yellow wool round his fingers. Tying a knot in the hair so it's easier to find, he lays it on the side of the plate. Unravelling more, he reveals himself, remade as a doll. His face has been drawn clumsy on stained cotton, and sewn onto straw with blue thread. He unbinds, and unbinds, winding the wool into a ball. An eyelash falls onto the white plate. He moves it carefully to the side.

There's a long strip of torn brown paper wound round the poppet's middle. He unwinds it carefully and reads:

Morrie –

If you've got this, you're a thief. Unbind yourself and burn all that you find. I'm not angry you didn't love me, as you never lied about that. I'm angry you thought the whole time you were getting one over on me. So this is my revenge: I've set three storms on you. Once they're done with, you're released.
Loretta

The first storm which forced him to stop last night is dying down outside.

The second storm: a storm of the mind: remembering a dream.

What will the third storm be?

He unbinds the rest of the poppet, and picks off the cushioned hump Loretta's made of his back. He removes the thin fabric she's rolled around a rusted screw for his member.

Straw, fabric and wool. Screw, stitches and ink. Hair, paper and eyelash. He burns these things in a metal bowl. When he clenches his hands shut, and opens them, they still feel bound by threads.

He can't travel the ether with this binding hex still in place. And Mag was right, he needs to keep his energy for the road.

Blue eyes shine from the shadows under the sink. He looks around for real things. The kettle, jug and the taps. Toothbrush, scissors and soap. Bread, carrots and sliced chicken. Meal, grains and mead. He'll eat and drink, then check Inferno is fit to take to the road. And then he'll travel onwards and await Loretta's third storm.

As he thinks of Loretta, she's got a devilish twist to her smile, and smoky anger in her eyes. She's wearing a mask of what she wants folks to see, prettifying and hiding herself away behind it. But he's not angry with her any more. Not for binding him, or speaking ill of him, or even for this hex of three storms. Sometimes there needs to be a punishment delivered for not thinking the right way. If he'd not been weakened, if he'd not thought he needed her help, if he'd not been starved of the closeness of any woman's body for so long . . . But his real crimes were in thinking she cared less than she did, and was less clever than she is.

Once the third storm arrives, however it comes, his guilt will be carried away.

But for now, he'll ride on through whatever's left of the first storm, and shake the second storm from his mind. He can still taste the salt and the blood and the sweat of those lily petals.

He brushes his teeth to get the flavour to change. If he barely stops and keeps going at the same pace, he can't be more than a week away from Matryoshka, but he wants days to be hours. He clothes himself in layers, a vest, thick trousers, jumpers and a fur jerkin.

Danu would never thread, ravel or bind him. She would never hex, spell or wish him ill.

He'd pass through a thousand storms if that meant he could be with her again. He remembers that one night Danu slept in his bed. The warmth of her body only inches from his. The scent of her unwashed hair. Her hand on his cheek, soft as breath.

The night before she's due to see Jude Crown again, Danu's performing at Kasabar. She stands on the edge of the platform, about to step onto the wire. But she can't step. She's staring at the platform on the other side. Opposite her, there's a pale shadow in the shape of a human figure. As Danu moves her arm, the shadow mimics her movement. It is a distorted silhouette of herself, a ghosted reflection, playing some foul trickery.

The piano must be playing by now but she can't hear it. The lights shine along the wire. Dust motes dance through the air in the dome like miniature fireflies. But where are the notes they're dancing to?

Danu raises her hands and the shadow matches her movement. Danu's arms are straight. The shadow's arms are crooked. It turns its head to the side.

It's not her reflection any more. It's in the shape of a bird with a sharp beak.

Is this Death, finally come to claw her away?

She looks away, and looks back.

Death is still there, poised like a bird.

The piano plays without sound. The pianist frowns, pauses, fingers hovering, and places them back on the black and white keys.

The expectant faces of the audience below her are raised.

What do they want from her?

She is meant to be singing but she's not even breathing.

Her mind says, step forward. Her legs won't do it.

Her mind says, dance on this wire. Her arms won't let her raise them.

If she walks the wire tonight, will Death walk towards her, twanging the wire with limping steps?

Will Death catch her as she falls, and pull her down into some hell she can't believe in?

Death is a shining bird. Static, watching her.

This is hell she's in now if that bird is the magpie who left her behind.

Danu opens her mouth and exhales an entire song.

The audience is made of scowls.

Opposite her, Death unfolds glowing wings.

Danu looks down at the audience again, searching living eyes. And now there is sound. The piano is playing, repeating a phrase. It sounds distant, and out of tune. Voices.

Someone shouts, 'No, she'll fall, look, she's dizzy!'

Someone else yells, 'Get on with it!'

Death becomes paler, more transparent.

Between them, the wire vibrates with light.

It gleams like a knife-edge.

Opposite her, Death watches her without eyes.

Danu's legs shake. Eyes lowered, she descends the ladder accompanied by jeers from the audience.

She pulls the lever to release the platform which will lower her from the stage. The lever isn't working so she thuds her fist on the trapdoor. Someone pulls another lever, underground.

The trapdoor clicks and she descends into the dressing room.

Her eyes fill with circles and everything turns black.

Danu's eyes open. Concerned faces. Hands reach down, lift her up, and seat her on a chair. Her head is pushed forwards. A cool cloth is pressed to the back of her neck.

Mikka's voice says, 'Sit here till you're better.'

Another voice. 'I'll walk you home after the show?'

Danu stares through the gap between her knees. She says, 'Did you see it too?'

Bo's voice speaks, 'Go home, Danu. You're ill.'

She looks up and his face blurs into a jigsaw puzzle of itself. She says, 'Up there. A crow. A raven. A magpie. A woman. Death. *Am* I ill?'

His voice is so far away. 'You should be in bed. I'll get the lighting engineer to walk you home soon, if you're up to it?'

Danu murmurs, 'No one's to know where I live . . .' The next act erupts onto the stage and the sound of tap shoes banging reverberates through her empty ribcage. Once everyone's attention is elsewhere, she lurches to her feet and gets her clothing.

Going into a cubicle, she pulls on her tunic. She bashes her knees against the walls as she draws on her trousers and boots, and emerges fully dressed.

Back in the dressing room, she puts on her coat.

One of the Antisocial Tricksters approaches her with a glass and tells her, 'Drink water. You look terrible.'

She shakes her head. 'Thanks.' Not knowing the right or wrong thing to do, she sits down and sips from the glass. Her head spins as she looks over at the door. Perhaps she *is* ill. Putting the glass on the floor, she rests her forehead against her knees.

Bo puts a hand on her shoulder, and asks if she's all right.

Danu murmurs, 'I'm vanishing.'

He replies, 'Panicking?' He's misheard her.

She says, 'Goodbye,' as if she's leaving. How can this thought scrape her mind like truth?

His hand squeezes her shoulder again. 'Just sit still for a while. You'll be fine. Breathe deeper.'

Is she sick, or panicking, or dying? Voices and footsteps clatter around her. She doesn't even want to look at the faces she's seen night after night. Memorialise them in her mind as the friends she didn't make, to remind herself that she should have forced herself to learn how to talk more. Or listen better. But if she dies tonight, she won't have to remember anything.

Where is Death now?

Still up on the wire, perched in the unlit dome?

Danu knows no one well enough to speak of this without sounding mad.

Part of her is still here in this dressing room, surrounded by noise. But part of her is out of reach.

She is in too many places:

She is in Mag and Sandy's caravan behind a yellow curtain, searching for the outlines of her parents' faces. They died only a few days ago. Where are their voices, where are their faces, where are their voices?

In Morrie's bed. She touches his back, willing him to roll towards her. He doesn't turn to face her though her fingertips trace his spine and tears roll from her eyes.

In the churchyard at Caderton, decorating the graves of her parents with leaves of ivy and witch hazel and elder. Acorns and grass seeds. She plants bluebells and snowdrops and these bulbs twist like keys in frosted soil. She plants nettles, thistles and bramble vines. She plants dock leaves and camomile. Plants which protect themselves, plants which soothe.

She is on the wire, facing a donkey, dressed as a moth.

Outside the entrance to Matryoshka, she exhales red petals into winds.

Easing her body through the kitchen window at Wringers Street, hoping she'll be able to make a home of this house, hoping she'll be all right on her own, hoping that hope is enough.

She is fractured through memories.

*　*　*

330

Danu opens the back door of Wringers Street and goes into the kitchen. She walked back from Kasabar with a numb fog all around her, seeing only the edges of the pavement. She picks up reels of yellow thread from the table and doesn't remember why she bought them. There are tin cans on the draining board. Dirty dishes soaking in the sink. Stained cardboard is stacked beside the back door. There is nothing of comfort here in this house. Why is the heart of a home supposed to be the kitchen, when the kitchen is the dirtiest place? She drops the yellow threads and steps over them.

Where is the heart of this house, if it isn't in the kitchen?

She descends stairs. Down. Basement deep.

There's no light in the basement. It reeks of bogs and she inhales the perfume of rot. Fungus, dead leaves, soil. Isn't this how graves smell? Or is she deeper underground than graves – are these the scents of hell?

She listens for the sounds of heaven above, but heaven is silent.

She remains in the dark, smelling rot, dirt, soil.

Thinking about heartbeats in houses, in ribcages, in coffins.

She imagines reading a letter which Morrie has never written and can't see the words.

Eventually, she climbs out of the dark and goes upstairs to the kitchen.

She writes Morrie a letter in her notebook.

It's finished. She never wants to re-read these words.

Tearing the letter out, she puts it in an overflowing bag of rubbish.

Bottle-edging her lips against green glass, Danu drinks too much wine, too fast. She slumps on a kitchen chair, head-pillowing the table till the wine soaks in so deep she can't feel what she is. She is a mirror, doubling herself and reflecting around into infinity, thinning along its curve. She is the picture that Jude Crown denies painting. She is a coincidence. A premonition.

Sitting up, the kitchen shifts around her, and shifts back. She's drunk, so now what?

The scissors on the table are blunt. The corners of the table are curved and she can't feel her elbows or knees. Danu never touched alcohol till after her parents died. Her father didn't like people drinking, though everyone around them drank all the time. He said, 'Gin, rum, wine, whisky . . . these things destroy dreams.' Clem kept his own dreams close by: a wife who would scold him whenever he was too adventurous. A daughter to play with. An imaginary dog he always wanted but never had. Sirius, their horse. These things held him in place. He was an anchor for Danu, because he needed anchors for himself.

And her mother? Adelaide needed to live in a way that kept her as cossetted as her past. She needed to avoid worry, to be protected from strangers, she needed everyone familiar to remain predictable. Sometimes she needed to be protected from her own sadness. Adelaide hid in their caravan for much of her adult life. She'd come out to sing, resentfully, and retreat again. A bird from a nest, a song to be sung, and then back to the nest. She was a nest for Danu, because she needed a nest for herself.

Her parents feared danger, but Danu's needed danger to feel alive. She's needed heights and the risk of falling. She's needed the wire. And now she needs to be able to numb herself when she's frightened of her own mind. She's never leaned on the solid things which kept her parents safe. The first thing she did was to sell their security – the horse and the caravan, and give away all their possessions.

No nest, no anchor.

She has a green bottle, but it's already empty.

So she opens another.

Cradling it, she makes slow progress up the stairway.

In the bathroom she scrawls words across the wall tiles in red lipstick:

Death has come for me.

She writes these words over and over again until her heart feels emptied. Then she climbs the stairs to the attic.

Drinking from the green bottle, she slumps into herself. She will sleep in the arms of a guardian angel named Wine who has wrapped her in burgundy numbness and red gratitude.

She can't harm herself or be harmed while she's numb in her world.

And there is much to be grateful for.

Thank you vine leaves. Thank you sunlight. Thank you soil. Thank you black grape. Thank you sugars. Thank you fermentation.

NINE FOR WEALTH

Jude Crown feels compassion as she thinks about Danu returning to her studio tomorrow morning. She also thinks about her daughter, Rosa. Rosa's physically smaller than Danu, and so clumsy that she could never dance on a wire. And yet while Danu stands tall and straight so she can walk along a thin line, Rosa can loosen her spirit from her body, and let it fly. She can travel wherever she wants to.

As long as Rosa can feel love, she is free. Jude made sure that her daughter was the most loved daughter in the Inner Circle. Rosa soaked that love into herself as she grew. Though she's now an adult, parts of her don't want to grow up. She wants to play, be naughty, tease, get angry, laugh too much, swim and fly. She loves too hard and falls too awkwardly and eats so much sugar she often reels from it. Jude smiles as she remembers a conversation in which Rosa said, *What is the point of seriousness? Seriousness binds people to rules, responsibilities, and the ground. As adults, we should still play.*

Danu might walk a wire through air, but that is as high as she can reach. Which of them has ultimately had the better life?

Rosa can travel over mountain ranges and roll down the dunes of deserts, as long as she feels love for rocks, and love for sand. She can caress dripping rainforests as long as she feels love for vines and creepers. She can crawl along ocean beds feeling unrequited love for hidden monsters, and sigh with elation inside the embrace of clouds. She can shoot faster than fireworks through the gaps between living and dying stars.

Jude has examined the surfaces of the sun and the moon, Neptune and Jupiter, Venus and Mars, and found many strange colours and crumbs to hanker for. She loves everything that she can imagine, and she has a vivid imagination. The ether is everywhere. Everything is the ether. People can send their spirits towards anyone and anything they love.

The ether's possibilities are limitless.

Jude nods to herself. Her daughter has a good life. A quiet, slow life when her feet walk along the ground, but freedom, speed, excitement, whenever she chooses to travel.

Jude closes her eyes. She is calm now and wants to travel to her daughter. It was embarrassing, last time, as Rosa was in bed with her boyfriend. Jude hopes Rosa didn't sense her watching for just a moment too long. Jude's spirit left her to it and sought out flowing waters. She swam the deepest river she could find. She met a dolphin that had lost its way, and though she couldn't touch it to guide it to freedom, the dolphin had a loosened spirit. It sensed her and followed her downstream and out into the ocean.

Jude's spirit shifts within her body as she separates out the part that feels emotions. She sees the line that connects her spirit to Rosa's as a flame-rope. A circle of light appears in front of her, and she steps through it. As she passes through the circle, she sees Rosa in the distance.

She's in the bathtub, reading a book.

With a burst of affection, Jude's spirit rushes along a burning corridor. She runs fast as a cheetah, straight towards her daughter. Once she's in the bathroom, she stands quietly next to her. Her spirit purrs as she watches her daughter's hands turning a page. She's got toothpaste in her hair. Jude's spirit glows with love as she remembers the orange shampoo Rosa liked when she was small.

Rosa smiles. 'Hello, Mum,' she says. 'I was wondering when you'd drop in.' Her smile broadens. She closes her eyes as she exhales, and says, 'You're warm tonight. I'm doing better, thanks. I'm not angry any more. Sorry it took me so long to calm down, yet again. They were splitegg traitors. She wasn't.'

Rosa drops her book on the bath mat and exhales. Her spirit slips out of her body and gathers itself beside Jude. Tonight, Rosa's spirit is made of thistledown. This young woman who's never run away from anything is formed from the softest, most airborne of seeds. She's beautiful with ether-light shining through her. Silver-grey and broken. Swirling, she mends herself. Jude's spirit is eased just from being beside her.

Jude's spirit becomes a swarm of admiral butterflies, fluttering wing-sounds through her daughter's airborne seeds. Flighty and excited at first, they calm themselves as they flit through clumps of thistledown. She diffuses her daughter's spirit. Her daughter's spirit diffuses hers. As they merge, they are simultaneously themselves and each other.

Now they're both spirit, they communicate in images and transformations:

Rosa becomes a wire shining like a knife-edge.

Jude becomes tiny handwriting on fragile paper.

Rosa becomes fear trembling through air with jagged brightness.

Jude waits. She becomes a handwritten advert for a life model.

And then she becomes her own painting of Danu.

Rosa pauses before changing, as she sees the image of Danu's face.

She pulses like two matching heartbeats and becomes teardrops made of blue ink.

Jude becomes the shape of a woman's body made entirely of hands. The hand nearest where her heart should be grips a paintbrush. It paints gold-lettered words down the side of the painting: *Your decision?*

Rosa becomes blue letters which hang in the air: *Bring Danu home to me.*

Jude Crown paces her studio. It is eleven thirty in the morning and Danu is late. What if she isn't coming? Jude wants to take Danu to meet Rosa as soon as she's ready. Rosa circles any major decision like a cross kitten, batting at her choice from all angles. Now Rosa's travelled to Danu on the ether, and Jude's met her, Rosa is finally certain.

Jude's suspected all along that this is what Rosa would decide. But she wasn't sure, hence sending an art student to seek out Danu. If Rosa had been travelling the ether to Jude, she would have witnessed the illusion of Jude meeting Danu purely by chance. No, Jude was never entirely certain what Rosa would decide. But she was certain enough.

Rosa's always believed she's different to other people in the Inner Circle. In many ways, she is. Though people are accepting of her, she doesn't want to be accepted. She wants to be understood. But the families who inhabit the Inner Circle have lived there for generations. They are kind and self-contained. They have grandchildren and grandparents to discuss and remember. Rosa only has Jude.

Jude can now be completely honest with Danu. If Rosa had decided she didn't want Danu to know about her, then Jude would have lied to Danu, to protect her from this rejection.

But how terrible it would be for Rosa if Danu decides that the choice Jude is about to present her with is too big a decision to make. Danu was brought up by travellers, and will have the heart of a gypsy. She's bound to value freedom more than anything else. She may see the Inner Circle as a prison.

The truth of it is that Rosa needs Danu. Now Jude has to make it happen.

The studio clock ticks loudly. Eleven thirty-four.

Seconds tick in time with Jude's heartbeats. Eleven thirty-five.

A knock.

Heavy air shifts as Jude's relief spreads through the studio.

She goes to the front door and opens it.

Danu's eyes are red-rimmed and she's so dishevelled she must have slept in her clothing. On seeing her in this state, Jude hugs her.

Her body trembles and the air around her vibrates with fear. She smells of stale wine.

Danu says, 'I can't remember the last time someone hugged me.'

Jude holds her as if she is Rosa.

Danu cries without making a sound.

Compassion surges through Jude. She says to Danu, 'It's all right.'

Danu shakes her head against Jude's shoulder. She says, 'No. It's not.'

Gently easing Danu away so she can look into her eyes, Jude says, 'What's wrong?'

Her words come rushing. 'I'm only here now because I said I would be and I don't know what else to do. I don't want to be needy – I don't really need anyone. Stop me. Stop me saying this. You were lying last time we met, but I like you too much to stay away. I'm disappearing. I'm – stop me talking.' She covers her mouth.

Jude speaks gently. 'Danu, there are things I should tell you—'

'Well, say them. If you know why your name hangs at my throat, tell me.'

With her arm around Danu's shoulder, she draws her into the studio and sits her in a chair. Taking a seat beside her, she presses her palms against Danu's hand and holds it firmly.

She speaks to her as if she is a child. 'Your mother must have wanted us to meet if anything happened to them. That's the only reason she would have carried my name in her locket, and made sure you had it when she died. Are you calm enough to hear this?'

'Just say it.' Danu lowers her eyes. Her hands are trembling.

Jude takes a deep breath. 'Your mother gave birth to twins. I adopted your sister. You stayed with your parents.'

Danu stares at Jude in disbelief.

Jude continues. 'Your sister was born, dying. It was an act of kindness, giving her up for adoption. Your parents were good people.'

'How could they—'

Jude speaks earnestly. 'She wouldn't have survived the nomadic life you must have had with them. She was born far, far too small. She spent the first year of her life in hospital.'

Danu's face drains of colour. 'And did she live?'

Jude smiles. 'Oh yes. I made sure of that.'

'So . . . I've got a twin?'

'The painting you thought was you? That will have been one of my portraits of her.'

Danu looks confused, as if unable to grasp what's been said. 'But why did they never tell me?'

'They did what they thought was best for you. Right or wrong, that's what parents do.'

'Where is she now?'

'She lives with me in the Inner Circle. She's been upset, confused, all kinds of things since getting your letter. I'm sorry I lied about that. She just needed time. But she really wants to meet you.'

'Is she sure?'

'Very. And once she's made her mind up about something, there's no dissuading her. You would be allowed to enter the Inner Circle with me, because of your relationship to her.'

Jude takes a deep breath. 'But this is what you have to consider: if you come in, you'll make vows. One vow is that you won't ever leave. It's not an easy choice. So you must take your time.'

Danu looks at the floor as if she's seeing something far beneath it. 'I don't have any time. I borrowed it.'

Jude frowns, unsure what she means. She rubs Danu's shoulder.

Danu still stares, pale-faced, at the floor. She whispers, 'I have a sister.' She tests the words again, 'I have a sister.' She laughs, but the sound is so raw that Jude wonders what she's really thinking.

For a while they sit quietly. Jude waits for Danu to speak.

Danu's eyes fill with wonder, and something clears in the air around her. She looks directly at Jude. 'I sometimes feel suddenly cold. When I was really little, I talked to someone who wasn't there. Was I missing her without knowing her – is that even possible?' She's barely breathing as she shakes her head, still trying to comprehend what she's heard. 'What's her name?'

'Rosa.'

Danu exhales. 'She was only ever a name. And then she was an unanswered question.' Her eyes become distant. She looks like she's searching memories for something she can't find. After a while, she asks, 'What's she like?'

Jude laughs. 'Other people say she's difficult, because she's feisty and angry half the time. But I've always thought of her as the sweetest thing in the world. She's got kindness in her, for anything she deeply loves. She used to have a lazy eye and had to wear an eyepatch for three years. She learned the recorder, and played the same tune over and over again till she'd mastered it. Then she'd never play it again. She hated any sign of cruelty in others. At school she'd stay in the classroom alone at playtime. She came home each day with a new drawing she'd copied out of a nature book. I've got at least a hundred of them, somewhere. And she used to—'

Interrupting her, Danu says, 'You're talking about memories. What's she like *now*?'

Jude replies, 'She cooks experimental meals that always turn out brilliantly. She's got a sweet tooth, she can swim like a fish, and goes to the swimming pool as often as she can. She plays guitar and writes nonsense songs. Really good ones, often about beetles, birds, rodents and ants. They're taught to children in our primary schools.' She smiles. 'All the kids call her *the singing lady*.'

Danu asks, 'Who gave her the name Rosa?'

'Your parents.'

'Did you ever meet them?'

Jude nods. 'Twice, with a social worker. I really liked them.'

'I wonder whose name they chose first.' Danu's expression is so vulnerable it springs tears in Jude's eyes.

Jude says, 'I told Rosa about you when she was four, because she kept telling me that someone was missing.'

'Did she?' Danu's voice is choked.

'But she can't leave the Inner Circle. So this isn't easy, but it's down to you. You'd be going into a closed community. It's not unlike entering a convent, in some ways. You should talk this through with someone who's more objective than me, or take advice from a close—'

Danu shakes her head. 'I don't need to. Rosa's the reason I was drawn to stay in Matryoshka.'

'I want to be sure it will be right for *you*.' She squeezes Danu's hand. 'What about the man you mentioned last time we met – I'm sorry I can't remember exactly what you said – could you talk to him about this?'

Sadness thickens in the air around Danu.

Jude rubs Danu's hand and lets go. She says, 'This is a lot to take in. You look like a little girl. So this is what happens next.

341

Go and either talk to others about this, or just take some time to think.'

Danu turns to look at her. 'I'm just shocked. I'll be fine . . .'

Shaking her head, Jude says, 'I'm sorry to treat you like a child, but sometimes it's needed. Go and do whatever you need to do.'

Danu says, 'If I come back tomorrow morning, will you be here?'

Jude smiles at her. 'I'm not going anywhere.'

Morrie's expecting Loretta's third storm to stop him travelling this fast, to halt him and ground him by hurling wild rages. He chases faster as if it's coming up behind him and the faster he runs, the further he'll get before it hits him.

But no third storm comes.

Along the sides of the narrow road heading north, scarred trees stretch their branches like arms, reaching dark veins to the sun.

The horse's breathing is ragged but Morrie's barely remembering to breathe. The caravan wheels grate against uneven stones. He's nearing the highest range of mountains now, and Matryoshka can't be too far away. A day, perhaps two?

He searches the skyline for buildings but sees mountains and mountains and mountains.

Hurtling ever onwards, closing the gap between him and her, his eyes fill with daylight's frazzles. It's got a strange light, this morning's sun. Silver as moonshine it glimmers on the racing horse's mane. The hairs on the back of Morrie's forearms look like small flames. He's left his gloves inside the caravan. He'll get them next time they stop. But he doesn't want to stop. His body feels made of burning fabric strands. Tightening things.

His hands are stones. Coals. Too warm. Too cold. Nothing feels right.

He thinks about the Double. The madness which could come from sighting something that's almost there, but not quite. He remembers Danu's drawing of the Gemini fish – one face clear, the other distorted. That sent a shiver through him when he stared at it, and it was no more than a picture. If she'd sensed a Double back then, she never spoke of it.

He should have talked to her about the ether. About otherness. About ghosts and reflections and projections of folk. But she was always so tied to the ground. Wouldn't even get her tarot cards or palm read. She never talked about what was designed for her in any map of stars. She never spoke of any kind of god. Aye, she was afraid of what could be out there, or frightened there was nothing at all.

His mind fills with pictures of Danu's face with different expressions; crying, confused, untrusting, sleepless. A clearer picture arrives: Danu's face underwater with her thick hair floating like seaweed. Eyes closed, holding her breath.

Shaking the picture from his mind, he lashes the reins.

The morning air is ice cold as if the whole sky is freezing.

Sunlight burns his forehead like heated sugar then freezes like frost.

Till this hex is done with, he'll not trust the lies of his body.

But fear is a cold thing. So is exhaustion. So is shock. Dread. It's dread that burns.

So close to her, now. Closing in.

Close enough to be afraid of what he'll find.

Jude anticipated that Danu would arrive at her studio fairly early this morning, so she slipped out at first light and bought pastries. Danu arrived fifteen minutes ago, and Jude told her immediately that they wouldn't talk till she'd at least eaten something. She made coffee and handed her a stuffed paper bag.

Now Danu's perched on a tall stool beside the window eating cinnamon swirls.

Jude doubts that Danu's slept much, if at all, by the looks of the dark rings beneath her eyes. But she's at least washed her hair and put on clean clothes. While she's focused on eating, Jude mentally compares her to Rosa. Danu's eyebrows are thicker. She's taller, physically stronger, but their shoulders are the same shape. Danu's cheekbones and nose are identical to Rosa's, but her eyes are more intense. Jude can't imagine what Rosa will feel like, if they meet, when she sees all these similarities. She's never met a blood relative, let alone a twin.

When Danu's finished eating, she folds the paper bag into a small square and throws it into the tin bin beside the door. Picking up her mug from the floor, she takes a slug of coffee.

She drinks just like Rosa, in huge gulps, with no regard for temperature. As she moves over to the sink and puts her mug down, Jude can't take her eyes off her. Danu is a strange thing to Jude today: her daughter, but not her daughter.

Turning to face her, Danu says, 'Thanks. I didn't realise I was so hungry.'

Her tone of voice is the same as Rosa's, though their accents are different.

Jude replies, 'It's a lot to take in.' From her paint-splattered chair on the other side of the studio, she continues to regard Danu. She's stronger today. She needs more physical space around her.

Danu paces up and down. 'So I've had time on my own to think. Or rather, draw lots of pictures, sleep fitfully, have a bath, and try to get my head set straight.'

'But you've not eaten anything till now?'

She shrugs. 'Can I ask you some questions?'

'Of course.'

Danu says, 'I never suspected that Rosa existed, but from what you said yesterday, it sounds like she was aware of me, long before you told her she had a twin?'

Jude nods. 'From a very young age.'

'That must have been hard for her. The constant feeling that someone is missing, then finding out that there *is* someone missing, but not knowing if you'll ever meet them.'

Jude says quietly, 'Yes, it was. It still is.'

'So why did you return my letter?'

'From now on, I'll only be honest with you. And you mustn't repeat anything I say about the Inner Circle.'

Danu nods. 'You can trust me.'

'I know. I can feel it.'

'So, my letter?'

'Rosa sent it back, I'm afraid. It hit her hard to discover that Clem and Adelaide had died. Really hard. She'd never heard from them and had always hoped that one day, she would. She wrote you so many replies and rephrased them, got me to read them, then wouldn't show me any more. She screwed each one up. Eventually she told me she couldn't find the right words and went off for a walk. She came back drunk and crying. She'd just posted your letter back to you.'

Danu folds her arms as she paces, and stares at the floor. 'I suppose I can understand that.'

'The next day she regretted it, which set her off all over again. She felt as if she'd lost her birth parents twice. She was also deeply jealous of you, and felt that she wasn't good enough to be loved by them. She imagined you as this perfect person, and herself as deeply flawed. But she's now done a lot of crying, a lot of thinking, and a lot of talking. She really wants to meet you.'

'I've never known what to do with jealousy.'

'Let it subside.'

'That doesn't always work.'

Jude smiles. So Danu's wise.

Danu says, 'What happens to me if she changes her mind? You could kick me out of your house and if I wouldn't be allowed to leave the Inner Circle – I'd have nowhere to go, and I don't even know if I'd be able to get a job there—'

Jude shakes her head. 'No one earns a living as such. We share the jobs that need to be done. And no one is homeless in the Inner Circle. The population is less than the rooms available to be slept in.' She laughs. 'And if there was ever a population surge because *all* women started giving birth to twins, we've got decent builders. We'd just build more rooms, upwards.'

Unsmiling, Danu meets Jude's gaze.

It's not yet the right time for jokes. Jude says, 'You're right to be asking all these things.'

'My instinct is to ask you to take me to Rosa today. Not waste a day more, not knowing her.'

Jude relaxes a little. 'I know her better than I know myself. She would never expect you to leave unless you had somewhere to go. We'd sort something out if either you, she, or even I, wanted to live independently of each other.'

Danu nods, and sits on the floor. She rests her chin on her knees, in a posture just like one of Rosa's when she's got things on her mind.

She's silent for a while.

When she speaks again, her voice is little more than a whisper. 'If Morrie was here, I couldn't make this decision.' She stares up at the thick grey clouds which are framed in the window. 'I've been thinking about never seeing him again. He's the one tie I've got to the world outside the Inner Circle, so he's the one thing that could stop me.'

'Where does he live?'

346

'On the road. In fields. On the edges of other places, like I did. In a cluttered caravan. He's probably lost that tiny scrap of paper with my address on it.'

Again Danu sinks deep into her own thoughts. Her eyes drift around the studio, lingering on the still life arrangement, the cushions on the floor, and they come to rest on Jude's bag. She stares at it for a while.

As she looks up at Jude again, her eyes are shining. The air dances around her as she asks, 'If everyone in the Inner Circle travels the ether, would I learn?'

Frowning, Jude says, 'How do you know about that?'

'I read a leaflet in your bag.'

Jude shakes her head. She should have checked it properly before leaving the Inner Circle. She asks, 'Have you mentioned this to anyone?'

'Of course not. Would I learn?'

'We'll teach you.'

'The last thing Morrie said to me was *watch for me on the ether*. If he's travelling to me, will I be able to travel to him?'

Jude nods. 'If you're both travelling and seeking each other out, your spirits can meet.'

Danu gets up from the floor and paces for a while again.

Eventually she sits in the chair beside Jude. She says, 'Then I have to come to the Inner Circle with you, to have any chance at happiness. I thought I'd got no family, but I have Rosa, and this might be the only way I can ever communicate with Morrie.'

'I'm so sorry you can't meet Rosa before you decide. So few of us are allowed out—'

'Why *is* that?'

'If our deep knowledge about the ether spread, the ether would be misused. The world is full of people who want power but don't have the wisdom to wield it. We need all kinds of people

347

in the world, some highly visible, but also those, like us, who are unseen.'

Danu frowns. 'Why choose to remain unseen?'

Jude says, 'It's far more common than you'd think. Even outside the Inner Circle.'

'In what way?'

'Think of all the neighbours you've never met, and people who barely speak. Think of bag ladies and their collections of things. Imagine what solitary mountaineers dream of, when they're up above clouds. Think of runaways and hermits. All these people have their own obsessions. Many artists, writers or sculptors spend years hidden away, privately making paintings, stories or sculptures. Everyone can either create their own world, or fit into a world that's been created by others. In the Inner Circle, our obsession is the ether. We treat it with love and respect. We cleanse it, so it remains pure. We are fully aware that it belongs only to itself.'

Danu smiles. 'That sounds like someone's had a dream of heaven, made it real, and then locked it away.'

'It didn't begin as a dream.' Jude laughs. 'It began as frustration and rebellion. A group of people feeling so incompatible with what was constantly called *the real world*, that they searched beyond it. And if the Inner Circle is a heaven, it's an imperfect version. We're as flawed as any other group of people. You should hear some of the arguments we have . . .'

'And Rosa? She wasn't born into the Inner Circle. How does she fit in?'

'I've done all I can, but she's always felt like an outsider. Like I said, we're all flawed. She loves travelling the ether but she needs more to anchor her. And, perhaps, so do you.'

Danu replies, 'I need Rosa exactly as much as she needs me.'

Jude smiles at her. 'I'm happy to hear you say that.' As she places her palm on Danu's shoulder, she feels the surge of an emotion she can't place.

Jude quietly says, 'You want to tell me something.'

Danu nods. 'I've believed for a long time that I should have died with my parents.' She looks at Jude with tears in her eyes. 'But if I have a sister, I want to live.'

How can Morrie have any strength left to kick in a locked door? This door, marked 19, is solid. This door won't open to him, even after this journey that's been so long, so hard to travel. He's checked and checked again that this is the address Danu wrote down for him. She should open this door now, but it remains shut.

He hammers, kicks, shouts her name up to the windows but no answer comes.

Two flatties come out of other houses.

He asks them, 'Is she out, will she return soon?'

They eye his caravan, parked up in the street. One of them says, 'No one lives here.'

He slumps himself onto the doorstep, thinking he'll wait for her.

They tell him again, 'No one lives here.'

He doesn't believe them. He looks along the street, wanting to see her walk along the pavement with a smile on her face as she sees him.

The flatties say, 'Are you sick? You look tired.'

He tells them, 'I'm knackered, but fine. I'll wait.'

Will she come back soon and let him in, take him upstairs to the attic room he's already seen, to the sofa she sleeps on? Will she put her arms around him and let him finally sleep?

The flatties walk away, looking back at him with suspicion.

He crouches, ear to letter box, but there's no sound inside.

What if she's in there hurt, unable to shout, make a sound? If he breaks in through the window and climbs stairways will he find her slumped on the floor, still breathing?

He gets up and rattles the handle. He calls her name through the letter box again.

There's still no sound but his own heartbeat, pumping.

Inferno stamps on the cobbles, and the sound wakes Morrie to the street.

Flattie children have gathered round the horse, but they're timid in petting him.

One of them calls, 'Does he bite?'

Morrie says, 'Is there a back door to these houses?'

They nod.

Morrie approaches them and their eyes widen in fear. He's unshaven and unwashed. He must look a fright.

One of the kids hunches over and mimics his figure. As Morrie clenches his fist, they scatter away towards other front doors which open so easy and close them away.

He tethers Inferno to the railings. From windows, flatties are staring.

Walking to the end of Wringers Street, he goes to the backs of the houses and climbs the wall. Counting numbers along, he wall-walks till he reaches 19. As he climbs down into the cluttered backyard, he kicks over a bucket filled with rainwater. Shelves of mushrooms fall out in slumps.

A hideous thought: that she's dead, and he's to be the one who finds her body.

What would he do? Cry enough tears to soak her with, and part with her yet again as some morgue claims her for burial or burning?

Shaking his head to spill thoughts, he takes a breath. Heart thumping, he pushes in through the back door and enters a kitchen.

There's a pile of dirty dishes in the sink, but how long have they been there? There's no mould to speak of, though the water smells rank.

He goes into a sitting room that no one's lit a fire in for hundreds of years. There's layers of dirt on the windows. There's been no flattie friends or neighbours seated on this sofa or on those chairs stacked in the corner. If Danu lives here, she's got herself no company. No company at all.

Anyone who lives in this cold house would get grim with misery being alone here. He remembers how she felt from the inside, that one time he occupied her body. All of her guilt. All of her grief. To feel like that, in this house that's slowly disintegrating . . . She must have felt derelict.

The high ceiling spun with webs feels lower than it is. This whole house feels like a trap. A trap that wants to snap and send him scuttling outside. The air's too thick.

Was she ever here at all?

No, she *was* here. There's the proof.

A letter in the top of a bag of rubbish. Her handwriting. His name.

He draws it out. Reads it.

Dear Morrie,

I'm so frightened. Death is finally coming for me.

I am in a pairing I don't understand. This could all be in my mind but now it's become real. I saw Death on the wire. Is this vision a prediction, like Cianto's cards? Have you ever seen illusions while walking? We never spoke of such things. I wonder if you'd see Death as male, whereas mine is female. My instinct is that she is testing me - she has moved away and I am certain this retreat is only for a short amount of time.

Morrie. I wish you could help. Tonight, I don't know where I am. I am in all of the places I ever have been, and all the places I have dreamed of. You know how odd my mind gets: you've seen my drawings, and heard my stories. My mind is stranger since being here alone. I am standing on a roof, throwing petals into the sky. I am in your caravan hanging on a hook beside your coat. I am the dirtied handkerchief in my father's pocket. I am my mother's thumbprint as she touches window glass. I am the dark earth my parents are buried in and the worms . . . I am the worms, twisting between their bones like a disease.

I should have died with them. Now Death has come to take back the time I've borrowed. She must want it for some other purpose.

If Death comes for me again, I will die too easily. I know no one well, here in Matryoshka, so there is no one to hurt. I can die as carelessly as snow melts. No one to apologise to. No one left grieving.

I'm sorry that I caused us to part. Without you, I have become too quiet in the world. Part of me wonders if Death was my ultimate destination all along, decided long before the moment I left you.

I should stop waiting for Death and choose for myself the moment and the method. I would use a knife and a tall building. There's wine in the kitchen and that will numb pain and the impact of falling. With no one to stop me, how high can I climb, how deep can I slice, how fast can I plummet? Or is it best to go somewhere quiet, outside of Matryoshka, take myself away to a deserted mountain cave, and let no stranger be shocked for the rest of their lives by discovering me dead?

Tonight I will drink myself down to wherever I land within the tang of grapes and sweet-bitterness. I'm not yet sure what's right to do. I trust no one, but I trust wine. It will take me in whatever direction I need to go in.

I'm sorry I was so frightened when I lived with you. I wish I hadn't been. I've never met anyone as trustworthy as you. Perhaps there isn't anyone in the whole world who is, but I'd assumed that there were many.

Tonight, it's myself I can't trust. And that, Morrie. That, is terrifying.

Danu

His hands are freezing. His arms are freezing. His lips are numb.

He climbs stairs, looking for her body in every damp-soaked room.

Through blurring eyes, he sees words scrawled on bathroom tiles:

Death has come for me.

Red words and madness.

She's gone somewhere he'll never find her, and killed herself.

He keeps climbing stairs, shivering. Unfeeling. Numb.

The last room he reaches is the attic.

She's removed her possessions, and left no trace of herself.

Crouching his cheek to the sofa, he catches her scent on the fabric. He sinks into the place where she slept. The sharpness of ice crackles through him.

Coldness spreads through his bones.

Frost covers his eyelids. His lips dry. His spine fuses.

Snow clumps in his liver, his kidneys, his heart.

This must be enchantment. Loretta's third storm freezes his own shock through his body.

Any slight movement will crack him.

He waits for the final storm to be over.

He waits, knowing Danu is dead, but not yet believing it.

He waits, to thaw.

Danu arrives before Jude at the gate to the Inner Circle. She hugs one of her bags to her chest, while feeling the heaviness of the other against the bumps of her spine. It's weightier now she's retrieved her wire and turnbuckles from Kasabar. Bo was there. She said goodbye to him, but didn't tell him why she was leaving or where she was going. At first he was annoyed and disappointed. By the time she'd dismantled the wire, he'd calmed down. He talked to her as though she was sick in her mind, and about to go into some hospital. She didn't reassure him. He said that she'd be welcome back when she felt better. He said that she was to remember that all of them loved her. And though she doesn't believe they liked her let alone loved her, his final hug made her cry.

She adjusts her bags and feels the weight of her mementos. The clothes and costumes she kept from her life with the circus are the skins of who she is, and who she has been. She examines her hand, noticing the colours within her flesh. This skin was once only a movement of cells as they split away from the twin she is about to meet.

There are footsteps on the stairway behind her, and Jude arrives breathless. She's carrying a small rucksack. She smiles anxiously as she greets Danu. She glances at the gate and says, 'You're sure?'

Danu matches the intensity of Jude's gaze. 'I've never been more certain.'

Jude nods, just once.

Behind the gate, a slight movement. Jude glances over her shoulder, checking no one has followed her, but the stairway is clear. She squeezes Danu's hand and lets go. 'Well, then. Let's do this.'

There's a tall figure on the other side of the gate, but Jude hasn't summoned anyone with a bell or a shout. Danu whispers to Jude, 'How do they know we're here?'

Jude says, 'They always know where I am.'

Facing the gate, she says, 'Jude Crown. With Danu Mock, blood-sister of my legal daughter Rosa. No one's followed. Let us in.'

Danu doesn't breathe as on the other side of the gate a key slides, and clicks in the lock.

The gate opens silently.

Jude goes through it.

Danu steps inside the Inner Circle. At the top of a steep staircase, minarets appear and disappear between thick clouds.

The gate closes behind her. The key clicks again in the lock.

A man clasps the elegant key against his chest. He's wearing loose linen clothing. His face is deeply wrinkled, yet his eyes are youthful and bright.

As he's about to speak, Jude says, 'We'll swear her in some time over the next few days. She's not had much time to get used to the idea of having a sister, let alone being here.'

He looks concerned as he replies, 'We should welcome her immediately.'

Jude says, 'She needs to meet her sister.'

He drops his eyes.

Jude rises to her full height. 'We'll do all the ceremonials soon, I promise.'

The man seems intelligent and gentle as he turns to Danu. 'Welcome. I look forward to knowing you well.'

Danu smiles at him. 'Me too.'

He climbs the staircase and disappears into a descending cloud.

Heart pulsing, Danu touches the gate. 'Is there only one key?'

Jude places her hand on Danu's arm. She says, 'It's all right – you might *feel* trapped, but you're not. Our house is just up this stairway and along to the right. Rosa's expecting us.'

'How does she know we're arriving now?'

'I've told her, or rather, shown her. Let's get you home.' Jude turns away and climbs the staircase.

Danu runs her fingertips along the edge of the keyhole.

She whispers, 'Goodbye Morrie. Watch for me on the ether.'

Number nineteen has been rudely reawakened. Its atmosphere spreads in pulses through air particles, and its woodworm burrow deeper into its stairs.

The man who's invaded is half-man, half-ghost. He rises from the sofa in an icy state, joints cracking as he stretches them and places his feet on the attic floor.

He rubs his arms till the ice changes from white to pale gold. He looks around with suspicion as if he doesn't remember where he is. Number nineteen wants him gone, so exudes musty scents within its atmosphere.

The man coughs, and covers his frost-bitten nose, appearing susceptible. But then he descends to the first floor, interested in nothing but the urge to pour warm piss into its toilet bowl. He flushes with a yank. Water gushes. He avoids looking at the words the girl scrawled on the tiles. He picks up the bar of soap she left on the edge of the bath and washes ice crystals off his chilblained hands. He inhales the smell of the soap, and leaves it in the sink.

He looks around its landing hopelessly, seeking something he wants but can't find.

Number nineteen hides its relics under shadows.

The man doesn't notice them. When he arrived, kicking and shouting at its front door, his atmosphere was burning with some kind of fire. Blue flames flickered from his hands before he crunched splinters from its floorboards, climbed to number nineteen's full height, and turned to ice.

He remained ice for three hours, three minutes and three seconds, according to number nineteen's hallway clock.

But now he thaws.

Slush falls from him in grey slumps. He's more-than-half man and less-than-half ghost as he drips down its stairs to the ground floor.

If he intends to stay, number nineteen will entice him into its basement.

But this man is leaving through the back door.

He steps outside, and is gone.

A warm draught comes in from the backyard. It blows strands of hair and dust across floorboards. Number nineteen's walls sink a millimetre. Not enough to dislodge the parts of it which rely on number seventeen and number twenty-one. But enough to make these neighbouring houses shift, extending their supportive and irritatingly comfortable atmospheres.

Number nineteen closes its back door and clicks the lock mechanism sealed. It is weary of invasions. If anyone else breaks in, number nineteen will seduce them into its basement and demolish them in septic rots.

As they walk up the copper stairway and turn into the street that leads towards Duffle Close, Jude looks closely at Danu. She walks as though blind, thoughts focused on meeting her sister.

Jude is desperate to ask her, *What are you thinking, how do you imagine it will feel?*

But Danu's locked inside her own mind.

Jude wants to ask, *Will you speak to her quietly, or call out to any god who's listening, or circle her?*

But anyone locked in their own mind needs to emerge at their own pace.

Jude breathes deeply. Someone needs to remain calm within this strange situation. Two sisters are about to meet who should never have been parted. This is something most people would never experience. She has no idea what will happen when they see each other for the first time.

Beside her Danu walks through her own thoughts, eyes blind to all else.

To distract herself, Jude imagines how she'd describe the Inner Circle to Danu if she really was blind. She'd say, feel this air on your face. It's so moist at the peak of this mountain. She'd say, raise your chin. That's the direction you need to tilt your head in to see all those domes, turrets and minarets punctuating the blurred horizon lines. She'd take her hand and place her palm against a wall. Feel this, she'd say. These walls are coated in matt grey metal and greening copper.

She'd encourage her to stamp on the ground and then tell her that these paving stones which barely echo are made from thick recycled glass. She'd turn her away from this street in the direction of the side street which leads up to the vast greenhouses which grow herbs and spices, flowers, vegetables and fruits. She'd tell her to sniff. She'd ask Danu to describe what she could smell and tell her that she smells tomatoes, wild garlic and flowering stocks.

She'd pause by this well, and ask Danu if she'd noticed the continuous sound of running water. Together they'd listen to the thudding of pumps which remove liquid from deep inside the mountain. Danu might catch the scent of disinfectant or meal, and ask Jude about these. Jude would explain that there are small pens for sheep and goats in one area, while chickens and ducks live in huts in another. She'd notice if Danu frowned as the sky darkened. And then Jude would tell her that up here the clouds are constant, and even sunsets are seen through a haze. She'd say that dawn mists hide all traces of sunrises, and the stars are so rarely seen that when they do emerge, they are celebrated as a great event.

She'd pause then, to see if Danu had any questions. If she was silent, she'd tell her that, no matter what you imagine other people's vision is like, we all live within our own clouds. Imagination is of greater value than anything that can be seen. She'd get her to reach both arms out and feel how narrow the streets are, and then she'd tell her that everyone here is a pedestrian. She'd finish this conversation by saying, *Over the years, we have learned to travel great distances. How far can you imagine? Take it a million miles further, feel anticipation, and you'll understand the possibilities of travelling the ether.*

That's how Jude would describe the Inner Circle if Danu was blind. But she's not. She's just closed away. Protecting herself, or frightened? She shouldn't be so focused on Danu. But she looks so like Rosa, she *is* so like Rosa, Jude feels protective.

But what is she protecting Danu from?

Her own daughter?

No. Confusing as this is, Rosa has to come first.

She'll have to decide what's best to do when she sees how they are together. Go by the feeling, the instinct. Follow their lead. Don't overthink.

As they turn into Duffle Close, Jude says, 'We're here.'

Danu exhales, and takes a deep breath. They walk a few more paces and Danu focuses on the front door.

Jude grips the door handle.

Danu clutches her bag tightly to her chest. Her arms are shaking.

Jude smiles at her and opens the door. 'Go on in.'

Jude steps back as Danu walks through.

Rosa's at the far end of the wide hallway.

Jude's heart thuds as she steps inside and gently closes the door behind her.

Rosa walks forward and holds out her arms.

Danu drops her bags on the floor and rushes towards her twin. She embraces Rosa.

In half-light, their bodies look like one thing as a tall body encloses a small one.

They are still for a long time. Holding. Silent.

Jude waits, barely breathing. Looking at them. Looking away.

They shouldn't have been parted. For the first time, Jude feels guilty. But if she hadn't been chosen by Danu's parents, one of the other three potential parents would have raised Rosa.

Jude wants to go to them. Wrap them both in her arms and tell them how moving this is. How sorry she is. How unbearable it is that they've been apart for all these years.

But she inhales. *Remain calm, hold back.* She tells herself: *Be here for Rosa first. Danu second. Put yourself to the side.*

Eventually, Danu speaks. She says, 'Forgive me for being the one they kept.'

Rosa's Achilles' heel. Jude can't breathe.

Rosa stiffens. She moves away from Danu as she says, 'Forgive me if I scared you. I didn't mean to make you think you were dying. I just wanted to dance with you.'

Perhaps this is Danu's Achilles' heel.

The air around them is tense, and it's coming from both of them.

Rosa says, 'I've always missed you,' and takes Danu's hands in hers.

They stare at each other in silence. They're barely blinking, looking into each other's faces. Their expressions change subtly, but their emotions are intense.

Curiousity. Recognition. Wonder.

Jude exhales, and slips off her shoes beside the long bookshelves.

Picking up Danu's bags, she passes the kitchen doorway which smells of onions and brandy. She climbs the curved stairway to the third floor.

Pausing for breath on the landing, she rests the heavier bag on the banisters. She listens. They're talking quietly, though she can't hear what they're saying.

She goes into the bedroom which Rosa has decorated and prepared for her sister.

Putting Danu's bags on the bed, she looks around.

She says, 'Yes, this will do. Well done, Rosa. Well done, home. This is exactly the atmosphere Danu needs. It's peaceful.'

Crimson roses are arranged in a vase, punctuated by curves of ivy. Danu looks at Rosa across the oak table in the kitchen where the three of them are eating a late dinner. An ivy leaf casts a shadow over Rosa's mouth. It's like looking in a mirror, but believing what she sees for the first time. Perhaps she's always hated looking in mirrors because a primal part of her was always looking for Rosa, but seeing herself.

Rosa's beautiful.

Danu shouldn't stare at her so much. She looks around the kitchen. Her mouth is filled with flavours of rosemary, orange and garlic. Seven candles flicker from a metal candelabra. The dresser displays blue and green hand-painted plates. There are framed pictures of phoenixes on the walls. Pots and pans hang from a rack near the cooker.

Danu says to Rosa, 'Are you all right?'

Rosa tilts her head, considering her. 'I think so. You feel more timid, now.'

Danu smiles at her across the table. 'I feel like you can see right into me.'

'So do I.' Rosa smiles and wipes bread across the juices on her plate.

Beside them, Jude slices through a roasted tomato. Yellow pips spill across her plate.

Danu wonders why they're not eating in the dining room which has four straight-backed chairs and a marble-topped table. She thumbs open her brown roll, and smears it in butter.

Rosa's eyes are fixed on Danu's. 'The kitchen's more informal. I hope you feel relaxed here soon. It must be much grander than living in a caravan.'

She's read her mind. Danu's overwhelmed by how clean and ordered this house is. Each individual piece of furniture has been skilfully handmade. She says, 'It's lovely. It's just not what I'm used to. Not just this house, but the Inner Circle – the curves and shapes of the buildings, the light shining off glass and metal. I don't deserve to live somewhere so exquisite.'

Rosa glances at Jude.

Jude speaks gently. 'Who exactly would benefit, if you sought out somewhere uncomfortable and ugly to live, because you felt that's what you deserved?'

Danu laughs. 'No one. Unless I wrote a really good story about it and performed it on a tightrope wire.'

Rosa asks, 'Do you like poetry? I've put some books in your room but you don't have to read them.'

'I like *some* poetry. I've not read much.' Danu lowers her eyes to her plate as she slices through a baked mushroom stuffed with hazelnuts. She hasn't yet cut into the lamb because she's intimidated by it. Lamb's far more expensive than mutton. It smells delicious. Smiling to herself, she thinks that perhaps Jude and Rosa think she deserves to eat lamb.

Rosa's already finished her meal. She runs her little finger over her plate, and sucks it.

As Danu wonders what kinds of poems Rosa likes, a picture comes into her mind. A poet reading aloud, standing in front of a small gathering. Arm gesturing as if illustrating the words. Danu chews, swallows, and is about to ask Rosa if she prefers hearing poems read aloud, or seeing them on the page.

But Rosa answers before Danu's spoken. 'It depends how they're read. We've got a lot of poets living here. Some of them have really irritating lilts.' She smiles. 'We should go to a reading.'

Perhaps it doesn't really matter what they're talking about. Their minds seem to be able to fill in any blanks.

Danu shifts in her chair. Rosa sees right into her, and she's starting to see right into Rosa.

She wants to push the vase of flowers out of the way, lean across the table and place her palms on Rosa's eyelids to force her to look away, just for a moment. Just so she can have the courage to say to her, *It's huge. This moment. We might pretend otherwise because we're trying not to offend each other yet, but no matter how small or big we talk with words, we can't lie. What will this be like – living together and being unable to hide anything?*

But she doesn't.

As if she's heard this thought, Rosa's cheeks flush and she averts her gaze. She tops up her wine glass and sips from it.

Jude's also now finished eating. As she refills Danu's wine glass, Rosa says, 'Sorry – I should have done that.'

Danu shakes her head. 'Please don't worry so much. Everything's perfect. But it doesn't need to be.' She immediately thinks she's said the wrong thing.

Focusing on clearing her plate as quickly as possible, Danu

slices into the lamb and it falls off the bone. As she eats, savouring the delicate flavour, she wishes she was sitting next to Rosa rather than opposite her. If she was beside her, she'd nudge her leg with her boot. She stretches her foot under the table in case she can reach from here, but the table's too wide. She's not yet sure why, but physically touching Rosa would make her feel less awkward.

Danu puts down her fork.

Jude slides her chair back, and gathers up their plates. 'Is there pudding, Rosa?'

Rosa looks worried. 'No . . .' she says. 'I didn't make any.'

Danu says, 'I don't usually bother with puddings—'

Rosa laughs. 'I do. Meringues are my favourite.'

Danu smiles. 'Jude said you liked sugar. Or sweets, was it sweets?'

Rosa frowns at Jude. 'Did she?'

Danu says quickly, 'I might be mistaken. Sorry. I'm a bit clumsy, sometimes. I used to talk to horses more than people.'

Rosa says, 'I talk to spiders.'

Danu laughs. 'I watch them for hours and think at them, very loudly.'

Jude says, 'You two need to get to know one another in your own time.'

Rosa's eyes narrow as she returns her gaze to Jude. 'And in our own words.'

Jude carries their plates to the sink and runs the tap.

Rosa's still watching Jude. She shakes her head. 'I'm sorry, Mum.'

The air clears.

But as Danu observes how Rosa watches Jude, she hears her thoughts. *You're my mother. Don't love her more than you love me.*

Jude turns off the tap and faces them. 'Ice cream?'

364

Rosa smiles. 'We're full.'

A frown crosses Jude's forehead, and disappears as she smiles.

Rosa looks at Danu with her eyebrows raised. 'We *are* full, aren't we?'

Biting her lip, Danu replies, 'I am. Are we, *we*?'

Rosa shakes her head. 'I don't know.'

'I'll light a fire in the sitting room.' Jude leaves the kitchen.

Danu gets up and goes round to Rosa's side of the table. There are so many things to ask and be answered, and so many answers with no questions.

She nudges Rosa's shoulder with her knuckles and sits next to her.

Rosa turns to face her, and takes her hand.

Both of them hunch over. Danu's fingers are longer and Rosa's are narrower, but they're the same shape. As they compare the shapes of their thumbnails, their foreheads rest against each other. For a moment, Danu feels as if she's resting her head against an animal which trusts her. Talking into its mind, but without words.

Jude comes back in and gets a bar of chocolate and another bottle of wine out of the fridge. She says, 'Shall we go and get comfy?'

As they go through the hallway and into the sitting room, Danu asks them to tell her about the ether.

Rosa says, 'I think of it as the universe.' Whispering to Danu, she says, 'But no matter what anyone else says to you, remember this: the universe is secretly made of love.'

She sits on a green sofa beside Jude, and Danu takes the soft chair next to the fire.

Jude says, 'Over time, you'll form your own opinion. The first step is to become more aware of your emotions—'

Rosa interrupts, 'To learn to name the darkest feelings and the brightest ones. You then have to train yourself to choose what you feel.'

Danu smiles at them. 'You'll have to tell me all of this again tomorrow. Tonight I'm overwhelmed with emotions I can't choose.'

They sit together watching the flames, talking and not talking, drinking pale wine and eating dark chocolate.

When the ashes glow in the grate, Rosa kicks off her shoes and lies back on the sofa. Her eyes close.

Jude gets a cream-coloured throw from a small chest near the door, and places it over Rosa's shoulders. She whispers to Danu, 'She's had one glass too many. She'll crawl upstairs when she wakes. Do you mind if I go off to bed?'

Danu shakes her head. 'Go and sleep.'

'And you know where your room, and the bathroom, and towels—'

'I'll be fine.'

After Jude's footfall turns to silence, Danu sits on the floor beside the sofa and examines Rosa's feet. Her middle toes are slightly longer than her big toes. A feminine version of Clem's. These are not buried skeletal toes, but skin-wrapped and warm-veined things with a pulse.

Danu watches Rosa's sleeping face.

Looking for her parents, looking for herself, looking for the parts which belong only to Rosa.

TEN FOR YOUR OWN TRUE SELF

Danu has been given a vast bedroom. The walls are white, the floor is white, and the dressing table is white. Two stems of blossoming willow curve from a vase on the windowsill. She puts her possessions away in drawers and shoves her emptied bags in the bottom of a tall wardrobe. Closing the night away behind thick curtains, she exhales. The room is illuminated by a circle of bright lightbulbs which hang from the ceiling. An intricate cornice spans the walls. This is a room small enough to contain her, and big enough to be a home.

She smooths her purple coverlet over the double bed. She leaves the lights on because tonight she needs to see everything, as if brightness illuminates the truth of things, and all shadows are lies.

In the wardrobe mirror, she sees parts of Rosa's face in her own. The angle of her jaw. The curve of her cheekbones. The eyebrow which is slightly higher than the other.

She removes her clothes. These are her own breasts, this is the dip between them where her heart is buried, somewhere to the left. This is her own belly, slightly swollen from their rich meal. She holds out her arm and moves her hand as if she's dancing with it. These are the bones of her wrist.

Danu is still looking for their similarities and differences. Which parts of her body belong to her alone? Which parts are shared?

Her mind is filled with Rosa. The sound of her voice, the way she moves, her facial expressions. Her twin: lost, unknown, found, rediscovered. Is Rosa still asleep on the sofa downstairs, or is she now sitting quietly in her own bedroom, thinking of Danu? Their thoughts feel like magnetised things rushing at each other through this house and finding things they already know are there.

Their thoughts clump together. Cling. Repel, stick.

As Danu thinks about what Rosa might be doing now, she sees black words dancing on a white page. Is Rosa lying in bed attempting to read but not quite seeing the words? Perhaps she's writing the lyrics for a new song. Danu smiles, because this feels like truth. And yet walls divide them, so how can she know this?

As she inhales, her thoughts clear. As she exhales, emotions fall away from her like discarded weights.

As Danu gets to know Rosa better, she'll hate her and love her and this must be the truth of all sisters.

But tonight, she loves her. She loves Rosa because as well as having Clem's toes, she has Adelaide's lips. These are not soil-buried dead lips, but living, speaking, parting lips. She has the kind of mouth which would sing sounds as wide as a bell. If she writes songs, she must know how to sing them.

She opens the window to let in air. The curtain dances with a light wind.

Danu unties the bootlaces from her ankles. Her skin is livid. She places her father's laces on the sideboard and stares at their knots and unravelling strands.

Releasing the tight catch at her neck, she places her mother's locket beside the bootlaces. It floats in the pool of its chain.

She's taken a sore kind of comfort from this bruising trinket and these stinging knots. But for the first time since her parents died, she wants to sleep naked.

She curls up on the bed and lets herself drift. Inside a red cave, the sound of twinned heartbeats is amplified. At the mouth of the cave there's a view of an ocean. There's a full moon behind slow-moving clouds. A fire burns on the beach. One heart flickers in the flames, singing a song about burning. As the clouds move away from the moon, Danu sees another heart. It's sewn onto a kite made of red feathers, which loops in chaotic circles. It lands at the fireside and listens to the song of the heart in the fire.

This room is intensely bright. With her eyes closed, Danu can see the inside of her eyelids. Reds shine as if her body is brightening itself from the inside, wanting to be fully seen and felt and known. Colours, light, emotion, air, wind, sound – all of these things have no edges. They flood through her body, filling it, filling it, filling it.

There's no rush to travel back to the circus, there's no rush for anything. Morrie is unbound from the hex of three storms but he's got nothing left to chase for.

It's just him now, as alone as he can be in this world that keeps turning. The sun rises and sets, scarring his eyes. Each night sky is a vast bruise. He stops a few nights here and a few nights there, wherever there's water for the horse: a well, a lake, a river. A village tavern, a woman who eyes him, a half-hearted brawl with her man, and he's back to the road again.

He turns off the main road and heads west for a time, seeking a cliff that's calling him to walk along it.

For countless days he watches the sea raging beneath rock faces under rain and storms. He lets gales blow through him and empty his head of thoughts. Then he sets off again, travelling the coastal road heading south. All along the way, the chimneys in fishing villages cease smoking after dark, and the fires are lit again at dawn.

On a white-skied day, black-clad women repair a fishing net

on a sandy shoreline. Morrie keeps his distance, perched on sharp rocks. He listens to the sadness in their constant singing.

Night after night the sun sinks into the sea, spreading a thousand flame colours.

Travelling inland again, Morrie goes back to the main road and heads further south.

In the larger towns, there's laughter and fuss in the main streets, but he never speaks a word. Further along the road, he takes another detour and stops in a forest. For over a week he hears nothing but the sounds of leaves and the rare yowls of vixen.

When he leaves the forest, he helps a stooped farmer hoik a ewe out of a ditch it's near on drowning in.

Morrie doesn't speak a word to him either.

The farmer thanks him by giving him a beef casserole from his own kitchen. He says, 'Must be a hard life you're living. Being a mute.'

It's deceitful not to correct the farmer's mistake, but he needs to be silent and stare at other horizons for a time.

When Morrie reaches Caderton, he stops at the graveyard and visits the graves of the circus folk. He places garden-thieved violets on Clem and Adelaide's graves.

He thinks of telling them that he loved their daughter. That he hopes they're all together now in some bright heaven. That she missed them too much, so that makes him glad for her.

But he's got no voice to speak with, even to ghosts.

He won't let himself talk till he can say, *She's dead*.

These words are stone-grindings in his throat.

Drawn towards the flatlands to the east, Morrie turns off the main road yet again. He stops beside a black lake with no reflections. The lake shows him nothing, so there's only the sky. For many nights he watches the moon pass through clouds, harvest fat and thinning.

A few lone walkers stare to see him here, and he wonders where they've come from and where they're headed.

He nods as they pass him, but now he's not spoken for so long, he can't speak at all.

And after a long while of travelling, he notices the half-square symbols carved into the fence posts and trees at the turning points of crossroads which mean *this way*. Sandy's been true to Mag's word, though it'll have slowed them up to keep stopping and starting. Morrie follows these marks, tracking where the circus has gone to without him.

The sun's not long risen when Morrie finally reaches the circus camp. They're in a field halfway between two small towns. A red flag flies from the top of the performing tent.

Morrie pulls down on the reins and the horse turns in through the gate.

He sees Loretta first. She's hand in hand with Tomas, who grins as he sees Morrie.

Morrie gets down from the front porch and leads Inferno as he draws the caravan into a space in the corner of the field.

Loretta comes forwards, drawing Tomas along with her. She looks at the caravan window as she says, 'Is Danu with you?'

Morrie unbuckles leather straps. He's still not spoken in all this while, and while there's things he could say to Loretta, silence holds him steady. He shakes his head.

She says, 'Why not?'

He looks at their joined hands, and back at her face.

As she flushes, he shakes his head again.

Tomas says, 'What a journey to travel, for nothing. Glad you're back safe.'

Morrie leads Inferno over to the horses' enclosure.

Loretta calls, 'I'm sorry. For *all* of it, Morrie. I was angry.'

He turns to face them.

Tomas is clever enough to see past Loretta's looks and bold talk.

And here's a strange thing. Her face is clearer now, as if she's taken off some devilish mask.

There's no trace of malice.

He nods to show he understands, and leads the horse away.

When Inferno's watered and fed, Morrie returns to his caravan.

Mag's there, waiting for him. She's still in her dressing gown. She puts her arms around him.

Rubbing his back, she says, 'I know, pet. Shall we go inside?'

He opens the door and lets her step in before him.

She sits at the table, and says, 'You got there too late.'

He sits opposite her.

She rubs his arm. 'Speak, Morrie.'

This is Mag, who's hurt and helped him, and now asks for his voice.

So he gives it to her. 'She's dead.' He's startled at the cracked sound of himself.

There's softness in Mag's eyes. And some kind of knowing.

She says, 'You've not travelled the ether, have you?'

He shakes his head.

'If you had, you'd know that Danu's lost to you, and to all of us. But she's not dead.'

He clenches his fists so the nails bruise his palms.

Mag speaks firmly. 'She's alive, Morrie. But she's shut herself away. To us, she's disappeared. But she's not lost to herself. She still thinks of us. Loves us. Loves you.'

He stares at her, still not believing what she's saying, but there's no lie in her face.

She says, 'You might not want to hear this yet, but she's finally content. Complete and peaceful. That's the picture I get.'

Words break from his throat. 'It was only ever Danu. If she's alive, I want her to be happy. But I won't be.'

Mag takes his hand and holds it tight.

Her eyes grow distant, as if she's searching through his future.

Finally, she speaks. 'No, you won't. Over time you might be able to pretend happiness. Lightness as well. But you'll never let yourself love like that again.'

Danu whispers into Morrie's ear through darkness, to wake him from sleep.

'You.'

He frowns as if straining to hear more.

His spirit rises and drifts above his body.

Danu hovers above him as a magpie made of light and dark.

Now fearless, she watches him changing.

His spirit becomes a river which twists around rocks.

She becomes a fish and swims him, shedding mirrored scales.

He becomes a pale cloud.

She becomes a flock of starlings, and swarms through him with the whirring of wings.

He becomes a sunset, glowing her a thousand colours.

She is one moon and many moons.

He becomes night as she slices through him, sickle thin and widening.

She crashes as an ocean against his distant shore.

He becomes stars which break apart and fall, dissolving in her waves.

She becomes a fog of moths and flits away, chasing the brightest light.

Acknowledgements /
The Story of This Story

Heartfelt gratitude to everyone mentioned below:

In the summer of 2013 I was at Cove Park in Scotland, on a Literature Residency. There was a beautiful view of water and hills, and pieces of old pottery were washed up on the shore. I was testing out some early ideas about Matryoshka – the story of the architect emerged like a bright flame. Polly, Julian, Emmie and many other wonderful people worked there, and were available to talk quietly with. In my final days at Cove Park, there was a phonecall from home, and my marriage ended.

I returned to Brighton and gave most of my possessions to charity shops. My friend Kate Adamson provided me with the sanctuary of her spare room while I dismantled my life. I left Brighton on a train to Devon where I was to teach fiction writing for Arvon at Totleigh Barton for the first time. As I lugged two enormous bags out of a taxi, my co-tutor, Cliff Yates, asked where I lived. I replied, 'Right now? I'm voluntarily homeless. So I live here.' We've been firm friends ever since. I went on to teach for all three Arvon Centres and Moniack Mhor, and am grateful to have worked with student writers with so much passion for writing.

I gained support to start writing this novel from Creative Scotland's Artist and Creative Talent Award Programme. Unsure of where to live, I explored house-sitting websites. I was trusted by many people across the UK to look after their homes and pets, including a snake. Part of me felt as if I was constantly running away, but couldn't stop. But as Danu was a transient, it seemed right, though hard at times, that while writing her story, I also lived a transient life. The strange atmospheres of other people's homes helped me to find a voice for number nineteen Wringers Street.

The Scottish Book Trust were generous in their support, and also published my blog, *Life Size*, on their website (and later on, *Undrowned*).

I was grateful for genuine friends who kept in touch via email. Also, Kathy Andrews and Sophie Khan read early ideas or chapters. Tom Fox visited me during two house-sits and spent much time discussing Matryoshka, dancing around lamp posts and singing. I am also grateful to Anne Richards for her advice on astrology, and letting me paint a room in her colourful house white. A white room is so tranquil, I wanted Danu to have this type of peace by the end of her journey.

Solitude was a joyful freedom and it was also lonely. I felt all the Anchoress' '15 Words for Loneliness'. Between two house-sits I called in on my best friend, Tim Bedford, who lives in the sky above Cumbria. With Badger, his dog, we went for walks through clouds up on his mountain. This helped in imagining the Inner Circle, but transience was becoming a physical and emotional strain. Sometimes Morrie and Danu became too dark, then too light, before settling back into being themselves.

By this point, I hated telephones but was still online. Online worlds are strange places. So is our own world, and all the ways in which we communicate with each other. There are tunnels which are best avoided, but there are also bright stars. Via Facebook, I reconnected with Sally J Morgan, an artist I'd met while she was a course leader at Dartington College of Arts in the early 1990s. While house-sitting in Cheshire, which became Caderton, where Danu's parents are buried, I discovered that Sally now lived in New Zealand. We wrote to each other about love and loss, creative writing and performance art. We wrote about the ether, and she would know the moment I woke up. I could tell when she was asleep though we were on opposite sides of the world.

When Sally visited the UK in October 2014, we met in York. Then I visited her in Chicago, where the skyscrapers made their way into the second circle of Matryoshka. On the flight back to Scotland I was happy and in love, but when I landed I was taken straight to a hospital. My dad had become suddenly ill.

To be near him, I rented a flat in Glasgow for three months. Sally flew across the world again and met my family for the first time at my dad's funeral. At this point, I realised that I'd lost too much in too short a period of time. If I was going to survive grief, I needed to stop running. Finding it hard to speak or write, I got on a plane to New Zealand, chasing happiness. Chasing love. With Sally's help, humour, and gentle care, I finished this novel in 2016. During the same year, we got married.

At its core, *City of Circles* is about love and grief. It's been a beautiful and truthful and difficult tale to write during my own strange journey. Perhaps all fiction is in some ways autobiographical, even while telling its own story. I am therefore immensely grateful for the sensitivity and intelligent advice from Francine Toon, my editor at Sceptre, and the patience and wisdom of my wonderful agent, Lucy Luck.

But the person I must thank most of all is my soulmate, Sally, for finding me when I was so lost. So Sally, thank you for giving me space, love and encouragement while I completed this novel. You are my home. X

Garlic

Garlic

Over 65 deliciously different ways
to enjoy cooking with garlic

Jenny Linford

photography by Clare Winfield

RYLAND PETERS & SMALL
LONDON • NEW YORK

Dedication
For my mother and father, with my love

Senior Designer Sonya Nathoo
Editors Gillian Haslam, Alice Sambrook
Production Controller David Hearn
Head of Production Patricia Harrington
Art Director Leslie Harrington
Editorial Director Julia Charles
Publisher Cindy Richards

Food Stylist Rachel Wood
Prop Stylist Jo Harris
Picture Manager Christina Borsi
Indexer Hilary Bird

First published in 2016
by Ryland Peters & Small
20–21 Jockey's Fields
London WC1R 4BW
and Ryland Peters & Small, Inc.
341 East 116th Street
New York NY 10029
www.rylandpeters.com

Text © Jenny Linford 2016
Design and commissioned photographs
© Ryland Peters & Small 2016 (see full photography
credits on page 159)

ISBN: 978-1-84975-707-2

10 9 8 7 6 5 4 3 2 1

Printed and bound in China.

CIP data from the Library of Congress has been
applied for. A CIP record for this book is available
from the British Library.

Notes
• Both British (metric) and American (imperial
plus US cups) are included in these recipes; however,
it is important to work with one set of measurements
and not alternate between the two within a recipe.
• All eggs are medium (UK) or large (US), unless
specified as large, in which case US extra large
should be used. Uncooked or partially cooked eggs
should not be served to the very old, frail, young
children, pregnant women or those with
compromised immune systems.
• When a recipe calls for the grated zest of citrus
fruit, buy unwaxed fruit and wash well before using.
If you can only find treated fruit, scrub well
in warm soapy water before using.

Contents

INTRODUCTION **6**
Feature: *The many forms of garlic*

CHAPTER ONE Mellow **10**
Feature: *Garlic preparation and storage*

CHAPTER TWO Sunshine **32**
Feature: *Garlic for health*

CHAPTER THREE Comfort **62**
Feature: *Garlic folklore*

CHAPTER FOUR Fiery **84**
Feature: *Meet the garlic farmers*

CHAPTER FIVE Go Wild **108**
Feature: *Growing garlic*

CHAPTER SIX Celebratory **132**
Feature: *Garlic festivals*

INDEX **156**
ACKNOWLEDGMENTS **160**

Introduction

Garlic is audacious. Its pungent scent and powerful flavour – with each small clove packing a huge punch – have aroused strong feelings throughout history. This is an ingredient which, at times, has been scorned by the upper classes in society and frowned upon by a number of the world's religions. On the other hand, garlic's extraordinary ability to transform and invigorate dishes has made it a much-loved and essential flavouring in kitchens around the world. There is a distinctly democratic streak to its universal popularity; eaten with relish by the poor in many countries for many centuries, it has long been known to ancient civilizations, including those of China, India, Egypt, Greece and Rome.

The name 'garlic' originates from the Anglo Saxon word 'gar' meaning spear, a reference to the shape of the plant's leaves, though the plant itself is thought to be native to Central Asia. Otherwise known as *Allium sativum*, garlic's powerful flavour is released through crushing and chopping. One of the pleasures of cooking with it is learning how to adjust the level of 'garlic power' as required. For example, keeping a garlic clove whole makes it less powerful than cutting it into small pieces, in order to subtly infuse but not overwhelm a dish. A whole garlic clove fried in oil but then discarded, with the flavoured oil then used for cooking, is an effective method of adding its distinctive taste discreetly. A whole garlic clove placed in the cavity of a chicken before roasting has a similar effect, as has adding one to a slowly simmered casserole or sauce. Rubbing a salad bowl with a peeled garlic clove is a classic and elegant way of adding garlic notes.

When asked to write this book, I was thrilled. I had realized some years ago that all my favourite dishes contained garlic, so my affection for this extraordinary flavouring is deep and long-held. There are so many different ways of using garlic that, when it came to inspiration, I was spoilt for choice. French, Italian, Lebanese, Indian, Portuguese, Chinese, Thai – there are very few cuisines in the world in which garlic does not play a part. It is a truly cosmopolitan ingredient that features in many of the world's classic dishes, from Italy's homely pasta carbonara or Egypt's rustic ful medames to luxurious French coq au vin and Thailand's aromatic green curry. In writing this book, I've also embraced garlic-flavoured ingredients, such as wild garlic/ramps and garlic chives, on the grounds that they, too, deserve a place in a celebration of garlic.

Affordable and readily available, garlic is an everyday, almost humble ingredient, yet, when one stops to think about it, a remarkable one. If I had to choose one desert island ingredient, it would be garlic.

The many forms of garlic

Garlic

Known botanically as *Allium sativum*, there are two main subspecies of garlic (hardneck and softneck) and many further varieties, with greengrocers, delicatessens and farmers' markets all useful sources for purchasing. Garlic's powerful flavour is released when the cloves are broken, producing sulphur-containing compounds within the plant's cell walls. Garlic is usually sold in bulbs or heads, each containing separate cloves wrapped in a papery skin.

Wet garlic

Most garlic sold has been dried to preserve it. Wet garlic (or green garlic) is freshly harvested and sold as a new-season specialty. These young bulbs have not yet formed skins or split into cloves, so the whole head and stalk can be eaten. The flesh is moist and white with a mild flavour.

Elephant garlic

Striking in appearance, *Allium ampeloprasum* var. *ampeloprasum* is botanically classified as a leek rather than a garlic, although it possesses a mild garlic flavour. The large bulb contains large cloves, which can be used whole in dishes to good visual effect.

Black garlic

Originally from Korea, black garlic is a form of preserved garlic, created by gently heating heads of garlic for a long period of time. During this process, the cloves blacken in colour and the garlic changes texture, becoming soft. The flavour also mellows, losing the pungency of garlic, taking on instead smoky and balsamic vinegar notes. In cooking, black garlic is used for its flavour and its striking black appearance.

A selection of garlic bulbs, in their many glorious forms.

Smoked garlic

Garlic is smoked to transform its flavour, rather than to preserve it, giving a subtle smokiness to the cloves – while muting their natural pungency – and adding a dark brown hue to the papery wrapping.

Deep-fried garlic

Available ready-made in stores/supermarkets, this is produced by deep-frying finely minced garlic in oil until golden brown and crispy. A popular ingredient in Thai cuisine, deep-fried garlic is used to add crunchy texture and garlic flavour to a wide range of dishes.

Pickled garlic

Peeled garlic cloves are preserved in brine and vinegar, these have a crunchy texture and retain a strong garlic flavour, as well as a salty tanginess.

Garlic salt

A seasoning made by mixing salt with ground dried garlic, this has a distinctive garlic flavour and is a store cupboard substitute for fresh garlic.

Garlic scapes

Garlic scapes are flower stalks produced by hardneck garlic. They are harvested in late spring and prized as a seasonal delicacy. Bright green in appearance, they have a pleasant juicy texture and a sweet garlicky flavour. They can be used as a herb or a vegetable.

Wild garlic/ramps

Also known as ramsons, wood garlic or bear garlic, the plant *Allium ursinum* grows wild in shady woodlands in Europe, with its edible long green leaves possessing a definite garlic aroma and a subtle garlic flavour. In North America, wild garlic is 'ramps' or *Allium trioccum,* a very similar plant to *Allium ursinum.*

Garlic chives

Allium tuberosum, also known as Chinese chives, have long, flat, narrow, green leaves and a distinctive garlic flavour. In Chinese and Korean cookery they are used as flavouring and as a vegetable in stir-fries.

Mellow garlic

Garlic preparation and storage

When it comes to cooking with garlic, part of its versatility as a flavouring is that you can adjust the strength as required. Breaking down the garlic cells as you chop or crush a clove causes an enzyme reaction creating the compound which gives garlic its distinctive smell and flavour. So, when just a discreet garlic touch is required, adding a whole clove, unpeeled or peeled, to a dish such as a ragu works well. For gloriously powerful garlic, however, crushed garlic is often called for.

There are myriad garlic presses, crushers and mincers out there to help you in this task. Their popularity is partly to do with people wishing to avoid their hands smelling of garlic, as well as their ease and speed of use. One way to get rid of the smell is simply to rub your hands on something made of stainless steel. It is possible to buy odour-removing stainless steel 'soap' bars specifically for this purpose.

Against garlic crushers is the fact that cleaning some of these gizmos can be fiddly and, all too often, pieces of garlic are left behind in the gadget. An easy, gadget-free way of crushing garlic, favoured by many chefs, is to place a peeled, chopped clove on a chopping board, sprinkle over a pinch of salt (which helps break it down), cover it with the broad side of a large knife, then press down hard repeatedly onto the blade, crushing the garlic into a paste.

When buying garlic, choose heads that are firm and plump, avoiding any that look dried out and shrivelled. The best way of storing garlic is to keep it in dry, cool and, ideally, dark conditions, for example, in a basket, ceramic pot or a breathable mesh bag inside a cupboard. Storing garlic in the fridge encourages it to sprout and is not advised. Usefully, whole garlic heads and loose garlic cloves stored correctly will keep well for several weeks. The majority of garlic we buy has already been allowed to dry out after harvesting by the growers. An exception to this is new-season 'wet garlic' (sometimes called green garlic), which is freshly harvested. Try and use this as soon as possible before it begins to dry out.

One traditional way of storing garlic is in plaits or braids, and garlic farms often sell their wares in this form. These are generally made by the garlic growers themselves from softneck garlic, using the long stalks of the garlic to plait/braid the heads together once it has been dried. Appealingly rustic, a plait/braid of garlic hung from a hook in the kitchen out of direct light is picturesque and allows for air to circulate and keep the garlic dry.

Garlic can be frozen peeled or unpeeled, as whole cloves, chopped, or in paste form. If freezing, bear in mind that the odour can permeate other ingredients, so be sure to store it in a well-sealed container or wrap it in a couple of layers of plastic sandwich bags, clingfilm/plastic wrap or parchment paper.

A delicious way of preserving the flavour of garlic is to make garlic-infused oil. While this is a straightforward process, a few simple but important steps need to be followed to make it correctly and safely and prevent any toxins from forming. Fry the garlic cloves gently in a little olive oil, stirring them often to prevent them browning, for around 3 minutes until fragrant. Add in the remaining olive oil for the quantity required to the pan and simmer for 20 minutes. Strain the oil well, allow to cool and pour into a dry, sterilized glass bottle. Store in the fridge and consume within a week.

It is also possible to infuse vinegar with garlic. Use a good quality vinegar and be sure to check the label to ensure that the vinegar has an acetic acid content of at least 5 per cent (which makes it hard for micro-organisms to survive) and for best results heat the vinegar before steeping the garlic.

Hummus

This tasty, nutty-flavoured Middle Eastern dip is so easy to make at home. Serve it with pitta bread, falafel or vegetable crudités as a snack or alongside other mezze dishes for a light meal.

125 g/¾ cup dried
   chickpeas/garbanzo beans
1 teaspoon bicarbonate of
   soda/baking soda
2 garlic cloves, crushed to
   a paste
4 tablespoons tahini
freshly squeezed juice of
   1 lemon
salt

TO GARNISH
olive oil
paprika or sumac
finely chopped fresh parsley

Serves 6

Soak the chickpeas/garbanzo beans overnight in plenty of cold water with the bicarbonate of soda/baking soda.

Next day, drain and rinse. Place in a large pan, add enough fresh cold water to cover well and bring to the boil. Reduce the heat and simmer for 50–60 minutes until tender, skimming off any scum. Season the chickpeas with salt, then drain, reserving the cooking water and setting aside 1 tablespoon of the cooked chickpeas/garbanzo beans for the garnish.

In a food processor, blend together the cooked chickpeas/garbanzo beans, garlic, tahini and lemon juice. Gradually add in the cooking liquid until the mixture becomes a smooth paste. Season with salt.

Transfer the hummus to a serving bowl. To serve, make a shallow hollow in the centre using the back of a spoon. Pour in a little olive oil, top with the reserved whole chickpeas/garbanzo beans and sprinkle with paprika and parsley.

Bean and garlic dip

A fresh-tasting dip, with a pleasant nutty flavour.
Serve with pitta bread or crudités.

250 g/9 oz. frozen broad/fava
  beans

2 roast garlic cloves
  (see page 23),
  peeled and mashed

1 tablespoon olive oil

100 g/½ cup ricotta cheese

2 tablespoons chopped fresh
  dill, plus fronds to garnish

salt and freshly ground black
  pepper

Serves 4

Cook the frozen beans in a saucepan of boiling water until just
tender. Drain, cool and pop the beans out of their tough skins.

Place the skinned beans, roast garlic and olive oil in a food
processor and blend together; alternatively mash together in
a bowl using a fork. Add in the ricotta, chopped dill, salt and
pepper and blend together briefly.

Cover and chill. To serve, garnish with dill fronds.

Roast garlic beetroot/beet soup

2 garlic cloves,
   unpeeled
500 g/1 lb. 2 oz. raw
   beetroot/beets
1 tablespoon olive oil
½ onion, finely chopped
a splash of red wine
   (optional)
600 ml/2½ cups fresh
   chicken or vegetable
   stock
salt and freshly ground
   black pepper
crème fraîche or sour
   cream, to serve
chopped tarragon, to
   serve

Serves 4

This striking soup has a pleasantly earthy sweetness to
it. Serve as a hearty appetizer or for a light lunch, with
some good crusty bread on the side.

Preheat the oven to 200°C (400°F) Gas 6.

Cut the tip off each unpeeled garlic clove, to just expose the clove
inside. Wrap the garlic and beetroot/beets together in foil, sealing well.
Place on a baking sheet and bake in the preheated oven for 1 hour.
Unwrap and set aside to cool.

Peel the beetroot/beets and roughly chop. Peel the garlic and mash it.

Next, heat the oil in a large saucepan set over a low heat. Add the onion
and fry gently until softened. Add the chopped beetroot/beets, mashed
garlic and a splash of red wine if desired. Cook for 2 minutes, then pour
in the stock. Bring to the boil, cover, reduce the heat and simmer for
30 minutes.

Leave to cool a little, then blend until smooth, using a stick blender or
a food processor. Season with salt and pepper, return to the pan and
gently heat through.

To serve, pour into bowls and garnish with crème fraîche or sour cream
and chopped tarragon.

Pan-fried gnocchi with garlic mushrooms and pancetta

A hearty, rustic dish, perfect for a comforting supper after a busy day. Use as many different mushrooms as you can find for a range of flavours and textures. When in season, a few wild mushrooms would add a touch of luxury.

500 g/1 lb. 2 oz. potato gnocchi

2 tablespoons olive oil

50 g/2 oz. pancetta, diced

2 garlic cloves, chopped

a sprig of fresh thyme

500 g/1 lb. 2 oz. assorted mushrooms (such as button, oyster and shiitake), small ones left whole, large ones roughly sliced

25 g/1 oz. dried and chopped porcini mushrooms, soaked in hot water for 15 minutes, then drained

a splash of dry white wine

freshly grated nutmeg

15 g/1 tablespoon butter

salt and freshly ground black pepper

chopped fresh parsley, to garnish

grated Parmesan cheese, to serve

Serves 4

Boil the gnocchi in a large pan of boiling salted water until cooked (check packet intructions for cooking time); drain and set aside.

Heat 1 tablespoon of the olive oil in large frying pan/skillet. Add the pancetta, garlic and thyme and fry, stirring often, for 2 minutes. Add the assorted mushrooms and porcini, mixing in well. Add the wine and cook, stirring, until evaporated. Season with salt, pepper and nutmeg and fry, stirring often, until the mushrooms are cooked through but retain their texture. Set aside.

In a separate large frying pan/skillet, heat the remaining olive oil and the butter. Once the mixture is frothing, add the cooked gnocchi, spreading them out in a single layer. Fry for a few minutes, turning now and then, until golden brown on all sides. Add the fried mushroom mixture, mixing it in well, and cook until the mushrooms are heated through.

Garnish with the parsley and serve at once with grated Parmesan cheese to sprinkle over.

Roast garlic crab tart

A rich treat of a savoury tart, studded with mellow roast garlic cloves. Serve with a refreshing fennel and watercress salad, for a pleasing contrast of textures.

250 g/9 oz. shortcrust pastry/pie dough

2 eggs plus 1 egg yolk, beaten together

300 ml/1¼ cups crème fraîche or double/heavy cream

a pinch of saffron threads, finely ground and soaked in 1 teaspoon hot water

250 g/9½ oz. picked crab meat (white and brown)

8 roast garlic cloves (see page 23), peeled, left whole

salt and freshly ground black pepper

22-cm/9-in. loose-based tart pan, greased

baking beans

Serves 6-8

Preheat the oven to 200°C (400°F) Gas 6.

Roll out the pastry/pie dough thinly and use it to line the greased tart pan. Line the pastry case with a square of parchment paper, then fill with baking beans.

Blind bake the pastry case in the preheated oven for 10 minutes. Remove the parchment paper and beans and bake uncovered for a further 5 minutes. Brush a little of the beaten eggs over the case and bake for a further 5 minutes. Remove from the oven, leaving it on at 200°C (400°F) Gas 6.

Meanwhile, prepare the filling. Whisk the crème fraîche or cream with the beaten eggs. Stir in the saffron liquid. Season with salt and pepper.

Spread the crab meat evenly in the part-baked pastry case. Dot over the roast garlic cloves. Pour over the crème fraîche/egg mixture.

Bake in the preheated oven for 30–40 minutes. Remove and serve warm or cool.

Roast garlic salt cod croquettes

These crisp, light-textured croquettes, with their subtle, salty, fishy flavour, are addictively good! Serve with either the parsley pesto or the roast garlic tartare sauce. Great with a crisp side salad for a light meal or enjoy as a snack.

1 head of garlic

600 g/1 lb. 5 oz. salt cod fillet, soaked for 24 hours, with water changed 2–3 times during soaking period

600 g/1 lb. 5 oz. floury potatoes, such as King Edwards, peeled and chopped

2 eggs, lightly beaten

2 tablespoons freshly chopped parsley

grated zest of 1 lemon

oil, for deep-frying

salt

PARSLEY PESTO

50 g/2 cups freshly chopped parsley

120 ml/½ cup olive oil

salt

ROAST GARLIC TARTARE SAUCE

200 g/1 cup mayonnaise

2 tablespoons finely chopped gherkins

1 tablespoon capers

2 roast garlic cloves, peeled and mashed (taken from head used in croquettes above)

2 tablespoons finely chopped fresh parsley

Makes 24 croquettes (serves 4–6 for a light lunch)

To roast the garlic, preheat the oven to 180°C (350°F) Gas 4.

Slice the top off the garlic head, to expose the cloves inside. Wrap in foil and bake the garlic head in the preheated oven for 1 hour. Unwrap the foil and set the garlic head aside to cool.

When the garlic is cool enough to handle, squeeze out the softened roast garlic from each clove. Set aside and then mash 4 cloves for the croquettes and 2 cloves for the tartare sauce.

To make the croquettes, drain the soaked salt cod and place in a pan. Cover generously with cold water, bring to the boil and cook over a medium heat until tender, around 20 minutes; drain.

Boil the potatoes in salted water until tender; drain, mash and allow to cool. Mix the 4 mashed roast garlic cloves into the potatoes.

When the salt cod is cool enough to handle, use your fingers to go through it and discard any skin and bones. Flake the fish.

In a large bowl, mix together the flaked salt cod, mashed potato, eggs, parsley and lemon zest, mixing well. Using 2 tablespoons, shape the mixture into 24 croquettes and set aside to cool completely.

If serving with parsley pesto, blitz together the parsley and olive oil in a food processor, then season with salt.

If serving with roast garlic tartare sauce, simply mix all the ingredients together and chill before serving. (This tartare sauce is also good with fish and chips, or fish-finger/fish stick sandwiches.)

Heat the oil for deep-frying in a large saucepan until very hot. Fry the croquettes in batches until a rich golden brown in colour, turning them over during frying so that they brown on both sides. Remove and drain on kitchen paper.

Serve warm from frying or at room temperature with the parsley pesto or roast garlic tartare sauce on the side.

Flowering Chinese chive prawns/shrimp

Flowering Chinese chives are a lesser-known variety of Chinese chives, both can be found in Asian stores/supermarkets. Either would work well in this recipe, providing a subtle garlic flavour and pleasant texture. Serve with noodles for a quick and tasty meal.

1 tablespoon sunflower or vegetable oil

2 cm/¾ in. fresh ginger, peeled and finely sliced

200 g/7 oz. flowering Chinese chives or Chinese chives, chopped into 2.5-cm/1-in. lengths

200 g/7 oz. raw prawns/shrimp, peeled

1 tablespoon rice wine or medium sherry

1 tablespoon light soy sauce

½ teaspoon sesame oil

Serves 2

Place the oil in a wok over a high heat. Add the ginger and stir-fry until fragrant. Next put in the Chinese chives and stir-fry briefly.

Add the prawns/shrimp and stir-fry. As soon as the prawns/shrimp turn opaque, add the rice wine and sizzle briefly. Lastly, throw in the soy sauce and sesame oil. Stir-fry for 2–3 minutes until Chinese chives are just wilted. Serve at once.

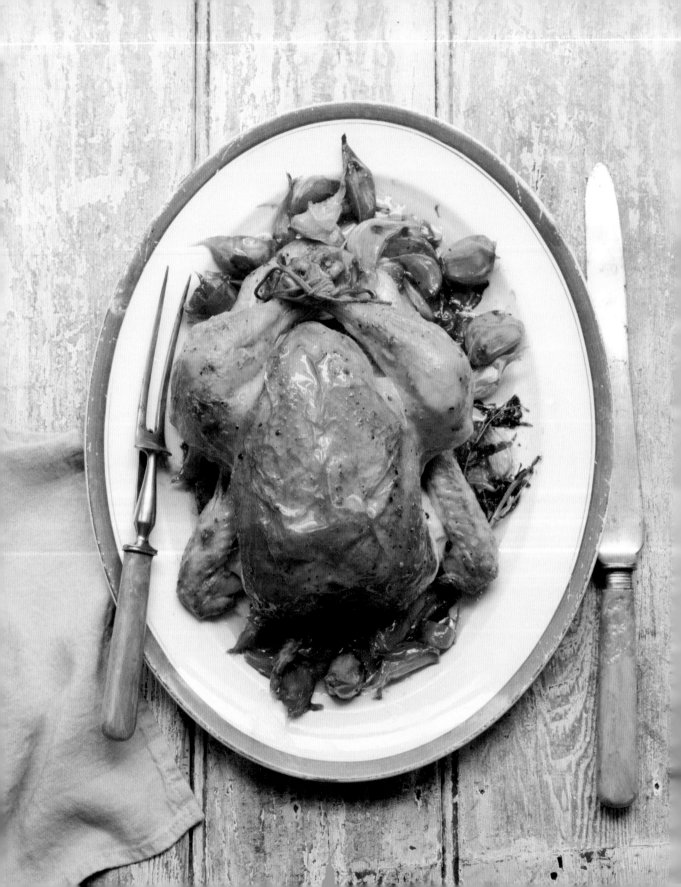

Chicken with 40 cloves of garlic

Yes, this is truly a dish for garlic lovers! Pot-roasting
the bird makes for tender, flavourful chicken, aromatic
with tarragon. Serve the cooked whole garlic cloves with
the chicken so that guests can squeeze the softened garlic
out of the skins as a rich and tasty accompaniment.

1.8 kg/4 lb. free-range chicken
25 g/1½ tablespoons butter
1 tablespoon olive oil
40 garlic cloves, separated but
   unpeeled
100 ml/⅓ cup vermouth or dry
   white wine
freshly squeezed juice of ½ lemon
200 ml/1 cup good-quality chicken
   stock

a handful of fresh tarragon sprigs
salt and freshly ground black
   pepper

*a lidded flameproof casserole dish,
   large enough to hold the chicken*

Serves 6

Preheat the oven to 180°C (350°F) Gas 4.

Season the chicken with salt and pepper. Heat the butter and olive oil
in a large frying pan/skillet. Add the chicken and brown on all sides. Save
the pan juices.

Meanwhile, heat the casserole dish on the stovetop. Transfer the browned
chicken to the casserole dish. Tuck some of the garlic cloves into the
cavity, sprinkle the rest around the chicken and pour over the vermouth or
wine. Allow to sizzle briefly, then pour in the buttery juices from the frying
pan/skillet, the lemon juice and stock. Add the tarragon, placing a few
sprigs inside the cavity.

Bring to the boil on the stovetop, then cover with the lid and transfer the
casserole to the preheated oven. Bake, covered, for 1 hour 20 minutes–
1 hour 30 minutes until the chicken is cooked through and the juices
run clear.

Transfer the chicken to a serving dish. Use a slotted spoon to transfer the
garlic cloves to the dish. Pour the juices into a serving jug/pitcher to use
as a gravy, skimming off any excess fat. Serve the chicken with the garlic
cloves and gravy.

Smoked garlic pulled pork

Slow-cooked, tender pork with its smoky garlicky flavour is a tasty dish, contrasting well with this tangy dressing. Serve the shredded pork in bread rolls or as a buffet dish with potato salad and coleslaw.

2.2-kg/5-lb. pork shoulder on the bone, skin scored for crackling
2 smoked garlic cloves, thinly sliced
2 teaspoons smoked garlic powder
2 tablespoons olive oil
8 bread rolls
salt and freshly ground black pepper

DRESSING
6 tablespoons red wine vinegar
2 tablespoons clear honey
2 roast garlic cloves (see page 23), peeled and mashed
salt

Serves 8

Preheat the oven to 220°C (425°F) Gas 7. Bring the pork to room temperature.

Pat the pork dry with paper towels and season the skin thoroughly with salt. Lightly score the flesh, then cut small incisions and insert the chopped smoked garlic pieces. Season the flesh with smoked garlic powder, salt and freshly ground black pepper.

Line a large roasting pan with a large piece of foil. Place the pork in the middle of the foil, pour over the olive oil, then wrap the foil up over the pork to form a parcel.

Roast for 15 minutes in the preheated oven, then reduce the temperature to 150°C (300°F) Gas 2. Cook the pork for a further 5 hours 45 minutes.

Unwrap the pork, saving the pan juices. Discard any fat, or if you want crispy crackling, remove the fat and place under a hot grill/broiler for 10–15 minutes. Using two forks, pull the soft cooked pork off the bone in long shreds. Toss the pulled pork with 3–4 tablespoons of the roasting pan juices for extra moisture.

Mix together the dressing ingredients and season to taste.

Fill the rolls generously with pulled pork, topping with the tangy dressing as required.

Garlicky goose fat roast potatoes

Everybody loves roast potatoes and these ones are irresistibly moreish. Serve with roast beef, lamb, pork or chicken.

1 tablespoon goose fat
a pinch of salt
700 g/1½ lbs. roasting potatoes, peeled and cut into large, even chunks
8 garlic cloves, unpeeled
sea salt flakes

*Serves 4
as a side dish*

Preheat the oven to 220°C (425°F) Gas 7. Place the goose fat in a roasting pan and preheat in the oven.

Bring a large pan of salted water to the boil. Add the potatoes and cook for 10 minutes to par-boil them; drain, return to the pan and shake to roughen their surface.

Add the par-boiled potatoes to the hot goose fat in the roasting pan, shaking to coat them well. Sprinkle in the garlic cloves and season with salt flakes. Roast for 30–40 minutes, turning over now and then to brown on all sides, until golden brown. Serve at once.

Italian-style garlic spinach

An elegant and easy vegetable dish, this garlicky spinach makes the perfect accompaniment for roast lamb or beef.

500 g/1 lb. fresh large leaf spinach, rinsed
2 tablespoons olive oil
1 garlic clove, peeled and left whole
a squeeze of fresh lemon juice
salt and freshly ground black pepper

*Serves 4
as a side dish*

Place the spinach in a large, heavy-based pan and season with salt. Cover and cook for a few minutes until the spinach has just wilted (no need to add extra water). Drain in a colander, pressing with a spatula to squeeze out excess moisture. Roughly chop.

Heat the oil in a large frying pan/skillet. Add the garlic and fry, stirring, until browned on all sides; remove and discard the garlic. Add the chopped spinach to the pan and fry in the garlic oil, turning to coat thoroughly. Season to taste, add a squeeze of lemon juice and serve at once.

Sunshine garlic

Garlic for health

Historically, human beings have had a very special relationship with garlic (*Allium sativum*). Not only has it been relished for its ability to add bold flavour to food but also as a traditional medicine attributed with numerous special healing powers. For centuries, doctors and alternative health practitioners have treated the natural world as a medicine chest, searching for remedies and using plants, including garlic, to treat illnesses.

Garlic is particularly striking because of the range of ailments it has been used to treat. Used both internally and externally, it has been prescribed raw, prepared in food, taken with vinegar or wine, applied to wounds in the form of poultices, rubbed on bruises or mixed with goose fat and applied to ears.

In Indian Ayurvedic medicine, garlic is highly valued, used as a diuretic, as a pick-me-up, to aid digestion and to treat heart disease and arthritis.

In Chinese medicine, garlic was considered as a stimulant and warmer (yang in the yin–and–yang view of the universe) and used to help relieve depression. The Ancient Egyptians used garlic as a fortifying medicine, with the slaves who built the pyramids given daily doses of garlic in order to keep them strong. This perception of it as a strengthening food continued with the Greeks and Romans, with garlic fed to Olympian athletes and soldiers. In Ancient Greece, Hippocrates (460–370 BC), the renowned physician, recommended garlic in treating pneumonia and other infections. The Roman author and naturalist Pliny the Elder (AD 23–AD 79) wrote that 'garlic has powerful properties', advising that it can be used to treat snake bites, applied to bruises and taken to induce sleep.

Through the centuries, garlic has continued to be valued in many countries for its healthy properties. In Europe during the Middle Ages, garlic was used to treat digestive disorders, constipation and the plague. The sixteenth-century Italian physician Pietro Andrea Mattioli (1501–1577) recommended that garlic be used to treat digestive disorders and worms. In nineteenth-century America, John Gunn's *Home Book of Health* recommended that garlic be used to treat asthma, lung disorders and infections. In Russia garlic was widely used to treat respiratory tract diseases.

As our scientific knowledge of plants and their medicinal properties has progressed, so has our understanding of garlic's antibacterial powers. In 1858 the French scientist Louis Pasteur experimented with garlic and noted its ability to destroy bacteria. Throughout World War I, garlic was used to dress wounds and during World War II, with conventional medicines in short supply, garlic was used instead by the Red Army to treat soldiers in Russia, hence its nickname 'Russian penicillin'.

Our age-old fascination with garlic as a healthy food shows no signs of abating. We now know that garlic contains the compound alliin and the enzyme alliinase which, when garlic is cut or crushed, come together to create allicin. This compound allicin (incidentally responsible for garlic's odour) is known to have antibacterial and antifungal medicinal properties.

Garlic also contains ajoene, which functions as an antioxidant and also has antithrombotic properties which helps to prevent blood clots from forming.

Garlic is recognized by medical authorities as reducing lipids (fats) in our blood, specifically cholesterol. When it comes to cardiovascular health, garlic's sulphur-containing compounds are thought to protect against inflammation and oxidative stress.

Garlic and garlic products are still widely prescribed around the world to treat a range of conditions. Scientific research continues to explore its health-giving properties, among them the potential it may have as a cancer-fighting anticarcinogen.

Roast garlic herbed labneh

Making labneh (also labne, labni or yogurt cheese) is very simple, but do bear in mind that it takes 24 hours to strain the yogurt. Serve this Middle Eastern cheese as an appetizer with vegetable crudités and hot pitta bread.

450 g/2 cups full-fat goat's milk yogurt
salt
2 roast garlic cloves (see page 23)
finely grated zest of 1 lemon
3 tablespoons finely chopped fresh parsley
1 teaspoon finely chopped fresh chives
1 teaspoon fresh thyme leaves
olive oil, to serve
pistachio nuts, finely ground, to garnish

a muslin/cheesecloth square and string

Serve 4–6

First, make the labneh. Season the yogurt with salt to taste, mixing it in well. Place the yogurt in the centre of the muslin/cheesecloth square, fold up the muslin/cheesecloth around the yogurt and tie tightly, forming a parcel. Suspend the muslin/cheesecloth parcel over a deep, large bowl by tying it with the string to a wooden spoon laid across the top of the bowl.

Leave in the fridge for 24 hours, during which time the excess moisture will drip out of the parcel.

Squeeze the roast garlic out of the papery skin and mash into a paste. Flavour the labneh by mixing it with the roast garlic, lemon zest, parsley, chives and thyme.

Transfer the labneh to a serving dish. Use the back of a spoon to make a little hollow in the middle of the labneh, pour in a little olive oil, sprinkle with ground pistachio nuts and serve.

Roast garlic rosemary focaccia

Freshly made focaccia is always a treat, with roast garlic adding a wonderful savouriness and rosemary an appealing aromatic note. Serve on its own or with Italian charcuterie, such as parma ham/prosciutto or mortadella, for a light meal.

500 g/3½ cups strong white bread flour, plus extra for dusting

1 teaspoon fast-action dried yeast

1 teaspoon salt

1 teaspoon sugar

300 ml/1¼ cups hand-hot water

5 tablespoons extra virgin olive oil

6 roast garlic cloves (see page 23), peeled and chopped

3 tablespoons rosemary leaves, finely chopped

a pinch of sea salt flakes

a large mixing bowl, oiled
a baking sheet, greased

Makes 1 loaf; serves 6

Mix together the flour, yeast, salt and sugar. Gradually add in the water and 2 tablespoons of the oil, bringing the mixture together to form a sticky dough. Turn out onto a lightly floured surface and knead until smooth and elastic. Then work in the roast garlic and 2 tablespoons of the rosemary. Transfer to the prepared mixing bowl, cover with a clean damp kitchen cloth and set aside in a warm place to rise for 1 hour.

Break down the risen dough and shape into a large oval on the prepared baking sheet.

Using your fingertips, press into the dough to make numerous small indentations. Spoon over 2 tablespoons of the oil, so that it fills the indents, and sprinkle over the remaining rosemary. Set aside to rest for 30 minutes.

Preheat the oven to 200°C (400°F) Gas 6.

Bake the focaccia in the preheated oven until golden brown. Spoon over the remaining oil and sprinkle with the sea salt flakes.

Serve warm from the oven or at room temperature.

Green garlic muffins

1 teaspoon olive oil

2 garlic cloves, chopped

225 g/1¾ cups self-raising/self-rising flour

1 teaspoon baking powder

1 teaspoon salt

1 egg

50 g/4 tablespoons natural yogurt

100–125 ml/⅓–½ cup whole milk

150 g/1¾ cups grated courgettes/zucchini

50 g/½ cup chopped pistachio nuts

50 g/½ cup grated Cheddar cheese

a 12-hole muffin pan, lined with paper cases

Makes 12

These tasty muffins, flecked with grated courgette/zucchini and chopped pistachio nuts, are great for brunch; serve warm from the oven with butter or cream cheese.

Heat the oil in a small frying pan/skillet and gently fry the garlic until golden, stirring and taking care not to burn it. Set aside to cool.

Preheat the oven to 200°C (400°F) Gas 6.

Sift the flour, baking powder and salt into a mixing bowl. In a separate bowl, whisk together the egg, yogurt and 100 ml/⅓ cup milk. Pour the egg mixture over the sifted ingredients and stir together, taking care not to over-mix. If the mixture appears very dry then add the extra milk. Fold in the fried garlic, grated courgette/zucchini, chopped pistachios and grated Cheddar.

Divide the mixture among the muffin cases. Bake in the preheated oven for 20 minutes until risen and golden brown. Serve warm from the oven or allow to cool.

Ajo blanco

Also known as white gazpacho, this classic Spanish cold soup, simply made from a few humble ingredients, has a delicate nutty flavour. Garnished, as is traditional, with fresh grapes or melon, it makes a visually appealing and refreshing first course or light lunch.

100 g/3½ oz. slightly stale white bread, crusts trimmed, sliced

700 ml/3 cups cold water

200 g/1½ cups blanched almonds

2 garlic cloves, crushed

6 tablespoons extra virgin olive oil, plus extra for serving

2 tablespoons sherry vinegar

salt

24 white seedless grapes, halved, or 200 g/7 oz. green or orange melon, cut into small chunks

Serves 4

Soak the bread in the cold water for 30 minutes until softened.

Finely grind the almonds in a food processor. Add the soaked bread and half the soaking water, reserving the remainder. Blitz until smooth. Add the crushed garlic, olive oil and sherry vinegar and blend together until smooth.

Add in enough of the remaining soaking water to give the soup a creamy texture. Season with salt. Cover and chill in the fridge for at least 2–3 hours.

Serve garnished with a drizzle of olive oil and grape halves or small chunks of melon.

Black garlic tricolore salad

Insalata tricolore – Italy's patriotic red, white and green salad – is a classic which, when made with good-quality tomatoes, ripe avocado and fresh mozzarella, is such a treat to eat. Adding black garlic is an unorthodox touch, but the smoky sweetness of black garlic works well with the balsamic vinegar and gives an interesting flavour to the dish.

6 tablespoons extra virgin olive oil

2 tablespoons balsamic vinegar

2 black garlic cloves, finely chopped

3 mozzarella cheese balls, drained and sliced

4 ripe tomatoes, sliced

2 avocados, sliced and tossed with a little lemon juice to prevent discolouring

a handful of fresh basil leaves

salt and freshly ground black pepper

Serves 4

Make the dressing by placing the olive oil, balsamic vinegar and black garlic in a small lidded jar, then shaking well to mix together. Season with salt and pepper.

Arrange the mozzarella, tomato and avocado in overlapping slices on a large serving plate. Pour over the black garlic dressing, scatter over the basil leaves and serve at once.

Thai prawn/shrimp pomelo salad with garlic and herb dressing

Pomelo is a thick-skinned citrus fruit with a distinctive flavour and juicy texture. It is often used in Thai salads. The contrast in textures works well, with the tasty dressing adding a pleasant piquant punch. If pomelo is unavailable, white grapefruit can be used instead.

½ pomelo, or
   1 grapefruit
1 ripe mango
200 g/7 oz. cooked, peeled king
   prawns/jumbo shrimp

DRESSING
15 g/1 cup fresh
   coriander/cilantro leaves
10 g/⅔ cup fresh mint leaves
1 garlic clove, peeled

1 green chilli/chile, chopped
grated zest of ½ lime
freshly squeezed juice of 1 lime
a pinch of salt

Serves 4 as an appetizer or 2 as a light meal

Make the herb dressing by blitzing together the coriander/cilantro, mint, garlic, chilli/chile, lime zest, lime juice and salt into a paste in a food processor.

Peel the pomelo and separate into segments (only half the pomelo is required). Peel each segment of its tough skin and slice into pieces.

Using a sharp knife, halve the mango, discarding the large central stone. Cut a criss-cross pattern across each mango cheek, then cut out the mango chunks, discarding the skin.

Toss together the pomelo, mango and prawns/shrimp with the herb dressing, mixing well. Serve at once or cover and chill until serving.

Spaghetti alle vongole

One for shellfish lovers, this simple yet classic pasta dish offers a taste of the sea, Italian style. Fresh clams have a distinctive sweetness and texture, flavoured here simply but effectively with olive oil, garlic, white wine and parsley.

1 kg/2 lb. 3 oz. fresh clams

400 g/14 oz. spaghetti

6 tablespoons olive oil

3 garlic cloves, finely sliced lengthways

6 tablespoons finely chopped fresh parsley

100 ml/⅓ cup dry white wine

salt and freshly ground black pepper

Serves 4

Prepare the clams by rinsing them under running water and sorting through, discarding any that are open. Keep in the fridge until you are ready to cook them.

Bring a large pan of salted water to the boil. Add the spaghetti and cook until al dente; drain.

Meanwhile, heat the olive oil in a large saucepan. Add the garlic and fry gently until just golden, stirring often. Take care not to burn the garlic, as this would give a bitter flavour. Add the clams, 2 tablespoons of the chopped parsley and the white wine.

Cover and cook for a few minutes until the clams have opened. Discard any that remain closed. Season with pepper.

Toss together the cooked spaghetti, clams and remaining parsley, adding just enough of the clam cooking liquor to moisten the spaghetti. Serve at once.

Spanish garlic prawns/shrimp

This quick-to-cook classic tapas dish, made from a few simple ingredients including garlic and smoked Spanish paprika, is addictively moreish. Cook and serve it at once as a first course or as part of a tapas feast. Do make sure you have plenty of bread on hand for soaking up the flavourful olive oil.

4 tablespoons olive oil

2 garlic cloves, chopped

2 small dried red chillies/chiles, crumbled

450 g/1 lb. raw prawns/shrimp, peeled, deveined, rinsed and dried

1 teaspoon sweet smoked Spanish paprika

1 tablespoon finely chopped fresh parsley

salt

crusty bread, to serve

Serves 4 as a tapas dish

Heat the olive oil in a heavy-based frying pan/skillet. Add the chopped garlic and fry briefly, stirring, until fragrant. Add the crumbled chillies/chiles, mixing well, then add the prawns/shrimp, mixing to coat them in the oil.

Fry the prawns/shrimp briefly, stirring, until they turn opaque and pink on both sides, taking care not to over-cook them and dry them out. Season with salt, then add the Spanish paprika, mixing in. Sprinkle with parsley and serve at once with crusty bread.

Garlic lime chicken

Flavoured with plenty of lime zest and juice, this is a true sunshine recipe, which would be perfect for a barbecue on a hot summer's day. Serve with griddled pineapple, a herby rice salad and an ice-cold mojito or margarita on the side.

4 garlic cloves, crushed
grated zest and freshly squeezed
　juice of 2 limes
2 tablespoons olive oil
2 tablespoons light soy sauce

2 teaspoons brown sugar
8 chicken thighs, bone in, skin on
salt and freshly ground black pepper

Serves 4

Mix together the garlic, lime juice and zest, olive oil, soy sauce and sugar to form a marinade. Season the chicken with salt and pepper, then place in a non-metallic bowl. Toss with the marinade, coating well. Cover and marinate in the fridge for 4 hours or overnight.

Fire up the barbecue or preheat the oven to 200°C (400°F) Gas 6.

Place the thighs on a rack in a tray and roast in the oven for 25–30 minutes or until cooked through. Alternatively cook the chicken on the barbecue, turning occasionally, until the juices run clear and the skin is nicely browned. Serve at once with griddled pineapple and herby rice salad.

Saffron garlic chicken kebabs/kabobs

Marinating chicken is a simple but effective way of adding flavour. These kebabs/kabobs would also be great for a barbecue. Serve with basmati rice, the Tzatziki dip (below) or a raita and a side salad.

a generous pinch of
   saffron threads
2 garlic cloves
3 tablespoons olive oil,
   plus extra for basting
freshly squeezed juice of
   ½ lemon
500 g/1 lb. 2 oz. chicken
   breast fillet, cut into
   approx. 2.5-cm/1-inch
   cubes
salt
torn fresh mint leaves,
   to garnish

8 wooden skewers,
   soaked in water

Serves 4

Grind the saffron threads, then soak in 1 teaspoon of warm water.

Pound the garlic into a paste and mix with a pinch of salt.

Mix together the garlic, saffron water, olive oil, lemon juice and salt in a large bowl to make the marinade. Add the chicken and toss, coating thoroughly in the marinade. Cover and marinate in the fridge for 4–6 hours, turning over the chicken pieces halfway through.

Preheat the grill/broiler until very hot. Thread the marinated chicken onto the skewers, dividing the pieces evenly.

Grill the chicken kebabs/kabobs for about 15 minutes until cooked through and the juices run clear, turning often and basting with a little oil if required. Serve at once, garnished with torn fresh mint.

Tzatziki

This delicate, refreshing and garlicky Greek dip is a classic. Serve with the chicken kebabs/kabobs or with pitta bread or crudités for a snack.

½ cucumber
1 garlic clove, crushed
250 g/1½ cups Greek
   yogurt
1 tablespoon chopped
   fresh mint leaves
1 tablespoon olive oil
1 teaspoon white wine
   vinegar
salt

Serves 6

Peel the cucumber and grate it.

Sprinkle with salt and set aside for 15 minutes to draw out moisture; drain and pat dry with paper towels.

Mix together the grated cucumber, garlic, yogurt, chopped mint, olive oil and vinegar. Cover and chill until ready to serve.

Roast garlic pork burgers

Making your own burgers is very simple and allows you to be creative with the flavourings. Adding roast garlic, fennel seeds and lemon zest gives a great depth of flavour to these tasty burgers, perfect for summertime barbecues. Serve with fries and crunchy coleslaw.

½ teaspoon fennel seeds
1 roasted head of garlic (see page 23)
400 g/14 oz. minced/ground pork
1 tablespoon finely chopped fresh parsley
1 teaspoon grated lemon zest
sunflower or vegetable oil, for frying
salt and freshly ground black pepper
4 brioche rolls or hamburger buns
mayonnaise, ketchup and sliced gherkins, as desired

Serves 4

Dry-fry the fennel seeds in a frying pan/skillet until fragrant, then cool and grind.

When the roasted garlic is cool enough to handle, squeeze out the softened pulp from each clove and mash into a paste.

Mix together the minced/ground pork, roast garlic paste, ground fennel, parsley and lemon zest, mixing thoroughly. Season well with salt and pepper. Shape the minced/ground pork into 4 patties.

Add a touch of oil to a large frying pan/skillet and heat through. Add the patties and fry for 15–20 minutes, or until cooked through, turning over as they cook.

Place the patties in the rolls, adding mayonnaise, ketchup and gherkins to taste and serve at once.

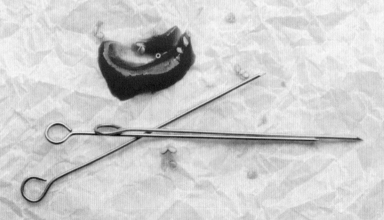

Garlic pilaf

Fragrant basmati rice, cooked with herbs and spices in chicken stock, becomes a tasty and elegant rice dish. This makes an excellent accompaniment to curries and meat or chicken dishes, such as the Saffron Garlic Chicken Kebabs/Kabobs (see page 55) and Fragrant Garlic Lamb Shanks with Apricots (see page 152).

250 g/1¼ cups basmati rice
1 tablespoon olive oil
1 garlic clove, chopped
1 bay leaf
½ cinnamon stick
10 g/2 teaspoons butter
300 ml/1¼ cups chicken stock or water
a good pinch of saffron strands, finely ground and soaked with 1 tablespoon hot water
salt
1 tablespoon pine nuts, toasted
1 tablespoon finely chopped fresh parsley

Serves 4

Rinse the basmati thoroughly in cold running water to wash out the excess starch; drain well.

Heat the olive oil in a small, heavy-based saucepan. Add the garlic and fry, stirring, until golden. Take care not to burn it, as it would become bitter. Add the bay leaf and cinnamon stick, then stir in the butter until it has melted.

Add the rice, mixing well to coat thoroughly in the oil/butter. Add the stock, saffron water and salt to taste.

Bring to the boil, then reduce the heat to very low, cover and cook for 15–20 minutes until the water has been absorbed and the rice is soft and fluffy. Discard the bay leaf and cinnamon stick. Sprinkle over the pine nuts and parsley and serve at once.

Garlic and almond purple sprouting broccoli

Cooking purple sprouting broccoli in this way retains its crunchy texture, while giving it a boost in the flavour stakes. Serve as a side dish alongside Garlic Butter Roast Chicken (see page 82) or with Garlic Anchovy Roast Lamb (see page 155), or toss with cooked pasta for a vegetarian meal.

300 g/10½ oz. purple sprouting broccoli, chopped into 2.5-cm/1-in. lengths, or broccoli florets
25 g/⅓ cup flaked/slivered almonds

2 tablespoons olive oil
1 large garlic clove, roughly chopped
salt and freshly ground black pepper

Serves 4

Bring a large pan of salted water to the boil. Add the broccoli and cook for 2 minutes, then drain thoroughly and refresh in cold water to stop the cooking process.

Dry-fry the almonds in a frying pan/skillet, stirring often, until golden brown; set aside.

Heat the olive oil in a large frying pan/skillet. Add the garlic and fry until golden and fragrant. Add the drained broccoli and fry briefly for 2 minutes, stirring to coat it in the oil. Add the almonds, season with freshly ground pepper and serve at once.

Garlic peas a la Française

This can be made with fresh peas and freshly harvested, new season wet garlic, but it works equally well with frozen peas and garlic. Serve as a vegetable side dish – it goes particularly well with roast lamb.

15 g/1 tablespoon butter
2 spring onions/scallions, chopped into 1-cm/½-inch pieces
1 rasher/slice bacon, chopped into strips
2 wet garlic cloves (or 1 garlic clove), chopped
75 g/2 cups lettuce leaves, such as Little Gem, shredded

400 g/3 cups fresh or frozen peas
150 ml/⅔ cup chicken or vegetable stock
salt and freshly ground black pepper

Serves 4

Melt the butter in a heavy-based saucepan. Add the spring onions/scallions, bacon and garlic and fry, stirring, for 2 minutes until the mixture smells fragrant and the bacon has turned opaque. Add the lettuce, peas and stock and season with salt and pepper. Bring to the boil, cover and cook for 5 minutes until the peas are tender.

Serve with the cooking juices, so it has an almost soupy texture.

Comfort garlic

Garlic folklore

Fascinatingly, this everyday ingredient has long been linked with magic, myths, folklore and superstitions. The association is closely intertwined with its historic reputation as a plant with health-giving properties (see page 34). In many cultures, garlic was traditionally thought to endow warriors with strength and potency and has often been regarded as a protective charm, with the Roman naturalist Pliny the Elder writing of its ability to ward off scorpions and snakes. The English herbalist Nicholas Culpeper assigned it to the planet Mars – with Mars being the

God of War – writing that garlic's heat 'is very vehement'. In Chinese folklore, garlic is also seen as protective. It was, for example, traditionally eaten at the dragon boat festival (or Duanwu festival) to fend off evil spirits. Bulbs of garlic were even discovered in the tomb of King Tutankhamun, as the ancient Egyptians believed that it would protect them in the afterlife.

One feels that garlic's powerful, penetrating scent must have played a part in its mighty reputation; certainly in the most notorious of its properties –

the ability to protect against vampires. This is an association so famous that its legend lives on, even now in the twenty-first century garlic-laden dishes are jokingly said to 'keep the vampires away'. The tradition is particularly associated with Slavic folklore and famously with Transylvania. During the eighteenth century in Transylvania, fear of vampires was widespread, graves were dug up and bodies staked to prevent them returning in vampiric form and preying on people. Garlic, long seen as a charm with health-giving properties, especially among Transylvania's rural communities, was widely used as a protection – hung in or spread on doorways and window sills as a deterrent to form a barrier and so ensure the safety of those inside. Such was its reputed power that garlic cloves were placed in the mouths of the dead bodies of suspected vampires in order to weaken them and prevent them preying on the living. Reputedly, garlic was also used as a way of detecting vampires hidden in the community, with anyone refusing to eat a clove of garlic in church falling under suspicion. In his influential, much-filmed novel *Dracula*, the best-known of vampire stories, author Bram Stoker referred to this ancient custom, describing how the vampire hunter Van Helsing seeks to protect Lucy from the Count by giving her a necklace of garlic and spreading it on the entrances to her room. Vampires were not the only evils to be safeguarded against with garlic, it was also said to protect against the 'evil eye', demons, witches and werewolves.

Garlic's long-held – indeed still current – reputation as an aphrodisiac is thought to be linked to the suggestive shape of the spear-shaped plant and its bulbs. It is particularly striking just how many cultures around the world associate garlic with lust and love, as an ingredient that inflames passions. In traditional Indian Ayurvedic medicine, garlic is categorized as rajasic and tamasic, that is a food which promotes passion and ignorance. So, while in Ayurvedic medicine garlic is recommended as a tonic for loss of sexual power, it is shunned as a food by those seeking to reach a higher spiritual plane, therefore avoided by Buddhists, devout Hindus and Jains. In Greek mythology, garlic inflamed the romantic desires of King Minos and his wife Pasiphaë, who gave birth to the Minotaur. Aristotle, the Ancient Greek philosopher (384–322 BC) listed garlic as an aphrodisiac. In the writings of the Talmud, garlic is credited with encouraging love and healing the sick. In popular culture and consciousness, garlic's reputation as a plant with potent power endures; it is an interesting aspect of our abiding fascination with this special ingredient.

Fettunta

The original 'garlic bread', this Italian dish is traditionally made using the new season's olive oil, although any good-quality extra virgin olive oil can be used. In classic Italian fashion, simple ingredients combine to great effect. The name translates literally as 'oily slice', but it is far more delicious than this name may suggest. Although quick and simple to make, it is incredibly tasty. Try it!

4 thick slices of rustic bread
1 garlic clove, peeled
4 tablespoons extra virgin olive oil
salt (optional)

a griddle pan

Makes 4 slices

Preheat a griddle pan until hot. Griddle the bread for 2–3 minutes on each side until golden-brown and nicely striped. If you don't have a griddle pan, preheat a grill/broiler and toast until golden brown on each side.

Immediately rub one side of each slice with the garlic clove. Pour a tablespoon of olive oil over each slice. Add a pinch of salt, if using, and serve at once.

Roast garlic tartiflette

This classic French dish is a fine example of comfort food, with roast garlic adding a mellow richness to the indulgent layers of creamy sliced potatoes and melted cheese. Serve with a crisp green salad. Reblochon is the traditional cheese used in an authentic tartiflette, giving it a distinctive flavour and texture.

1 tablespoon vegetable oil

1 onion, halved and finely sliced

100 g/3½ oz. pancetta or bacon, cubed

300 ml/1¼ cups crème fraîche or sour cream

300 ml/1¼ cups whole milk

3 sprigs of fresh thyme, leaves picked

3 roast garlic cloves (see page 23), peeled and crushed to a paste

800 g/1¾ lbs. waxy potatoes, such as Charlottes, very finely sliced

½ Reblochon cheese, thinly sliced with rind left on

salt and freshly ground black pepper

1.5-litre/50-fl oz ovenproof dish, greased

Serves 4

Preheat oven to 200°C (400°F) Gas 6.

Heat the oil in a frying pan/skillet. Add the onion and fry, stirring often, until lightly browned and softened. Add the pancetta and fry, stirring, for 2–3 minutes.

In a large saucepan, mix together the crème fraîche, milk, thyme leaves and roast garlic paste. Season with salt and pepper. Bring to the boil and add the potato slices. Reduce the heat and simmer, covered, for 8 minutes. Mix in the fried pancetta and onion.

In a greased ovenproof dish, layer in a third of the crème fraîche and potato mixture. Top with a layer of Reblochon slices. Repeat the process, finishing with a layer of cheese.

Bake for 1 hour in the preheated oven until the potato slices are tender and the dish is golden brown.

Serve warm from the oven.

Spanish garlic soup

Garlic is at the heart of this rustic Spanish soup, sopa de ajo. The chicken stock is the key to its success, so if not making your own, buy the best quality stock you can find. Don't be tempted to use a stock cube!

2 tablespoons olive oil
4 garlic cloves, sliced
salt
1 teaspoon sweet Spanish paprika
4 slices of rustic bread
chopped fresh parsley, to garnish

CHICKEN STOCK
700 g/1½ lbs. chicken wings
1.2 litres/5 cups water

1 onion, chopped
1 carrot, chopped
2 celery stalks, chopped
1 garlic clove, peeled
5 peppercorns
(or 1 litre/4¼ cups good-quality chicken stock)
a handful of fresh parsley, to garnish

Serves 4

First make the stock. Place all the stock ingredients in a large pan. Bring to the boil, then cover, reduce the heat and simmer for 1 hour. Strain and reserve the chicken stock.

To make the soup, heat the olive oil in a large saucepan. Add the garlic and fry gently, stirring, until it turns pale gold. Take care not to burn it, as this would make it bitter. Add the stock and season with salt. Bring to the boil, then reduce the heat and simmer for 10–15 minutes, until heated through. Stir in the paprika.

Toast or grill/broil the bread. Place a slice in each of four soup bowls, pour over the soup, garnish with parsley and serve at once.

Roast garlic mac 'n' cheese

This is a luxurious take on traditional macaroni cheese, with the roast garlic adding a richness to the cheese sauce, elevating it from an everyday supper dish to something rather special. Serve with a crisp green salad.

200 g/1¾ cups macaroni or short penne pasta

1 teaspoon sunflower or vegetable oil

75 g/2¾ oz. pancetta or bacon, finely chopped

50 g/3½ tablespoons butter

50 g/6 tablespoons plain/all-purpose flour

600 ml/2½ cups whole milk

50 ml/3½ tablespoons double/heavy cream

125 g/1½ cups Cheddar cheese, grated

freshly grated nutmeg

3 roast garlic cloves (see page 23), peeled and crushed

75 g/½ cup cooked frozen peas

2 tablespoons grated Parmesan cheese

25 g/½ cup fresh breadcrumbs

salt and freshly ground black pepper

a shallow ovenproof dish, greased

Serves 4

Cook the macaroni in a large saucepan of salted boiling water until al dente; drain.

Meanwhile, heat the oil in a frying pan/skillet. Add the pancetta and fry, stirring often, until lightly browned and crisped.

Preheat the oven to 200°C (400°F) Gas 6.

Make the cheese sauce. Melt the butter in a heavy-based saucepan. Add the flour, whisking in well and cooking for 1 minute, stirring. Gradually add in the milk, stirring well with each addition to prevent any lumps forming. Bring to the boil, stirring, until thickened. Stir in the cream, then mix in the grated Cheddar cheese (reserving 2 tablespoons for the topping), stirring until melted. Season with salt, pepper and grated nutmeg. Mix in the roast garlic.

Mix together the macaroni, pancetta, peas and cheese sauce and transfer to the shallow ovenproof dish. Top with a layer of the remaining Cheddar, the Parmesan cheese and breadcrumbs.

Bake in the preheated oven for 20 minutes until golden brown on top, then serve at once.

Roast garlic fish pie

This luxurious version of a fish pie, with its creamy filling contrasting with the savoury mash, is perfect for dinner parties. Serve with the Italian-style Garlic Spinach (see page 31) as an accompaniment.

500 ml/2 cups good-quality fish stock

800 g/1¾ lbs. white fish fillet, skinned, cut into 4-cm/1½-in. chunks

1.5 kg/3¼ lbs. floury potatoes, such as King Edwards, peeled and chopped into chunks

a dash of milk

4½ tablespoons butter

3 roast garlic cloves (see page 23), peeled and mashed to a paste

freshly grated nutmeg

1 shallot, finely chopped

40 g/4¾ tablespoons plain/all-purpose flour

150 ml/⅔ cup double/ heavy cream

2 tablespoons finely chopped parsley

grated zest of ½ lemon

200 g/7 oz. cooked peeled prawns/shrimp

8 quail's eggs, hard-boiled/ hard-cooked, shelled and halved

25 g/¼ cup grated Cheddar cheese

salt and freshly ground black pepper

Serves 6

In a large saucepan, bring the fish stock to the boil. Add in the fish and simmer for 2–3 minutes until cooked through. Strain, reserving the stock, and set the fish aside to cool.

Make the roast garlic mash. Boil the potatoes in salted boiling water until tender; drain. Add the milk, 1 tablespoon of the butter and the roast garlic paste and mash together well. Season with pepper and nutmeg to taste.

Make the sauce. Heat the remaining butter in a heavy-based saucepan. Add the shallot and fry gently for 1–2 minutes until softened. Mix in the flour and cook, stirring, for 1 minute. Gradually add the fish stock, stirring to incorporate the flour well and ensure a lump-free sauce. Bring to the boil, stirring until it thickens. Stir in the cream, parsley and lemon zest. Set aside to cool.

Preheat the oven to 200°C (400°F) Gas 6.

Place the cooked fish, peeled prawns/shrimp and quail's eggs in a large ovenproof dish. Pour over the sauce and gently fold together. Spread over the garlic mash in an even layer. Sprinkle with the Cheddar cheese.

Bake for 30–40 minutes in the preheated oven until golden brown and piping hot. Serve at once.

Cider and garlic roast belly pork

A splendid and succulent slow-cooked pork dish, with the apple flavours of the cider cutting nicely through the richness of the pork. Stuffing prunes with mellow, smoky black garlic adds an extra tasty touch. This dish is great served with mashed potato and buttered cabbage.

2 kg/4½ lbs. belly pork on the bone, skin scored for crackling

6 garlic cloves, 4 left whole and 2 crushed

1 tablespoon finely chopped fresh thyme

2 large carrots, halved lengthways and chopped

1 onion, cut into chunks

500 ml/2¼ cups dry cider

300 ml/1¼ cups apple juice

8 pitted prunes

8 black garlic cloves

butter, for frying

salt and freshly ground black pepper

Serves 8

Bring the pork to room temperature and pat dry with paper towels. Preheat the oven to 220°C (425°F) Gas 7.

Season the flesh of the pork with salt and pepper, rubbing the salt generously into the scored skin. Mix together the crushed garlic and thyme into a paste. Rub the paste over the pork flesh.

Place the carrot, onion and whole garlic cloves in a roasting pan, then top with the seasoned pork belly so it rests on the vegetables. Pour the cider into the roasting pan.

Roast the pork for 30 minutes in the preheated oven then reduce the heat to 180°C (350°F) Gas 4 and roast for a further 2 hours, adding the apple juice to the roasting pan halfway through the cooking time.

Rest the pork in warm place. Blend the roast vegetables, garlic and cider mixture until smooth to form a gravy. Season with salt and pepper.

Fill each of the pitted prunes with a whole black garlic clove. Heat the butter in a small frying pan/skillet and fry the prunes briefly to heat through.

Serve the roast pork with the cider gravy and black garlic prunes.

Spanish-style garlic baked beans

My Spanish-inspired take on baked beans is a hearty, full-flavoured dish. Serve hot, warm or at room temperature with rustic bread to mop up the tasty sauce, and with a green salad on the side for contrast.

400 g/2½ cups borlotti/
    cranberry beans
1 tablespoon olive oil
1 onion, finely chopped
1 celery stalk, finely
    chopped
2 garlic cloves, chopped
1 tablespoon freshly
    chopped rosemary
    leaves
2 cooking chorizo
    (200–300 g/7–10 oz.),
    sliced
150 g/5½ oz. pancetta
    or bacon, diced
1 teaspoon sweet Spanish
    smoked paprika
400 ml/2 cups
    passata/strained
    tomatoes
salt and freshly ground
    black pepper
2 tablespoons freshly
    chopped parsley

*a lidded flameproof
    casserole dish*

Serves 6–8

Soak the beans in plenty of cold water overnight. Drain, place in a large pan and cover generously with cold water. Bring to the boil, reduce the heat and simmer for 45–60 minutes, until the beans are tender. Drain and set aside, reserving the cooking water.

Preheat the oven to 150°C (300°F) Gas 2.

Heat the olive oil in a flameproof casserole dish. Add the onion and celery and fry gently for 2 minutes, until softened. Add the garlic and rosemary, fry briefly until fragrant, then add the chorizo and pancetta. Fry, stirring often, for 3–5 minutes. Sprinkle over the paprika, and stir in the passata/strained tomatoes and 400 ml/1¾ cups of the reserved bean water (keep the remaining bean water to top up). Season with salt. Add the beans.

Bring to the boil, cover and transfer to the preheated oven to bake for 2 hours, checking now and then whether the beans are drying out during this stage and adding more bean water if necessary.

Transfer the dish from the oven to the stovetop, uncover and simmer gently for 30 minutes, stirring now and then, to reduce and thicken the sauce. Taste and season with salt and pepper as required. Garnish with parsley and serve at once.

Italian sausages with garlic lentils

Sausages and lentils make the perfect partners. This is an easy, filling meal full of robust flavours – comfort food Italian style! If possible, use fresh Italian pork sausages, which are often flavoured with garlic and fennel, as their texture and taste work well with the lentils.

400 g/2 cups Castelluccio or Puy lentils, rinsed
1 carrot, finely diced
300 ml/1¼ cups red wine
1 litre/4¼ cups cold water
3 garlic cloves, peeled and left whole
1 fresh bay leaf
3 fresh sage leaves
½ tablespoon vegetable oil
8 Italian sausages (or good-quality meaty sausages)
3 tablespoons extra virgin olive oil
4 tablespoons freshly chopped parsley
salt

Serves 4

Preheat the oven to 200°C (400°F) Gas 6. Place a roasting pan in the oven to preheat.

Place the rinsed lentils and diced carrot in a large saucepan. Add the red wine, water, garlic, bay leaf and sage. Bring to the boil, then reduce the heat and simmer for 20–25 minutes until the lentils are tender but retain some texture. Add salt to the lentils to season, then drain.

While the lentils are cooking, heat the vegetable oil in a large frying pan/skillet. Add the sausages and brown quickly on all sides. Transfer the browned sausages to the preheated roasting pan and bake in the oven for 20–25 minutes until cooked through.

Pick out and discard the bay leaf and sage leaves from the lentils. Mash the garlic cloves. Toss the cooked lentils with the mashed garlic, olive oil and parsley. Top with the sausages and serve at once.

Boeuf bourguignon

This classic French dish is a rich combination of slow-cooked, tender, wine-marinated beef, flavoured with herbs, bacon, mushrooms and garlic. Serve it with creamy mashed potatoes and green beans. As it can be made in advance, this is an ideal dish for entertaining.

800 g/1¾ lbs. braising steak, cubed

750 ml/3¼ cups red wine, ideally Burgundy

1 onion, roughly chopped

1 carrot, roughly chopped

3 garlic cloves, chopped

4 fresh thyme sprigs

2 fresh bay leaves

2 tablespoons olive oil

1 shallot, chopped

2 rashers/slices smoked bacon, chopped into fine strips

400 ml/1¾ cups beef stock

15 g/1 tablespoon butter

200 g/7 oz. button mushrooms

salt and freshly ground black pepper

chopped parsley, to serve

a lidded flameproof casserole dish

Serves 6–8

Place the steak in a large bowl with the red wine, onion, carrot, garlic, thyme and bay leaves and marinate in the fridge for at least 3 hours, or ideally overnight.

Preheat the oven to 150°C (300°F) Gas 2.

Remove the beef from the marinade and pat dry with kitchen paper. Discard the onion and carrot, but reserve the rest of the red wine marinade (i.e. the garlic and herbs). Place the reserved red wine marinade in a pan, bring to the boil and cook uncovered until reduced to about 600 ml/2½ cups.

Heat 1 tablespoon olive oil in a casserole dish. Add the beef and fry for 3–5 minutes until browned on all sides. Set aside.

Wipe out the casserole dish with paper towels. Add the remaining olive oil, heat through and fry the shallot and bacon for 1–2 minutes, until fragrant. Add the browned beef, reduced red wine and the beef stock. Season with salt and pepper. Bring to the boil, cover and cook in the preheated oven for 2 hours.

Towards the end of the casserole's cooking time, heat the butter in a frying pan/skillet and fry the mushrooms until golden brown. Stir the mushrooms into the casserole and serve garnished with chopped parsley.

Garlic butter roast chicken

Roast chicken is an all-time favourite and always makes a great family meal. Adding the butter under the skin results in a moist, tasty chicken, aromatic from herbs and garlic. Serve with Garlicky Goose Fat Roast Potatoes (see page 31) or Garlic and Almond Purple Sprouting Broccoli (see page 60).

3 garlic cloves, 2 peeled and 1 unpeeled
70 g/5 tablespoons butter, softened
2 tablespoons finely chopped fresh parsley
1 teaspoon lemon thyme leaves or thyme leaves
grated zest and freshly squeezed juice of ½ lemon (save the lemon half after squeezing as it will be used in the recipe)
1 oven-ready chicken, approx. 2 kg/4½ lbs.
salt and freshly ground black pepper

GRAVY
½ tablespoon olive oil
½ onion, finely chopped
1 fresh bay leaf
splash of white wine
300 ml/1¼ cups chicken stock

Serves 4

Preheat the oven to 200°C (400°F) Gas 6.

Make the garlic butter by pounding the peeled garlic into a paste with a pinch of salt. Mix together 50 g/3½ tablespoons of the butter with the garlic paste, parsley, lemon thyme and lemon zest.

Season the chicken with salt and pepper. Place on a rack in a roasting pan. Place the unpeeled garlic clove and the squeezed lemon half inside the chicken cavity. Pour over the lemon juice.

Using your fingers, gently pull the skin away from the chicken breast. Insert the garlic butter under the skin and on to the flesh, pressing down to spread it evenly over the chicken breast. Dot the remaining butter over the chicken legs and wings.

Roast the chicken in the preheated oven for 1 hour 20 minutes – 1 hour 30 minutes, basting often with butter juices, until cooked through and the juices run clear. Rest for 15 minutes.

Meanwhile, use the roasting juices to make a gravy. Skim off excess fat from the roasting juices. Heat the oil in a pan, add the onion and bay leaf and fry gently until the onion has softened. Add the wine, cook briefly, then add the stock and the roasting juices. Bring to the boil and cook until slightly reduced. Season as required. Discard the bay leaf and serve at once with the chicken.

Fiery garlic

Meet the garlic farmers

South West Garlic Farm, Dorset, England

Farmer Mark Botwright's interest in growing food dates back to his days as a boy, when he looked after the family's vegetable plot. His fascination with garlic, however, dates back to a birthday present of elephant garlic from his wife. Mark planted them in his garden, grew them, dried them and replanted the cloves, growing his garlic collection until he had thousands of bulbs and a range of varieties.

Such was his obsession that Mark decided to switch from sheep farming to garlic farming and has now established a flourishing business on his Dorset-based South West Garlic Farm, growing Iberian, Morado, Violet Spring and (naturally) elephant garlic. His customers include top British restaurants and high-end food stores, attracted by both the provenance and the exceptional quality of his fresh produce.

Mark's genuine interest in ingredients and cooking, together with an adventurous willingness to innovate, have fed into his business. The cult popularity among chefs of garlic scapes – the edible stalks of garlic (which had been previously discarded by garlic growers in the UK) – is something he has pioneered. He also offers black garlic, created by gently heating

garlic bulbs for 40–50 days until the cloves darken and soften, taking on a distinctive sweet-sourness.

Filaree Garlic Farm, Omak, Washington, USA

Filaree was founded in 1977 by Ron Engeland, initially as an heirloom apple orchard. During the mid 1980s, however, Ron began growing garlic in between the trees. His fascination with heritage varieties saw him contacting university researchers in a quest for unusual garlic varieties, and the farm at one stage grew a staggering 300 varieties.

Today, this organic farm grows over 100 varieties of garlic and supplies seed garlic to other growers. Now owned by Alley Swiss, Filaree is North America's largest privately owned collection of garlic, deeply committed to its self-proclaimed mission to preserve and promote its diverse range of unique garlic varieties, many of which trace their origins to Germany's Gatersleben seed bank. Growing so many varieties of garlic allows for the diversity of garlic to be revealed and appreciated. Among the strains cultivated by Filaree are hot-flavoured, purple-striped Turban strains, large-cloved Porcelain strains, rich-tasting Rocambole and sweet Creole.

The farm's location in an arid desert region means that they are free from many of the hazardous pests and diseases normally associated with garlic. The crop is lovingly tended, with the weeding done by hand, irrigation from mountain-fed spring water, the fields regularly walked to check the health of the plants and much of the garlic selectively harvested at the peak of its maturity.

La Maison de l'Ail, Saint-Clar, France

France has a venerable tradition of protecting its historic foodstuffs and garlic is among the ingredients recognized in this way. It has long been cultivated in the department of Lomagne in south-west France, thriving in its favourable climate and ideal clay and

limestone soils, and becoming an important crop in the area. Since 2004, Lomagne white garlic has been granted Indication Géographique Protégée (IGP) status. Around 300 growers in the region grow this highly regarded white garlic, used in local dishes such as *tourin*, a simple, rustic garlic soup.

Among them are farmers Monsieur and Madame Gamot who, in 2000, founded La Maison de l'Ail in an old barn on their farm to celebrate the region's garlic. Exhibitions, sculptures and festive events such as a market and an annual garlic competition, attended by local garlic farmers, offer a chance to learn about garlic and how it is cultivated in the region.

The Gamots are firm believers in the healthy virtues of garlic, both for humans and for the soil. On their farm they grow white garlic, planted in the autumn, then harvested on the Feast of St John on June 24th, and also violet garlic, harvested in late summer. The garlic is picked, dried for a month, plaited and sold from July through to October.

Piquant peanut and garlic relish

Peanut butter lovers will appreciate this savoury, nutty, chilli/chile-piquant relish. It makes an excellent accompaniment to grilled meats or fish.

25 g/1 cup freshly chopped parsley stalks and leaves

2 heaped tablespoons peanut butter

1 tomato

1 red chilli/chile, chopped

2 garlic cloves, chopped

2-cm/¾-in. fresh ginger, peeled and chopped

1 tablespoon groundnut or sunflower oil

Makes about
220 g/8 oz.

Place all the ingredients in a food processor and blend into a paste. Cover and chill to store, but serve at room temperature.

This relish is best eaten fresh when the flavours are strongest. However, any leftovers can be stored in the fridge, covered with a thin layer of oil to prevent discolouring, for up to 2 days.

Herb and garlic chutney

Tangy with a kick of chilli/chile, this fresh chutney has an exuberant zing to it. Serve as a relish alongside Indian dishes such as tandoori chicken.

100 g/2 cups fresh
   coriander/cilantro, stalks
   and leaves
2 garlic cloves, chopped
50 g/⅓ cup blanched
   almonds
1 teaspoon cumin seeds,
   toasted and finely ground
1 green chilli/chile, chopped
freshly squeezed juice of
   1–2 lemons
1 teaspoon salt
1 teaspoon sugar

Makes about
220 g/8 oz.

Rinse the coriander/cilantro well, discarding any wilted leaves, and chop. In a food processor, blitz together the coriander/cilantro, garlic, almonds, cumin and chilli/chile to a paste. Gradually add in the lemon juice, salt and sugar, blitzing to mix well and tasting to ensure a balance of sweetness, sourness and saltiness.

Cover and chill until serving. This chutney is best eaten fresh when the flavours are at their strongest. However, any leftovers can be stored in the fridge for up to 2 days. Cover with a thin layer of oil to prevent discolouring.

Smoky garlic baba ghanoush

This Middle Eastern-inspired dip has a pleasant, subtly smoky garlic flavour. Roasting aubergines/eggplant until the skin is charred softens the flesh and mellows their flavour. Serve it with warm pitta bread and crudités as a vegetarian appetizer, or with other dishes, such as Hummus (see page 14) or Tzatziki (see page 55) as part of a mezze meal.

2 aubergines/eggplants
2 smoked garlic cloves
freshly squeezed juice of ½ lemon
3 tablespoons extra virgin olive oil, plus extra to serve
salt

TO GARNISH
1 tablespoon natural yogurt
a pinch of ground sumac
freshly chopped parsley

a foil-lined baking sheet

Makes about 400 g/14 oz.

Preheat the oven to 200°C (400°F) Gas 6.

Place the aubergines/eggplants on a foil-lined baking sheet and roast in the preheated oven for 1 hour, turning over halfway through, until charred on all sides. Place the hot aubergines/eggplants in a plastic bag (so that the resulting steam will make the skin easier to peel off) and set aside to cool.

Peel the roasted aubergines/eggplants and chop the flesh into chunks. Crush the smoked garlic with a pinch of salt into a paste. In a food processor, blend together the roast aubergines/eggplants, smoked garlic paste, lemon juice and olive oil into a smooth purée. Season with salt.

Place in a serving bowl and spoon over the yogurt. Top with sumac, a little olive oil, add parsley and serve.

Kimchi pancake with black garlic crème fraîche

My take on this popular Korean dish contrasts the chewy-textured, chilli/chile-hot pancake with the subtle coolness of crème fraîche, enriched with the mellow sweetness of black garlic. Kimchi is a traditional Korean fermented relish, usually made with cabbage.

100 g/¾ cup plain/all-purpose flour
½ teaspoon salt
100 ml/⅓ cup water
3 tablespoons kimchi liquid (reserved from kimchi)
130 g/1 cup kimchi, finely chopped
1 spring onion/scallion, finely chopped
150 ml/⅔ cup crème fraîche or sour cream

3 black garlic cloves, finely chopped
1 tablespoon sunflower or vegetable oil
thinly sliced spring onion/scallion, to garnish

Serves 4 as an appetizer or 2 as a main course

Make the batter by whisking together the flour, salt and water into a thick paste. Stir in the kimchi liquid, then mix in the kimchi and spring onion/scallion.

Mix together the crème fraîche and black garlic and set aside.

Heat a large frying pan/skillet until hot. Add the oil and heat well. Pour in the batter, which should sizzle as it hits the pan, spreading it to form an even layer. Fry for 3–5 minutes until set, then turn over and fry the pancake for a further 3–4 minutes until it is well browned on both sides.

Cut the kimchi pancake into portions and serve topped with the black garlic crème fraîche. Sprinkle with extra spring onions/scallions to garnish.

Spaghetti con aglio, olio e peperoncino

So simple but so good, this homely pasta dish of garlic, oil and chilli/chile is an Italian classic. Made in minutes using store–cupboard staples, it's a great speedy meal. A generous quantity of garlic is traditional as it is the dish's key flavouring.

450 g/1 lb. spaghetti

150 ml/⅔ cup extra virgin olive oil

8 garlic cloves, finely chopped

6 pepperoncini (small Italian dried chilli/chile peppers), chopped

6 tablespoons finely chopped fresh parsley

salt and freshly ground black pepper

grated Parmesan cheese, to serve

Serves 4

Cook the spaghetti in a large pan of salted, boiling water until it becomes al dente.

Meanwhile, heat the olive oil in a small, heavy-based frying pan/skillet. Add the garlic and pepperoncini and fry gently over a low heat, stirring often, until the garlic turns golden brown. Take care not to burn the garlic as this would make it bitter. Set the garlic pepperoncini oil aside to infuse.

Once the spaghetti is cooked, drain well and return to the saucepan. Gently reheat the oil and pour over the spaghetti, mixing well. Sprinkle with parsley and serve at once with Parmesan cheese.

Malay garlic and chilli/chile prawns/shrimp

A quickly cooked, piquant king prawn/jumbo shrimp dish, fragrant with lemongrass and kaffir lime leaves. Serve with coconut rice as a soothing contrast.

2 lemongrass stalks

150 g/1 cup tomatoes, chopped

1 onion, chopped

2 garlic cloves, chopped

2 tablespoons tomato purée/paste

1 red chilli/chile, de-seeded and chopped

a pinch of sugar

2 tablespoons sunflower or vegetable oil

2 kaffir lime leaves, central vein discarded, finely shredded

300 g/10½ oz. raw king prawns/jumbo shrimp, peeled and deveined

salt

finely chopped spring onion/scallion, to garnish

Serves 4

First make a paste. Remove the tough outer casing from the lemongrass stalks and finely chop the white, bulbous part, discarding the rest. In a food processor, blend together the lemongrass, tomatoes, onion, garlic, tomato purée/paste, chilli/chile and sugar, set aside.

Heat a wok until hot. Add the oil and heat through. Add the shredded kaffir lime leaves and blended paste and fry, stirring often, for 7–8 minutes until cooked through and reduced.

Add the prawns/shrimp, season with salt, and stir-fry, until the prawns/shrimp turn opaque and are cooked through – this takes just a few minutes. Serve at once, garnished with the finely chopped spring onion/scallion.

Thai-style fish with fried garlic

This recipe is a great way of cooking a fish fillet, with the crisp garlic flakes adding both flavour and texture. Serve with rice and a green vegetable, such as spinach or pak choi/bok choy.

1 lemongrass stalk
500 g/1 lb. 2 oz. white fish fillet (such as cod)
2 tablespoons sunflower or vegetable oil
1½ tablespoons fish sauce
1 shallot, finely chopped
1 red chilli/chile, de-seeded and finely chopped
4 garlic cloves, sliced finely lengthways
freshly ground black pepper

Serves 4

Preheat the oven to 200°C (400°F) Gas 6.

Remove the tough outer casing from the lemongrass. Finely chop the white, bulbous part, discarding the rest.

Place the fish skin side-down in a shallow ovenproof dish or roasting pan. Mix together 1 tablespoon of the oil, the fish sauce, shallot, chilli/chile and lemongrass, season with pepper and pour evenly over the fish, coating it well. Bake the fish for 15–20 minutes until cooked through.

Just before the fish has finished cooking, heat the remaining oil in a small frying pan/skillet. Add the garlic and fry until golden-brown, taking care not to burn it, as this would make it bitter. Pour the hot garlic and oil over the cooked fish and serve at once.

Garlic chive meatballs

500 g/1 lb. 2 oz. ground pork
25 g/1 oz. Chinese or garlic chives, finely chopped
1 garlic clove, finely chopped
1 cm/½ in. fresh ginger, peeled and finely chopped
1 egg white
1 tablespoon light soy sauce
1 teaspoon salt
½ teaspoon ground white or black pepper
1 teaspoon sesame oil
2 teaspoons cornflour/ cornstarch

DIPPING SAUCE
3 tablespoons light soy sauce
1 teaspoon sesame oil
½ red chilli/chile, de-seeded and finely chopped

a steamer

Serves 4

This is a simple, homely dish. Steaming the meatballs, rather than frying them, is an easy and healthier way of cooking them. Serve with rice or noodles and Chinese greens such as pak choi/bok choy or gai lan (also known as Chinese broccoli or Chinese kale).

Blend all the meatball ingredients together in a food processor until thoroughly mixed. With wet hands to prevent sticking, shape the mixture into small meatballs, each the size of a large marble.

Steam the meatballs for 20 minutes until cooked through.

Mix together the dipping sauce ingredients. Serve the meatballs with the dipping sauce.

Thai-style fried garlic minced/ground chicken

A truly tasty dish, inspired by Thai flavours. Serve with steamed rice for a simple, yet satisfying meal, ideal for a midweek supper. If green beans are not available, tenderstem broccoli would make a good substitute.

2 tablespoons sunflower or vegetable oil

2 garlic cloves, finely chopped

1 shallot, finely sliced

100 g/3½ oz. green beans, topped, tailed and cut into 1-cm/⅜-in. pieces

4 button mushrooms, chopped

400 g/14 oz. minced/ground chicken

1 red chilli/chile, de-seeded, finely chopped (optional)

1 teaspoon dark brown sugar

1 tablespoon fish sauce

1 tablespoon dark soy sauce

3 tablespoons chicken stock

freshly ground black pepper

Thai basil or basil leaves, to garnish

Serves 4

Heat a wok until hot. Add the oil and heat through. Add the garlic and shallot and fry, stirring, until garlic turns pale gold. Add the green beans and fry, stirring, for 1 minute. Add the mushrooms and fry, stirring, for 1 minute.

Add the minced/ground chicken and fry, stirring with a spatula to break up any lumps, until lightened on all sides. Add the chilli/chile, if using, and mix in well. Add the sugar, fish sauce and soy sauce and mix in. Add the stock and stir-fry for 5 minutes until the stock has cooked off and the ingredients are well mixed.

Season generously with black pepper, garnish with basil leaves and serve at once.

400 g/14 oz. rump steak,
finely sliced into short
strips

MARINADE
2 tablespoons sesame seeds,
dry-fried until golden
brown
3 garlic cloves, crushed
with pinch of salt to make
a paste
1 teaspoon sugar
3 spring onions/scallions,
sliced into 2-cm/
3/4-in. lengths
4 tablespoons light soy
sauce
2 tablespoons sesame oil
2.5-cm/1-in. fresh ginger,
peeled and finely chopped

DIPPING SAUCE
3 tablespoons light soy sauce
1 tablespoon sesame oil
1 tablespoon rice wine or
medium sherry
1 teaspoon Korean soy bean
paste
1 tablespoon sesame seeds,
dry-fried until golden
brown
1 spring onion/scallion,
finely chopped
1 garlic clove, finely chopped
1 teaspoon sugar
1/2 teaspoon dried chilli
flakes/hot pepper flakes

Serves 4

Bulgogi

This famous Korean dish, consisting of savoury,
tender beef strips, is addictively good. Make sure you
allow sufficient time for marinating, as this is essential
for locking the flavours in. Serve with rice or noodles
and Chinese greens on the side.

Mix together the marinade ingredients. Add the steak strips and
toss to coat thoroughly. Cover and marinate in the fridge for at least
6 hours, ideally overnight.

Mix together the dipping sauce ingredients and set aside.

Bring the marinated beef out of the fridge 30 minutes before
cooking, to allow it to come to room temperature.

Preheat a large, heavy-based frying pan/skillet or griddle pan until
very hot. Add the beef strips in one layer to the pan. Cook briefly on
one side, then turn over to cook the other side, until browned on
both sides – this takes just a few minutes in total.

Serve the beef at once with the dipping sauce.

Spicy Indian garlic meatballs

Minced/ground beef doesn't have to be dull, as this recipe proves with its array of spices. Serve these little meatballs with basmati rice and a vegetable side dish.

500 g/1 lb. 2 oz.
  minced/ground beef
1 garlic clove, crushed with
  a pinch of salt
1 teaspoon ground cumin
2 teaspoons ground
  coriander
2 tablespoons sunflower
  or vegetable oil
1 onion, finely chopped
1 garlic clove, chopped
2-cm/¾-in. fresh ginger,
  peeled and finely chopped
1 cinnamon stick
4 cardamom pods
handful of fresh or frozen
  (not dried) curry leaves
  (optional)
400-g/14-oz. can of chopped
  tomatoes
¼ teaspoon ground turmeric
¼ teaspoon chilli powder/
  hot red pepper powder
  (optional)
300 ml/1¼ cups water
salt and freshly ground black
  pepper
torn fresh coriander/cilantro
  leaves, to garnish

*a large lidded frying
  pan/skillet*

Serves 4

First, make the meatballs. Mix together the beef, crushed garlic, cumin and coriander and season well with salt and pepper. With wet hands to prevent sticking, shape the mixture into small meatballs, each roughly the size of a large marble.

Heat 1 tablespoon of the oil in a large, lidded frying pan/skillet and fry the meatballs until browned on all sides. Set aside.

Add the remaining oil to the pan. Fry the onion, chopped garlic clove, ginger, cinnamon stick and cardamom pods, stirring, until the onion has softened. Mix in the curry leaves, if using, frying briefly, then add the chopped tomatoes. Add in the turmeric, chilli/hot red pepper powder and water. Season with salt. Bring to the boil.

Add the browned meatballs, bring to the boil once more, then cover, reduce the heat and cook for 15 minutes, stirring now and then. Uncover and cook for 10 further minutes, stirring often, until the sauce has reduced and thickened. Serve at once, garnished with fresh coriander/cilantro.

Go wild garlic

Growing garlic

One of the reasons for garlic's universal popularity is the plant's ability to thrive in a range of climates and soils. Just as it is versatile in the kitchen, so garlic is adaptable as a plant, growing in both cold northern climates and in tropical countries. While garlic grows well in the ground, it does not require a lot of space and can also be grown successfully in pots, making it an excellent addition to a potted herb collection.

Choosing your garlic

Garlic is grown from individual cloves. While it is possible to simply plant garlic cloves bought from a food shop, because of the risk of disease it is recommended that you source your seed garlic from a plant nursery or grower.

Bear in mind that the larger the clove, the larger the plant will be, so choose the biggest cloves, keeping on their papery husk. Separate cloves from the bulb just before planting, rather than in advance.

There are several varieties of garlic to choose from, with variations including white and violet-coloured bulbs and flavour ranging from mild and sweet to hot and fiery. Garlic (*Allium sativum*) has two subspecies: softneck (*Allium sativum sativum*) and hardneck (*Allium sativum ophioscorodon*). Unlike softnecks, hardnecks produce a straight, central edible stalk. Traditionally, in order to produce larger bulbs, these stalks were cut; they are known as scapes.

When to plant

In cold climates, garlic is usually planted before the winter, to give the plants a chance to establish their root systems before the arrival of frosts. Spring planting, depending on the climate and variety, is

also possible. Plant the cloves root-end down about 5 cm/2 in. deep in soil, spaced 15 cm/6 in. apart if planting in a row. Garlic enjoys well-drained, rich soil but can grow in a variety of soils. The plants can be smothered easily by weeds, so be sure to weed the soil around them thoroughly.

As softneck garlic grows, it sends up green leaves, with hardnecks also sending up a straight stalk. Water garlic evenly, taking care not to overwater. When the leaves have grown, the plant will set its bulb. Once the bulb is established, the advice is not to water the garlic otherwise you risk rotting the bulb.

Harvesting

Garlic is harvested in the summer months, between June and August depending on the variety. When the leaves turn yellow, this is a sign that the bulb is ready to harvest. Many growers harvest when the lower leaves have turned yellow but the ones above are still green. Harvesting too early risks an underdeveloped bulb, while harvesting too late can result in a looser bulb, which won't store as well. To harvest, carefully loosen the soil around the plant, making sure you do not damage the bulb, and gently lift out the bulb by hand so as not to damage it.

Once the garlic has been lifted from the soil it needs to be dried or cured. Remove clumps of soil from the roots, but leave the roots on the bulb. Spread or hang the garlic in a cool, dry place, with good air circulation; hanging the garlic is ideal as this allows it to dry out evenly. Leave the garlic in these conditions for two weeks, so that the outer layer has dried but the garlic retains its moisture, then trim the roots and remove any dirty outer layers. Your garlic is ready to use.

Wild garlic/ramps hazelnut pesto

Wild garlic (or ramps) combined with hazelnuts gives this simple-to-make pesto a wonderfully distinctive flavour. Stir it into Pasta Primavera (page 120), spread it over chicken or fish before baking or use it as a tasty garnish for soups, such as sweet potato or carrot.

80 g/⅔ cup hazelnuts
80 g/3 oz. wild garlic leaves/
 ramps, thoroughly rinsed,
 roughly chopped
150 ml/⅔ cup extra virgin olive
 oil

50 g/⅔ cup grated Parmesan
 cheese
salt

*Makes about
350 g/12 oz.*

Dry-fry the hazelnuts in a heavy-based frying pan/skillet over a medium heat, stirring frequently, until golden brown. Set aside to cool, then finely grind.

If using a food processor, blitz the wild garlic/ramps into a paste. Add the ground hazelnuts and olive oil and briefly whizz together. Mix in the Parmesan cheese, then season with salt, bearing in mind the saltiness of the cheese.

If using a pestle and mortar, pound the wild garlic/ramps into a paste. Add in the ground hazelnuts and olive oil and pound to mix together. Mix in the Parmesan cheese, then season with salt.

If any of the pesto is left over, it can be stored in the fridge for up to 2 days; covering the surface with a thin layer of oil helps to preserve it. Alternatively, it can be frozen.

Wild garlic/ramps dough balls

Enjoy these truly tasty, savoury bread rolls freshly baked and warm from the oven. Serve them with soup for a first course or a light meal.

500 g/3½ cups strong bread flour, plus extra for dusting

1 teaspoon fast-action dried yeast

1½ teaspoons salt

1½ teaspoons sugar

300 ml/1¼ cups hand-hot water

2 tablespoons olive oil, plus extra for greasing

75 g/⅓ cup butter, softened

25 g/1 oz. wild garlic leaves/ramps, rinsed well and finely chopped

2 baking sheets, lightly greased

Makes 24

First, make the bread dough. In a mixing bowl, mix together the flour, yeast, salt and sugar. Gradually add the hand-hot water and olive oil, bringing the mixture together to form a sticky dough. Turn out onto a lightly floured surface and knead well until the dough is smooth and elastic. Place in a clean, oiled mixing bowl, cover with a damp, clean kitchen cloth and set aside in a warm place to rise for 1 hour, during which time it should rise noticeably and almost double in size.

While the dough is rising, mix together the butter and wild garlic/ramps thoroughly.

Preheat the oven to 220°C (425°F) Gas 7.

Gently heat the wild garlic butter in a pan until just melted.

Break down the risen dough and divide it into 24 even-sized portions, shaping each into a rounded ball shape. Place the dough balls on the greased baking sheets, spaced well apart. Brush each dough ball generously with the melted wild garlic/ramps butter.

Bake the dough balls for 15–20 minutes in the preheated oven until golden brown. Brush the freshly baked dough balls with the remaining wild garlic/ramps butter and serve at once.

Wild garlic/ramps goat's cheese flan

This stylish savoury tart, combining subtle goat's cheese with earthy wild garlic, has a delicate, moist texture. Serve with a crisp-textured salad for a light meal.

300 g/10½ oz. shortcrust
pastry/pie dough
2 eggs plus 1 egg yolk
300 ml/1¼ cups crème
fraîche or sour cream
25 g/1 oz. wild garlic
leaves/ramps, thoroughly
rinsed, finely chopped
freshly grated nutmeg
200 g/7 oz. white rind goat's
cheese, sliced
salt and freshly ground black
pepper

24-cm/9½-in. loose-based
flan tin/quiche pan, lightly
greased

Serves 6

Preheat the oven to 200°C (400°F) Gas 6.

First make the pastry case. Roll out the pastry/pie dough on a lightly floured work surface, then line the greased flan tin/quiche pan. Press it in firmly and prick the base several times to stop the pastry bubbling up. Line the case with a piece of parchment paper and fill with baking beans. Blind bake the pastry case for 15 minutes. Carefully remove the baking beans and paper and bake for a further 5 minutes.

While the pastry is baking, lightly whisk together the eggs, egg yolk and crème fraîche. Stir in the wild garlic/ramps and season with grated nutmeg, salt and pepper.

Layer the goat's cheese slices in the pastry case. Pour over the egg mixture. Bake for 40 minutes until risen and golden-brown. Serve warm or at room temperature.

Wild garlic/ramps cheese scones

Freshly baked scones, served warm from the oven and spread generously with butter, are always hard to resist. These savoury scones, with their earthy flavour, are no exception.

250 g/1¾ cups self-raising/self-rising flour

1 teaspoon baking powder

a pinch of salt

50 g/3½ tablespoons butter, diced, plus extra to serve

75 g/1 cup finely grated Cheddar cheese

1 egg

125 ml/½ cup buttermilk (or 100 ml/⅓ cup whole milk with 25 ml/2 tablespoons yogurt mixed in), plus extra for glazing

25 g/1 oz. wild garlic leaves/ramps, thoroughly rinsed and finely chopped

6-cm/2-in. cookie cutter
a baking sheet, greased

Makes 8

Preheat the oven to 220°C (425°F) Gas 7.

Sift the flour and baking powder into a mixing bowl. Mix in the salt. Rub in the butter with your fingertips until absorbed, then mix in the grated Cheddar.

Whisk the egg into the buttermilk. Pour the egg mixture into the flour mixture, add in the chopped wild garlic/ramps and mix together to form a soft, sticky dough.

Roll out the dough on a lightly floured work surface to a thickness of 2.5 cm/1 in. and use the cookie cutter to cut out the scones, reshaping and re-rolling the trimmings, to form 8 scones.

Place the scones on the greased baking sheet. Brush lightly with buttermilk.

Bake the scones for 10–15 minutes in the preheated oven until they have risen and are golden brown. Serve at once, split in half and spread with lashings of butter.

Wild garlic/ramps pasta primavera

Primavera means 'spring' in Italian and this simple yet elegant recipe makes use of seasonal ingredients to create a lovely fresh and light garlicky pasta dish.

1 tablespoon pine nuts
100 g/1 cup fresh asparagus, sliced into 2.5-cm/1-in. lengths
75 g/½ cup fresh peas (or frozen if preferred)
75 g/⅔ cup green/French beans, topped, tailed and sliced into short lengths
200 g/3 cups farfalle pasta

100 g/½ cup Wild Garlic/ Ramps Hazelnut Pesto (see page 112)
2 heaped tablespoons mascarpone cheese
grated Parmesan cheese, to serve

Serves 4

Put the pine nuts in a dry heavy-based frying pan/skillet set over a medium heat and toast, stirring often, until golden brown. Remove the pan from the heat and set aside.

Cook the asparagus, peas and green/French beans in separate pans of boiling water until just tender – you want them al dente. Drain at once, immerse in cold water to stop the cooking process, then drain again thoroughly.

Bring a large pan of salted water to the boil. Add the pasta and cook until al dente; drain.

Toss the freshly drained pasta first with the wild garlic/ramps pesto, then the mascarpone cheese, coating well. Add the asparagus, peas and green/French beans and toss together thoroughly. Scatter over the toasted pine nuts and serve at once, with Parmesan cheese sprinkled over the top.

Grilled wild garlic/ramps mussels

A rich, tasty way to serve mussels, this offers a great contrast of textures between the crunchy crumb crust and the juicy mussel flesh below.

1 kg/2¼ lbs. mussels
30 g/⅓ cup fresh breadcrumbs
15 g/¼ cup wild garlic leaves/ramps, thoroughly rinsed and very finely chopped
60 ml/¼ cup extra virgin olive oil
salt and freshly ground black pepper

Serves 4 as an appetizer or 2 as a main

Rinse the mussels well under cold running water, discarding any which are open or cracked. Scrub well to remove any beards or grit.

Put the cleaned mussels in a large pan, adding cold water to a depth of 2.5 cm/1 in. up the side of the pan. Set the pan over a medium heat, cover and cook the mussels for around 5 minutes, until they have steamed open.

Drain the mussels, discarding any that haven't opened during the cooking process.

Once the mussels are cool enough to handle, pull one half of each shell off each mussel, leaving the mussel anchored in the remaining half. Place the mussels, shell-side-down, on a baking sheet.

Mix together the breadcrumbs, wild garlic/ramps and olive oil, seasoning with salt and freshly ground pepper. Spoon a little of the breadcrumb mixture over each mussel, so that it forms a topping.

Preheat a grill/broiler to its highest setting and cook the topped mussels for 2–3 minutes until the crumb topping turns golden brown. Serve at once.

Wild garlic/ramps salmon en papillote

Cooking fish en papillote, that is 'wrapped in a parcel', is a great way of retaining both flavour and moisture. This recipe is for salmon, but other fillets of fish, such as sea bass, would also work well. Serve the salmon with new or mashed potatoes and green beans as an elegant dinner party dish.

40 g/3 tablespoons butter, softened

10 g/½ oz. wild garlic leaves/ramps, finely chopped

grated zest of 1 lemon

4 salmon fillets (each around 175 g/6 oz.)

2 tablespoons dry white wine

salt and freshly ground black pepper

4 squares of parchment paper, 30 x 30 cm/ 12 x 12 in.

Serves 4

Preheat the oven to 220°C (425°F) Gas 7.

Mix together the butter, wild garlic/ramps and lemon zest.

Fold each piece of baking parchment in half. Place each salmon fillet, skin-side-down, on one side of the crease in the paper. Season each fillet with salt and pepper, spread with a quarter of the wild garlic/ramps butter and spoon over a quarter of the wine. Fold the paper over the fillets and crimp the edges together, folding tightly.

Place the parcels on a baking sheet and bake for 15 minutes until puffed up. Serve at once, opening each parcel at the table.

Beef ale stew with wild garlic/ramps dumplings

A traditional dish of stew and suet dumplings, perfect for a hearty supper when you want something warming and substantial. Serve with a simple green side vegetable, such as the Italian-style Garlic Spinach (see page 31).

700 g/1½ lbs. braising beef, cubed

2 tablespoons olive oil

6 shallots, blanched and peeled

1 bay leaf

2–3 sprigs of fresh thyme

2 carrots, peeled and chopped

300 ml/1¼ cups brown ale

300 ml/1¼ cups beef or chicken stock

1 whole garlic clove, peeled

1 tablespoon freshly chopped parsley

salt and freshly ground black pepper

DUMPLINGS

125 g/1 cup self-raising/self-rising flour

75 g/¾ cup shredded suet

15 g/½ oz. wild garlic leaves/ramps, finely chopped

cold water, to mix

a lidded flameproof casserole dish

Serves 6

Preheat the oven to 180°C (350°F) Gas 4. Bring the beef to room temperature.

Heat 1½ tablespoons of the olive oil in a casserole dish until hot. Add the beef and fry, browning on all sides. Remove the beef and reserve.

Add the remaining olive oil to the casserole dish and heat through. Add the shallots and fry until lightly browned.

Return the browned beef to the casserole and add the bay leaf, thyme, carrots, brown ale, stock, garlic and parsley. Season with salt and pepper. Bring to the boil. Cover and cook in the preheated oven for 1½ hours until the beef is tender.

Towards the end of the cooking time, make the dumplings. In a bowl, mix together the flour, suet and wild garlic/ramps, seasoning well with salt and pepper. Add in cold water, 2–3 tablespoons at a time, and bring together to form a sticky dough. Shape into 6 even-sized round dumplings.

Add the dumplings to the casserole dish, allowing them to rest on the surface of the stew. Cover the casserole dish and return to the oven. Bake for a further 20 minutes until the dumplings have cooked and expanded. Serve at once.

Wild garlic/ramps miso pork stir-fry

Wild garlic/ramps has a great affinity with Asian flavourings, such as ginger, soy sauce and Japanese miso paste. Cooked in just minutes and served simply with rice or noodles, this pork dish makes a perfect midweek supper. If you wish, tofu could be used instead of pork.

1 tablespoon sunflower or vegetable oil

1 cm/½-in. fresh ginger, peeled and finely chopped

400 g/14 oz. lean pork fillet, sliced into 1-cm/½-in. strips

1 tablespoon rice wine or Amontillado sherry

1 tablespoon dark soy sauce

1 tablespoon dark miso paste

40 g/1½ oz. wild garlic leaves/ramps, rinsed well and chopped into 2.5-cm/1-in. lengths

Serves 4

Heat a wok until hot. Add the oil and heat through. Add the ginger and fry briefly, stirring, until fragrant.

Add the pork strips and fry, stirring, until lightened. Pour in the rice wine and allow to sizzle briefly. Add the soy sauce and miso paste and stir-fry for 2–3 minutes.

Add the wild garlic/ramps and stir-fry until just wilted. Check the pork has cooked through and serve at once.

For a vegetarian version of the dish, cube 400 g/14 oz. of firm tofu and pat dry. Add to the wok once the ginger is fragrant and stir-fry for 2–3 minutes until the tofu takes on a little colour. Proceed with the recipe as directed.

Wild garlic/ramps stoved new potatoes

This traditional, stovetop method of cooking potatoes results in a great combination of textures, with the crispy 'crust' and the soft, steamed potato. The potatoes take on a nutty sweetness flavoured by the wild garlic/ramps.

500 g/1 lb. 2 oz. new
  potatoes
2–3 tablespoons clarified
  butter, or 2
  tablespoons olive oil
  mixed with 10 g/
  2 teaspoons butter
sea salt flakes, to season
25 g/1 oz. wild garlic
  leaves/ramps (or garlic

chives if wild garlic
  is not in season),
  thoroughly rinsed and
  chopped into 2.5-cm/
  1-in. lengths

*a heavy lidded frying
  pan/skillet*

Serves 4

Chop the potatoes into even-sized chunks, roughly 3 x 2 cm/1¼ x ¾ inches.

Heat the clarified butter in the heavy, lidded frying pan/skillet until hot. Add in the potato pieces, flesh side down, arranging them in a single layer in the pan. Season with sea salt flakes and sprinkle over the chopped wild garlic/ramps.

Cover the pan and cook over a medium heat without disturbing the potatoes for 30 minutes until they are soft and tender. Carefully turn over the potatoes, revealing their crispy golden brown side and serve them this side up.

Wild garlic/ramps sweet potato mash

Wild garlic/ramps gives a savoury lift to mashed sweet potatoes. Serve with sausages or a chicken casserole for a tasty meal. As you peel the potatoes, place in water acidulated with a touch of vinegar or lemon juice to prevent discolouration.

900 g/2 lb. orange-
  fleshed sweet
  potatoes, peeled and
  chopped into even
  chunks
3½ tablespoons butter
50 g/2 oz. wild garlic
  leaves/ramps,
  thoroughly rinsed and
  finely chopped

splash of single/light
  cream
freshly grated nutmeg
salt and freshly ground
  black pepper

Serves 4

Boil the sweet potatoes in salted water until softened; drain well and return to the pan. Melt the butter in a small frying pan/skillet, add in the wild garlic/ramps and cook, stirring, until slightly wilted.

Add the wild garlic/ramps with the butter to the potatoes and a splash of cream. Mash together well. Season with freshly ground pepper and grated nutmeg. Serve at once.

Celebratory garlic

Garlic festivals

Garlic has always aroused strong emotions, with people either loving or loathing it. The conviction of those who love it is demonstrated by the number of festivals celebrating this pungent ingredient around the world, from Europe to North America.

Amongst the most famous of these is the Gilroy Garlic Festival, held each summer in the city of Gilroy in California, USA. It was well-respected Gilroy resident Dr Rudy Melone who, in 1978, came up with the idea of a festival celebrating the garlic harvest. He approached Don Christopher of the Christopher Ranch, a local grower and shipper of garlic, and

together the two of them co-founded the festival. Such has been the festival's success that it has become one of the largest food festivals in the US, attracting tens of thousands of visitors each year and raising large amounts of money for local charities. Run with both brio and professionalism by a committed team of volunteers, the event is a massive garlic-themed jamboree in the best American style. As one might expect, there is a plethora of garlic-flavoured foods on offer, including garlic gator, garlic burgers, garlic calamari, pesto and a signature garlic ice cream. Culinary garlic creativity is encouraged by the Great

Garlic Cook Off, which is open to amateur chefs across the US who must create original recipes using at least six cloves of garlic. Professional chefs are catered for with a garlic-themed Iron Chef-style showdown.

The Gilroy Garlic Festival has inspired festivals in other parts of the world, among them the Isle of Wight Garlic Festival, held on the British island since 1983. The community of Newchurch were looking for fundraising events to raise money for the local school. Farmer Colin Boswell, who had visited Gilroy, suggested the idea of a similar event and so the Isle of Wight Garlic Festival came into being. Offering a characterful combination of a 1960s-style pop festival and a country fair generously laced with all things garlic, the event attracts thousands of visitors and has become a fixture in the island's summer calendar.

As one might expect, garlic festivals usually take place in areas where garlic is cultivated, offering the growers a chance to both celebrate and promote their crop and the work that goes into growing it. Voghiera, near Ferrara in Italy, has long been noted for its garlic, which has bright white large cloves and a delicate flavour, in 2007 it was granted a Protected Designation of Origin. Each summer the local authority holds the Fiera dell'Aglio di Voghiera DOP offering farmers the chance to sell their recently harvested garlic to the public and to talk about garlic's properties, while the garlic can be sampled in traditional dishes.

In Lautrec in France, late summer sees a festival celebrating the famed pink garlic of Lautrec. The garlic had traditionally been grown on a small scale but 1959 saw the founding of the splendidly named Defence Committee of the Pink Garlic of Lautrec, aimed at promoting and protecting this local speciality, with the garlic given Protected Geographical Indications status (PGI) in 1996. The Pink Garlic Festival, which has taken place since 1970, is held in August and features events such as a contest for the longest garlic plait and the chance to sample the local delicacy of garlic soup. It is a picturesque event to mark the harvest of a special local crop.

Crispy garlic chive chicken wontons

Deep-frying these dumplings until they are crisp transforms them into an appetizing snack – when served with the dipping sauce, they go perfectly with pre-dinner drinks. Chinese black rice vinegar is available from Asian stores.

1 chicken breast fillet (approx. 140 g/5 oz.), finely minced

4 tablespoons finely chopped fresh Chinese chives

a pinch of ground Sichuan pepper

1 teaspoon light soy sauce

½ teaspoon sesame oil

16 wonton wrappers

sunflower or vegetable oil, for deep frying

salt and freshly ground black pepper

DIPPING SAUCE

2 tablespoons Chinese black rice vinegar

1 teaspoon sugar

1 garlic clove, finely chopped

½ red chilli/chile, finely chopped (optional)

Serves 4

Thoroughly mix together the minced chicken, Chinese chives, Sichuan pepper, soy sauce and sesame oil. Season well with salt and pepper.

Mix together the ingredients for the dipping sauce and set aside.

Take a wonton wrapper and place a teaspoon of the chicken mixture in the centre of the wrapper. Brush the edges with a little cold water and bring the wrapper together over the chicken to form a parcel, pressing together well to seal properly. Set aside. Repeat the process until all 16 wrappers have been filled.

Heat the oil in a large saucepan until very hot. Add four of the wontons and fry for a few minutes, until golden brown on both sides, turning over halfway through to ensure even browning. Remove with a slotted spoon and drain on kitchen paper. Repeat the process with the remaining wontons.

Serve at once with the dipping sauce.

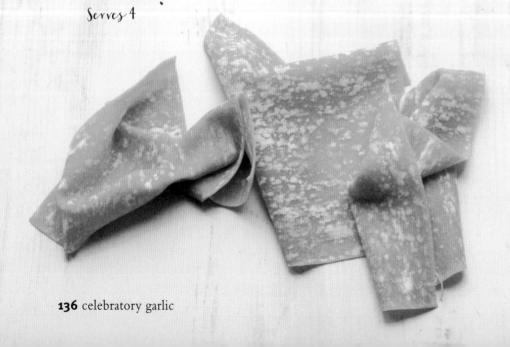

Steamed black garlic scallops

A luxurious seafood dish, with the natural sweetness of the scallops contrasting nicely with the savoury, smoky saltiness of the garlic dressing.

3 tablespoons dark soy sauce

2 black garlic cloves, finely chopped

2-cm/¾-in. fresh ginger, peeled and finely chopped

1 spring onion/scallion, finely chopped

12 king scallops

4 tablespoons groundnut or sunflower oil

2 black garlic cloves, finely chopped

a steamer

Serves 4 as an appetizer

Mix together the soy sauce, black garlic, ginger and spring onion/scallion in a bowl and set aside.

Steam the scallops until they turn opaque and are cooked through.

Heat the oil in a small frying pan/skillet, add the garlic and fry, stirring often, until fragrant. Pour the hot garlic oil into the soy sauce mixture, mixing well to form the dressing. Spoon the garlic dressing over the freshly steamed scallops and serve at once.

Risotto nero with garlic prawns/shrimp

A well-made risotto is always a treat. Black rice, cooked with squid ink and flavoured with fish stock, combined with pink prawns/shrimp makes a striking dish – one which tastes as good as it looks and is ideal for dinner parties.

1 litre/4 cups good-quality or homemade fish stock

3 tablespoons olive oil

1 shallot, finely chopped

3 garlic cloves, 2 finely chopped and 1 peeled but left whole

200-g/7-oz. squid, cleaned and chopped into small pieces

8-g/¼-fl .oz. sachet of squid ink

350 g/1 ¾ cups risotto rice

50 ml/3½ tablespoons dry white wine

25 g /1¾ tablespoons butter

12 raw tiger prawns/shrimp, heads removed, peeled and deveined

salt

chopped fresh parsley, to garnish

Serves 4

Bring the fish stock to a simmer in a large pan.

Heat 2 tablespoons of the olive oil in a separate, heavy-based saucepan. Add the shallot and chopped garlic and fry gently, stirring, until the shallot has softened. Add the squid and fry, continuing to stir, until whitened and opaque. Mix in the squid ink. Stir in the rice. Pour over the wine and cook, stirring, until reduced.

Add a ladleful of the simmering stock to the rice and cook, stirring, until absorbed. Repeat the process until all the stock has been added and the rice is cooked through. Taste and season with salt as needed. Stir in the butter and set aside to rest briefly.

Heat the remaining oil in a frying pan/skillet. Once frothing, add the whole garlic clove and fry, stirring, until fragrant. Add the prawns/shrimp with a pinch of salt and fry, stirring, until the prawns/shrimp have turned pink and opaque and are cooked through. Discard the garlic clove.

Serve each portion of the risotto rice topped with prawns/shrimp and garnished with parsley.

Griddled tuna with garlic bean purée and gremolata

Gremolata – traditionally served with osso buco – also goes very well with fish. Here firm-textured tuna steaks contrast nicely with the soft bean purée, while gremolata adds a refreshing zip. A great dish to make for dinner parties.

2 x 400-g/14-oz. cans
  of butter beans/lima beans
  in water
2 tablespoons olive oil
1 onion, finely chopped
1 garlic clove, finely chopped
4 tuna steaks, each
  approx. 200 g/7 oz.
salt and freshly ground black
  pepper
extra virgin olive oil, to garnish

GREMOLATA
2 garlic cloves
pinch of salt
finely grated zest of 2 lemons
6 tablespoons finely chopped
  fresh parsley

a griddle pan

Serves 4

First, make the gremolata. Crush the garlic cloves with a pinch of salt to a paste. Mix together with the lemon zest and parsley and set aside.

Drain the beans, reserving 4 tablespoons of the bean water. Heat 1 tablespoon of the olive oil in a heavy saucepan. Add the onion and garlic and fry gently, stirring, until softened. Add the drained butter beans and reserved bean water, mixing in. Cover and cook gently for 10 minutes, stirring now and then. Mash into a purée, season with salt and pepper and keep warm until serving.

Preheat the griddle pan until very hot. Coat the tuna steaks with the remaining olive oil and season with salt and pepper. Griddle the tuna steaks until cooked to taste (about 2–3 minutes per side), turning occasionally to ensure even cooking.

Spoon the gremolata over the griddled tuna steaks and serve on a bed of bean purée, spooning over a little extra virgin olive oil for flavour and moisture.

2 tablespoons olive oil

2 shallots, finely chopped

1 celery stalk, finely chopped

2 garlic cloves, chopped

2 bay leaves

5 sprigs of thyme

½ teaspoon fennel seeds

50 ml/3½ tablespoons
   Pernod or dry white wine

400-g/14-oz. can of chopped
   tomatoes

50 ml/3½ tablespoons
   freshly squeezed orange
   juice

1 teaspoon grated orange
   zest

a pinch of saffron strands,
   finely ground and soaked
   in 1 tablespoon hot water

a pinch of Turkish chilli/
   Aleppo hot pepper flakes

500 ml/2 cups fish stock

a handful of freshly chopped
   parsley, plus extra to
   garnish

500 g/1 lb. 2 oz. fish fillet,
   skinned and chopped into
   chunks

200 g/7 oz. raw prawns/
   shrimp, peeled and heads
   removed, deveined

150 g/5½ oz. squid rings

salt and freshly ground
   black pepper

chopped fresh parsley,
   to garnish

a deep sauté pan

Serves 4

Mediterranean garlicky fish stew

An appealingly colourful dish, perfect for a hot summer's day and ideal for entertaining. Serve with slices of baguette to soak up the fragrant broth.

Heat the olive oil in the deep sauté pan. Add the shallots and fry gently, stirring often, until softened and lightly browned. Add the celery, garlic, bay leaves, thyme and fennel seeds and fry, stirring, for 2 minutes until fragrant.

Pour in the Pernod or white wine and fry, stirring, until largely reduced. Mix in the chopped tomatoes and cook, stirring often, until thickened and reduced. Stir in the orange juice and zest, saffron soaking water and chilli/hot pepper flakes. Add the fish stock. Taste and season with salt and pepper accordingly. Mix in the parsley.

Bring to the boil and cook for 5 minutes. Add in the fish, prawns and squid rings and simmer until just cooked through – this takes just a matter of minutes. Garnish with parsley and serve at once.

Braised garlic pork bao

Smooth-textured, pillowy Taiwanese-style buns contrast beautifully with the gutsy, succulent braised pork, making this a memorably tasty treat.

BRAISED PORK

1 tablespoon oil

1 onion, finely chopped

2 garlic cloves, chopped

2-cm/¾-in. fresh ginger, peeled and chopped

400 g/14 oz. pork belly, cut into 2.5-cm/1-in. cubes

1 tablespoon Korean soy bean paste

1 tablespoon Korean chilli paste

1 tablespoon dark soy sauce

1 tablespoon rice wine or medium sherry

1 teaspoon sugar

300 ml/1¼ cups chicken stock or water

BAO (TAIWANESE BUNS)

250 g/1¾ cups plain/all-purpose flour

2 teaspoons caster/granulated sugar

½ teaspoon fast-action dried yeast

½ teaspoon baking powder

¼ teaspoon salt

100 ml/⅓ cup hand-hot water

50 ml/3½ tablespoons whole milk

2 teaspoons white wine vinegar

shredded carrot and spring onion/scallion, to garnish

a large lidded frying pan/skillet or casserole dish

a steamer

Makes 8

First make the braised pork. Heat the oil in a large lidded frying pan/skillet or casserole dish. Fry the onion, garlic and ginger for 2 minutes, stirring, until the onion has softened and the mixture is fragrant. Add the chopped pork belly and fry, stirring often, until the pork is lightly browned.

Add the soy bean and chilli pastes and mix to coat thoroughly. Add the soy sauce, rice wine and sugar and cook, stirring, for 1 minute. Add the stock or water and bring to the boil.

Cover with a lid, reduce the heat and simmer for 1 hour until the pork is tender. Uncover the pan, increase the heat to bring the liquid to the boil and cook uncovered over medium heat, stirring often, until the sauce has considerably reduced. Set aside.

To make the bao, mix together the flour, sugar, yeast, baking powder and salt in a large bowl. Add in the hand-hot water, milk and vinegar and mix together to form a soft dough. Knead for 10 minutes until the dough is supple and smooth.

Place the dough in an oiled bowl, cover with oiled cling film/plastic wrap and set aside in a warm place for an hour to rise.

On a lightly floured surface, knock back the risen dough and roll to form a thick sausage shape. Cut into 8 even-sized pieces and shape each piece into a ball.

Roll each dough ball into an oval, roughly 12-cm/5-in. long. Fold each oval in half over a small rectangular piece of parchment paper. Cover with oiled clingfilm/plastic wrap and set aside to rest for 20 minutes.

Line the steamer with oiled parchment paper. Steam the buns in batches, spaced apart, for 10 minutes or until cooked through.

Handling the hot buns carefully, remove the parchment paper. Fill each bun with braised pork, garnish with shredded carrot and spring onion/scallion and serve at once.

Rosemary, garlic and fennel roast pork

Fragrant rosemary, aromatic fennel and tasty garlic combine to good effect with this simple but flavourful roast pork dish.

1.8-kg/4-lb. pork loin, skin
    scored for crackling,
    chined*
1 tablespoon fennel seeds
1 teaspoon olive oil
2 garlic cloves, peeled and
    cut into slivers
3–4 rosemary sprigs,
    chopped into short pieces
salt and freshly ground black
    pepper

*Note: the chine is a tough
    cut of meat which is
    usually removed in
    supermarket meat but
    may need to be trimmed
    if bought from the butcher,
    or you can ask your
    butcher to do this
    for you.

Serves 4–6

Preheat the oven to 220°C (425°F) Gas 7. Bring the pork to room temperature.

Dry-fry the fennel seeds until fragrant, then cool and finely grind.

Pat the pork dry with paper towels. Season with salt and plenty of pepper, rubbing the salt into the skin.

Rub the pork with the ground fennel, then cut small incisions in the flesh. Rub the flesh with olive oil, then insert the garlic slivers and rosemary into the incisions. Place the pork in a roasting pan.

Roast the pork for 15 minutes in the preheated oven, then reduce the oven temperature to 180°C (350°F) Gas 4 and roast for a further 1½ hours until cooked through. Set aside to rest in a warm place for 20 minutes before carving. Serve with the roasting juices.

Garlicky chicken livers with pomegranate molasses

A classic from Lebanon, this simple but tasty dish of soft, tender chicken livers is given a pleasant sour tang by the pomegranate molasses and lemon juice. Serve as an appetizer or as part of a mezze meal.

3 tablespoons olive oil

1 garlic clove, sliced lengthways

400 g/14 oz. chicken livers

1 tablespoon pomegranate molasses

freshly squeezed juice juice of ½ lemon

1 tablespoon pomegranate kernels (optional)

salt and freshly ground black pepper

chopped fresh parsley, to garnish

bread, to serve

Serves 4

Heat the olive oil in a large, heavy frying pan/skillet. Add the sliced garlic and fry briefly, stirring, until fragrant. Add the chicken livers and fry, stirring frequently, for 3–5 minutes. Don't overcook the livers, as this would make them tough to eat. Season with salt and pepper.

Add the pomegranate molasses and lemon juice to the frying pan/skillet. Cook briefly, stirring to coat the livers in the liquid.

Serve at once, garnished with pomegranate kernels, if using, and parsley with bread on the side to soak up the juices.

Fragrant garlic lamb shanks with apricots

Slow-cooking is ideal for lamb shanks. This recipe delivers great results with tender, aromatic spiced meat. Serve this flavourful, fragrant lamb dish with couscous or rice.

2 tablespoons olive oil

4 even-sized lamb shanks

2 onions, finely chopped

2 garlic cloves, chopped

1 celery stalk, finely chopped

1 carrot, peeled and finely sliced

1 cinnamon stick

1 teaspoon ground ginger

½ teaspoon ground cinnamon

a pinch of saffron strands, ground and soaked in 1 tablespoon warm water

½ teaspoon freshly ground black pepper

3 tablespoons tomato purée/paste

salt

12 dried, unsulphured apricots

1 tablespoon clear honey

½ teaspoon rose water, optional

3 tablespoons flaked/slivered almonds, dry-fried until golden

chopped fresh coriander/cilantro, to garnish

a large lidded casserole dish

Serves 4

Preheat the oven to 150°C (300°F) Gas 2.

Heat 1 tablespoon of the olive oil in a large frying pan/skillet. Add the lamb shanks and fry until browned on all sides. Remove from the heat.

Heat the remaining olive oil in the large casserole dish. Add the onions, garlic, celery, carrot and cinnamon stick and fry gently, stirring, until the onion has softened and the mixture is fragrant. Mix in the ginger, ground cinnamon, saffron water and black pepper, then the tomato purée/paste. Add the browned lamb shanks and mix to coat well.

Pour in enough water to just cover the lamb. Season with salt. Bring to the boil. Cover and transfer to the preheated oven to cook for 2 hours, adding the dried apricots after 1½ hours of cooking time.

When the lamb is tender and cooked, stir in the honey and rose water, garnish with flaked almonds and chopped coriander/cilantro and serve at once.

Garlic anchovy roast lamb

Adding a few classic flavourings to lamb before roasting it is a simple step that transforms the finished dish. As the lamb cooks, the anchovy fillets 'melt' into the dish, adding an extra umami touch to the tender lamb. Serve with new potatoes and broccoli, green beans or brussel tops.

1 leg of lamb, approx.
   1.5 kg/3¼ lbs.

2 garlic cloves, chopped into slivers

5 anchovy fillets, chopped into short pieces

3 fresh rosemary sprigs, cut into short pieces

40 g/3 tablespoons butter, softened

150 ml/⅔ cup red wine

salt and freshly ground black pepper

GRAVY
300 ml/1¼ cups chicken stock or water

Serves 4–6

Preheat the oven to 230°C (450°F) Gas 8. Bring the lamb to room temperature.

Season the lamb with salt and pepper. Using a small, sharp knife, cut little incisions in the lamb flesh on all sides of the leg. Take a piece each of garlic, anchovy and rosemary and insert the flavourings into an incision, making sure to push the garlic into the flesh. Repeat the process until the garlic has been used up.

Mash any remaining anchovy and rosemary leaves into the softened butter. Place the lamb in a roasting tray and smear the butter over the fleshy part of the lamb. Pour over the red wine.

Roast the lamb in the preheated oven for 15 minutes. Reduce the oven temperature to 180°C (350°F) Gas 4 and roast for a further 45 minutes for medium rare or 30–35 minutes for rare, basting now and then with the wine roasting juices.

Remove from the oven and rest in a warm place for 30 minutes.

To make the gravy, de-glaze the roasting pan – place it on the stovetop, add the stock or water and bring to the boil. Scrape the pan with a wooden spoon to release the flavoursome brown residues so they combine with the liquid.

Serve the lamb with the roasting juice gravy on the side.

Index

A

ajo blanco 43
allicin 34
almonds: ajo blanco 43
  garlic and almond purple
    sprouting broccoli 60
  herb and garlic chutney
    89
anchovies: garlic anchovy
  roast lamb 155
aphrodisiacs 65
apricots, fragrant garlic
  lamb shanks with 152
asparagus: wild
  garlic/ramps pasta
    primavera 120
aubergines/eggplants:
  smoky garlic baba
    ghanoush 91
avocados: black garlic
  tricolore salad 44
Ayurvedic medicine 34, 65

B

baba ghanoush, smoky
  garlic 91
baked beans, Spanish-style
  garlic 77
bao, braised garlic pork 147
bean and garlic dip 17
bear garlic see wild
  garlic/ramps
beef: beef ale stew 127
  boeuf bourguignon 81
  bulgogi 105
  spicy Indian garlic
    meatballs 106
beer: beef ale stew 127
beetroot/beets: roast garlic
  beetroot soup 18
black garlic 8–9
  black garlic tricolore
    salad 44
  cider and garlic roast
    belly pork 75
  steamed black garlic
    scallops 139

boeuf bourguignon 81
borlotti/cranberry beans:
  Spanish-style garlic
    baked beans 77
bread: ajo blanco 43
  fettunta 66
  roast garlic rosemary
    focaccia 39
  Spanish garlic soup 70
  wild garlic/ramps dough
    balls 115
broad/fava beans: bean
  and garlic dip 17
broccoli (purple sprouting),
  garlic and almond 60
bulgogi 105
burgers, roast garlic pork
  56
butter, garlic 82
butter beans/lima beans:
  griddled tuna with garlic
    bean purée 143
buying garlic 12

C

cheese: bean and garlic
  dip 17
  black garlic tricolore
    salad 44
  green garlic muffins 40
  roast garlic mac 'n'
    cheese 71
  roast garlic tartiflette 69
  wild garlic/ramps cheese
    scones 119
  wild garlic/ramps goat's
    cheese flan 116
chicken: chicken with
  40 cloves of garlic 27
  crispy garlic chive chicken
    wontons 136
  garlic butter roast
    chicken 82
  garlic lime chicken 52
  saffron garlic chicken
    kebabs/kabobs 55
  stock 70

Thai-style fried garlic
  minced/ground chicken
    102
chicken livers with
  pomegranate molasses
    151
chickpeas: hummus 14
chillies/chile peppers:
  Malay garlic and chilli
    prawns/shrimp 96
  spaghetti con aglio, olio
    e peperoncino 95
Chinese chives: Chinese
  chive prawns/shrimp 24
  garlic chive meatballs 101
Chinese medicine 34
chives see Chinese chives;
  garlic chives
chutney, herb and garlic 89
cider and garlic roast belly
  pork 75
cilantro see coriander
clams: spaghetti alle
  vongole 48
cod: roast garlic salt cod
  croquettes 23
coriander/cilantro: garlic
  and herb dressing 47
  herb and garlic chutney
    89
courgettes/zucchini: green
  garlic muffins 40
crab tart, roast garlic 21
cranberry beans see
  borlotti beans
crème fraîche/sour cream,
  black garlic 92
croquettes, roast garlic salt
  cod 23
crushing garlic 12
cucumber: tzatziki 55

D

deep-fried garlic 9
dips: bean and garlic dip 17
  dipping sauce 101, 105,
    136

hummus 14
  smoky garlic baba
    ghanoush 91
  tzatziki 55
dough balls, wild
  garlic/ramps 115
dressing, garlic and herb
  47
dumplings, wild
  garlic/ramps 127

E

eggplants see aubergines
eggs: roast garlic fish pie
  72
elephant garlic 8

F

fava beans see broad
  beans
festivals 134–5
fettunta 66
Filaree Garlic Farm, Omak,
  Washington 86–7
fish: Mediterranean
  garlicky fish stew 144
  roast garlic fish pie 72
  Thai-style fish with fried
    garlic 99
flan, wild garlic/ramps
  goat's cheese 116
flowering Chinese chive
  prawns/shrimp 24
focaccia, roast garlic
  rosemary 39
folklore 64–5
French beans see green
  beans

G

garlic chives: crispy garlic
  chive chicken wontons
    136
  garlic chive meatballs
    101
garlic salt 9
garlic scapes 9

gazpacho, white 43
gnocchi: pan-fried gnocchi with garlic mushrooms 20
goat's cheese flan, wild garlic/ramps 116
goose fat: garlicky goose fat roast potatoes 31
grapes: ajo blanco 43
gravy 82
green garlic muffins 40
green/French beans: wild garlic/ramps pasta primavera 120
gremolata 143
growing garlic 87, 110–11

H
hands, removing smell 13
harvesting garlic 111
hazelnuts: wild garlic/ramps hazelnut pesto 112
health benefits 34–5
herb and garlic chutney 89
history of garlic 34
hummus 14

I
Italian sausages with garlic lentils 78
Italian-style garlic spinach 31

K
kebabs/kabobs, saffron garlic chicken 55
kimchi pancake with black garlic crème fraîche 92

L
labneh, roast garlic herbed 36
lamb: fragrant garlic lamb shanks with apricots 152
garlic anchovy roast lamb 155
lentils: Italian sausages with garlic lentils 78
lettuce: garlic peas à la Française 60

lima beans see butter beans
limes: garlic lime chicken 52

M
mac 'n' cheese, roast garlic 71
La Maison de l'Ail, Saint-Clar Gers 87
Malay garlic and chilli/chile prawns/shrimp 96
mayonnaise: roast garlic tartare sauce 23
meatballs: garlic chive meatballs 101
spicy Indian garlic meatballs 106
medicinal uses 34–5
Mediterranean garlicky fish stew 144
muffins, green garlic 40
mushrooms: boeuf bourguignon 81
pan-fried gnocchi with garlic mushrooms and pancetta 20
mussels: grilled wild garlic/ramps mussels 123

P
pancakes: kimchi pancake with black garlic crème fraîche 92
pancetta: pan-fried gnocchi with garlic mushrooms and pancetta 20
roast garlic tartiflette 69
Spanish-style garlic baked beans 77
parsley: parsley pesto 23
piquant peanut and garlic relish 88
pasta: roast garlic mac 'n' cheese 71
spaghetti alle vongole 48
spaghetti con aglio, olio e peperoncino 95
wild garlic/ramps pasta primavera 120
peanut butter: piquant

peanut and garlic relish 88
peas: garlic peas à la Française 60
wild garlic/ramps pasta primavera 120
pesto: parsley pesto 23
wild garlic/ramps hazelnut pesto 112
wild garlic/ramps pasta primavera 120
pickled garlic 9
pie, roast garlic fish 72
pilaff, garlic 59
pistachio nuts: green garlic muffins 40
pomegranate molasses, garlicky chicken livers with 151
pomelo: Thai prawn/shrimp pomelo salad 47
pork: braised garlic pork bao 147
cider and garlic roast belly pork 75
garlic chive meatballs 101
roast garlic pork burgers 56
rosemary, garlic and fennel roast pork 148
smoked garlic pulled pork 28
wild garlic/ramps miso pork stir-fry 128
potatoes: garlicky goose fat roast potatoes 31
roast garlic fish pie 72
roast garlic salt cod croquettes 23
roast garlic tartiflette 69
wild garlic/ramps stoved new potatoes 131
prawns/shrimp: flowering Chinese chive prawns 24
Malay garlic and chilli/chile prawns 96
Mediterranean garlicky fish stew 144
risotto nero with garlic prawns 140

roast garlic fish pie 72
Spanish garlic prawns 51
Thai prawn pomelo salad 47
preparing garlic 12–13
prunes: cider and garlic roast belly pork 75

R
ramps see wild garlic
ramsons see wild garlic
relish, piquant peanut and garlic 88
rice: garlic pilaff 59
risotto nero with garlic prawns/shrimp 140
roast garlic: roast garlic beetroot/beet soup 18
roast garlic crab tart 21
roast garlic fish pie 72
roast garlic herbed labneh 36
roast garlic mac 'n' cheese 71
roast garlic pork burgers 56
roast garlic rosemary focaccia 39
roast garlic salt cod croquettes 23
roast garlic tartare sauce 23
roast garlic tartiflette 69
rosemary: roast garlic rosemary focaccia 39
rosemary, garlic and fennel roast pork 148

S
saffron: garlic pilaff 59
saffron garlic chicken kebabs/kabobs 55
salads: black garlic tricolore salad 44
Thai prawn/shrimp pomelo salad 47
salmon: wild garlic/ramps salmon en papillote 124
salt cod: roast garlic salt cod croquettes 23
sauces: gravy 82

roast garlic tartare sauce 23
sausages: Italian sausages with garlic lentils 78
scallops, steamed black garlic 139
scones, wild garlic/ramps cheese 119
shrimp see prawns
smell of garlic 13, 64
smoked garlic 9
smoked garlic pulled pork 28
smoky garlic baba ghanoush 91
soups: ajo blanco 43
roast garlic beetroot/beet soup 18
Spanish garlic soup 70
sour cream see crème fraîche
South West Garlic Farm, Dorset 86
spaghetti: spaghetti alle vongole 48
spaghetti con aglio, olio e peperoncino 95
Spanish garlic prawns/shrimp 51
Spanish garlic soup 70
Spanish-style garlic baked

beans 77
spinach, Italian-style garlic 31
squid: Mediterranean garlicky fish stew 144
risotto nero with garlic prawns/shrimp 140
stews: beef ale stew 127
boeuf bourguignon 81
Mediterranean garlicky fish stew 144
stock, chicken 70
storing garlic 12–13
sweet potatoes: wild garlic/ramps sweet potato mash 131

T
tahini: hummus 14
tartare sauce, roast garlic 23
tartiflette, roast garlic 69
tarts: roast garlic crab tart 21
wild garlic/ramps goat's cheese flan 116
Thai prawn/shrimp pomelo salad 47
Thai-style fish with fried garlic 99
Thai-style fried garlic

minced/ground chicken 102
tomatoes: black garlic tricolore salad 44
Malay garlic and chilli/chile prawns/shrimp 96
Mediterranean garlicky fish stew 144
Spanish-style garlic baked beans 77
spicy Indian garlic meatballs 106
tuna: griddled tuna with garlic bean purée and gremolata 143
tzatziki 55

V
vampires 64–5

W
wet garlic 8
garlic peas à la Française 60
storing 12
wild garlic/ramps 9
grilled wild garlic/ramps mussels 123
wild garlic/ramps cheese scones 119

wild garlic/ramps dough balls 115
wild garlic/ramps dumplings 127
wild garlic/ramps goat's cheese flan 116
wild garlic/ramps hazelnut pesto 112
wild garlic/ramps miso pork stir-fry 128
wild garlic/ramps pasta primavera 120
wild garlic/ramps salmon en papillote 124
wild garlic/ramps stoved new potatoes 131
wild garlic/ramps sweet potato mash 131
wine: boeuf bourguignon 81
wontons, crispy garlic chive chicken 136
wood garlic see wild garlic

Y
yogurt: roast garlic herbed labneh 36
tzatziki 55

Z
zucchini see courgettes

Picture credits

All photography by Clare Winfield apart from pages:

Acknowledgments

My loving thanks to my family and friends who gave me feedback and support as I tested the garlic recipes for the book.

Many thanks for their help in sourcing ingredients to Nicola Lando of the brilliant Souschef, the wonderfully helpful John and Elena at Spa Terminus and Parkway Greens. Thank you, too, to committed garlic growers Mark Botwright of Southwest Garlic Farm, the Gamots of La Maison de l'Ail and Alley Swiss of Filaree Garlic Farm.

A book is a team effort and working with Ryland, Peters and Small is always a pleasure. Thank you, Cindy Richards and Julia Charles for commissioning this book on an ingredient I love and to Gillian Haslam and Alice Sambrook for your work editing it. It's a beautiful book – thank you, Clare Winfield for your delicious food photography, Rachel Wood for food styling, Jo Harris for prop styling and Sonya Nathoo for her art direction and design.